Once More
with
Feeling

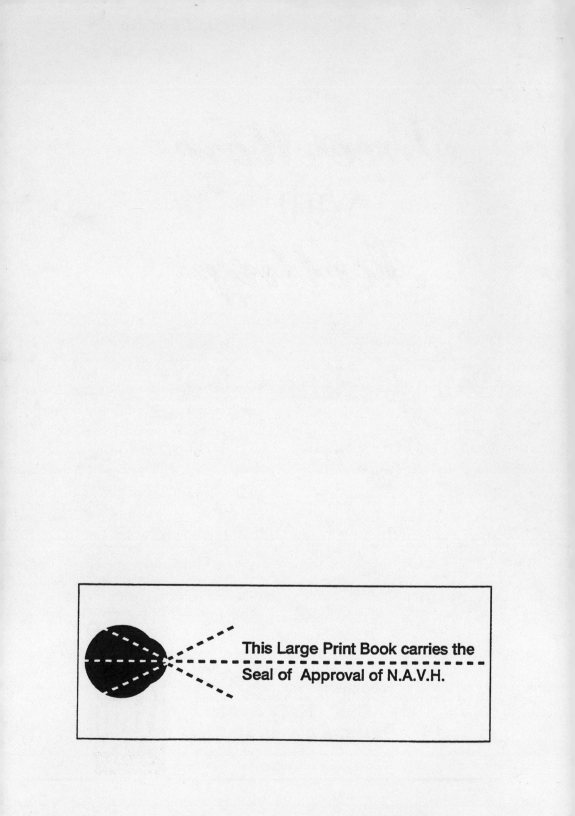

This Large Print Book carries the
Seal of Approval of N.A.V.H.

Once More with Feeling

Cynthia Blair

LP
111

G.K. Hall & Co.
Thorndike, Maine

Published in 1996 by arrangement with Ballantine Books,
a division of Random House, Inc.

G.K. Hall Large Print Romance Collection.

The text of this Large Print edition is unabridged.
Other aspects of the book may vary from the original edition.

Set in 16 pt. Bookman Old Style.

Printed in the United States on permanent paper.

Library of Congress Cataloging in Publication Data

Blair, Cynthia.
    Once more with feeling / Cynthia Blair.
        p.   cm.
    ISBN 0-7838-1942-0 (lg. print : hc)
    1. Large type books. I. Title.
[PS3552.L34624O5 1996]
813'.54—dc20   96-32969

To Mike

Chapter One

"Tablecloths, flowers, paper goods, food, hired help, food *for* the hired help . . ."

Chewing the end of a Bic, Laura Briggs scanned the list in front of her. She let out a deep sigh, then took a sip of coffee from her Forty-and-Still-Pushing mug. Planning an anniversary party, she thought, was as much work as planning the wedding had been fifteen years earlier. And the uncomfortable gnawing in her stomach, the nagging feeling that something was wrong with this picture, wasn't making it any easier.

She tried to ignore her Pepto-Bismol moment, instead concentrating on her monumental task. Menus from a dozen of Long Island's best restaurants and caterers, stacked on the dining room table, offered everything from the slimming *nouvelle cuisine* to the food of third-world countries in which the natives were lucky to eat at all. Pushed aside were the flyers from rental agencies proffering gigantic coffeemakers, tanks of helium, and bubble machines.

Then there was her own list, without which the entire project would fall apart. It had been scrawled across the back of a brochure from an environmentalist organization printed on dingy recycled paper. Immediately to her right sat a telephone and the Yellow Pages.

The Pages were open to *Party Supls. — Retail & Rental*, with red check marks next to the places she'd already tried. Finding just the right paper goods was turning out to be more challenging than coming up with the plot of one of the children's books she wrote. I need a break, she thought, gazing out the dining room window.

The Long Island suburb of Clover Hollow, meandering roads dotted with an odd mixture of whimsical Victorians and cookie-cutter ranch houses, was at its best in late September. The sky was a soft shade of blue, the trees covered with patches of orange and gold. Laura found herself fighting an almost overwhelming urge to borrow a golden retriever and take a long walk in the woods.

Reminding herself she was determined to put this party together this afternoon, she turned back to the phone. Ever since she'd packed away the lawn chairs and bought her son, Evan, a brand-new back-to-school wardrobe consisting of enough tie-dyed T-shirts for a Woodstock revival, she'd been fantasizing about this soirée. She wanted it to be a tribute to Roger and her as a couple, a celebration of the fact that they'd made it through a decade and a half despite their many ups and downs.

Ups and downs was an understatement, Laura reflected pensively as she ran her finger down the handle of her coffee mug. She was talking the Swiss Alps here. Since the very beginning, the marriage of Laura Briggs and Roger Walsh had been less than perfect. More than once she'd been driven to the Self-Help section of the bookstore to buy thick paperbacks with titles like *You CAN Make Your Marriage Work!* and *He Said, She Said: Translating the Language of Couples.*

Awareness of their rocky history created an ambivalence in Laura every time she sat down to make a list of people to invite or lay in bed trying to estimate exactly how many stuffed mushrooms and crudité platters she'd need.

But we made it, she reminded herself stubbornly. Fifteen years together is no small achievement . . . one that deserves recognition.

And the right paper napkins. Pushing back her hair, which was straight and blond and just long enough to brush her shoulders, she turned her attention to the phone book.

"Hey, Ev?" she called into the living room once she'd located the next paper emporium in line. "It's a beautiful day. How about finding a friend and tossing a football around? A softball? A Frisbee? The neighbor's cat?"

Her eight-year-old son, looking like Oliver Twist with his shaggy blond hair and his carefully constructed outfit of ripped jeans, a T-shirt seven sizes too big, and a scuffed pair of L.A. Lights, didn't even glance up. She found it frightening, the way his angelic blue eyes zeroed in on the TV, his fingers moving frantically over the plastic Nintendo control. On the screen, one of the Mario Brothers was racking up points by smashing his head against blocks. The computerized bleeps and squawks set Laura's fillings vibrating.

"Evan," she pleaded, "the sun is shining, the air is crisp. . . . I've seen enough Tide commercials to know you should be outside, breathing fresh air and grinding grass stains into your jeans."

No response.

"Tell you what. Two bucks if you rake up every leaf on the property."

His eyes still fixed on the television, he said, "Make it three and we've got a deal."

"That's highway robbery!"

"Two seventy-five."

"Two-fifty."

"Deal."

He was already bounding out of the room, the Nintendo game gone from the screen.

"Thanks, muffin," she called after him.

10

"Mo-o-om! I told you not to call me that anymore!"

"Thanks, killer."

It was all she could do to keep from going over and ruffling his hair. Or worse, kissing him. Yet those days were over. Already Evan was less interested in cuddling with his mom than in massacring bad guys on the video screen, shooting hoops with balled-up socks, and drinking milk straight from the carton. Her little boy, she reflected sadly, was growing up.

As she turned back to her party plans and punched in a phone number, Laura happened to glance at the television screen. Instead of the Mario Brothers, Phil Donahue was earnestly making eye contact with the camera.

"Today we're talking with men who, to the people who know them, seem like the typical guy next door. Yet they all have one thing in common: they're leading secret lives —"

"Oh, please!" Laura groaned. "Evan! Will you turn off —"

Behind her, the back door slammed.

"Great. Now I've got Phil Donahue — hello, Paper Trail? Do you carry paper napkins printed with — yes, I'll hold."

"Norm has been living with his terrible secret for years," Phil told her, lowering his voice to a conspiratorial tone. "To his friends and neighbors, he looks like an average Joe. He's a plumber, a volunteer fireman, and a Little League coach. He's always known his secret life would bring pain to the people who love him, yet he claims he's powerless in the face of his desires."

The camera cut to a balding man built like an automatic banking machine. His eyes were cast downward, glued to his beefy thighs.

"For the past four years," reported Phil's voice-over, "Norm has been having an affair with his mother-in-law."

"Oh, Norm," Laura breathed. "Have you no shame?"

"It all just kind of happened," Norm confessed, his eyes still fixed on the two massive fields of wool-and-polyester blend. "One day I go over my mother-in-law's house to unclog her toilet, and the next thing I know, we're in bed."

Laura shook her head in disbelief. "Why on earth would anyone go in front of millions of people like that and spill his — yes, I'm still here. I'm calling to find out if you carry paper napkins for fifteenth wedding anniversaries. Oh, I don't know, something catchy like 'Happy Fifteenth Wedding Anniversary.'

"Uh-huh . . . yes, I have thought of going with solid colors, but . . . Yes, peach and mint green *are* very nice. . . . Thanks, I think I'll try someplace else."

Grimacing, Laura hung up. Putting this anniversary party together was taking up too much time. She'd already reached the *P*s and her dream napkins had yet to materialize.

"Paperazzi," she read from the telephone book. "Six-seven-four . . ."

Glancing at the TV while she waited, Laura saw that another distraught man, this one with more hair and less body fat, was pouring his heart out to America. Emblazoned across the screen were the words DWAYNE. LIKES TO WEAR PANTY HOSE.

"Good Lord," Laura muttered. "I'd be much more interested in seeing a *woman* who enjoys wearing panty hose — hello? Can you tell me if you have paper napkins printed with 'Happy Fifteenth Wedding Anniversary'? No, 'Happy Anniversary' isn't specific enough. Sure, I'll hold for the manager.

"You'd think I was trying to find the Holy Grail," Laura complained to Dwayne, who was peering out at her from the screen, tears streaming down his cheeks.

"If you're watching this, Marva," he was saying, "I hope you'll forgive me. Please try to understand. I never wanted to hurt you."

Laura, the phone receiver still clamped against her ear, checked her watch. It was

13

after four, and she hadn't even begun to tackle "Food."

Her ruminations were cut short by a cheerful yet commanding voice at the other end of the phone line.

"Paperazzi, the place for all your disposable needs. How may I help you?"

"Hi, is this the manager? I was wondering if you had 'Happy Fifteenth Wedding Anniversary' napkins in stock. . . . You're kidding! You *do?*"

Suddenly she froze. Dwayne was gone from the screen. In his place was an attractive man. Thick, dark hair, well-proportioned features, the handsome cragginess that good-looking men develop somewhere in their mid-forties. He was a man she recognized. His head was distorted, the colors a bit off, the flatness disconcerting, but his identity was unmistakable.

Her husband. That was Roger's face on the screen.

For a moment Laura was puzzled. Desperately she struggled to figure out what was going on.

"You, too, have been living with a secret." Phil's voice-over reverberated in Laura's ears. "Tell us, Roger, what you haven't been able to tell anyone else — not even your own wife."

"They come in packages of twenty-four or fifty."

It took Laura a few seconds to figure out that the manager of Paperazzi was speaking to her.

"Could you please hold on a minute?" Her mouth was so dry she could barely get the words out. One hand gripped the receiver a few inches from her ear, the other clutched her chest. The room was suddenly odd-looking, the walls and windows tilting at strange angles like those in a fun house. The tightness in her stomach had graduated to an intense pain.

"I haven't been working for the past seven months," Roger told Laura, Phil, and millions of faceless, nameless television viewers. He looked surprisingly at ease, sitting up there with Norm and Dwayne. Laura couldn't help noticing how good-looking he was.

"You've been unemployed . . . and your own wife hasn't known about it?" Phil's bushy eyebrows were furrowed.

"That's right."

"Wait a minute. Let me get this straight. You got fired —"

"I wasn't fired. I quit." Roger was indignant. "I had no choice. Not when my boss was so unreasonable."

"Exactly what did he expect of you?" Phil asked.

"He wanted a robot. Somebody who'd do what he was told, no questions asked."

Roger snorted contemptuously. "I don't know who he thought he was."

The audience was growing restless. Hands were shooting up like weeds along a highway.

"It's not the first time I've run into that attitude, either," Roger went on. "Before this, I worked for a small company for about a year. Oh, sure, it sounded good at first. But it turned out to be the same thing. I had no choice but to leave. There was no outlet for creative expression, no room for individuality —"

"What was that job?" Phil interrupted.

"Selling water-purifying systems. Anyway, the job I had before *that* —"

Wearing a look of incredulity, Phil asked, "Roger, how many jobs have you had?"

"Let's see." Roger began counting on his fingers.

"Oh, boy," breathed Norm.

"And you've kept the fact that you quit this last job a secret from your wife?" Phil asked.

Laura watched, vaguely aware that she'd lapsed into a state of suspended animation: her heart stopped, her blood frozen in her veins, her brain in an eerie holding pattern.

"I've been keeping this secret since last spring. She wouldn't have understood how unhappy I was. That job compromised my integrity. She'd have blamed me." Bitterly he added, "She always does."

Phil strode over to the audience, brandishing his microphone.

"I have a question for Roger," said a well-groomed woman dressed completely in beige. "How did you keep your wife from finding out you'd quit another job?"

"I'd pretend I was going off to work, but instead I'd go to IHOP."

"The International House of Pancakes?" It was hard to tell whether Phil was appalled or sympathetic.

"Right. I'd sit there for hours, drinking cup after cup of coffee. They give unlimited refills."

Phil seemed to be having trouble comprehending. "Didn't your wife notice you weren't getting a paycheck?"

Roger waved his hand in the air. "I dipped into our savings a little. That's what it's for, isn't it? A rainy day?"

"Roger," asked Phil, "how much of your savings did you go through?"

"Pretty much all of it."

Abruptly Laura's life functions recommenced, leaping into overdrive. "All our money?" she gasped.

"All of it?" Phil echoed.

"After I went through our savings, I cashed in a couple of IRAs."

"And your wife didn't know a thing about any of this?"

17

"Jeez." Dwayne was shaking his head. "You got a real problem, man."

It's not real, Laura was thinking. It can't be real. It's a trick. Or a crazy new game show.

But she was already on her feet, heading toward the desk in the living room where Roger stashed the household papers. A terrible dizziness had come over her. Her heart pounded so hard her chest hurt. With trembling fingers she opened the bottom right-hand drawer and pulled out a stack of bank statements.

One by one she looked into the envelopes, something inside her collapsing a little further with each discovery. The mutual funds: liquidated. Two of their IRAs: liquidated. The passbook savings . . .

Laura felt as if all the breath, all the life, had been taken from her in one fell swoop.

The money was only part of it. What mattered even more was the lying. The duplicity. The betrayal.

Gradually she became aware that across the room, the telephone was still off the hook. Moving like a zombie in a low-budget movie, she headed back to the dining room. As she did she glanced at the TV one more time. Passionate violin music played as a handsome actor slid a diamond-studded band of gold onto a woman's finger.

"Show her you'd marry her all over

18

again," the voice-over urged.

Laura picked up the phone. "Hello?" she said dully.

"Ma'am?" the Paperazzi manager said patiently. "I could hold some of these napkins for you."

She opened her mouth, but no words came out.

"Hello? It'd be no trouble for me to put some aside."

"Uh —" Her voice was hoarse, barely recognizable even to her.

And then she took a deep breath, a mysterious strength suddenly rising from deep within.

"Thank you," she said slowly, "but I don't think I'll be needing them after all."

"Come on, you guys!" Evan cried in frustration, racing after a swirl of dried leaves, moving just fast enough to elude the clawed ends of his bamboo rake. His oversized sneakers were festooned with small clumps of bright orange, and a brown oak leaf stuck out of his hair like a feather on an Apache brave.

Gazing out the kitchen window, Laura thought that any other day, she would have been amused by her eight-year-old's awkward attempts at corralling the leaves strewn across the backyard. Today, however, Evan's antics offered only an ironic contrast to the tears streaming down her cheeks.

As she gripped the counter she was surprised to find that her hands were trembling. She simply stared at her ragged fingernails, at the cuticles that three chipped layers of Hard As Nails had done little to protect. Then she noticed her entire body was shaking. She shuffled across the room and sank into a kitchen chair. Blinking hard, Laura tried desperately to focus on something — anything.

Through the blur created by her tears, she took a mental inventory of the items surrounding her. The coffeepot, the microwave, the cheerful ceramic canisters filled with tea bags and sugar and flour. The decorative touches she'd so painstakingly added: the wreath made of dried herbs and flowers hanging next to the back door; the houseplants lining the windowsill; the cheerful curtains, a perky shade of blue that with the bright yellow walls gave the room the happy feeling of a kindergarten. She'd tried so hard to create a home. Yet sitting here, trying to stop shaking, Laura realized she had no home.

She finally had no choice but to admit that her marriage was a sham. She and Roger had done an excellent job of fooling the rest of the world. The two of them routinely showed up at PTA events. They had collected all the usual gadgets and photographs and memories over the years. She even made a point of mentioning him in the author's biography inside the back covers of the dozen children's books she'd had published, the adventures of a jungle sleuth named Gertrude Giraffe and her sidekick, Carol Cobra. Yet their household was like a tree that had died: still standing, continuing to give the appearance of a strong and substantial entity but, underneath its thin layer of bark, completely rotted away.

Now, suddenly, she could no longer pretend. No longer rationalize. No longer convince herself that their marriage would be wonderful . . . if only this or that happened. If only Roger got a job that satisfied him. If only she made enough money from her chirpy accounts of Gertrude's adventures that it no longer mattered whether or not he worked. If only they could find a common language that would enable them to communicate. If only she lost ten pounds or made herself over into a more fascinating woman or became a better lover. If only, if only, if only . . .

There was no magical *if only*. No quick fix. No one thing — or five things or ten things or one hundred things — that could breathe life back into a marriage that she now admitted had been kept alive not by love, not by honesty, not by commitment, not even by loyalty, but by nothing more noble than inertia.

Wrapping her arms around herself protectively, Laura reflected on the fact that this moment had been a long time coming. For months, even years, she'd woken up every morning with a heaviness in her chest, the nagging feeling that something was wrong. She would lie in bed, struggling to clear the cobwebs of sleep from her mind. And then she'd remember.

Today I'm going to make this marriage work, she'd resolve with the same regularity with which she brushed her teeth. Somehow, I'm going to find a way to get through to Roger.

Yet she never did. The distance between them stopped being painful, instead becoming the norm. Too many times she lay in bed alone late at night, after Roger had insisted he wasn't tired. From downstairs she would hear *Star Trek* reruns, the voices of Mr. Spock and Captain Kirk fading to background noise until she finally succeeded in drifting off.

Now, sitting at the kitchen table, the house strangely silent, Laura waited, curious to see what she would feel. It was like being at the movies, watching the lead actress confront a horrible truth, wondering, What's she going to do now? How is

22

she going to react? She had that same sense of anticipation, the feeling that any minute she was going to be surprised. Her heart pounded and adrenaline rushed through every vein. What next?

Watching herself this way, Laura braced for a rush of anger. There was so much to be angry about. One more in a long line of financial fiascoes, the continuation of a trend that had started even before their marriage. The way Roger had kept it all from her, ignoring the fact that husbands and wives were supposed to be partners. The bizarre way she'd discovered that, all melodrama aside, her husband really had been living a secret life.

But Laura felt no anger. Surprised, she waited to see if perhaps she would be overcome by sadness. As she clasped her hands, still struggling to quell the horrible trembling, a long-forgotten memory flashed into her mind. It was from the first year she and Roger were married, when she'd still basked in the certainty that she'd found her happily-ever-after.

The two of them were in bed, limbs intertwined, cloaked in perspiration and body heat and the intoxicating air of intimacy that lingers after making love. She delighted in the sensation of his hard, muscular thigh pressing against hers, marveled over how perfectly her head fit into the gentle slope between his shoulder and his collarbone. In those days, she and Roger lighted candles, wanting to banish the brightness of electric lights but still be able to read the subtlest changes in each other's expression by the soft, flickering light.

Running her fingertips lightly across his chest, she had reflected that her commitment to him and their marriage was so strong it could withstand anything.

Drowsily she told him, "We won't be like everybody else. I won't let us. This marriage is going to work because I'm going to *make* it work."

She had truly believed it, that day and every other that followed. Only now, looking back and recognizing how tenaciously she'd been clinging to her vow, she realized that holding a marriage together wasn't something a person could do alone.

She should have been filled with sadness. Yet she felt none, just as she'd felt no anger. Instead, sitting alone in a silent house, Laura was filled with fear.

She was frightened because she knew that deep inside — in her heart, her soul, that undefinable part of herself from which it was impossible to hide the truth — she had finally made her decision. She could no longer remain married to Roger. Having made that decision, she had no choice but to take action. And that was guaranteed to

24

throw her entire life into turmoil.

Slowly Laura rose. Standing in the doorway of the dining room, she caught sight of the party brochures strewn across the table. They seemed to mock her. What a fool she'd been, planning an event meant to celebrate a man and a woman who hadn't really been a couple at all.

"Oh, my God!" she cried, a deep, painful sob rising up out of her chest. In one swift, unanticipated motion, she swept all the papers onto the floor.

Suddenly Laura felt a strange sense of calm. Of finality. Of the relief that came from resolution — a resolution that was long overdue.

She was finally free to admit the truth.

Chapter Two

"Okay, tiger. Hop into bed."

Sitting on the edge of Evan's bed, waiting while he decided which of his two dozen stuffed animals would be his sleeping partner that night, Laura was amused by the way both her son's past and his future were mixed up in his room. A wide-eyed teddy bear was pushed in the corner with his rap-singer-style sneakers. Picture books about bunnies and squirrels were lined up next to wrestling magazines. Hanging above his dresser were two posters, one of Curious George, one of a sleek race car.

He's at an in-between age, she thought. Just a few more years and he'll be a teenager. As she tucked the blankets under his chin she noticed he was growing so tall that soon there'd hardly be any room for her to sit at the end of his bed.

But for now, he was much more of a child than he was a man. He lay in bed with his arm wrapped around the neck of a polar bear named Snuffles, staring up at her expectantly. Looking into his clear blue eyes, Laura swallowed hard. It took every bit of her self-control to keep back the tears.

Yes, I'm lying to him, she admitted. Pretending nothing's changed, calmly discussing which book I'm going to read to him tonight. . . . But I've been lying to him all along. Every day for months. For years. Instead of feeling guilty, I should be grateful. After all, the lying is about to end.

She reached over and smoothed back his hair, forcing herself to smile. "You did a terrific job today, Ev. Raking leaves, I mean."

"Thanks, Mom." Earnestly he glanced over at the money he'd earned, stacked up in full view on his night table.

"You're getting pretty big. Before you know it, you'll be mowing the lawn, shoveling snow, digging cesspools —"

"Mo-o-om! I don't want to —" He cut his protestations short. "You'd pay me, right?"

"Look at you. Eight years old and ready to join a union."

He handed her the slim paperback they'd been working on together all week. "Not until you finish reading me and Snuffles this book."

Once the house was quiet, Laura settled onto the living room couch, covering herself with the afghan her mother had crocheted the first Christmas she and Roger celebrated as a married couple. Turning on the television for background noise but unable to concentrate on the sitcom unfolding before her, she waited.

All evening she'd been trying to imagine the scene that would play out when Roger came home. Yet even with her overdeveloped writer's imagination, she couldn't bring it into focus. Instead, she agonized over the details that were under her control: how she would act, what points she'd make . . . even where the confrontation would take place.

This last concern was of no small consequence. She certainly didn't want to conduct such an important conversation lying in bed, barefoot and vulnerable, even though that was the obvious place to be at this hour. As for the kitchen, it had already been the scene of too many late-night discussions, with Roger delivering endless monologues justifying his latest escapade and Laura ending up apologetic, if confused, by the time they went to bed.

So Laura sat on the couch, her heart pounding as she attempted to calm herself. Desperate for some distraction, she looked around the room. She scanned the rows of novels she'd already read, neatly lined up on the bookshelves. Untouched sections from the previous Sunday's *New York Times*. Haphazard piles of papers, Evan's schoolwork and junk mail and obsolete telephone messages that begged to be sorted. Finally her eyes lit on a thick white volume, tucked away on the bottom shelf of the bookcase. Her stomach lurched. Her wedding album.

Maybe she *should* take a look, she thought, sort through the pieces of her life and evaluate them in the same way she so matter-of-factly sifted through the clutter that accumulated on the end tables and kitchen counters.

Slowly she rose, letting the afghan fall onto the carpet. She hesitated before retrieving the white photograph album from the bottom shelf, then reminded herself, Ebenezer Scrooge reviewed his past. Look what it did for him.

She settled back down on the couch and ran her hand over the smooth white leather. She'd rejected the idea of a professional photographer who lined up warm bodies according to size and arranged them in stiff, unnatural poses, like the inmates of a wax museum. Instead, she'd asked her friends to take personal, informal pictures. One long, rainy afternoon a few weeks after her wedding, she'd painstakingly arranged the scores of photographs to tell a story.

As she opened the album, Laura was instantly whisked back in time. First came snapshots of the huge ramshackle Victorian mansion on eastern Long Island where the wedding was held, the summer home of friends of Roger's who were as generous as they were wealthy. The Darlings' summer home was like something out of a movie. It had, in fact, been the setting for one, a tragic, terribly romantic story filmed in soft focus, its pastel shades blending together like the paint in a watercolor.

Laura had wanted to recapture the same poetic feeling created by the director and his cameramen and set designers — without the overlay of tragedy, of course. At the same time she was determined to plan a wedding as unique as the newly formed unit called Laura-and-Roger.

In each photograph there were signs that every element had been personalized, every detail carefully thought out. The house itself was funky, right out of a Grimms' fairy tale, with its wonderful towers and turrets and gingerbread trim. Huge windows opened onto impressive views, not only of the rich oranges and reds of autumn trees, but also of the sea. The water was a calm expanse of blue dotted with sailboats that, from so high up on the cliff, looked like toys. Dark, old-fashioned oil portraits of stern-faced strangers, picked up at auctions and garage sales, lined the house's walls. Wicker chairs and love seats, mismatched tables and lamps, and a scattering of throw rugs furnished the interior. The mansion's most notable attribute, its porch, wrapped around three sides of the house over her shoulder for Roger's approval, made a point of asking her mother-in-law-to-be for advice.

"Sylvia, I need help ordering flowers. Nothing ostentatious. In fact, I'd prefer something simple . . . like wildflowers."

"Flowers? Don't worry about flowers," Sylvia insisted with a wave of her hand. "I'll take care of it. I'd love to help out."

Laura was touched, and the fact that Sylvia was willing to do some of the legwork was only part of it. Laura was paying for her own wedding, and with Roger out of work — a temporary situation, he assured her — her budget was already tight. "*Thank* you. Sylvia, that's so sweet of you. I also need something to wear in place of a veil. was thinking of a wreath of flowers, some-ing with baby's breath —"

"I'll take care of it."

aura smiled shyly. "What about a bou-niere for Roger? You're already being so rous, but isn't that fairly standard?"

, yes. And one for his brother, and one ed, and one for your father . . . but ven think about it. I'll take care of

enough, the flowers arrived right on . Huge bouquets, more luxurious thing Laura could ever have envi-ozens of roses, yellow and white. for her hair, exotic blossoms

34

and afforded an even more magnificent view of the water.

The photographs showed how Laura had superimposed over this dramatic backdrop her own interpretations of all the traditional elements of a wedding. The three-tiered cake was chocolate. Her bouquet was a cluster of colorful wildflowers. As for the food, it wasn't catered by some slick or-ganization that descended like a SWAT team, administering hummus and chicken cordon bleu with coldhearted efficiency. In-stead it had been made with love by the friend of a friend with a knack for preparing tricolor pasta salad and teriyaki chicken in cauldron-sized quantities.

Even her wedding dress, on page three directly underneath a shot of the wooden arch Roger had built for the outdoor cere-mony, showed Laura's characteristic touch. She'd had no interest in a traditional wed-ding dress, one of those white creations, all ruffles and lace and fussiness. Nor had she been lucky enough to have an antique wed-ding dress stashed in a trunk somewhere, its lace yellowed, its satin ribbons fraying.

And so she'd searched endlessly for the right dress, finally finding it in a boutique in New York's trendy SoHo district. Because it was meant to be worn at parties without a "Till Death Do Us Part" theme, her selec-tion wasn't white or even cream-colored. It

31

was pale yellow, with large pink flowers and mint green leaves and, around the waist, a floppy green sash. Made of soft rayon, the dress hung flatteringly, the bodice clingy, the skirt giving way at the hips to generous folds that swished and swirled deliciously when she moved.

Yes, she'd been determined that she and Roger were going to do things their own way. They were both going into this with their eyes open. They would avoid the traps other couples fell into. They would be open with each other. They would talk . . . and they would listen. Above all, they would never lose the feeling of connection, the conviction that they were two kindred spirits who'd banded together against whatever the rest of the world would be throwing their way.

There'd been compromises, of course. Looking back, Laura could now see the early signs of the problems that would come to haunt them. The first had arisen, of all things, over beverages.

She and Roger had agreed that the only alcohol they wanted served at their wedding was champagne. Champagne was so light and bubbly. So sophisticated. So French. Yet his parents, Sylvia and Fred, were appalled when they learned there'd be no scotch, gin, or other such staples for their friends. After all, the freshly retired men in

kelly green pants and their wives, thick-waisted yachting and golf widows, constituted a segment of the population that never embarked upon a social event without a drink in hand.

"Let us take care of it," Sylvia had insisted. "It'll be our contribution."

"They're your parents. Just tell them we want to do it our own way," she pleaded. How desperately she wanted him to side with her. To stand up for what was supposed to be their wedding, custom-designed by this brand-new entity, separate and strong.

Instead, Roger simply shrugged.

"Let's just do it their way," he said, pa her on the shoulder. "If having an op for their friends is that important t let them have it. After all, they di pay for it."

And so instead of the delica champagne glasses tinkling ground, the Walsh-Briggs aff panied by the clunk of ice into gin and tonics and S Even more of a presenc male laughter as Fred would slap one of his and bark out the p joke.

Roger's parents as well. Sylvia, in pa

interlaced with baby's breath. For the men there were white carnations. When the florist delivered them all to the Darlings' house on the morning of the wedding, Laura was overwhelmed by their opulence. It wasn't quite what she'd had in mind, of course, but she hardly felt in a position to complain.

After the flowers were brought inside, the florist pressed the bill into the palm of Sylvia's hand. Without even glancing at it, she handed it to Laura.

"Here, Laura. Take care of it."

An hour before the wedding, Laura headed out to a field to pick her own bouquet, pink and purple wildflowers, which she tied together with a scrap of ribbon pulled off the florist's version. In the end, she decided not even to mention it to Roger. She'd already learned an important lesson from *Champagne* v. *The Hard Stuff*.

Not that he was around. Though Laura and Roger had agreed to see to all the last-minute details together, he was no-where to be found. Mystified about his whereabouts, growing more and more fidgety by the minute, she finally decided to take it on faith that he'd show up for his own wedding. She retreated to her hotel room to dress.

As the hour of the ceremony drew close, he still had not appeared. Wearing her wedding dress, her hair hanging halfway down her back and crowned by the somewhat overdone wreath Sylvia and her chichi florist had cooked up, she searched the Darlings' property. She finally discovered him in the garage, bent over a stack of wooden slats, sawing. He was wearing jeans and a ripped T-shirt, covered in sweat, and badly in need of a shave.

"What are you doing?" she gasped. "It's three-thirty, and the wedding's at four!"

"I'll make it," he assured her, not even glancing up. "I thought it'd be a nice touch to have an arch for the judge to stand in front of. Isn't that a great idea?"

The local judge showed up a few minutes later, looking spiffy in his suit, playing the role of small-town bureaucrat with impressive skill. Laura, her stomach in knots, tried her best to be gracious. She handed him a copy of the ceremony she'd written. She considered it one of the most important tokens of her desire to personalize her wedding and was proud of it.

Everything was ready. The guests were seated in a collection of odd chairs — folding, lawn, wooden dining room ones — set out in uneven rows on the back lawn, overlooking the harbor. The arch was in place, with yellow roses — incredibly expensive yellow roses — interwoven into the latticework. As four o'clock gave way to five after, then ten after, the crowd whispered and squirmed in their seats. Roger's scraggly-haired brother, Dirk, wearing shades and what looked dangerously like a white Nehru jacket, was supplying the music for the occasion. He strummed his guitar, glancing around nervously as he launched into his fourth rendition of "Here Comes the Sun."

"It's after four," the judge complained.

"I know," Laura replied, her head spinning. "But we can't start yet. The groom isn't here."

He checked his watch. "If we don't get started in five minutes, I'm going to have to leave."

"You can't leave!" Laura cried, clutching her bouquet of wildflowers so tightly that a few of the purple blossoms up and died. "There are a hundred fifty people out there! They're all expecting a wedding. A lot of them drove out here all the way from the city. Most of them brought presents!"

The judge didn't look impressed. With a shrug, he told her, "Five minutes."

"What's going on, man?" asked Dirk.

"Just keep playing," Laura hissed.

The judge was still engaged in his countdown when Roger finally appeared, surprising Laura by coming up behind her and throwing his arms around her waist.

"See?" he said playfully. "I made it. And

the arch looks fantastic, if I do say so myself."

Like so many brides before her, Laura took the long, measured walk down the aisle, which in this instance was a somewhat rocky trek from the back of the Darlings' garage to the handcrafted wooden arch. Standing in front of it was the judge with his Brooks Brothers look. Beside him was Dirk with his Allman Brothers look. She tried to float, rather than merely walk, and to adopt an appropriately serene expression. It wasn't easy, given her state of agitation over Roger's tardiness, the judge's surliness, and the fact that if she heard "Here Comes the Sun" one more time, she was certain she'd scream.

"Friends of Laura and Roger," the judge began, reading from the crumpled piece of paper in his hands, "today we have gathered together to share in the new life upon which these two kindred spirits are about to embark together. . . ."

Laura relaxed. Glancing to the side, she could see Roger, looking handsome indeed in his borrowed suit. There was an odd expression on his face, a sort of smirk, that she attributed to nerves. She could hardly blame him. After all, she was feeling the same way.

The fact that she was taking a giant step was only part of it. What seemed even more significant at the moment was the fact that the two of them were the center of attention. More than a hundred people had showered and shaved, made up and perfumed, dressed and overdressed, all on their behalf. Over three hundred chicken parts were piled high in the Darlings' kitchen, smothered in a special teriyaki sauce that had been created in their honor. An embarrassing number of presents were stacked up on the window seat in the dining room, enough glassware, silverware, ceramicware, and small appliances to outfit an embassy.

At that moment, in a blinding flash, Laura came to a terrible realization. All the drama of weddings, the pomp and circumstance, the engraved invitations and the quest to find the perfect shoes and the decisions about flowers, napkins, music, the number of tiers in the cake, the type of filling in between the layers of the cake, the color of the sugar roses on top of the cake . . . it was all meant to be a distraction. A distraction from a truth so monumental, so terrifying, so incredibly overwhelming, that to confront it head-on would have been devastating.

That truth was that she and Roger, this man who suddenly seemed like a total stranger, were about to intertwine their lives forever.

When she'd sat down to write her own wedding ceremony, Laura had made a point of omitting the clichés. All that business about sickness and health, better or worse, richer or poorer. Especially the part about death. Yet standing in front of the judge, listening to him stumble over words that had sounded so beautiful and so sincere in her own head, she understood that whether those words were spoken as part of the ceremony or not, they still spelled out what she was in for.

What am I doing? The thought was accompanied by a wave of panic so great that for a fraction of a second she was tempted to flee. But it was too late. Struggling to focus on what the judge was saying in a voice as lyrical as that of a newscaster reciting the Dow Jones report, she realized he was almost at the end.

They were getting to the "I do" part. This was her last chance to change her mind. To back out. Yet through the fog that had enveloped her, she heard herself say the words. "I do."

There were more of the judge's mumblings, and then Roger echoed those same words. "I do."

And she heard, "I now pronounce you man and wife."

Snapping out of her reverie, Laura opened her mouth to protest. Wait a minute! she wanted to cry. I wrote that *husband* and wife! We're both changing our status here, not just me!

She didn't have a chance to voice her protest. Roger was kissing her. A crowd was surrounding them, cooing like a flock of pigeons. Dirk had launched into a spirited version of "You Are the Sunshine of My Life."

It was over. She was married. This man who was kissing her was her partner for life.

Laura Briggs was no longer simply Laura Briggs. She was a wife.

As she heard Roger fit his key into the backdoor lock, the pounding of her heart increased alarmingly. She stashed the wedding album back on the shelf.

"I figured you'd wait up," Roger said.

Laura just nodded. She couldn't help noticing he was even better looking than he'd been on TV. It wasn't only his tall, dark, and handsome look; it was also the way he carried himself, with a confidence that bordered on arrogance.

"You saw the show?"

"Yes."

"You're mad, right?" Both his tone and his posture was defiant. Laura was struck by the fact that he was actually daring her to react.

"I'm too tired to be mad." She sat down

41

on the arm of the couch, her eyes downcast. "To tell you the truth, I've already spent too much emotional energy being angry at you, Roger." She took a deep breath. "I think I've had enough."

He didn't seem to have heard her. He sank into a chair, his eyes fixed on the ceiling.

"I just know being on that show is going to turn out to be a good thing. It's a great way of breaking in."

"Breaking in?"

"Television. The way I figure it, a few million people saw me on TV today. All I need is for one of them to have been the right person. A producer, or maybe an advertising executive —"

"What are you talking about?"

"TV commercials." He looked at her as if she were the one not making sense. "That's what I've decided to do. I've always been interested in acting. Hell, I was in half a dozen plays when I was in college. Then there was that summer I spent at the Downington Theater Festival when I was sixteen. Anyway, there's a lot of money to be made doing commercials. I just need my first big break —"

"You didn't hear what I said."

Roger looked puzzled. "You said you weren't mad."

"No. I said *mad* wasn't the right word. I said what I am is tired."

"Well, sure. It must be almost eleven."

"It's past eleven."

"So go to bed. What are you waiting for?"

What are you waiting for? Laura would have laughed if she hadn't been so close to tears.

"I want out, Roger."

"Out of . . ." he prompted.

"Out of this marriage." Correcting herself, she said, "Out of this poor excuse for a marriage. I — I can't do it anymore."

Roger stared at her, a look of incredulity on his face. "All this because I went on some stupid television show?"

She struggled to find something to say, but there were no words. She felt as if something were lodged in her throat — something that had been stuffed deep inside her for a very long time, but was finally coming to the surface.

Her husband continued staring at her, his eyes wide. "You mean it, don't you?"

She nodded. The tears she'd been fighting to hold back began sliding down her cheeks. Laura covered her face with her hands, unable to look at him. When his response was nothing but silence, she peered at him through parted fingers.

She saw that he was angry. Not penitent, not distressed, not even shocked. Just angry.

"Fine," he said coldly, already heading

toward the stairs. "Do what you have to do."

Laura watched him walk away. This was her husband, the man with whom she'd lived for fifteen years. Roger Walsh, with whom she'd bought a house, created a child, established a credit rating, filed joint tax returns, experienced nearly every variety of foreplay imaginable . . . and envisioned a future that by definition would include each other. A decade and a half together, and this is what it came down to: "Do what you have to do."

To Laura, left alone in the living room, the air suddenly felt so cold that she retrieved the afghan from the floor and wrapped it around herself. As she curled up on the couch, she knew sleep wouldn't come for a very long time.

Chapter Three

The words on the menu of the Sassafras Café were difficult to decipher under the best of circumstances, given the loopy calligraphic style the management used as one more way of justifying its inflated prices. Today they were just a blur to Laura as she sat at a corner table waiting for her two closest friends. Even with half a Valium in her system, she couldn't keep the tears from her eyes.

Don't you dare cry, she scolded herself. You can't. You demolished your last tissue fifteen minutes ago.

Desperately she tried every trick she could remember. Biting her lip. Taking deep breaths. Counting to a hundred. Thinking happy thoughts . . .

The last one was her downfall. There *were* no happy thoughts. Reminding herself of that painful reality sent two fat tears running down her cheeks.

"Something to drink?" the waitress chirped, pouring ice water into a glass. When she glanced at Laura, her expression changed to one of sympathy. "I'll get the wine list."

Laura shook her head. Even though the

Valium was doing little besides making her feel as if she no longer had feet, she'd heard too many coma stories on the six-o'clock news to take a chance.

"Just ginger ale, thanks."

Glad to be left alone again, Laura looked around the restaurant. The Sassafras Café was a good choice, the perfect setting for ladies who lunched. The interior was all soft pinks and yellows, with tea roses on each table and such a profusion of ferns it was a wonder tick warnings weren't posted. The menu included all the current food fads: sun-dried tomatoes, goat cheese, arugula at every turn. The other patrons certainly seemed to be enjoying themselves. Everywhere Laura saw happy faces, bright eyes, animated gestures, lively conversations. The scene depressed her immeasurably.

She turned her eyes to the window, seeking the comfort of the outside world. In the parking lot, people got in and out of their cars, making their way to and from the restaurant and the other stores in the shopping plaza. She spotted a few solo flyers, but mostly there were couples. Men and women strolled along, talking and laughing together, paired off like passengers on the ark.

Laura shut her eyes. No matter how hard she tried, she couldn't block out the bad feelings. For the past two days she'd felt as if she'd stepped onto a roller coaster. The car was moving slowly but already picking up speed, embarking on a ride she knew would raise her up to exhilarating highs only to plunge down to valleys far below. Yet she had no choice but to hang on, clinging to the thought that, in time, it would all be over.

She cast a grateful smile at the waitress who placed an icy glass of ginger ale in front of her. All the tears she'd shed had left her feeling drained and dehydrated. The surge of sugar, she discovered, was even more comforting than the Valium.

Telling the people closest to her was apparently the first gut-wrenching drop on the roller-coaster ride. She'd put off calling her two best friends, Claire and Julie. She hadn't been ready to speak the words, but she wasn't able to lie, either, to act as if everything were the same as it had been a mere forty-eight hours earlier. And so she'd avoided them, wincing at the cheerful sound of their voices on her answering machine, dreading the moment she'd have to tell them.

Saying it out loud, she knew, would make it real.

The idea of ending her marriage, discarding what had been her life for well over a third of her nearly forty years, was something she wanted to keep inside a little longer. Until she went public, she could still turn back. Change her mind. Tell Roger she had simply been angry, neatly putting everything back the way it had been before.

Then, suddenly, she found she could no longer put it off. She'd told Julie first, suspecting that Claire would be miffed but feeling it safer to try it out first on her softer, less judgmental friend.

Julie Cavanaugh, with her cascades of long, wavy red hair, pale skin, and soulful green eyes, looked as if she'd just stepped out of a Pre-Raphaelite painting. Her manner complemented her waiflike appearance. Her voice was soft and breathy, her movements graceful. She had a reassuring way of focusing on people as she elicited every detail of their problems, listening intently, sighing with indignation, then spooning out solid, commonsense advice.

People who didn't know her well were surprised at the competence with which she performed the duties of her rigorous job as a massage therapist. Giving expert massages was only the beginning. Her devoted clientele contended that she not only worked the knots out of their muscles, but out of their minds as well. That had certainly been Laura's conclusion three years ago, when too much time hunching over a word processor had brought her to Julie's massage table.

"Laura, where have you been?" Julie's voice had been filled with concern the day before when she discovered who was on the phone. "Didn't you get the message I left yesterday?"

"Yes, I —"

"Oh, that's right. Weren't you signing autographs at a new bookstore?"

"The signing's tomorrow night. Julie, listen to me." Laura took a deep breath. "I'm getting divorced." She'd promptly burst into tears, her resolve about staying calm forgotten.

"Oh, Laura! Are you all right? What do you need me to do? Have you told Evan? How's Roger taking it?" Julie paused to catch her breath. "You must be a bundle of nerves. Would you like me to come over and walk on your back?"

Telling Claire had been more difficult. On the one hand, Laura mused, hesitating before dialing, Claire was bound to be better at empathizing, since she herself belonged to the sisterhood of divorced women. On the other hand, while Claire Nielsen meant well, her sledgehammer style was sometimes hard to take.

"Well, it's about time!" she'd exclaimed over the phone in response to Laura's announcement. "I never could figure out what you were waiting for."

Despite Laura's impulse to hold the phone

away from her ear, she knew Claire was right. This bit of news was long overdue. For years Claire had been hearing about Laura's unhappiness. She'd provided a well-padded shoulder for her to cry on, as well as a steady stream of no-nonsense advice.

The two of them had been friends since college. During their senior year, Claire dropped out right after second-semester midterms. While Laura was scrawling an essay on the three most notable characteristics of Byzantine architecture, Claire was eloping with a student from the business school.

From the start she worked alongside her new husband, channeling the energy that was a by-product of her type A personality into making his computer consulting business a success. She was the unofficial "silent partner." The firm had exploded like a sky full of fireworks in the techno-explosion of the 1970s and early eighties. Yet during their entire marriage, she required nothing more than an occasional pat on the head and a "Thanks, honey."

When, after six years, Claire discovered that her husband's frequent dinners out weren't always spent entertaining clients, her response had been immediate. First she took off with the Mercedes, the Sony Trinitron, and the Rolodex containing his list of

50

clients. Then she cut her hair to a length somewhere between Kevin Costner's and Sinead O'Connor's, bleaching the brown stubble a blinding shade of platinum blond. Along with her new look came a new identity. She switched back to her maiden name and became Claire Nielsen once again.

As for the client list, that proved more useful than either the television or the car. Claire set up her own computer consulting firm, and managed to lure away enough clients to become dangerous to her ex — or at least to his bottom line.

Along with her success as a solo act came a harder edge. Even so, Laura knew her well enough to see through her defenses. Underneath her crisp facade, Claire was a loyal, concerned friend. She was also protective, anxious to spare the people she cared about some of the despair she'd experienced.

Laura was tense as she sat with her napkin neatly spread across her lap, waiting for her friends. Telling them her news on the phone had been difficult enough. Confronting them face-to-face, bearing both their pity and the anger they were bound to feel on her behalf, was going to be even harder. Her heartbeat quickened as Julie and Claire burst into the restaurant, zeroed in on her, and made a beeline for her table.

"*There* she is," Claire cried, zigzagging

through the café, arms outstretched.

"We're here, Laura," cooed Julie, a few paces behind.

For the occasion, Claire had decked herself out in black. On the surface, anyway; underneath the dark, loose-fitting jacket was a swirl of purples and blues. Beneath her midthigh hemline were long, purple legs and a pair of spike heels precisely the same shade as the stockings. Blue enameled earrings contrasted sharply with her white-blond crew cut.

Every element of Claire's outfit was matched, coordinated, or otherwise carefully thought out; Julie, on the other hand, looked as if she'd gotten dressed in the dark. With her long, flowered rayon skirt, a throwback to the Age of Aquarius, she wore a denim jacket, a man's undershirt, and four different strands of beads. Her wild red hair cascaded around her like an aura. Still, on Julie, it somehow all worked.

"That beast!" cried Claire, pulling out a chair and dropping into it. "I want you to tell us every detail. Every single, solitary detail of what that — that *cretin* did to you."

"Hello, Claire. Hi, Julie." Blinking, Laura put down her menu.

"The first thing we have to do is get you a good lawyer," Claire insisted.

"The first thing we have to do," Julie said softly, "is ask Laura how she's handling this."

52

"Actually, not too badly," Laura said in an even voice. "I feel kind of calm. Accepting. A little dazed . . . Of course, it could be the Valium."

"Poor Laura." Julie reached over and patted her hand. "I knew I should've come over last night and walked on your back."

Laura shook her head slowly, unable to look her friends in the eye. "I've known for years it would come to this," she told them. "I didn't want to admit it, but deep down, I never doubted it. Not when Roger and I haven't been able to talk to each other since . . . since . . . ever."

"I know." Claire was nodding enthusiastically. "Men really are like creatures from another planet, aren't they? They think differently, they talk differently . . . and they certainly have a different standard for table manners."

"Not all of them," Julie said quietly. "Not George."

Julie had been living with George Stanton — a man Laura invariably thought of as "sweet, gentle George" — for close to five years. From what Laura could see, they were the ideal couple, often held up as an example of how a man and a woman really could sustain a loving relationship.

"Just remember, Laura," Claire went on, "you're not alone. You've always got us."

"You've got Evan, too," Julie reminded

her. "And your writing. Don't forget that."

Claire rolled her eyes upward. "Thank God for work. If it hadn't been for that, I don't know how I ever would have gotten through my divorce."

"Just don't be too hard on yourself," Julie said soothingly. "It's going to be a long process, full of ups and downs. Expect to go through a grieving process. You've heard of Elisabeth Kübler-Ross's theory, haven't you? That there are five stages of grief?"

Laura nodded. "Denial, bargaining, anger, depression, and finally acceptance."

"Hah!" Claire countered. "Listen, ladies, I've been through this. And I'll tell you what the five stages are. First comes giving all his fifteen-hundred-dollar suits away to the Salvation Army. Second is consuming every ounce of chocolate in the entire state. Third is going on a shopping spree, buying gold-sequined halter tops and black leather jeans. Four is lying in bed for two weeks with nothing but six boxes of Kleenex. Five is —"

"Claire," Julie protested gently, "I'm not sure Laura needs to be hearing all this right now."

Claire waved Julie away with her hand. "I've got something better than advice. Here, Laura. I brought you the name of my lawyer." Reaching into her purple shoulder bag, she pulled out a business card. "If you're looking for revenge, he's your man."

"Revenge?" Laura repeated. So far, the concept hadn't even occurred to her.

"Of course. You want to get back at the louse, don't you?" Claire's expression was poisonous.

"I — I hadn't thought about it. I've been too busy thinking about more concrete concerns. Like where I'm going to live. What's going to happen to the house." She swallowed hard. "How we're going to tell Evan."

"You'll work all that out over time," Julie assured her. "But for now, I've got a suggestion, too."

"Another lawyer?" asked Claire, looking interested. "One who's even more ruthless than Irwin Hart?"

Julie reached into her purse and pulled out a tattered clipping from a newspaper.

"Don't tell me," said Claire. "A recipe for chicken soup."

"It's an article about a support group for people going through a divorce," Julie replied, smoothing out the crumpled piece of paper on the pink linen tablecloth. "It meets once a week, at the Y. I think you should go, Laura. Or at least consider it."

Pushing the article toward Laura, her eyes moist and filled with concern, Julie added, "It might help."

"Thank you." Laura tucked both contributions into her wallet. "Now, how about ordering? Getting divorced makes a person hungry."

"I told you!" Claire cried. "You're in Stage Two, the chocolate-eating stage!"

Laura stared out the window at an autumn evening that was already fading to night. October had always been her favorite month, but this year she found the drying leaves and early dusks threatening, a reminder that winter was looming in the wings. She longed to hibernate — or at least spend the evening curled up in bed with an engrossing novel and a bag of M&M peanuts.

Tonight she was expected to shine, however. Months earlier she'd arranged to do a book signing at the grand opening of a new Book Bonanza. Back then, garnering a little publicity had seemed like an exciting opportunity. At the moment she would have preferred having several teeth pulled.

The clock next to the bed warned her that it was getting late. In addition to finding a suitable outfit and a pair of shoes she wouldn't be embarrassed to wear in public, she had to put something in her stomach.

That meant venturing into the kitchen.

Ever since she'd told Roger she wanted a divorce, the tension in the house had been like that of an embassy under siege. Laura vacillated between trying to avoid him at all costs and wanting to fight. "This is my house, too" resounded through her brain a dozen times a day.

Laura usually opted for avoidance. She spent hours lying low in her bedroom, busying herself with tasks like organizing her earring collection. Tonight, however, she had no choice but to head downstairs. As she did, she put on the same mean expression she wore whenever she rode the New York City subways.

Her worst fears were realized. Roger was standing at the counter, microwaving the last hunk of leftover lasagne that Laura had had her eye on. She headed toward the refrigerator. Studying its contents, however, she realized tonight's dinner was going to consist of a bowl of Cheerios. As she moved around the kitchen, gathering the things she needed, Roger pointedly ignored her.

Then she reached for a spoon out of the silverware drawer at the same moment he grabbed a fork. Their hands brushed against each other. Instantly both of them withdrew.

"You know," Roger said evenly, "I think it'd make sense for us to work out a schedule for using the kitchen. That way we won't have to run into each other."

"If you moved out, we wouldn't have to go through this," Laura countered through clenched teeth.

"Oh, sure," he shot back, his tone instantly icy. "You'd love that, wouldn't you? That's exactly what you'd need to turn around and sue me for abandonment."

"I wouldn't do that, Roger! I just want to ease some of the tension around here. Not only for my own sake, but for Evan's as well!"

"Right. I can just picture your lawyer rubbing his hands together greedily."

"I don't have a lawyer."

"You will."

"All right; I will. But I have no intention of getting anything more out of this divorce than my fair share."

"Hah! The key word here is *fair*."

"I'm not going to accuse you of anything." Laura's voice had become pleading. "Don't you know me well enough to believe that?"

He stared at her coldly. "I thought I did. But it turns out I don't know you at all."

While Laura sat hunched over at the kitchen table, mechanically shoveling Cheerios into her mouth, Roger stomped around the kitchen. He slammed the door of the microwave. He rifled through the knives in the drawer with such ferociousness that it sounded like clashing armies, punctuating his movements with angry snorts.

By the time Laura was backing the car

out of the driveway, she wondered how she was going to get through the evening. What she wanted to do was indulge in a good cry, not gossip about giraffes and snakes.

Her only hope was for a meager turnout — so pathetic, in fact, that the store manager would take pity on her and cancel the event. And so her heart sank when she drove into the strip mall's parking lot and saw Book Bonanza's neon lights blazing through the dark autumn night, beckoning to the literate wayfarer. The blown-up faces of famous writers, most of them long dead, gazed out earnestly from the store windows. As if all that weren't enough, the Book Bonanza people had even brought in a cappuccino machine and a huge glass jar of *biscotti.*

Standing with her nose pressed against the window, Laura watched the throngs that had turned out for the store's opening night. Customers perused the stacks of best-sellers piled up near the front door, lovingly fondling the pages of Danielle Steel and Dean Koontz and John Grisham. They leafed through magazines with obscure titles like *The Organic Herb Gardener* and *Wood-Look Office Furniture Monthly*. A few stood half-hidden behind shelves, surreptitiously reading cartoon books.

Laura swallowed hard. She didn't know how she'd ever get through the evening. A tribe of butterflies began doing gymnastics routines in her stomach.

"Excuse me," she said with all the enthusiasm she could muster, cornering a young woman in an official-looking navy blue blazer and white name tag. "I'm Laura Briggs."

The woman stared at her blankly.

Run! thought Laura. Get out while you can!

Instead, she pointed to the four-foot poster six inches away from the woman, featuring a full-color blowup of the cover of *The Mystery of the Missing Mangoes*. "The author who's autographing tonight?"

"Oh, right! I'll get the manager." The woman's smile quickly vanished. "What was your name again?"

Laura recognized the person who ran the show right away. She was the energetic one, the woman who looked as if she knew what she was doing. She walked quickly, purposefully, pausing every so often to tuck a book further back on the shelf so that it was lined up with the others or to prop up a fallen volume on a display table.

"Laura?" she said, sensible heels clicking efficiently against the floor. "I'm Jennifer Norris. Thank you so much for coming tonight. We appreciate your taking time out of your hectic schedule to be here."

Laura suddenly realized how lucky she

was to be out of the house for the evening. And here the manager of Book Bonanza thought Laura Briggs, author, was doing *her* a favor.

"I'm hoping you'll autograph my copy of *Helena Hyena Has the Last Laugh*," Jennifer went on. "I made a point of bringing it from home. Of all your books, that's my favorite. I adore that part where Helena Hyena gets back at Johnny Jaguar and Lenny Leopard by laughing all the way to the riverbank."

Laura felt better already.

"But for now, come on back here. I'll show you where you'll be reading —"

"Reading?" Panic rose up. "I thought I was just autographing."

Jennifer waved her hand in the air casually. "Oh, we always like to start off with a short reading."

"How short?"

"Fifteen or twenty minutes, for children's books."

Laura gulped. For the past few days, ever since she'd so innocently invited Phil Donahue and guests into her living room, she'd been unable to focus on words on a printed page. Even instructions on a cake-mix box had been beyond her. An air of surrealism hung over everything. It was like living in Salvador Dali's world. Now, without the slightest bit of preparation, she was expected to act out the roles of a prim giraffe, a couple of troublemaking cats, and — if Jennifer had anything to do with it — a giddy hyena.

"I, uh, hadn't realized —"

"There's no problem, is there?" The store manager frowned.

"Oh, no." Laura forced a smile, and began planning her reward for getting through the evening. It was a toss-up between Pepperidge Farm and Häagen-Dazs.

"Attention, book lovers," a loud voice blared over the loudspeaker system. "Tonight Book Bonanza is pleased to present Lauren Briggs, reading from one of her best-selling children's books."

"Uh, that's Laura, not Lauren." She cleared her throat. "And, to be honest, none of my books were actually best-sellers. Of course, the Norwegian translation of *Lizards Need Hugs, Too* sold remarkably well —"

"Take a seat up here." Jennifer gestured toward a podium. "Here's my copy of *Helena Hyena*. You *will* indulge me, won't you?"

Laura nodded meekly.

"Tell you what. Get yourself settled, and I'll be back in a few minutes."

You've read to eight-year-olds before, Laura reminded herself, sitting on the thronelike seat in the middle of an elevated platform. All around her were brightly painted wooden cutouts of well-known characters from children's literature: Curious George, the Berenstain Bears, the ubiquitous Barney. Their presence made her nervous. In the first place, they were all better known — and better loved — than she was. In the second place, those characters were stars to *small* children, those who tended to steer clear of books with words in them. Still, she willed herself to be calm, reminding herself that it was only an hour out of her life. Two, at the most.

Wearing a self-conscious smile, Laura waited. Looking down at the huge store spread out before her, she felt she understood what the expression "lonely at the top" was all about.

At that moment she couldn't possibly feel worse. Her throat thickened as she took a brief inventory of her life. She was trapped in a house with a maniac who was taking out years' worth of anger on an unsuspecting microwave. Her son was so confused about all the tension in the house that he spent more time interacting with imaginary superheroes than with his own parents. And here she was, relegated to the humiliating role of supplicant, sitting alone in a corner of a bookstore, forcing a smile, wishing desperately that someone — anyone — would pay attention to her.

Finally a lone figure appeared, a woman

wandering out from the cookbook aisle. She did a double take when she caught sight of Laura. The woman's face lit up.

She recognizes me, Laura thought, smiling warmly. A fan.

The woman hesitated, then began walking over to the platform.

Things are already getting better. She's going to ask me for my autograph. Laura sat up a little straighter.

"Excuse me." The woman leaned toward Laura.

"Yes?"

"Could you please tell me where the ladies' room is?"

With a growl, Laura sent the woman off to find someone who got paid for spending time in the store.

Yet, surprisingly, she felt better. The situation suddenly seemed so absurd she had no choice but to enjoy the ridiculous aspects of it.

A few shoppers eventually straggled over. Two of them were men — divorced fathers, she speculated, desperate to find free entertainment for their fidgety offspring. Between them, they had three kids. The other adult was a woman, the doting mother of a beautiful blond-haired girl dressed completely in pink ruffles. Gingerly the adults lowered themselves into the teensy-weensy chairs arranged in a half circle in front of the stage. As for the children, they looked as if they had no intention of sitting at all, not for at least another six or eight years.

The average age of the children, Laura estimated, was two.

"Uh, Jennifer?" she whimpered, and began formulating her argument. Her books were geared toward much older children. Children who no longer sucked on book covers. Children who were able to refrain from scribbling with crayons across their favorite illustrations.

But Jennifer was nowhere to be seen. Laura was on her own.

She cringed when one of the fathers glanced at his watch and scowled.

"I guess we'll get started," she said brightly. After clearing her throat, she began, " 'Not long ago, in a jungle far, far away —' "

"Bah-nee!" a high-pitched voice suddenly screeched.

Laura glanced up. She saw that the little girl was pointing gleefully at the purple dinosaur behind her.

"Yes!" her adoring mother gushed loudly. "That's right, Brittany! That *is* Barney! Good for you!"

Laura cleared her throat once again. " 'Not long ago, in a jungle —' "

"I want to hug Bah-nee!" Goldilocks was already rushing onto the stage, her sticky fingers stretching toward the wooden model of the hottest TV celebrity since Big Bird.

"Isn't it past her bedtime?" Laura muttered through clenched teeth.

But the little girl had already climbed up onto the platform, right behind Laura. She grabbed hold of the purple figure, throwing her pudgy arms around its neck. "Bah-nee! Bah-nee!"

"Now, Brittany, you shouldn't run away like that." Brittany's mom, looking more proud than annoyed, crossed the stage in front of Laura to retrieve her bouncing baby girl. "We have to be polite to the lady who's reading us the nice story."

My story, Laura thought petulantly. *I* wrote it, Brit.

She was about to cast them both a scathing look when she remembered that another five pairs of eyes were watching her. Instead, she did her best to smile indulgently at little Brittany, now wailing at the top of her lungs as her mother dragged her away from her dino love.

"Let's see, where was — oh, yes." One more time, Laura cleared her throat. " 'Not long ago, in a jungle far, far away, there lived a giraffe named Gertrude. As all the animals knew, Gertrude was very good at —' "

"Attention, book lovers!" the loudspeaker suddenly blared. "Tonight Book Bonanza is pleased to announce that we're taking an extra twenty-five percent off all Stephen King novels. The supply is limited, so hurry over."

A restlessness instantly arose in the audience. Glancing up, Laura saw the two fathers exchange nervous looks.

" 'As all the animals knew, Gertrude was very good at solving mysteries. Everyone — including Helena Hyena.' "

The shuffling of feet and the scraping of chair legs against the linoleum floor caused Laura to look up one more time. The two dads were wandering off, the adventures of good-natured Helena Hyena proving to be no match for those of Stephen King's demonic characters. Sheepishly they slunk away, taking with them three quarters of the audience.

Laura surveyed the half circle of chairs, now empty except for Brittany and her mom. She was about to beg off when the woman raised her hand.

"Excuse me," she said. "Do you think instead of reading that book, you could read one that has Barney in it?"

By the time Laura put her autographing pen away, she'd decided that the winner of the contest for tonight's reward would have to be Häagen-Dazs. After this ordeal, only something with nuts, chips, and a three-digit fat-gram count would do.

As she zipped up her purse she became aware that someone was standing in front of her. She glanced up, expecting Jennifer.

"Ms. Briggs?" a woman about Laura's age asked shyly.

"Yes?"

"I wasn't sure if it was really you. I mean, the sign said you'd be here tonight, and, of course, I recognized your book on that poster over there. . . . But I could hardly believe I'd actually have the chance to meet you in person."

Laura just blinked.

"You see, all three of my children are big fans of yours. Of course, the two older girls are reading chapter books now. But David still can't get enough of Gertrude and Carol. In fact, promising to read your books is the only way I can get him into bed."

Tentatively the woman handed over a well-worn copy of Laura's first book, along with spanking-new copies of the two latest ones. "If you'd be kind enough to sign these for my children, I know they'd be absolutely thrilled."

Laura reached for the books. "I'd love to."

Maybe I'm not a wife anymore, she thought as she opened the book on top. But at least I'm still a writer.

Chapter Four

"Today, Laura Briggs Walsh, well-known author of more than a dozen children's books, was charged with first-degree murder at her home in Clover Hollow, an upscale suburb on Long Island's north shore. The victim: her husband, forty-five-year-old Roger Walsh."

The newscaster is speaking earnestly into a video camera, trying her best to look dignified as she stands in the middle of Laura's front lawn, strewn with roller skates, Roller Blades, a bicycle, and half a dozen other artifacts of an eight-year-old boy's life.

Laura takes a moment to wish she'd gotten on Evan's case about picking up after himself as she's led out the back door by a police officer. The video cameras are still whirring. She tries, unsuccessfully, to shield her face with the collar of her raincoat, the one she's been meaning to bring to the dry cleaner for weeks. Photographers from all the Long Island and New York papers are there. The New York Times. Newsday. Even the local edition of The Pennysaver. Flashbulbs explode in her face.

"She's an animal!" cries one of the dozens

of onlookers, a man in an undershirt and drooping jeans who's brandishing his beer can.

"She's not an animal," counters a woman clutching a bag of groceries. "She's a woman who needs a good lawyer!"

"She was merciless!" someone else cries.

"All she wanted was her just revenge," claims the woman.

Laura can remain silent no longer. "I didn't mean to kill him!" she cries. "It just happened! One minute I was arranging the steak knives in the drawer, and the next thing I knew —"

"Mo-o-o-om!" Evan's whiny voice pulled her out of her nightmarish reverie. "Today's gym, and I can't find any clean sweatpants."

For once, Laura was actually glad for the excuse to drag herself out of bed. Not that the fantasy she'd been spinning as she lay in bed was entirely rooted in fiction. Today she was making her initial foray into the world of the legal jungle. The day before, she'd made an appointment with a lawyer. A *divorce* lawyer. She'd dialed three times before she was able to keep herself from hanging up. It was such a monumental step. Such a definitive step. Above all, such a final step.

The fact that Irwin Hart had been Claire's lawyer bothered her, too. Laura's instincts told her that following Claire's recommendation for anything would be like borrowing one of her Lycra miniskirts: it would turn out to be much too much for Laura. Still, with no other ideas about whom to try, she'd decided to check him out.

She felt as if she were about to sneak off on a secret mission as she slapped peanut butter and jelly on white bread for Evan's school lunch and tried to carry on a meaningful discussion about why the Teenage Mutant Ninja Turtles no longer held the same cachet they once had. Through it all, Roger remained silent. He sat at the kitchen table, drinking coffee and looking sullen. Laura tried to quell her irritation — with him, of course, and with the fact that despite her decision to get out of her marriage, she was still living with the same husband in the same house, with the same anger gnawing away at the half-chewed bagel sitting in her stomach — by reminding herself that things weren't that different from what they'd been all along. On the upside, she realized that her days of breakfasting with a hostile, brooding husband were numbered.

She was standing in front of the mirror in Irwin Hart's reception area, looking with dismay at the sad, tired face staring back at her, when she remembered that this wasn't just any day. Today was her fif-

71

teenth wedding anniversary.

She was supposed to be buying champagne. Wrapping either a cappuccino maker or a bathrobe in colorful gift paper. Maybe even plotting a few surprises for the bedroom: reintroducing candles, perhaps, or even throwing caution to the wind and removing her socks. Instead, she was taking a mental inventory of their possessions, struggling to remember who'd originally owned the collection of Byrds albums, agonizing over who was entitled to the margarita glasses.

Looking at her reflection in the mirror, Laura watched her face crumple. "Oh, my God," she cried. "This is really happening!"

Even in her despair, she found herself thinking back, appreciating the tragedy of her marriage's end but not for a minute glossing over the realities that had brought her to this point. Today, on her wedding anniversary, she couldn't help but remember where she'd been fifteen years earlier.

Maybe planning and executing the wedding hadn't been enough to tip her off. But from where she now stood, Laura realized that the honeymoon should have opened her eyes to the fact that marrying Roger Walsh had been a bad choice in the cosmic game of Let's Make a Deal.

"If this is what it feels like to be married,

I'm going to love being a wife." Reaching across the front seat of the car, Laura placed her hand on Roger's thigh. When he rewarded her with a contented purr, she settled back in her seat, taking care not to spill the glass of lukewarm champagne she'd been nursing ever since they'd crossed the border into Canada.

This, she was certain, was sheer bliss: the two of them trundling down a country road in the vintage Volkswagen bug they'd borrowed from Dirk, the silhouettes of peace signs and oversized daisies still visible in bright sunlight. The late-afternoon sun beamed down approvingly, and while the champagne could easily have passed for a Woolite wash, the idea of drinking something French in broad daylight was even more intoxicating than the alcohol. Then there was the scenery. Here a barn, there a cow . . . Their surroundings were so pastoral it was difficult to believe they were less than an hour from Toronto, their destination for an intensive five-day training program for the marriage business.

A Canadian honeymoon had been her idea. A trip up north contained the exotic elements of a foreign vacation without such annoyances as passports, phrase books, and astronomical Visa bills. She was looking forward to tackling a new city armed with comfortable shoes, a good guidebook, and unwavering enthusiasm. Even more, she was filled with anticipation over the prospect of trying on the mantle of *wife* in neutral territory. It would take time to get used to the idea of traveling with a partner, not only through another country, but more important, through her own life.

When she and Roger had climbed into the car at dawn, they'd both been excited. The icing on the cake was finding the bon voyage present Claire had left on the backseat: a huge wicker basket containing crackers, cheeses, chocolates, and a modest-sized bottle of icy champagne. Also tucked into the tissue paper was a pair of tulip glasses. One sported a tiny black bow tie, the other a white satin ribbon.

"I hope the hotel's nice." Laura slid her fingers across Roger's leg. "Then again, as long as our room has a big, comfortable bed, I guess the rest doesn't matter much."

Suddenly the Volkswagen lurched. The car shuddered and the engine lost power. Laura automatically assumed that the provocative dip her stroking fingers had just taken was responsible. But then the car veered off to the side of the road. Anxiously she glanced over at Roger. His expression was dark.

"Damn!" he barked, slapping the steering wheel with the palm of his hand. "I told Dirk to have this stupid car checked out before we took it on such a long trip."

Laura dropped her hand primly into her own lap. "Why didn't he?"

Roger grimaced. "He probably didn't have the cash."

"Gee, and he gave us such a generous wedding present," Laura commented dryly. The Ziploc bag containing three ounces of marijuana had been left at home, along with the hand-crocheted coasters and the silver ice bucket engraved with a monogram that ignored Laura's decision to keep her own name. "Now what?"

Roger sat slumped behind the wheel, his arms folded across his chest. "We sit back and hope the Canadian people are friendly."

While Laura couldn't vouch for the entire population, the aging farmer who pulled his dusty pickup truck alongside and asked if they could use a hand was certainly helpful. The driver of the tow truck was downright palsy-walsy. As for the proprietor of Cyril's Auto Repair, he was grinning like a jack-o'-lantern as they said good-bye, leaving him their disabled vehicle.

"Look at it this way," Roger said with uncharacteristic cheerfulness as they stood on the corner in front of a scone shop, waiting for a bus. "We've already gotten to see a part of Toronto most tourists never get to see."

The Royal York Hotel was not only nice;

it embodied the kind of old-world elegance and charm that Laura had only experienced in Edith Wharton novels. She was almost able to forget about the Great Auto Disaster that evening as she lay back in an oversized bathtub beneath a mound of scented bubbles. She hoped that while she was untying knots in muscles she hadn't even known she possessed, Roger was turning back the bedspread, spraying on deodorant, and carrying out all the other preparations a groom on his honeymoon would be apt to make. So when she heard him speaking through the closed bathroom door, she sat up and listened.

"Hello? This is room seven-eighteen. I'd like to order movie number three. . . . Uh, I believe it's called *The Harder They Come.* . . ."

Dripping bubbles all over the floor, Laura went to the bathroom doorway, a towel concealing as much of her body as possible.

"Roger?" she demanded, incredulous. "What are you doing?"

He glanced up at her, his hand covering the receiver of the telephone. "Just ordering up some entertainment. I figured — Yes, I'm here. Eight o'clock sounds fine. Go ahead and bill it to the room."

"Roger, I don't think —"

Before she could manage to say more, the telephone rang. She hoped it was the front desk, informing them that due to technical difficulties, the wayward cheerleaders or stewardesses or whomever room seven-eighteen had ordered would be unavailable. Instead, it was Cyril.

"Whoooo," Roger breathed into the phone, his back turned to Laura. "That much, huh?"

"What did he say?" she demanded, perching on the edge of the bed. By then, she'd abandoned the idea of a long, hot soak in the tub. Instead, she was pulling clothes over her still damp limbs.

"The car needs a new engine. Cyril says the old one —"

"How much is 'that much'?"

Roger swallowed hard. "Five hundred bucks."

She stared at the carpeting, waiting for the rising panic to subside. "Whose five hundred bucks?" she finally asked.

"We'd better call Dirk."

So it was that the first night of Laura and Roger's honeymoon was spent in the company of romping cheerleaders . . . and the second night with Dirk and his pal Igor stretched out in sleeping bags on the floor of their honeymoon hideaway. Dirk, after all, was the rightful owner of the ailing VW. If he chose to tow it all the way back to Pennsylvania behind Igor's truck so he could personally fiddle with the recalcitrant engine, that was his business. Of course, where they spent the night was also Laura's. Still, she was a new bride, on her very best behavior, and she couldn't bring herself to exile her brother-in-law of two days to the Y when she was enjoying such luxurious accommodations.

That escapade, it turned out, was merely a precursor of the even more symbolic event that was to follow. On day three, over breakfast, Roger had a suspicious glint in his eyes, unlike anything Laura'd seen since he'd watched the cheerleaders video.

"I had a great idea," he told her. "How about renting a sailboat and taking it out on Lake Ontario? You and I haven't had a chance to go sailing together yet. So far," he added with a wink, "you've only heard about my prowess at sea. I'm anxious to show off."

Lounging on the back of the fourteen-foot sailboat that was theirs for the day, Laura couldn't remember the last time she'd felt so relaxed. Even though it was October, the day was unseasonably warm. She had no duties but to be appreciative. Roger, meanwhile, bustled around, trying to impress his new bride with his knowledge of peculiar knots and sails with names that sounded like acronyms.

"Mmm, that sun feels good," she commented, pulling off her sunglasses and squinting in the bright light. "I think I'll take a dip in the lake."

"Good idea," Roger said, flashing her a smile.

Standing perched on the edge of the boat, about to dive in, Laura noticed her wedding ring. Feeling a rush of protectiveness toward both her new status and her new jewelry, she pulled it off her finger.

"Here." She handed it to Roger, saying, "Hold this for me," as she jumped into the lake.

She never did fully understand the sequence of events that followed. It had to do with changing sails, fiddling with those knots Roger prided himself on knowing so much about. All she knew was that as she shivered in the icy water, wondering what on earth she'd been thinking, she noticed something gold glinting in the sunlight. With a tiny splash, it dropped into the water.

It only took her a few seconds to figure out what had happened. The look on Roger's face, the fact that there were only so many substances capable of catching the light in just that way . . . As she treaded water Laura's stomach cramped.

Her wedding ring. Gone.

"I hope what happened today isn't a bad sign," Roger said later that evening, chuckling. The two of them sat at a small table in a dark corner of a Basque restaurant, the plump couple who owned it watching anxiously to see if they were duly appreciative of the excellent cuisine. The tiny restaurant seemed to have been designed with honeymooners in mind. Candles dripped wax over wine bottles. The large china plates looked hand painted, the occasional chip only adding more to the ambience. As for the food, it couldn't have been tastier even if its ingredients had been identifiable.

Laura's smile was the cheeriest one she could manage. The last thing she wanted to do was cast a shadow over what was supposed to be a romantic evening.

"Don't worry about the ring," she insisted. "It's just a piece of metal, forty dollars worth of gold. I can replace it easily enough once we get home."

She reached for her glass of champagne, much drier than Claire's choice and served icy cold. Somehow, it didn't taste nearly as wonderful as the tepid stuff she'd sipped in the front seat of the car only days earlier.

Laura never did admit to Roger how much her feelings had been hurt by his carelessness with her ring, the first important thing he'd ever given to her, a symbol of a union that was meant to last. She'd never even admitted it to herself. Yet while the event was something she hadn't thought about for years, as she stood outside a divorce lawyer's office, it suddenly seemed of monumental importance.

Laura tried to concentrate on the present as she sat down in a hard wooden chair opposite Irwin Hart, folding her hands in her lap anxiously. Her focus, she reminded herself, should be not on herself, but on the man on the other side of the desk.

What struck her most were his small, dark eyes. She immediately thought of the word *beady*, and found herself considering adding a vulture to the cast of characters in her jungle books.

Irwin Hart had an odd way of looking at people, staring not into their eyes but just a bit higher. Laura found it disconcerting. Self-consciously she smoothed the top of her hair.

"So you want out of a marriage," he said, in a low monotone.

"Uh, yes." Laura squirmed in her chair. "I don't really know what steps I have to take —"

"Leave all that to me. That is, if you decide to avail yourself of my services." He leaned forward, forming an inverted V with his hands. He wore a big ring on either pinky. One was a solid band of gold, so thick it reminded her of a Life Saver. The other had a diamond as big as a Ritz cracker.

Clearing her throat, Laura continued.

"There are a few questions I'd like to ask before I decide —"

"Of course, of course." Irwin Hart spoke so quickly that she wondered if he had someone waiting in the next room.

"First of all," she said, her pen poised over the pad she'd taken out of her purse, "I'd like to know what percentage of your law practice is devoted to, uh, divorce."

"All of it." Irwin Hart reached into the center drawer of his desk and took out two shiny silver balls, smaller and smoother than golf balls. He held them both in his right hand, moving them back and forth, back and forth, tapping and grinding them against each other.

"I see. Well, that's good. Uh, I guess I'll need to know what you require as a retainer —" She stopped, suddenly aware of another noise in the room, less grating but distracting nevertheless. "Do you hear tapping?"

"Hmm? Oh, that's just my foot. Mrs. Walsh —"

"I go by the name Laura Briggs."

"Wise decision, keeping your maiden name. Makes a lot of things . . . simpler. Do you have credit cards in your name?"

"Yes, I made a point of —"

"Good credit rating?"

"Yes, I always —"

"Own checking account?"

"Uh, no, we —"

"Open one immediately. First thing tomorrow. Today, if you can get to the bank. Own savings account?"

"No, I —"

"How about bugs?"

"Excuse me?"

"Do you know how to plant a bug in the phone?"

"Of course not!"

He shook his head. "Child's play."

Laura opened her mouth to protest. But she stopped when she saw that for the first time since she'd entered his office, Irwin Hart's eyes had met hers. "Ms. Briggs, these are all mere details, things we can work out over time. What I started to say is that what's important here is for you to know that should you choose to have me represent you in your divorce, I can guarantee that I'll get your husband by the . . ."

He lowered his eyes to his right hand, an eerie smile creeping slowly across his face.

Laura opened the back door quietly late that afternoon, hoping to sneak up to the bedroom undetected. The last thing she was in the mood for was a confrontation with Roger.

She'd left her brief meeting with Irwin Hart seriously unnerved. Instead of feeling calm and in control, as if she now had a pillar of strength on her side, she felt as if she'd stepped into a Fellini movie. She headed for the first phone booth she could find, and made desperate calls to friends and friends of friends. Fortunately, they were able to come up with the names of half a dozen lawyers. She set up three firm appointments with likely prospects, which took the edge off her anxiety.

Her mission completed, she'd been at a loss as to how to spend the rest of the day. While her word processor beckoned, she couldn't bring herself to go home. Roger was bound to be there. It was her wedding anniversary, and the last person she wanted to spend the day with was her husband.

So she'd done what any other woman living in the suburbs would do: she headed for the mall. Aimlessly she'd wandered about, fondling merchandise she had no intention of buying. Glancing around, she saw she was hardly the only one spending the day this way. The place was amazingly filled with people just hanging out.

Finally, Laura slunk into the house as silently as a jungle cat, ruminating about the plot of her latest book.

So she was completely caught off guard when she discovered she'd just stepped onto the set from *Fantasy Island*.

The dining room was dark except for the pale, flickering light cast by the candles in the middle of the table. There were four, mismatched, lopsided, half-burned. Laura recognized them immediately. They were the ones she and Roger used during their first months of marriage, back when making love still seemed like one of the basic necessities of life. Seeing them again made her cringe.

A bottle of champagne sat alongside two glasses, white with frost. Roger, standing in front of the little surprise he'd concocted, had to have grabbed them out of the freezer as she was pulling into the driveway. Behind him, in a tall vase, was a big bouquet of long-stemmed red roses, the official flower of people in love.

"Roger, you shouldn't have —"

"Happy anniversary."

"But —"

He held up both hands. "Don't say a word, Laura. Just listen. You owe me that much, after fifteen years of marriage, don't you?"

"I suppose so." Her voice quivered.

"Okay. I admit that what I did, going on *Donahue* like that and spilling my guts, probably wasn't the brightest thing I've ever done."

"I bet Norm and Dwayne feel the same way."

"As for lying to you, not to mention going through most of our savings —"

"Please." Laura shut her eyes tightly. "I

can't even bear to think about that."

"I admit I was wrong. I really screwed up. But now that everything's out in the open, we can start to talk."

She sighed. "Roger, I've been trying to find a way to talk to you for fifteen years. I've tried being nice. I've tried being direct. I've even tried ignoring you, concentrating on my own life and trying not to be too bothered by the fact that ever since the beginning, our marriage has caused me nothing but heartache. . . ."

"We can start again."

"It's too late."

"What about the house?"

Laura looked around the dining room, cast in shadow by the flickering candles. She expected to feel pangs of remorse. And so she was startled by the absence of even the slightest reaction.

"We'll sell the house."

"Laura, this is our house."

"It's just a building."

"What about Evan? Or is he 'just our son'?"

Laura drew in her breath sharply. Evan. That was the part she couldn't bear to face. Every time she thought about what this was going to do to him, her heart felt leaden. Breaking up her marriage meant breaking up his family. He'd done nothing to deserve such a loss. He was only eight years old.

During all those years of rationalizing, calling upon every available resource to keep her marriage going, Evan had played a starring role. With a certain smugness Laura had read the magazine articles on the problems faced by children of divorce, relieved that this was one difficulty her son would never have to deal with.

The mere thought of telling him Mom and Dad were tearing his family apart made her knees weaken and her stomach cramp. Yet while in her heart she was distraught over what a divorce would do to him, in her mind she knew she couldn't be a very good mother to her child if she was angry and unhappy.

Besides, she'd reached the point where there was simply no other choice.

"Living in a family that's unhappy isn't good for Evan, either," she finally replied, grasping the back of a dining room chair for support.

"Unhappy? *I* wasn't unhappy. *He* wasn't unhappy."

"*I* was. It never worked right. I've felt alone for years." Laura burst into tears. "Don't you get it? I can't live with you anymore!" She flipped the light switch, casting the room in light so bright it caused them both to blink.

"I don't want this," Roger insisted. "I'm not going to let it happen."

"You can't stop it. It's already happening."

"Laura —"

"I saw a divorce lawyer today."

She took a deep breath. She could see the pain her words caused him. For a brief second her heart felt as if it were being crushed. But she knew she had to be strong. She had to remember her own pain. Even more, to hold on to the conviction that protecting herself from it counted, too.

"I'm sorry, Roger. I really am. But I suggest that you get yourself a lawyer, too."

He just stared at her until she looked away, no longer able to meet his eyes with her own.

Chapter Five

Laura ran her finger along the smooth edge of her coffee mug, watching the hands of the kitchen clock edge toward seven.

Her hair hung limply in her face and her shoulders were slumped. Sitting alone in the kitchen, weighed down by the silence of the house, she wondered if she would ever feel whole again. Her decision to leave the marriage that had dragged her down for so many years had been hard, but it was nothing compared to living with the aftermath. Shutting her eyes tight, she felt the roller coaster.

If only I can hold on, she told herself, I'll get through it. One day it'll all be over. I'll be my old self again. I'll be the star of an exciting new movie: *Laura's Life: Part Two.*

What terrified her was that she still didn't have the faintest idea what the plot would be.

She couldn't even be sure of the setting, since Roger had yet to agree to move out of the house. Glancing around the kitchen, Laura tried to imagine leaving it behind. Right now, giving up something so familiar was unimaginable. With everything else in her life shifting beneath her feet, she clung to whatever constants she could find.

As for the cast of characters, she'd been slowly working down her checklist of those who had to be told. While she'd been certain Julie and Claire would be supportive, she wasn't as sure about her parents.

"Mom, Dad, there's something I need to talk to you about."

When she had told them, sitting on the living-room couch in the house where she'd grown up, Laura had felt ten years old again. It was as if she were confessing to her parents that she'd been sent to the principal's office for passing notes. Only this time, not only was she bringing herself down, her actions affected her child, as well.

The tense, somewhat confused look on her parents' faces prompted her to lower her eyes. Quickly she replayed in her mind the speech she'd carefully planned: "Mother, Father, Roger and I are splitting up. Yes, I know it's a big decision, but I want you to know I've given this a great deal of thought. . . ."

"Oh, Mom!" Laura gasped instead, bursting into tears. "I'm getting divorced!"

She braced herself for a barrage of "I told you so's." At the very least, her parents were entitled to indulge in a little tearing down of Roger. Yet her mother came over and put her arms around her. She hugged her for a few moments, then smoothed back her hair, just as she'd done whenever Laura came to her after suffering a scraped knee or a slight at school.

"Honey," her mother told her, "whatever you decide to do is right."

Taking a sip of coffee now, Laura forced herself to confront the painful fact that things wouldn't go nearly as smoothly with Evan. In fact, the prospect of telling her son his mom and dad were getting divorced was what had kept her awake all night, tossing and turning like a wooden ship in a storm. Of everyone concerned, an eight-year-old boy who'd done nothing to create this situation was going to suffer the most.

When she heard Roger coming upstairs from the basement where he'd begun sleeping on the foldout couch, she tensed. Simply being in the same room with him was difficult. And this morning she had something much more important to talk to him about than whose turn it was to take out the garbage. The coffee sloshing around in her stomach picked that moment to turn to acid.

"You look terrible," Roger commented, glancing at her before he headed over to the coffeepot.

Laura wondered if she was imagining the gleeful undertone to his words. "I didn't sleep last night."

"Join the club."

"Roger, we have to tell Evan." Laura swallowed hard. "And we should tell him soon. I don't want him finding out from someone else."

Roger cast her a stony look. "All right," he said slowly. "Why don't we tell him tonight?"

"Tonight?"

"You said we should tell him soon." Roger's mouth twisted into a sneer. "Tonight's not a good time for you?"

Her stomach churned. "Tonight's fine."

Laura yearned to point out there would never be a good time to tell their son his parents were getting divorced. Instead, she picked up her coffee cup and retreated to her bedroom.

Sitting on the edge of her bed, staring out the window at the colorless sky, Laura attempted to will away her sick feeling. She wanted so badly to make sense of it all. Over and over again she replayed scenes from her life with Roger, trying to figure out what they could have done differently.

Almost from the very start she'd recognized that something wasn't right. Early in their first year together, when she was still insisting to herself that anytime now her new husband would tire of the "break" he was taking and get a job, she had casually opened a bank statement that came in the mail. She froze. Of course, she was aware that she'd dipped into her savings account several times since the wedding, anxious to support the freewheeling lifestyle she and Roger were quickly adapting to. Yet it wasn't until she was forced to confront the bottom line on a page of computer printout that she understood just how badly off they were.

She found Roger in the bedroom of their small apartment. He was clipping his toe-nails, using the classified ads of *The New York Times* as a catchall.

"Roger," she said as evenly as she could, "I just got a statement from Citibank. I must admit, I haven't been paying very close attention to how much money we've been going through."

"Yeah?" He paused, his nail clipper poised in midair, the toes on his right foot fanned out. "And?"

She took a deep breath. "My savings account is almost wiped out."

He looked at her expectantly. "What's your point?"

"I think you should get a job!"

Roger resumed his nail clipping, shaking his head. "I'm too busy. I've got too many other important things to do."

Laura stared at him. "All I want," she said, still trying to remain calm, "is a little bit of security. Some money coming in on a regular basis. Some savings in the bank for a rainy day. Maybe it's even time to start tucking something away for our future."

"If that's what matters to you," Roger shot back with an air of finality that sent chills down Laura's spine, "then you're ordinary."

Was it that early on that he'd closed off to her? Laura wondered. She stood up, listlessly tugging at the sheets in a half-hearted attempt at making the bed. Was it at that point he'd begun criticizing everything she did? Fifteen years worth of incriminations played through her mind like a tape. She ate too much sugar. Her friends were uninteresting. Her housecleaning wasn't up to his standards — at least his theoretical standards, since he rarely got involved in any household chores besides depositing his dirty clothes on the floor of the closet.

The criticism that hurt the most was his insistence that her skill at lovemaking simply didn't measure up.

By the time they'd reached their six-month anniversary, Laura was already pouncing upon magazine articles like "Celebrities Speak Out: Surefire Tips That Keep the Fire Burning." Roger had no qualms about telling her he wanted their sex life to improve. And according to him, it was always Laura, not he, who needed remedial work. Afraid that she was letting him down, she became more and more determined to live up to his expectations.

One Friday evening, as she waited for him to come home from a freelance job, she anxiously surveyed the scene she'd set. A cream-colored linen tablecloth covered the dining-room table, an attractive complement to both the pair of tall, slender candles and the bouquet of fresh spring flowers, their colors as intense as their fragrance. As for the menu, she'd carefully included all Roger's favorites: spareribs, herbed biscuits, a bottle of wine.

Her heart was pounding as she heard his key in the lock. Roger paused in the doorway, his expression changing from haggard to surprised. "What's this?"

"Oh, just a little something I cooked up." Laura didn't bother to mention that the inspiration for her romantic evening *à deux* was rooted in the latest issue of the *Ladies' Home Journal.* "I thought we deserved a quiet evening all to ourselves."

"Great." Roger sat down at the table, peeking under the cloth napkin that covered the basket of rolls. After casting her an appreciative glance, he grabbed a biscuit.

By the time Laura had served the Boston cream pie, the candles were burned halfway down, the wine bottle was empty, and her bare feet were in his lap.

"Let's go into the bedroom," she murmured.

This time, she told herself, shuffling down the hall with her arm slung around his waist, Roger and I will connect. We'll be closer than we've ever been before. I *know* we can. I can make it happen.

Lying with him in bed, she forced herself to shut out every defense, every reservation, every thought of anything besides the here and now. She even put aside her usual self-consciousness about her body. She knew Roger wished she were thinner, more graceful, more agile . . . freer. Tonight she refused to worry about any of that.

Instead, she concentrated on the sensation of the taut skin on the familiar curves of his shoulders. She pressed her breasts against his chest and felt a rush of excitement when she was rewarded with a satisfied smile. Her body responded to his in a way it never had before. As he pushed inside her she moved against him hard, giving in to the longing to have him as close to her as possible.

Afterward, Laura lay with her head on his stomach, her hair splayed out on his chest. One arm was flung across his waist while with her other hand she caressed him. When she heard his breathing turn heavy and even, she, too, fell asleep.

She woke up alone. Yet she was still glowing as she followed the sounds of coffee being made and found Roger in the kitchen.

Coming up behind him, she wrapped her arms around his waist.

"Hmmm," she purred, nuzzling the back of his neck. "That was nice last night, wasn't it?"

"Well," he replied matter-of-factly, "it was better."

As she finished making the bed, Laura sank down onto it. Whatever energy she'd awoken with was already sapped.

"I was never good enough," Laura said aloud. "No matter what I did, it was never enough."

Tears stung her eyes. Annoyed, she wiped them. Desperate for an antidote to the ache in her heart, she switched on the radio on the night table.

Bonnie Raitt was mournfully singing "I Can't Make You Love Me."

"Listen to that," Laura muttered. "They're playing our song."

She let out what was meant to be a laugh. Instead, it came out a sob.

There was an unreal quality to the scene that Laura found herself in that evening: three reluctant participants gathered in the kitchen, Laura and Roger sitting at the table, Evan standing in the doorway, impatient to get back to his Nintendo game. Part of her was shrieking, No! I don't want this!

97

I can't do it! Yet she knew this was just one more part of the roller-coaster ride. She had to hold on. If she could only hold on . . .

"What, Dad?" Evan said, his body present but his mind clearly in the living room with the Mario Brothers.

Something in Laura switched off. What she was experiencing was like an out-of-body episode. Her flesh was here, but her mind had departed, unable to accept the fact that this horrible moment was real. She felt as if she were watching a movie. Everything seemed to be moving in slow motion. Above all, she felt the urge to run away, or at least to do something — anything — to stop what was about to unfold.

We don't have to do this, she thought. Roger and I can put our arms around each other and laugh and tell Evan to go back to his Nintendo game. We can say that Mom and Dad were just kidding. . . .

But it was too late for that. Mom and Dad *weren't* just kidding. And so there was nothing she could do to set time back to its normal speed. Or make the wrenching pain in her gut go away.

"Evan," she heard Roger say, his voice sounding very far away, as if he were at the other end of a tunnel, "your mother and I have decided we can't live together anymore. We're going to get a divorce."

Through the tears welling up in her eyes,

Laura watched her son. He looked so small, standing in the doorway in the bright red shirt he'd picked out himself to wear that morning, his idea of an antidote to a gray, cheerless autumn day. He looked so alone.

"Can I go back to my game now?" he asked, his voice thin.

"Sure," said Roger.

And then, still standing in the doorway, Evan's face crumpled. He began to cry. His shoulders shook. The entire house seemed to tremble from his high-pitched, plaintive wail.

Suddenly Laura's tears were flowing freely as well. This is the worst, she told herself, her arms wrapped around herself. This is the worst moment in the whole process. It will never be this bad again. Nothing in my entire life will ever be this bad.

She longed to take Evan in her arms, to cry with him. But Roger had already grabbed him, holding him in a crushing embrace, his head next to Evan's, almost humorously large by comparison.

"It'll be all right, Ev," Roger assured him, his own voice cracking as he, too, let his tears fall. "Mom and I both still love you. That won't change. That'll never change."

"No-o-o-o!" Evan wailed. "I don't want it! No! You can't do it!"

Laura closed her eyes tightly, wishing she could banish this scene from her mind forever. She knew she never would. Evan, his small shoulders shaking, his wispy blond hair falling into his eyes . . . He was really still just a baby. It was unfair that the foibles of grownups could inflict so much pain on someone so innocent, so powerless.

She wondered if he, too, would remember this moment forever. She wondered if he would ever wear that shirt again, having learned that even the brightest, reddest garment was, in the end, a useless weapon.

Walking into the Divorce and Separation Support Group for the first time, Laura felt the way she had on her first day of junior high school. Would everybody else already know each other? Would anyone talk to her? Was she dressed appropriately? Would she turn out to be younger than everyone else — or older or quieter or louder or taller or shorter or any number of points of comparison on which she had the potential to fall short?

Despite her fears, she knew she had to rise above her own sophomoric concerns. The trauma of telling Evan that his family was about to fall apart had left her completely deflated. Walking around with a weight on her shoulders and a sick feeling in her stomach, she was desperate for relief. A way of putting everything into perspective. Perhaps even some answers.

She'd held on to the newspaper clipping Julie had given her, keeping it in one of the piles of papers that ended up occupying seven-eighths of her desk no matter how many times she pledged to get herself organized. Finally, sitting alone in her bedroom a few days after she and Roger had had their little talk with Evan, listening to the rain pound against the windows, she remembered it. Suddenly crazed, she began rifling through invitations to speak at local libraries, bits of dialogue suitable for large mammals scrawled on the backs of memos from Evan's school, and telephone numbers without any names attached to them, until she finally found it.

She scanned the article, curious but maintaining a certain skepticism. The idea of exposing herself in front of a roomful of strangers was nothing short of terrifying. Doing it at the word processor, with an entire jungle full of characters to hide behind, was one thing. Laying bare her soul to a real live audience was another.

Another factor that had kept her from making the initial telephone call earlier, responding to the invitation in the article's final paragraph to *call Marilyn for further information*, was her concern over the value of sitting around with a group of fellow divorcées and separatées, complaining.

What insights could possibly be provided by people who had also tried their hand at marriage . . . and failed? The prospect reminded her of chatting with the other cruise ship passengers huddled in the lifeboat about how they all should have been learning to operate a radio instead of spending so much time playing shuffleboard.

In the end, her desperation got the better of her. After spending the day debating whether or not she would actually be able to go through with it, Laura found herself turning in to the parking lot of the Y, butterflies wreaking havoc with the Budget Gourmet entrée she'd wolfed down at dinnertime.

Marilyn had explained over the phone that the evening started off with a coffee hour. Laura expected a small gathering, so she was shocked to see how crowded the meeting room actually was.

She stood in the doorway for a few seconds, taking deep, calming breaths as she surveyed the room. Nearly a hundred people had gathered, some of them standing around in small groups, cocktail party style, others sitting at big round tables, as if they were at a bar mitzvah . . . or a wedding. Just inside the door, a table held an industrial-sized coffee urn, and a tray of store-brand cookies that she immediately pronounced not worth the calories. A pool table and a couch had been pushed to the back of the room.

Edging her way in, Laura strove to maintain an expression that was friendly yet detached. She helped herself to a cup of coffee she didn't really want, then sat down at a table in the corner, as far away from the action as she could get without sitting in the hall. She felt like a wallflower. Her worst fantasies were coming true. It appeared that everyone knew each other. Everybody was chattering away happily, chuckling at inside jokes and slapping each other on the back and making brunch dates. As if that weren't bad enough, from where she sat it appeared that everybody else even had a better eye for jewelry.

Still, she'd come this far. Laura leaned forward, eavesdropping on other people's conversations. After all, she argued with herself, you might as well get a feel for what this is all about before deciding whether to stick it out or grab your coat and make a run for the door.

She heard a large woman declare in a voice that would have made Ethel Merman sound like an angel, "So I says to him, 'Ya don't send your child-support checks, ya don't see your kids.' "

Behind her, a tall man in a brown suit with a distinct polyester sheen was confiding in another man, ". . . nothing but a hot plate and one of those bar-sized refrigerators. If I ever want to invite a woman over for dinner, I'm going to have to send out for Chinese."

A petite woman with flame red hair declared, "I feel so strong. So . . . so powerful. I never knew I could feel this way."

An older man, probably close to seventy, was shaking his head slowly. "It's hard. It's just so hard."

Coat grabbing was becoming a stronger possibility. But Laura was distracted from plotting her escape when she felt someone pull out the chair next to hers. Automatically she jerked her seat away, scooping up her coat. It was the moment of truth. After a second's indecision, she slung the coat across the back of her chair and, glancing over in the newcomer's direction, smiled. "Hello."

The woman beside her sat clutching her pocketbook as tightly as if she were on a bench in a bus station. While she wasn't particularly attractive, she looked as if she had put a great deal of time into achieving whatever effect it was she was after. Every article of clothing she wore was dark green. Her sweater, her pants, her shoes, the scarf around her neck, the headband around her dark hair . . . Unfortunately, none of the greens went with the others. Her makeup was similarly self-conscious. Cheeks slashed with two streaks of pink. Lips colored the same ruby red as Snow White's. Eyes outlined in black, a dramatic effect apparently inspired by raccoons.

Even more noticeable than her *Night of the Living Dead* look, however, was her nervousness. Her hands moved constantly in a fluttering motion that reminded Laura of a nest of baby birds.

The woman peered at her. "What time do these meetings usually end?"

"Sorry," Laura replied with a shrug. "This is my first time."

"Mine, too!" The woman's glee over having found a kindred spirit faded quickly. "I'm kind of nervous. Are you?"

"A little. I —"

"I'm not good at speaking in front of large groups."

"I don't think everyone's required to speak. I imagine you're welcome to just listen until you feel comfortable enough to —"

"I just don't see the point of exposing yourself in front of a bunch of strangers."

"No one could expect you to say anything too personal —"

"I hope not." The woman blinked a few times. "I'm very shy."

Laura was relieved when someone who was clearly in authority — Marilyn, no doubt — clapped her hands and begged for everyone's attention. With crisp efficiency she explained that there were three different groupings. Group One, those who were newly separated, met in the room where they were sitting. Group Two, those who'd gotten over their initial trauma and were beginning to get on with their lives, met in the library.

Group Three, those who were already divorced, gathered in the lounge across the hall. That group, from what Laura could see, was the party group. They practically formed a conga line as, laughing and joking and doing an inordinate amount of touching, they moved, en masse, across the hall.

"Hey, Marilyn?" called one of the Group Two-ers, a mustached gentleman in a purple paisley shirt. "What about the group for people who hate their lawyers?"

"That group meets in Madison Square Garden," Marilyn shot back.

Laura had already decided she belonged in Group One. Longingly she watched the rest of the already-divorced group prance out. After them the separated-and-getting-their-lives-together crowd left, not quite kicking their heels in the air but still pretty chipper.

Those who remained looked as if they were suffering from battle fatigue.

She was having second thoughts as she

studied the seasoned members who were forming a circle with their molded plastic chairs, as dutiful as a class of eager-to-please first graders. There were four men and seven women, their ages ranging from late twenties to late sixties. The one thing this motley crew had in common was their downcast expressions. The woman with the raccoon eyes actually turned out to be one of the cheerier people in the room.

Their leader, Laura assumed, was the one with the clipboard. That was the only way to identify her, since her expression was as forlorn as everyone else's. She had large, soulful brown eyes and dark, unruly hair that was shoved back with a wood-and-leather barrette. Peeking out from underneath the hem of her long batik skirt was a pair of Chinese canvas slippers.

"Welcome," she said in a wispy voice. "My name is Merry, and this is Group One. First of all, I'd like to tell you all that you deserve a round of applause for coming here tonight. When you're going through a difficult time, it's easy to cut yourself off. But each and every one of you has taken a positive step by saying, 'Hey! I'm going to take care of *me*. I deserve it!' "

Laura had to resist the urge to curl up at Merry's batik knee and sob.

"Now, let's begin by going around the circle and telling everyone our names."

Once that had been accomplished, Merry rewarded the group by forcing a brave smile. Laura couldn't be sure, but she thought she saw tears in her eyes.

"Who'd like to start tonight?" asked Merry. "Does anyone here have something to share?"

The silence that followed was long and deadly. It reminded Laura of her seventh-grade social studies class, in which her sadistic teacher used a terrorist version of the Socratic method to drill New York State history into twelve-year-olds. Of course, the fear in this room came not from making a mistake about which town was the elevator-manufacturing capital of the world, but of exposing some far more personal inadequacy.

Finally a man raised his hand. He was large, probably six foot four in his stocking feet, and something about him screamed appliance salesman.

"Last Friday night," he said, his thick accent marking his birthplace as one of New York City's outer boroughs, "when I went to the place where my wife is livin' now to pick up my kids, she was all dressed up." He swallowed hard. "My daughter — she's fourteen — told me her mom was goin' out on a date."

"How did that feel, Arnie?" Merry prompted.

"How d'you think it felt?" another man answered for him. "It felt like shit."

"Uh-huh." Merry was nodding encouragingly. "Have you had a similar experience, Tom?"

"Hah!" snorted Tom, folding his arms across his dark blue work shirt with JO-JO'S BMW AND VOLVO REPAIR embroidered over the pocket in gold. "My wife left me for another guy! My best friend, as a matter of fact. Would you believe she left me for a guy that works on *Volkswagens?*"

"Now, *that* would make you feel like shit," Arnie mumbled.

"Okay," Merry said in her usual near whisper. "Tom, Arnie, it sounds as if you're both feeling a lot of anger. And that's *okay.*" Her eyes traveled around the circle. "It's *okay* to feel anger, isn't it?"

Laura, along with all the others, nodded obediently.

"Let's all tell Arnie and Tom that it's *okay* to feel anger."

Automatically Laura mumbled along with the rest of the group. "It's *okay* to feel anger."

"Hey, thanks, everybody." Tears had welled up in Arnie's eyes.

Tom, not quite as much the sensitive New Age guy, simply pounded his fist into his hand. Laura told herself she was probably imagining the growling sound coming from the back of his throat.

"There." Merry was beaming trium-phantly. "Anyone else? Dawn?"

A plump woman draped in gold jewelry, apparently real, shot her arm up into the air. "I had a bad experience this week, too. I was cleaning out my husband's things —"

"To pack them up so he could come by and get them?" Merry asked encouragingly.

"To throw them out the window the next time we get a really good rainstorm. Anyway, I was going through his papers — sorting them, I mean — and I found a diary he'd been keeping our last year of mar-riage."

Laura moved closer.

"I'd been a wreck since Jerry told me he wanted out. But then I started reading about some of the stuff that'd been going on. I had no idea he'd been gambling. For months he'd been hanging out at OTB with those degenerates who look like they live there. Stupid me, I thought he'd been work-ing late at his podiatry practice, and it turns out the only feet he was looking at had horseshoes on them.

"He lost thousands. Tens of thousands, even." Dawn bit her lip. "And he never told me a thing about it."

Laura was doing some lip biting of her own.

"*You* must have felt some pretty heavy-duty anger," commented Arnie. There was triumph in his tone.

"Actually," said Dawn, "finding that diary turned out to be the best thing that ever happened to me. I was finally able to face who he was. At last I understood." She was nodding energetically. "It helped me get past the fantasies about what I'd lost."

"My ex-husband never lied to me like that." The tiny woman with the flame red hair spoke up. "Even so, in the end, I was the one who left him."

Finally, thought Laura, breathing a little more easily.

"And what was it that pushed you over the edge, Carolyn?" Merry asked.

"He was cheap," she replied matter-of-factly.

"Hey," cried Tom, clearly offended. "What's wrong with a guy bein' thrifty?"

Carolyn cast him a cold look. "He used to water down my makeup so it'd last longer. He would soak used stamps that hadn't gotten canceled off envelopes so he could reuse them. He'd drive around town for half an hour until he found a parking meter that had time left on it." She took a deep breath. "He used to wash out condoms so we could reuse them."

"Wait a sec." Tom's eyes narrowed. "You mean his . . . or somebody else's?"

Merry had grown agitated. "Carolyn is

certainly feeling a lot of anger. What else do you think she's probably feeling right now?"

"Frustration, I guess," Tom volunteered with a shrug.

"Sadness," Arnie tried.

"Relief," breathed Dawn.

Laura was surprised when the woman with the Rocky Raccoon look timidly raised her hand.

"Oh, good!" Merry exclaimed. "A new person! Stella, isn't it?"

"Estelle."

Merry nodded. "You deserve credit for speaking out. It's hard, being new. Now, what would you like to share with us tonight?"

"First of all," Estelle began, clearing her throat, "I'd like to say that I'm not very comfortable speaking in front of a group. I — I'm not even sure this is something I'll be coming back to. I'm basically very shy —"

"You're doing something good for yourself by coming here tonight," Merry assured her. "We're all here for you. We've all been where you are."

Estelle hesitated. Laura found it painful, watching her try to get up the courage to speak. "We've all had difficult experiences," she began slowly. "That's why we're here. Separation is one of the most difficult things anyone ever has to go through."

Merry was nodding. Tom, Laura noticed, had resumed punching his fist against his other hand.

"But I think it's important for all of us to keep in mind that we *will* get through this, and there *will* be another person in our lives. Someone to care about. Someone to love. Maybe our love for this one particular person who disappointed us is dead, but that doesn't mean our capacity to love died with it."

Several other heads in the group were bobbing up and down. The level of tension was dissipating rapidly.

"When we find that person to love," Estelle went on, "all the parts of us that are on hold right now will reawaken. Positive feelings, sexual feelings . . ."

Laura was shocked at how quickly her use of the "s" word shot the tension level right back up again.

"In the meantime it's important for us all to think of ourselves as loving, caring beings. Sexual beings, as well. It's important for everyone in the room to know how to pleasure themselves."

Laura's eyes widened to the size of dinner plates.

"Women, especially, need to learn how to pleasure themselves. Men, too. It's an important part of being human, especially now, when we're all hurting so much. I know I pleasure myself regularly, and I'd like to impress upon everyone here how important a part of the human experience it is."

It took everything Laura had to raise her eyes up off the floor. Sneaking a surreptitious glance around the circle, she saw that she was not the only one who'd spontaneously developed an all-absorbing interest in footwear. No one moved. Even Tom's fist was frozen in midair.

For once, Merry was at a loss for words, even those memorized off bumper stickers. "Uh, thank you, Estelle. Does anyone else have something to, uh, share?"

If the awkward silence at the beginning of the session had been cavernous, the one that had now fallen over the room was Grand Canyonesque. Much to her own amazement, Laura found herself slowly raising her arm into the air.

Perhaps it had been Estelle's bravery, her willingness to share such a personal side of herself — even though she would no doubt be getting phone calls from every male in the room — but Laura suddenly wanted desperately to share something she'd been holding back.

"Another new person," Merry said, smiling uncertainly. "Do you, uh, also have something you'd like to share with the rest of us?"

Laura nodded. Her heart was pounding so loud she was certain all the others could hear it, especially since the room was still bathed in shocked silence.

"You're Laura, right?"

"That's right. There's something that's been bothering me, but I'm hoping that talking about it might help." She drew in her breath, preparing to bare her deepest, darkest, ugliest secrets. "Every night I lie in bed, thinking up awful things to do to my husband." Laura's voice trembled. She kept her gaze fixed on the metal feet of Arnie's chair, not able to look any of the others in the eye. "I've thought of putting dishwashing soap in his morning coffee. Adding castor oil to the maple syrup he puts on his pancakes. I've — I've even fantasized about putting sugar in his gas tank."

A heavy silence had fallen over the room. They must think I'm evil, Laura was thinking. Slowly, fearfully, she raised her eyes, expecting to see shock, disapproval, even disgust, in the faces of her confessors.

Instead, she saw they were laughing. *Laughing.* Not at her, either. They were laughing with her.

"Those are great ideas!" cried Arnie.

"We'll have to add them to our list!" said Dawn, the heavy gold chains draped across her massive chest glinting in the fluorescent light as they moved up and down in time with her loud guffaws.

Laura eyed them with astonishment. What surprised her even more than their reaction, though, was her own. What a relief it was to be spilling her guts and finding out she wasn't alone. Almost as if she were experiencing a physical sensation, she could feel her anger slipping away. For the first time in weeks she truly believed that at some point she would actually begin to feel better.

Laura grinned at the others. And it's *okay* to feel anger.

Chapter Six

Laura closed the door of the bedroom firmly, steeling herself for one more long night, holed up in her room . . . alone. It was Halloween, and Evan, disguised as a pirate who shopped at The Gap, had already been out for hours, prowling the streets in search of tiny Milky Ways and Snickers bars. Glancing out the window, she saw that her quiet residential street was alive with ghosts, goblins, and ghouls, trick-or-treat bags clutched tightly in their greedy little hands.

Zigzagging across the street was a little girl, ten or twelve, dressed like a hippie in a crocheted vest, bell-bottoms, and love beads. It depressed Laura to think that what had been her favorite outfit back in high school was now passing for a costume. Outside her front gate were three older boys dressed like the villains from her books, Johnny Jaguar and Lenny Leopard, complete with black leather jackets, combat boots, and bracelets with metal studs. Laura hoped they were only in holiday attire.

As for herself, she was determined to get some work done. But when she sat down at her word processor — the blinking cursor commanding, "Create! Create!" — she couldn't help going off into her own world, the one in which she, not a giraffe, was the main character.

There was one important lesson she'd learned from skimming all those magazine articles while standing in line at the super-market. And that was that it took two to tango.

Here I am, blaming Roger for the failure of our marriage, she thought, staring at the blank screen. But what about me? What was my role?

Looking back, replaying scenes she'd much rather have erased from the hard drive of her mind, Laura was forced to face the fact that, in her marriage, she'd become someone she didn't like very much. She'd taken on the role of victim, a person no longer in control of her own life. And it had changed her.

Her desperation had been reflected in the sound of her voice. Underlying her pleas to be heard was a current of frustration and anger, giving it a harshness that, for some reason, always made her think of the farmer's wife as she ran after the three blind mice, brandishing her famous carving knife.

Her resentment was apparent in her ac-tions as well. The way her husband kept

118

sending out messages that said she simply didn't count, year after year after year, was bound to affect her. Attempting to live in a situation like that was comparable to stuffing more and more garbage into a brown paper bag. Sooner or later the seams were bound to burst, leaving you with a monumental pile of coffee grounds and banana peels all over your shoes.

The way in which her own peels and grounds had periodically come rushing at her without any warning frightened her. Laura could feel her cheeks burning, red with shame, as, sitting alone in her bedroom, she remembered one particular instance, a year and a half earlier. Roger was still working for the water-filter company, a job that paid an hourly wage in addition to commissions. It was late at night, and the two of them lay in bed without touching, having tacitly agreed to designate the center crease in the sheet a demilitarized zone.

The topic, as was so often the case, was money — the fact that there wasn't enough of it. Laura was attempting to conduct a brainstorming session with Roger. This was much more than an intellectual exercise. April fifteenth was only a few weeks away. Not only was it time to pay taxes; it was also the season for stashing away a few thousand dollars in the form of IRAs, anticipating the time when both Laura and

Gertrude Giraffe would be ready to retire.

As usual, she had earned most of the money that kept the Briggs-Walsh household running. But she was careful not to dwell on that point as they lay side by side in the dark. Long before, she'd learned that doing so served no purpose except to make further discussion impossible.

"I know one thing I could do." Roger was surprisingly forthcoming. His usual response in this type of discussion was defensiveness. Laura's ears perked up at the optimism she heard in his voice. "I could show up at work an hour earlier. Instead of leaving at nine, I could leave at eight. If I put in an extra hour every day, that would add up to . . . let's see."

Maybe there really is a way out of the financial mess we're in, thought Laura. Maybe Roger and I really can work it out . . . together.

To celebrate, they'd made love. She'd felt much freer than usual, doing things with her fingers and lips and tongue she'd never dreamed she was capable of. It was one of the few occasions when Laura was able to forget that someone was keeping score.

The next morning, she was humming as she trotted downstairs at ten minutes to eight. Their night of passion was only partly responsible. Even more was the fact that, for once, she and Roger had seen eye to eye. They had confronted a problem and worked out a solution. They were moving toward something better . . . *together*.

She found him sitting at the kitchen table in his bathrobe, unshowered and un-shaven, sipping coffee and reading Evan's *Kid City* magazine.

"Roger!" she cried. "It's ten to eight!"

Lazily he glanced at the clock. "Yeah . . . so?"

"I thought we'd decided you were going to start leaving for work earlier."

He cast her an odd look. "I didn't mean *today!*"

The fury that rose up inside her was instantaneous and uncontrollable. It was only partially directed at him. She was angry at herself for allowing herself to be duped again. For believing in Roger . . . only to be proven a fool. For being naive enough to believe they'd actually made a step forward, when in reality they were still knee-deep in quicksand.

Before she even had a chance to contem-plate what she was going to do, she grabbed the magazine out of his hands and hurled it through the kitchen doorway. It landed in front of Evan, sitting cross-legged on the living-room floor, stuffing fistfuls of Cheerios into his mouth as he built a Lego missile launcher.

Evan let out a shriek, sending a shower

of Cheerios all over the room. Laura barely noticed. She was too busy screaming at Roger. And then her anger completely took over. She grabbed him by the lapels of his bathrobe and shook him, yelling something she could no longer remember.

Oddly enough, she remembered perfectly well what she'd been thinking. *Listen to me!* her heart cried out to him, aching to be heard. *Hear me! For once, make me feel that what I think, what I want, matters!*

The encounter left her shaken. Has it really come to this? she wondered, distraught as she picked Cheerios out from between the cushions of the couch after Roger and Evan had left the house. Have I actually resorted to violence — me, a woman who routinely lures renegade spiders onto an index card so I can return them to the great outdoors rather than squishing them with a rolled-up newspaper?

Sitting at her word processor, aware that a full fifteen minutes had passed and not a single word had appeared on the screen, Laura came to the conclusion that while it did indeed take two to tango, someone had to lead.

The sound of the doorbell prompted Laura to peek out the window. Down below, Swamp Thing and a Teenage Mutant Ninja

Turtle were shuffling impatiently on her front steps. Their beaming mother stood at the gate. Laura waited to hear the heavy tread of Roger's footsteps hurrying across the living room. Instead, she heard the doorbell once again — this time two short, irritated blasts. The amphibians were getting restless.

Where's Roger? she wondered. As far as she was concerned, she'd done her share. She'd bought the candy, put it in a big bowl near the front door, and turned on both the porch light and the string of plastic blinking pumpkins to let seekers of sugar know this household was ghoul-friendly. Now it was his turn.

When the doorbell rang half a dozen more times in quick, annoying succession, Laura tore down the stairs.

She flung open the front door just in time. The disappointed trick-or-treaters were only too happy to make a quick comeback, even though they openly registered their disapproval of candy bars that contained nuts. Laura marched right back into the house, fury rising inside.

"Roger? Roger, where are you?"

She found him in the kitchen, sipping a cup of decaf and perusing the newspaper.

"What do you think you're doing?"

His eyes never left the sports page. "What does it look like I'm doing?"

"Didn't you hear the doorbell?"

"Of course." When he finally glanced up at her, his look was so hostile she almost wished he hadn't.

"It *is* Halloween."

Roger stared at her blankly. "So?"

"So? *So?* So answer the door, for heaven's sake! You *are* still living here, after all! Drop a few Snickers bars into some poor little kid's trick-or-treat bag —"

He lowered his newspaper onto the kitchen table. "Do you honestly expect me to lift a finger to help you?"

She stared at him, taking a few seconds to regain her composure. "Good point. Why should things be any different now?"

"Oh, sure. I never did a thing around here, right?"

"Something like that. Even when you were home — which was rare, since you always seemed to have someplace more important to go — you were so turned off to what was going on around you that you wouldn't even have noticed if . . . if Elvis was living in our basement. You refused to have the slightest bit of involvement with me or Evan —"

"And why do you think I turned off to you? Whose fault was that?"

"Maybe your defenses were just too strong for you ever to open up to anybody."

"Me? What about you?"

"What *about* me?"

124

"You certainly never opened up to me sexually."

It took Laura a few seconds to recover from that one. "How could I," she said evenly, "when you were always so critical of me? You didn't like my body, you were always telling me I was fat, that I could never please you —"

"Well, let me tell you something. You know all those nights I told you I was going downstairs to watch *Star Trek?* That's not all I was doing, lying there alone on the couch in the dark!"

Slowly the meaning of his words sank in.

"It's just as well," she shot back. "At least on those nights, I didn't have to bother having to fake an orgasm!"

Bull's-eye. Roger's shock registered openly on his face. "You've been faking orgasms?"

Laura recoiled. "Sometimes."

"Since when?"

"Since the beginning."

"The beginning?"

"Starting on our wedding night."

"You faked an orgasm on our *wedding* night?"

She was grateful when the doorbell rang once again. She dashed off, relieved to leave Roger alone to digest that one.

"Oooh, the Little Mermaid!" she cooed with forced cheerfulness. She never let on that her head was spinning. She'd scored a victory, but instead of feeling better, she felt worse. She wished the Ninja Turtles would come back so she could follow them into the sewer. "Don't you look sweet. And what are you supposed to be?"

The little boy in the dark suit and striped Harvard tie opened up his huge plastic shopping bag, much bigger than any of the other kids' had been. "An IRS agent."

Laura wished Roger would leave. When she saw him still sitting in the kitchen, as much a fixture as the dishwasher, a tremendous rage rose up inside. It wasn't rooted only in the moment, either. Too many weeks living in the same house with the one person in the world she wanted most to get away from was finally taking its toll.

"Look," she breathed, trying to remain in control, "we can't go on living like this. It's crazy, all this fighting, all the tension in this house. You have to move out."

"*I* have to move out? Why me?"

"In the first place, most of the mortgage payments came out of my paychecks, not yours. Or weren't you aware that the International House of Pancakes doesn't pay dividends to its regulars?"

He opened his mouth to protest, but Laura didn't give him the chance to speak.

"In the second place, since I'm the one

126

who takes care of our son, I'm the one who needs to provide him with a home. The only house he's ever lived in seems like an obvious choice to me. And I have a feeling any judge in the world would agree with me."

"Great." Roger folded his arms across his chest and stuck his chin up in the air. "So I'm supposed to slink away, just disappear, leaving you with everything —"

"Not everything! You're welcome to take half. Isn't that what's in style these days? To split everything right down the middle?" The rage was growing, taking on a life all its own. Laura strode across the dining room, picking up one of the decorative hurricane lamps. "Here, take this. Lisa gave us two, so one of them is yours."

When he sat there, staring at her as if she'd lost her mind, she thrust it at him. "*Take* it!"

Her eyes darted around the kitchen, lighting on the loaf of French bread on the counter. She grabbed it and tore it in half. "Here!" she shrieked. "You want half? Take half! Take it and get out!"

"Laura, stop it!"

She knew she was out of control. But that feeling of being on a roller coaster was stronger than ever. This time the car was plummeting down, down, down, so fast she couldn't catch her breath. Her heart was pounding like a jackhammer. Adrenaline set her muscles tingling and her mind racing. It was as exhilarating as it was terrifying. She gave in to it, deciding that for once she wasn't going to resist. . . . The feeling of release was as intoxicating as the high from a drug.

"You want half of this?" she cried, grabbing the salt out of the cabinet. "Here. You got it." She turned the cylindrical carton upside down on the table in front of Roger, experiencing a bizarre sense of satisfaction as she watched a white mound form.

"Laura, you're acting crazy! Get a hold of yourself!"

"Here, take half of these, too." She'd taken a bunch of overly ripe bananas down from the wooden bowl on top of the refrigerator. Tearing off two, she hurled them at Roger. "Take them!"

They came flying too quickly for him to react. Instead, the bananas hit the floor — and exploded.

Suddenly everything was coated with banana. Mushy white bits clung to the counters, the floors, the baseboards. Smaller clumps stuck to the coffeepot, the ceramic canisters, even Evan's red plastic lunch box, tucked next to the microwave.

Laura froze. Part of her wanted to laugh — the throaty, hysterical laugh that, in the movies, always elicited a slap in the face.

But she was afraid that if she started, she'd never be able to stop.

"All right," she heard Roger say, his voice strangely quiet. "You've made your point. I'll move out. I'll start looking for a place right away." Casting her a peculiar look, partly amazed and partly fearful, he added, "But it's only because I'm afraid of what you might do if I don't."

A sudden loud rapping at the back door startled them both.

"Trick or treat!" several high-pitched voices called happily.

"At least you got your 'awful wedded husband' to agree to move out," Claire said, handing Laura a glass of white wine. "That's quite an accomplishment, believe me."

"But I was completely out of control!" Laura protested. "I threw bananas at the man!"

"That's not so terrible," Julie assured her in a soothing voice. "It's not as if you have a whole history of throwing fruit."

With a long, tired sigh, Laura leaned back against the soft cushions of Claire's couch. As upset as she was, she still felt she'd come to a place of refuge, surrounded not only by friends and the biggest bottle of chardonnay she'd ever seen, but also by a warm, familiar environment.

Laura had always found Claire Nielsen's

apartment to be very much like Claire herself: stark, angular, no-nonsense. The predominant color was a creamy white, so much like her hair it could have come out of the same Clairol bottle. The shade had been used on the walls, in the carpeting, the important pieces of furniture, and even the bricks in the fireplace, which Laura had never once seen used during the decade or so Claire had lived in Oyster Bay.

That was just the backdrop. Superimposed over this blank canvas were splashes of color, undoubtedly designed to shock, if not actually to cause migraine. The throw pillows on the white couch were hot pink, purple, and jade green. The silk-screened prints on the walls, meaningless blobs and rectangles that Laura could have sworn changed shape every time she saw them, favored colors like orange and lime green. An ottoman covered in a fabric that was halfway between a Hawaiian print and a Matisse rested underneath a windowsill.

The effect was startling, to say the least. Despite the decor, Laura had always felt comfortable here. Even if Claire wasn't the most competent hostess — making a pot of coffee but forgetting to mention she had neither milk nor sugar; serving muffins that were still frozen in the middle — the argument that "Claire meant well" always went a long way.

Tonight, as she sat curled up on the white couch, taking tiny sips from her glass of wine, Laura thought about how lucky she was to have such good friends. Both Claire and Julie were in a particularly upbeat mood, or were at least pretending to be for her benefit. When Laura had called Claire earlier that day, in tears over the argument she and Roger had had the night before, Claire had insisted she and Evan come over for a Chinese take-out dinner. At the moment Evan was happily watching television in Claire's bedroom, the impressive amount of General Ching's chicken he'd consumed slowing him down to couch-potato speed.

"Think of it this way," said Julie, perched on the ottoman, sipping a cup of Chinese tea, which fortunately required no sugar. "Last night's fight may have been one of your worst, but maybe it'll end up being your last." She was dressed in a flowered granny dress that came almost to her ankles, giving her a reassuring maternal look.

"It certainly was one of the worst," Laura agreed with a shudder. "After fifteen years, one person really knows the other's weak spots. When Roger and I were married, we always had an unspoken agreement about leaving certain things alone, no matter how angry we were. But boy, now that we're no longer pretending to be a couple, there are no limits."

"What do you mean?" asked Julie, puzzled.

Laura hesitated. "Well, one of the things he accused me of last night was having never opened up to him sexually —"

"Oh, *that's* original." Claire snorted. She stretched her long legs across the oversized, overstuffed easy chair that looked as if it should belong to Papa Bear. Tonight she was wearing nothing but purple, a startling contrast to the jade green canvas that covered the chair. "Right off page twelve of *Everything You Always Wanted to Know About How to Hurt Your Wife.*"

"There was something else, too. . . ." Laura swallowed hard. "He told me he used to go downstairs late at night, pretending to watch *Star Trek* reruns when what he was really doing was, um, masturbating."

"Oh, my." Julie covered her face with her hands.

But Claire's face lit up. "You're kidding!" she cried, wide-eyed. "Now I understand why there are so many Trekkies running around!"

Laura laughed. "And you thought it was Mr. Spock's ears that had all those middle-aged men so intrigued."

She was trying her best to sound light-hearted. Tough, even. But all of a sudden she could no longer control her tears. They started by running down her cheeks unobtrusively, but before long she'd succumbed to a sobbing fit.

"I — I — I'm sorry," she sniffled. "The last thing I want to do is ruin everybody's evening."

"You're not ruining our evening!" Claire insisted.

Julie had already come over to the couch to hug her. "Cry, if it makes you feel better. Don't hold back, Laura. Let it all out." Glancing up at Claire, she said, "Get her some tissues."

"I don't actually have any tissues. . . ." Claire, standing by helplessly, looking like a disoriented flight attendant in her purple space-age-style cat suit, thought for a few seconds. "How about a paper towel?"

"That'll have to do." Julie smoothed Laura's hair. "This is such a difficult time. Just remember that it will pass. Think of it as something you have to go through to get yourself to a much better place —"

"And you will," Claire reassured her. "Take it from somebody who's been there."

"Laura," Julie asked gently, "how is Evan handling all this?"

"I think he's pretty angry. Every once in a while he explodes. But most of the time he's just quieter than usual." Laura bit her lip. "I think it's better when he's crying and yelling and throwing toys all over the room."

Julie nodded. "You might think about

finding him somebody to talk to. A counselor, somebody who knows how to talk to kids."

"I've thought about it. I'll probably act on it one of these days, too. I've just been so busy trying to find myself a lawyer. . . ." Laura shrugged. "I'm feeling so overwhelmed by all the stuff that's going on with me that I can't even bear to think about how much it's affecting Evan."

"Poor Laura!" cried Claire. "You've got so much to deal with right now!"

Julie was nodding. "I've been thinking. This is a time in your life when what you really need is to be nice to yourself. To concentrate on Laura Briggs."

"She's right," Claire agreed. "You shouldn't be sitting around, marveling over how crummy it's possible for a fairly well-adjusted human being to feel. You need to get out, to have some fun. You know what they say."

Laura and Julie stared at her blankly. "No," Laura finally said. "What *do* they say?"

" 'Living well is the best revenge,' " Claire replied. "Although I still think you can come up with a much more creative form of revenge, Laura. More dramatic, too." She smiled sweetly. "How about something involving permanent scarring?"

"Forget revenge," insisted Julie, waving her hand in the air. "How about concen-

134

trating on having some fun? Speaking of which, I've come up with the perfect solution. Can you field Evan out to your parents' house some weekend soon?"

Laura nodded. "They said they'd do anything they could to help. I don't think parking him in front of their TV for three days is too much to ask."

"Perfect." Julie's face lit up. "Laura, have you ever been skiing?"

"Skiing?" Laura blinked. "Well, no, I —"

"I think it's exactly what you need. Going to a place you've never been before, trying something new . . . It's precisely what the doctor ordered."

"Skiing!" Claire looked alarmed. "Where'd you come up with that idea?"

"It's one of my favorite sports," Julie replied, slightly indignant.

"But Laura is . . . She and I are . . ." Claire waved her hands in the air. "Let's face it, Julie. You may be an old hand at slip-sliding around on the snow, but aren't Laura and I a little old to start schussing?"

"Not at all. Just today I was talking to a new patient who didn't take up skiing until he was in his late forties."

"Don't tell me," Claire said dryly. "His twenty-year-old wife — his *second* wife — got him into it."

Julie frowned. "He didn't say anything about a wife. He is divorced, though."

Rolling her eyes and shaking her head, Claire let out an exasperated sigh. "What is it with these guys? During their first marriage, you can't get them to do anything but sit in front of the boob tube. If you even suggest anything the least bit adventurous — like going to the movies or trying a new salad dressing — they fight you so hard you'd think you were trying to talk them into getting a tattoo.

"But when the second wife comes along, they go skiing, they go bungee-jumping —"

"He didn't say anything about bungee-jumping," Julie said thoughtfully.

"I guess the thing to do is be a second wife," Laura commented.

"Well, this man hasn't remarried. At least I don't think he has."

Claire cast Julie a meaningful look. "Or maybe he just wants you to think he's single."

"Don't you think you're being a tad cynical?" asked Julie. "He's a nice guy, that's all."

"I take it this 'nice guy' isn't exactly Jean-Claude Killy," Laura observed.

"Poor Bob twisted his knee. He told me all about it while I was massaging his pectineus."

Claire's eyebrows shot up. "Why, Julie Cavanaugh! You wicked thing!"

"Relax. It's a thigh muscle."

"Not nearly as interesting as the image that first came to mind."

"Anyway," Julie went on, "the reason I brought him up in the first place is that I think he's doing the right thing."

"What, pulling muscles with obscene names?"

"Trying new things. Bob got divorced a while back, and now, instead of sitting around, feeling sorry for himself, he's going out and enjoying life. He's exploring, expanding his horizons —"

"Sounds like a real going-for-the-gusto kind of guy," Claire observed with a wry smile.

Julie ignored her. "Laura, I think you should be doing the same thing as Bob. All three of us should. Together."

"If we're going away for the weekend," said Claire, "why don't we at least pick a place where we can sit on a beach, drinking mai-tais and ogling men's butts? We've got all those islands with the 'Saint' names so close to us. Surely we can find one where there's not much political unrest." With a shrug she added, "Why would anyone go somewhere where the whole point is to be cold?"

Julie ignored her suggestion. "Laura, it's really important that you break out of your rut."

"I'm not in a rut."

"What did you do last weekend?"

"Let's see. Evan was out of the house with Roger most of the weekend, so I . . ." Laura struggled to reconstruct two days. "I cleaned the attic."

"I rest my case," said Julie.

"That's not all." Laura was quick to defend herself. "I also rented three videos and baked chocolate-chip cookies." Lowering her voice to a conspiratorial tone, she added, "With nuts."

Claire shook her head. "The woman is out of control."

"Laura," Julie said with exaggerated patience, "we all need downtime. It's an important part of healing. But you really should be getting out more."

"Maybe, but skiing? Isn't that awfully . . . dangerous?"

"It certainly is!" Claire exclaimed. "Do you have any idea what those clingy ski pants can do to a pair of hips?"

"It's settled," Julie said firmly. "We're going. I'll lend you some of the clothes you'll need. I can probably get a hold of some discount lift tickets. And I know a great travel agent who can get us a reasonable rate at one of the ski lodges upstate, probably the Robin Hood Inn. We just have to decide on a weekend."

"Great," muttered Laura, trying to sound enthusiastic but still not completely convinced. "Now all I have to do is pay a visit to the Wizard of Oz. I just hope he's still got some courage in stock."

Chapter Seven

During the long bus ride to the ski lodge, Laura stared out the window, half listening to Claire and Julie's happy chatter. She couldn't stop thinking about the fact that while she was traveling north in search of adventure, Roger was packing up his things to move out. She was glad to be away and not have to witness the physical dismantling of their house — and, in essence, their life together. She only hoped that hiding out in the Catskills, pretending to be a mountain goat, wouldn't turn out to be a mistake. Especially one that resulted in expensive visits to an orthopedic surgeon.

When they finally arrived, Laura filed into the lobby behind Claire and Julie, suitcases in hand. She studied the place with curiosity. The Robin Hood Inn didn't quite fit her fantasy of what a ski lodge should be like. Her first impression was that the Inn had been designed by a renegade architect from Disneyland, with its mock-stone exterior, numerous decorative towers, and groin vaults. Observing the interior filled with plush red velvet, she assumed that the look it was striving for was medieval castle . . . a *luxurious* medieval castle, the kind in which even the dungeons had wall-to-wall carpeting.

"Gee, think it's big enough?" Claire commented, looking around the cavernous space.

"It seems quite . . . clean," Laura added. For a moment she wished she'd brought Evan along. He'd have adored the two knights with swords and battle-axes flanking the door to the men's room.

She had to remind herself that the whole point of this weekend was to get away from her familial duties. It was her breakout weekend. Her chance to do something for herself. An opportunity to be on her own, without worrying about peanut-butter sandwiches and clean soccer shirts and separation agreements.

Kurt, the red-haired, ponytailed tour guide for the group from Bellinski Ski Tours, of which the three of them were officially members, checked them in. Tucking her room key into her pocket, Laura felt a surge of excitement. This really was an adventure, a chance for her to have a good time — without anyone looking over her shoulder. She'd never skied before. She'd never gone for the weekend with her girlfriends, either, at least not in fifteen years. The trips she'd taken had either been business trips, giving speeches or signing autographs at conventions, or else family jaunts, during which she constantly wondered why she and Roger were spending money to fight in hotels when they could do that perfectly well at home.

Their room was designed with the same faux-medieval flavor. Stumbling through the door with her suitcases, Laura was overwhelmed by all the massive wood-look furniture that had been stuffed into the compact space, to say nothing of the red shag carpeting, the red drapes, and the red flocked wallpaper in a fleur-de-lis pattern.

"This looks quite comfortable," Julie said. She'd opened her suitcase and, with great meticulousness, was putting neatly folded clothes into drawers.

Claire had embarked on a more thorough tour. "Oh, look!" she called from the bathroom. "Ye Olde Velvet Toilet!"

"Let me see." Laura giggled. The toilet itself wasn't fuzzy and red, but just about everything else in the bathroom was.

"Gee," Claire commented, "I don't know whether to take a shower or behead somebody."

"I know what I'm going to do." Julie, having finished her unpacking, was stripping down. "I'm going to soak in a hot tub for at least an hour, and then snuggle up in bed with a good book. I hope to be asleep by ten."

Claire's eyebrows shot up. "Aren't you the party girl."

"Skiing is quite demanding," Julie explained. "I want to make sure I'm relaxed and rested when we get that eight o'clock bus to the slopes tomorrow."

"Not me," Claire insisted. "I came up here to have *fun*. And you," she went on, pointing at Laura, "are going to come with me."

"Fun?" Laura repeated. Eyeing her warily, she asked, "What exactly do you mean by *fun?*"

Claire shook her head slowly. "Ah, Laura. You've been married too long."

It was only a matter of minutes before Laura learned what that three-letter word translated to, at least in the eyes of a forty-year-old divorced woman imprisoned in a fake castle with hundreds of people in purple and green Gore-Tex.

"There's a huge social scene that's associated with skiing," Claire explained, leading Laura down the corridor to the hotel's lobby. "Most of the people here have no intention of skiing. In fact, they've never even been on a ski slope."

"Then why bother?"

"Because they want to *meet* people who ski. What better place than a ski lodge?"

"Why would anyone work so hard just to meet someone who skis?"

"Demographics, my dear. We're talking

143

upscale, educated, *single* people. People with money to burn. People with time on their hands. This Robin Hood fantasyland is exactly the kind of place singles flock to."

Laura was impressed. "How do you know so much about this?"

"I read *Cosmo*."

In the lobby, an enormous fireplace in one corner had drawn a crowd, mostly men. At least Laura thought it was the fireplace, until she looked more closely and saw that the television next to it, tuned to a football game, was the real crowd pleaser.

"I can't believe people come all the way up here and then spend the evening watching TV!"

"It's a good way of separating the sports addicts from the guys sincerely interested in meeting women," Claire said matter-of-factly. "You might even say it's a service provided by the hotel."

"I hope you didn't bring me here with the idea I might be interested in mingling with any of these people." Laura studied the TV crowd. "My God! Most of them still have acne!"

Claire ran her fingers through the champagne-colored stubble that constituted her hair. "What's wrong with a little meeting and greeting?"

"I think Julie had the right idea. A nice, hot bath and a good night's sleep are beginning to seem better every minute."

"You sound like my grandmother. No, even my grandmother's more fun than that. Come on, Laura. This is your chance to party! What good is sitting alone in your room —"

"Surely you're not about to suggest I come to the cabaret?"

"I think Maid Marian's Bar and Grill is a much better choice." Claire had already lured her as far as the doorway of the hotel bar. Peeking inside, Laura saw that beyond lay a cavern of darkness, reeking of beer and cigarette smoke. The music was turned way up, the bass throbbing so hard the glassware vibrated. "You've got to get your feet wet sometime, as they say."

Laura surveyed the scene before her. "Obviously the people who say that have never been confronted with a roomful of drunk college students rubbing up against each other and trying not to vomit in each other's presence."

"There are some grown ups here," Claire insisted. "Look at that man over there. He must be pushing fifty."

"He's the bartender." Suddenly Laura froze. "Uh-oh. Check out that man over there. *Discreetly.*"

"Which man? Where?"

"The handsome one, by the mock Tiffany lamp. Tall, blond . . . looks like he just stepped out of a men's underwear ad?"

Claire directed her gaze in the direction Laura indicated. When she gasped, Laura knew she'd spotted the right guy.

"Laura, he's gorgeous! God, everything about him is perfect. The way he's holding his brandy snifter, that Rhett Butler smile, those broad shoulders underneath that Icelandic sweater —"

"How do you know it's Icelandic?"

"Hell, Laura. It could be from Sears for all I care. My main interest is how he'd look with it off."

"I thought you weren't interested in having a relationship with a man."

"Who said anything about a relationship? You're right; that's the last thing I need. You let a man into your life, and the next thing you know, your toilet-paper roll's installed backward." Claire's eyes narrowed. "That doesn't mean I'm above treating one as a sex object every now and then."

"Sorry to burst your bubble, but it looks like I'm the apple of his eye, not you."

"You're right. And he's coming this way."

"Tell me you're joking!"

"If I'm joking, a lot of very attractive women on this side of the room are drooling for no good reason."

"Oh, no! What should I do?"

Claire cast her a look of incredulity. "Bat your eyelashes, laugh a high, tinkling laugh, and tell him you're a millionairess."

"Get serious, Claire."

"I *am* serious."

The tall, blond man stopped mere inches away, and smiled down at Laura. His blue eyes sparkled. "Hello."

Laura was unable to come up with anything equally clever. She was relieved when Claire filled in for her.

"You know," she said, batting her eyelashes and laughing a high, tinkling laugh, "my friend and I were just wondering about something. Maybe you could help us out."

"Perhaps I could." His words were meant for Claire, but his eyes remained fixed on Laura. She was beginning to wonder if she had food on her face.

"Who do you think make better skiers? Men, who have most of their strength in their shoulders . . . ?" Pointedly Claire stared at his. "Or women, who have their strength in their hips?" She thrust hers out for show-and-tell.

"Actually, I haven't the faintest idea," he replied. "I work for the tour company that brought up the group from New Jersey." With a shrug he added, "I just drive the bus."

Claire only looked crestfallen for a fraction of a second. Laura guessed that was how long she'd taken to remind herself she wasn't looking to have this man's children

. . . only to work on some of the preparatory steps.

But it was too late. The man's attention was by now concentrated completely on Laura. "Don't I know you from somewhere?"

Claire rolled her eyes.

"Well," said Laura, "I've been to New Jersey."

"No, no. Let me see. I used to work for UPS, so I got around quite a bit. . . ." He peered at her for an embarrassingly long time, then snapped his fingers. "I know! The Cachet Modeling Agency!"

Laura could feel herself blushing. "Heavens, no. I —"

"Yes, that's it. I know I've seen you there."

"Really, I never —"

"Weren't you the receptionist?"

Laura grabbed Claire's arm. "Will you excuse us? It was nice talking to you, but, uh, our boyfriends are waiting for us back at the room."

"They're millionaires," Claire added, allowing herself to be dragged away.

Once they were out of earshot, Claire groaned. "Laura Briggs, what is wrong with you?"

"What did I do?"

"That . . . that Nordic god was trying to pick you up!"

"I know what he was doing."

"So?"

148

"Claire, I still feel married!"

Claire sighed impatiently. "It's been over a month since you told Roger to kiss off."

"I think it's like having a foot amputated. You can still feel it, even after it's long gone."

Claire shook her head. "The problem with you is that you're not angry enough."

"I'm angry!" Laura insisted feebly. "I'm very angry. I never told you how I lie awake nights, trying to think up ways of killing him without getting caught. Ways of getting back at him for all the time he stole from me."

"And you don't think a long night of sweating up the sheets with Loki the God of Fire is a good way of getting back?"

Laura held out her hands in a gesture of helplessness. "I'm just not ready."

Claire slung a sisterly arm around her. "Okay. I've been there. I guess you're entitled to a little time. A little space. A king-size bed, all to yourself.

"But once you've passed through this phase . . . watch out, single men! None of you will be safe! Not the short, fat, bald ones, not the skinny, nerdy ones with pens in their shirt pockets . . . I predict that one of these days you're going to wake up and be like the proverbial kid in a candy store."

Laura wasn't convinced. "Believe me, Claire," she said, grimacing, "it's going to be some time before I manage to forget what a bad effect candy can have on your teeth."

"Look at us." Claire marveled, staring into the mirror. "We look like bionic Barbie dolls."

Studying their reflection, Laura had to agree with her. What set skiing apart from all other sports, she'd learned, was not the need for skill, balance, coordination, or even nerves of steel. It was owning a complete wardrobe specially designed to keep people warm and dry as they foolishly ventured outdoors where it was cold and wet.

To outfit themselves for trying on the persona of Frosty the Snowman, Laura and Claire had begged, borrowed, and shopped the sales at Ski Bum Warehouse. Julie, the experienced one, already owned two or three of each required garment. Now, inspecting the threesome one last time before heading out to the Bellinski Ski Tours bus, revving its motor in the parking lot right outside their window as it prepared to head for the slopes, Laura had to agree with Claire.

"It's quite dramatic," she said. "Me all in purple and green, Julie in navy blue —"

"And me in hot pink." Claire groaned. "I look like the first forty-year-old snow bunny in history. Honestly, I don't know how I ever let you talk me into buying this."

"It was on sale, remember?" said Laura. "Seventy percent off is a *very* compelling argument."

The one saving grace was that everyone else on the tour bus looked more or less the same. But Laura forgot all about how absurd she felt once they headed up the mountain, past some of the most dramatic scenery she'd ever seen. Everywhere she looked, the theme was ice. The mountain streams they passed were frozen over. Huge icicles, six, eight, ten feet long, hung down from cliffs menacingly. Of course, she couldn't help wondering if the narrow road that meandered along a very steep drop was also covered with ice. Rather than contemplate that possibility, she concentrated on Kurt, moving about the bus distributing ski boots with the good cheer of a flight attendant.

"Okay," he announced, once the bus had crept off the horrifying mountain road and into a parking lot that looked considerably more safe. "It's now eight-forty. We'll be leaving here promptly at four-thirty."

"That's eight hours away!" whimpered Claire, sitting beside Laura.

"It'll speed right by," Julie assured her. There was a glaze in her green eyes and a flush to her cheeks that scared Laura. She reminded Laura of the mad scientists in science-fiction films. "Once you get up to the top of the mountain —"

"Uh, you're not going to rush right off, are you?" Laura asked nervously. "You did promise to give us a few pointers."

Claire was nodding. "That's right. Don't forget that this was your idea. Yours . . . and that patient of yours with the midlife crisis."

"Just one more thing," Kurt was saying. "The temperature outside is seven —"

"Seven?" Claire croaked. "Did he say *seven?*"

"With the windchill, it's way down below zero. You'll notice frostbite warnings have been posted —"

"I *told* you we should have gone to one of those islands where they hate Americans!" hissed Claire.

"Just remain alert, folks. If you notice any numbness, any tingling sensation in your extremities, go inside and get warmed up."

"No," Claire shot back, "we'll just stay outside until we turn into snow angels."

"Oh, Claire," chirped Julie, shooing Claire and Laura off the bus, "once you get moving, you won't even notice the cold."

"Right," Laura muttered. "We'll all be too busy trying not to slide down a five-hundred-foot mountain slope covered in six feet of ice."

While Laura would never have admitted it to the cynical Claire, she was actually overcome with Christmas-morning excitement as she shuffled off the tour bus with the others. She was about to test herself in a way she'd never been tested before, to go one-on-one with Mother Nature, the most formidable opponent of all. The icy air blasting through the open door of the bus was her call to battle. The mountain beckoned, tall and proud and ready to be conquered.

It wasn't until she tried climbing off the bus that she realized just how difficult it was going to be.

"How are you supposed to walk in these things?" she demanded. Not only did the ski boots weigh as much as the concrete shoes gangsters use for drowning their adversaries, but with her feet encased entirely in the hard, shiny synthetic material, they had no choice but to remain at ninety-degree angles to her shins.

"You're not supposed to walk in them," Julie replied calmly. "You're supposed to attach your skis to their bottoms and *ski* in them."

"I'll never again complain about new shoes," Laura muttered. Steeling herself against possible disaster, she clomped around the parking lot. Keeping her balance was no easy task. Yet, moving with all the grace of a rhino in roller skates, she made her way to the side of the bus, where

Kurt was patiently distributing skis to the members of the group.

After an hour on the bunny slope, the nickname for the gentle incline where small children were taught the ups and downs of skiing, Julie pronounced Laura and Claire ready to try the real thing.

"But I haven't even mastered the rope tow!" Claire protested. "If the attendant with the potbelly and the cigar comes over to help me up out of the snow one more time —"

"The rope tow is the hardest part of skiing," Julie insisted. "No one should be subjected to it. You'll find the T-bar much simpler."

"Oo-o-o-o-oh . . ."

Riding up the T-bar alone, Laura could hear Claire behind her. She tried to rise above her friend's fear, preferring to side with Julie on this one. If Julie could do it, Laura reasoned, so could she. Of course, Julie's job demanded a working knowledge of how every single part of the body functioned, something that was bound to be helpful while plunging down a mountain with nothing for protection except two skinny little ski poles and more waterproof layers than a fish.

Hopping off the T-bar, sliding down a little slope designed to put the fear of God into people about to descend the mountain, literally took Laura's breath away. Still, she had to admit it wasn't an entirely unpleasant experience. By giving in, letting it simply happen, she sensed, from somewhere deep inside, she would pull it off. As she waited for Julie and Claire to catch up, she was exhilarated over the prospect of her first ski run.

Claire apparently did not share her enthusiasm.

"You can't be serious," she said tartly. "This is all a cruel joke, right?"

"You're going to love it," Julie insisted. "The crisp white snow, stretching on as far as the eye can see, the sensation of icy air on your face —"

"Don't forget all those cute, single guys out here on the ski slopes," Laura reminded her.

"True," Claire admitted. "After all, I did notice that the parking lot back at the ski lodge looks like a Mercedes dealership."

"There's more to a man than his checkbook," Julie retorted.

"Reading *Iron John* again?" Claire shot back.

"She doesn't mean any of it," Laura insisted to Julie, wanting to keep the peace. "Look, I think we need to stick together. Right now we've got a lot more to worry about than who's taking us to the prom.

We have to get from here . . . to *there*."

Swallowing hard, Laura took her first real look at the ski trail ahead of her. Never before had she seen anything quite so long — or quite so steep.

"You've got a point." Claire followed her gaze. "On second thought, I think I'll take the lift back down. I don't think I'll look particularly attractive showing up at tonight's happy hour in a body cast."

"You can't take the lift back down," said Julie. "It only goes one way."

"You're joking, right?" Claire's face was the same shade of hot pink as her bunny suit.

"No, Claire. Nobody rides down. The whole point is to ski down."

Laura, who had been entertaining her own thoughts about following Claire to the down escalator, quickly realized that panicking wasn't going to solve anything.

"Come on, Claire. We can do it. Kurt thought so."

"Kurt's probably so stoned he thinks we're all capable of flying." Cautiously Claire peered over at Laura. "Are you really going to do this?"

"We've come this far." Laura was trying so hard to sound jovial that she reminded herself of a scout leader. "Come on, Claire. Race you to the bottom."

"I'll catch up with you two later." Julie,

finally losing patience, suddenly took off. She slid away with such ease that Laura and Claire simply stared, dumbfounded.

"We're not going to let her show us up, are we?" Laura said. "One, two, three —"

Suddenly she felt herself moving. Through no conscious decision of her own, she had pushed off. She was sliding down the mountain, picking up speed.

She was skiing.

I'm doing it, she thought, both alarmed and astounded. I might end up with my face in the snow. Or my arm in a cast. But I'm really doing it!

Her adrenaline pumping as she recited the rules Julie had drummed into her, Laura moved smoothly down the side of the mountain. Surprisingly, she managed to remain upright. She even had some control over where she went — and how quickly she got there. Most remarkably, not once did she tumble into the snow, despite a few close calls when she felt herself losing her balance or picking up speed too quickly. Every time she managed to ward off disaster, instinctively knowing what to do.

Finally she reached the bottom. She was slowing down; gravity no longer grabbed at her quite so greedily now that the slope had leveled off.

I did it! she thought, wrapped in a glorious euphoria, feeling more alive than she had in months. I came down the mountain!

Blinking in the bright sunlight reflecting off the white fields of snow, Laura looked around for her friends. Julie was way ahead of her, already in line for her next ski-lift ride. But Claire was still halfway up the mountain, trying without much success to pull herself out of a snowbank. She looked like a giant pink turtle that had landed on its back.

Laura was thrilled she'd done so well. Not as well as Julie, but certainly better than Claire. She'd survived. She'd had her doubts, experienced fear . . . but gone ahead and, in the end, triumphed.

Pausing only a moment to catch her breath, she headed toward the ski lift, ready for more, awed by the discovery that she was capable of things that she'd never dreamed of.

Chapter Eight

Laura pushed the back door open slowly, afraid of what she might find — or what she *wouldn't* find. Her worst fantasy was that she'd come home from her weekend of picking icicles out of her collar and cuffs to find that her house had been stripped bare, her microwave, the doors of the kitchen cabinets, and even the switch plates carted off like booty from the Crusades.

So she was greatly relieved when she turned on the light and saw that not only was the switch plate firmly in place but that the kitchen was precisely as she'd left it. Her coffee cup from breakfast two days before sat in the sink, half-filled with murky water. The dish towel she'd dropped on the counter was still wadded up into a ball. The microwave and all the other accoutrements of her well-stocked kitchen appeared to have spent the weekend unmolested.

Even so, Laura held her breath as she went into the dining room. There, she began to see subtle signs of her husband having moved out. One of the ceramic hurricane lamps was gone. Half the wineglasses, displayed in a wooden case with sliding-glass doors, had vanished. The only sign of the hand-painted pitcher from Mexico, a wedding present from Roger's best friend from college, was a space on the shelf where it used to be.

Growing more and more uneasy, Laura stepped into the living room. Books were missing from shelves, leaving behind gaping holes. The swivel chair was gone. The TV and the VCR were still in place, but where the stereo had once been there was nothing but a bare rectangle outlined by dust.

She sank onto the couch, suddenly overwhelmed by the fact that Roger was gone. She felt his absence as strongly as she had once felt his presence. She was once again struck by the momentousness of what was happening. Everything in her life was changing. Elements that had once been stable were suddenly shifting, moving under her feet like the ground during an earthquake.

She told herself it was for the best. That it had to be this way.

As she leaned her head back, she hit the hard edge of the couch, instead of the pillows. She closed her eyes, partly to fight the tears that threatened to fall, but even more to concentrate on a vision that was pushing its way up from her unconscious. Suddenly it was clear, a memory that had been tucked away for more than three decades, a moment that had once meant so much to her that it had burned itself indelibly into her brain.

She was just a girl, no more than ten or twelve, walking home from a friend's house. It was the beginning of December, just as it was now; early evening, probably not much later than five o'clock, but darkness had already fallen. Hurrying down the street where she lived, Laura peered into the windows of the brightly lit houses she passed.

Sneaking peeks into other people's lives was a game she'd invented. She enjoyed imagining the scenes inside. That night she conjured up jovial fathers, just home from work, relieved finally to be home. She pictured safe, secure children, freshly bathed, well fed, swathed in contentment as comfortable as their soft flannel pajamas.

Most of all, she imagined the mothers. The women who were at the core of each household, the soul of the family. She remembered musing about how good it must feel to be in the center, surrounded by a loving family, a cozy house, the feeling that everything was just as it should be: fresh-smelling sheets and towels folded neatly in the linen closet, scented soap in the bathrooms, cookies still warm from the oven spread out on a plate.

How desperately she wished that one day she'd be a woman like that! Laura experienced a yearning so great it manifested itself in the form of a pain, a tightness near her heart. She could see herself in that role. She needed to believe that one day she would be that woman.

The way her life was turning out, the brightly lit house with the fragrant towels and the freshly baked cookies and the loving family united under one solid roof would never be hers.

Laura dragged herself off the couch, bracing for the trip upstairs. She could picture what lay ahead. The half-empty closet, the bare drawers that were usually weighed down by stacks of T-shirts and sweaters and white shorts . . . and the bed, once theirs, now permanently hers. She dreaded it, but at the same time wanted to see for herself that it was real, that Roger really was gone.

She'd climbed only two steps when she heard the back door swing open.

"Mom?" Evan torpedoed into the house, zeroing in on her like a heat-seeking missile. His face lit up when he caught sight of her. His blue eyes were shining, his cheeks pink with cold. Triumphantly he held up a toy car.

"Look what Grandpa bought me! Here, Mom, watch. You turn it on here, and it moves like this. . . . Watch, Mom! Isn't it cool?"

"Very cool." Laura went over and gave him a big hug. "I missed you, monkey."

Not sounding particularly convincing, he echoed, "I missed you, too." His eyes still fixed on the four-wheel wonder jerking around on the carpet, he asked, "Where's Dad?"

Laura's mother chose that moment to poke her head in through the doorway. "Here's Evan's stuff. Nintendo, Crash Dummies, Key Force . . . Oh, his pajamas and his toothbrush are here somewhere, too."

"Thanks, Mom. Want to come in and —"

"No, no. Daddy's waiting in the car. How was the ski trip?"

"Great."

"That's good." She glanced around the living room. "Is everything okay?"

"Everything's fine." Laura feigned interest in Evan's new toy, not wanting her mother to see the tears that chose that moment to well up in her eyes. "Thanks for baby-sitting."

"I'm glad you had the chance to get away." Her mother didn't have to express the concern she was feeling. It was clearly reflected in her face.

After the two women had chatted briefly about the hazards of winter sports, the even more treacherous hazards of traffic, and Evan's impressive junk-food consumption during the previous forty-eight hours, Laura was left alone with her son once again.

She sank onto the couch, watching him while he played with the latest miracle from Toys "R" Us. "Sounds like you had fun at Grandma and Grandpa's."

He didn't glance up. "Where's Dad?"

Laura hesitated. "Ev, this is the weekend your dad moved out, remember?"

"Oh. Right." In an instant the new toy was forgotten. He was silent for a few minutes, staring at his shabby sneakers. "Hey, Mom? Whose idea was it to get a divorce?"

She swallowed hard. "It's really for the best —"

"But whose idea was it?"

"Mine."

Evan jerked his head up. "Why?" he demanded, his voice edged with hysteria, his face tense. "Why did you do it? Why can't we just keep everything the same?"

"Because, Evan." It took every ounce of energy Laura possessed to remain calm. "Daddy and I weren't getting along. We feel too differently about too many things —"

"Daddy told me he doesn't want to get a divorce."

Thank you, Roger, Laura thought grimly. And thanks, Evan, for setting me up, ask-

164

ing me a question you already knew the answer to.

"Honey, I know it's hard for you to understand. And it's not easy for me to explain. I know it's not fair that grown ups' mistakes end up affecting their kids. . . ."

She could tell from the look on his face that her words, meant to be soothing, were having no effect. Her son looked angry. Confused. Most of all, hurt.

"Oh, Ev." She reached over and took him in her arms. "What's important is that Daddy and I both love you. We'll always love you. If only you could understand that that's something that's never going to change."

As she held him close against her, Laura's eyes lighted upon the empty spots on the bookshelf in front of her. They were a glaring reminder of what had once been here, a part of this house, but was now gone. For Evan, these bare spots, these holes, were just the beginning. Overcome with sadness, she buried her face in her son's neck, clinging to him as hard as he clung to her.

Laura walked into her local CVS drugstore, and was startled to see that Christmas was in full swing. An irritatingly "lite" version of "God Rest Ye Merry Gentlemen" assaulted her the moment she pushed through the glass doors. Passing through the "Seasonal" aisle, she noted that the usual decorations were crammed onto the shelves, boxes of glittery tinsel and shiny glass ornaments and red velvet bows, their cheesiness magically elevated to something glorious. Candies that only weeks earlier had been packaged in orange and black for Halloween now sported foil wrappers in blue and green and red, with snowflakes on the Milky Ways and sprigs of holly on the Nestlé's Crunch. Even the cologne bottles looked positively irresistible in their festive gift boxes.

It was a shock to realize that while she'd been changing her life, the rest of the world had been up to business as usual. Laura dreaded Christmas, certain that the joy and goodwill toward men that everyone else was apparently feeling would only make her feel more alone. As she waited in line, cradling a box of tampons, a package of minipads, and an industrial-size jar of Advil, she couldn't envision experiencing the excitement that, in past years, had accompanied all the wonderful, corny traditions she'd grown up with: The first glimpse of a Christmas tree. The fragrance of pine. Bright colored lights, especially the blue ones. Stacks of presents in silver paper tied with red satin ribbons.

The salesclerk rang up Laura's purchases, then flashed her a big smile as she handed over the bag of menstrual paraphernalia. "Have a nice day!"

Laura couldn't get out of the store fast enough. So her first reaction was annoyance, when, as she stood by the door, fumbling in her purse for her car keys, the person behind her suddenly turned and tapped her on the arm.

"Laura? Hi!"

The woman was one of the mothers who routinely hung around school, dropping her kids off and picking them up with the dependability of a Buckingham Palace guard.

"Oh, uh, hello." Laura never had been very good at remembering names. While the other mothers had apparently developed close friendships hanging out at the playground and hovering outside the school waiting for the final bell to ring, Laura had never quite edged her way into their society.

Still, this mother — Mary Ann or Mary Lou or maybe just plain Mary — had always been one of the friendlier ones, smiling and saying hello every time their paths crossed.

"Are you and Roger going to the PTA Family Dinner Friday night?" asked Mary. "I've still got some tickets left."

Laura hesitated for only a moment. She'd been dreading this sort of situation, knowing that sooner or later she'd have to go public.

"I guess you haven't heard. Roger and I are splitting up."

Splitting up. She'd given a lot of thought to which phrase to adopt. What was required was a word that people would understand, but one that was not overly descriptive. One that skirted the issue, avoiding pinning a label on something that was too threatening for many people to feel comfortable around.

Still, none of her backup work had prepared her for Mary's reaction. The woman's face grew pale before Laura's eyes. Her expression changed, her mouth turned down, her eyes looked at the floor. Laura felt as if she were watching high-tech morphing in a horror movie.

It was that word, the one for which *splitting up* was a euphemism. *Divorce.* Mary — happily married Mary, or at least Mary who wanted to believe she was happily married — was afraid divorce might be contagious.

"I'm sorry, I hadn't . . . No one . . . Well, uh, I . . ." Frantically Mary glanced around the store. Relief crossed her face when she spotted a display of socks.

"Oh, look! Socks! I've been desperate to find socks! You know how they always get lost in the dryer. I swear mine must *eat* them. . . . See you, Laura!"

Later, waiting outside Evan's school with all the other moms, Laura was still slightly dazed from the encounter. She was partly amused, partly astonished, and, she had to admit, hurt. When she caught sight of Mary halfway across the schoolyard, chatting happily with a woman in a nylon jogging suit, she made a point of standing behind a tree.

She thought she was alone, but Grace, the mother of one of Evan's best friends, sauntered over.

"Matthew's been bugging me about when we can have Evan over," she said congenially. "How about this weekend?"

"That's probably okay. I'll have to call you." Laura hesitated. "I guess you've heard the news."

"About you and Roger? Sure."

Laura held her breath.

"You know," said Grace, leaning forward and lowering her voice to a conspiratorial tone, "half the women in this town would kill to be in your position."

Laura just stared at her. "What, without a date for New Year's Eve?"

"Having the financial freedom to walk out the way you are. Oh, sure, a lot of them would never admit it. They'd do anything rather than face it."

Grace's eyes narrowed as she stared off into space at something too far away for Laura to see. "I know I'd do anything to be in your shoes."

Laura inhaled the fragrance of the steaming coffee before her, making a point of appreciating not only its taste but every one of its other sensual aspects as well. At ten dollars a pound, Kona coffee was worth savoring.

Whether Hawaii's finest was actually worth the price, she couldn't say. What she did know was that she'd been unable to resist splurging the day before. After finishing up her usual Friday-afternoon errands, she'd stopped in at the gourmet shop across the street from the supermarket. Food, Glorious Food was a delightful emporium where she'd done her share of drooling, but had never actually parted with any money. Before she had a chance to remember that a penny saved was a penny earned, she'd filled a basket with a pound of the coffee, a box of Scottish shortbread, and a hunk of cheese so foul smelling it was bound to be tasty.

Now, sitting in her kitchen, alone on a Saturday afternoon, she was about to sample the loot from her shopping spree. She closed her eyes and took a sip of coffee.

Yes, she decided, it was worth the price. *I'm* worth the price.

Laura realized she'd entered a brand-new phase. No longer feeling as if she'd been run over by a large vehicle with four-wheel drive, she'd begun looking at herself — and her life — differently.

Perhaps it was the fact that she had begun talking more openly about her decision to get divorced. Mary's horrified reaction to her news had stuck with her, as had Grace's contention that Laura Briggs was Clover Hollow's newest idol. They were bizarre extremes. Still, she realized that while she was amused at having become Topic of the Week for the curbside gossips hanging around outside the schoolyard, her own conviction that she was doing what was best for her enabled her to let the opinions of others run off her like rain off a slicker. What was more likely was that her change in attitude was simply due to the passage of time.

Wanting to be nice to herself was only part of it. Suddenly she wanted to look good. Not only good; fantastic. Better than she'd ever looked before. That morning she'd put on mascara and blush, even though she had no plans to go anywhere more glamorous than 7-Eleven for milk. She'd studied her earring collection for a good five minutes, agonizing over which pair to wear. Finally she'd settled on porcelain flamingos, a gift from Claire that up until now she'd never had the courage to wear. She'd even tossed a scarf around her neck, a flamboyant touch that would have been much too Isadora

Duncan for the old Laura.

She walked around humming, feeling as if a great weight had been lifted from her shoulders. With Roger out of the house, she was free to do the things she'd yearned to do for years but had never dared try because of the conflicts she knew were bound to erupt.

Using her wedding china, for example. It was hard to believe that such pretty dishes, pure white trimmed with a thick border of cobalt blue and edged in gold, could have been the source of so much tension.

When they'd first gotten engaged, Laura had casually announced her intention of registering at Bloomingdale's. Roger was outraged.

"Registering?" His voice was dripping with disdain. "I don't believe in that."

"Why not?" Laura's bafflement was sincere. "It's no secret that everyone we invite to the wedding is going to buy us a present. Why not help them get us things we want? Otherwise we're going to end up with eleven woks and eighteen fondue pots."

"The people who know us and care about us should just *know* what we want," Roger insisted.

In the end, Laura had gone ahead and registered. And while she never would have admitted it to Roger, it was one of the most pleasurable hour and a halfs she'd ever spent. Sauntering around Bloomingdale's housewares department, making a list of everything she wanted, was tantamount to living out the fantasy of every woman who'd ever thumbed wistfully through a mail-order catalog. She felt like Lady Di when things between Chuck and her were still good.

"I'd like a dozen of those wineglasses. . . . No, make that two dozen. They break so easily. And a set of these place mats. Oh, look! Matching napkins! And napkin rings! I want them all. Now let's see what you've got in frying pans. . . ."

Choosing the china pattern had been the greatest challenge. So many lovely designs, so many factors to consider. In one set, she adored the plates but hated the cups. In another, the pattern looked wonderful on every piece except the serving platters. A third didn't come with dessert dishes.

Not that it mattered. She had attempted to use the set only once, at a New Year's Eve dinner for six she put together during their first year of marriage. Roger froze when he emerged from the shower and found her teetering on a kitchen chair, taking the good china out of the cabinet above the refrigerator.

"I can't believe you registered," he muttered. "Especially since you knew how I felt about it."

Her holiday spirit drooped instantly. Still, when the doorbell rang a few minutes later and Claire and her husband stood in the doorway with three huge bottles of champagne, Laura did her best to play the role of the party girl. All evening she laughed too loudly and ate too much. She flirted with Jim Tiller and paid his wife, Lynn, too many compliments on her new haircut. She even made a few jokes about Roger's angry silence, kidding him about the effects of too much champagne.

Despite her bravado, she couldn't keep her stomach from tightening as she noticed the clock's hands edging toward midnight.

"Hey, quiet down, everybody," Jim Tiller urged at one minute before twelve. He leaned over to turn up the television's volume. "The ball's about to come down."

"Oh, no!" groaned Lynn. "Surely you're not serious! That Times Square scene is so corny —"

"Sh-h-h-h!" Claire insisted. "Ten, nine, eight . . ."

As the crowd on television exploded, a cacophony of cheering and whistling and noisemakers rising up as the ball of fire hit its mark, the other two couples cried, "Happy New Year!" and kissed. Laura stood next to Roger, her eyes cast downward as she traced the stem of her champagne glass. He stood stiffly, not looking at her, not moving.

"Happy New Year," she said in a soft voice.

He turned away, heading toward the coffee table and grabbing a handful of chips.

Laura didn't use the dishes again for the next fourteen years. Instead, she took them out of the cabinet every few months, washed them carefully, checked to see that none of the pieces was cracked or chipped, then regretfully put them away again in a place where Roger wasn't likely to encounter them.

Now that he was gone, she delighted in using the fine china. She had her morning coffee in one of the delicate cups and her low-fat lunch on a dessert plate. She even served Evan his Frosted Flakes and his peanut-butter sandwiches in them.

Her decision to treat herself better than she'd been treated in years was facilitated by one more change, something she hadn't anticipated. For the first time since Evan's birth, Roger was suddenly being forced to take his responsibilities as a father seriously. Now there were "Daddy days." Every other weekend plus one evening a week, Roger and Evan spent long, uninterrupted hours together. Laura was convinced that the enthusiastic reports Evan gave upon his return, tales of ice-cream cones and PG-rated movies and baseball-card shows, only partly accounted for the way his eyes were lit up and his cheeks were flushed. He was excited to be with Roger; a rare thing in his life. As for her, her initial reaction of missing Evan quickly passed. Instead, she began enjoying the time to herself.

Through all the changes, Laura was pleased about how well she was able to focus on her writing. Just as in Claire's case, her work was proving to be a lifesaver. Sipping her coffee, Laura gloated over the new pages she'd turned out that day. Evan's departure for an afternoon of video games at a friend's house had provided her with an unexpected block of free time, which she'd put to excellent use.

She was about to reach for the new pages of the manuscript, sitting on the kitchen table, waiting to be proofread, when the doorbell rang. She experienced a pang of resentment. She'd been luxuriating in the time alone, and having no distractions besides her glee over her literary coup and her Rosenthal cup of designer coffee. Figuring it was probably only the UPS man, she shuffled toward the front door.

"Hi," Roger said as casually as if his return to the marital residence were an everyday occurrence. "Can I come in?"

He'd already breezed inside, making a beeline for the kitchen table, the traditional site of their negotiations.

Automatically Laura braced herself for a fight. Instead, as she lowered herself into the chair opposite his, she saw the expression on his face was calm.

"Laura, we have to talk."

"Okay." The familiar wrenching feeling gripped her stomach. She pushed aside her coffee cup, thinking, So much for bliss.

"Is Evan here?"

Laura shook her head. "He's at Matthew's house."

"Good." Roger took a deep breath. "Look, I'll get right to the point. These past couple of months have been really tough on me. Getting divorced was your idea, not mine. Since the beginning, I've been hoping you'd change your mind. I only agreed to move out because I figured giving you some time to yourself would make you see what a mistake you were making.

"But being forced out of the house, out of our marriage, has given me time to think. And I've come to the conclusion —"

The coffee burned in Laura's stomach like lava.

" — that getting a divorce really is the best thing. You were right, Laura. We *have* been miserable for a long time. I was simply afraid to admit it. But now that I've gotten out, I have a much better perspective. We're bad for each other. Neither of us has been able to support the other. It's sad, of course, and it's going to hit Evan the hardest, but it's the way it's got to be."

Laura just nodded. She expected to feel released, or in some way triumphant. Instead, a wave of sadness washed over her, so strong that even her caffeine-induced high couldn't combat it.

Chapter Nine

"That positively smacks of another woman," announced Claire, kicking off her shoes and tucking her long legs, squeezed into turquoise skintight stretch pants, underneath her. "I'm telling you, Laura. There could only be one thing behind good old Roger's change of heart. I'd bet anything he's found himself somebody new to keep his feet warm at night."

Laura's eyes widened. "Do you really think so?"

"No question. Look, all along Roger's been fighting the idea of getting divorced. Now, suddenly, he decides it's — what was that phrase? — 'for the best.' " Claire pushed up the sleeves of her baggy turtleneck sweater, a blinding shade of yellow. "What else could be responsible for his one-hundred-eighty-degree turnaround?"

It was early evening, and Julie, Claire, and Laura were at the small house on the edge of Clover Hollow that Julie shared with George. Laura had been desperate for female companionship. Her conversation with Roger and his conclusion that her decision to end their marriage really was for the best had left her reeling.

Of course, he was right. And she knew, intellectually, at least, that she truly wanted to hear him say the words he'd finally spoken. Yet it was one more step in letting go. One more of those moments in which she was forced to face the fact that this was really happening.

The antidote was friendship. At Claire and Julie's insistence, she'd recited the conversation she and Roger had had as accurately as she could. And as she'd expected, they'd been eager to dissect every word.

"Maybe Roger's finally come to recognize his role in all this." Julie, sitting cross-legged on the floor in front of the fire, pulled her nubby oatmeal-colored cardigan around her more tightly. It was an odd complement to the rest of her outfit: a flowered cotton skirt, a faded blue work shirt, and canary yellow high-tops. Tonight she was wearing her long red hair pulled back into a loose braid. "Maybe he's finally taking a good, hard look at himself. Getting in touch with his inner child, owning some of the ways he was responsible for your marriage not working out . . . Maybe he's actually learned from all this."

Claire shook her head. "In your dreams. Trust me; some female is sniffing around our boy Roger. It's the only explanation."

"Claire," Laura protested, "I really can't believe that. I *know* Roger. If he were seeing somebody else, I'd know."

"We'll see." Claire cast her a meaningful look.

Laura sipped her coffee, thinking about Claire's prediction and looking around. Julie's house was as different from Claire's sleek apartment as the two women were from each other. While Laura was pleased that she was able to feel at home in a stark, modern place like Claire's, she often thought that no one could help but feel comfortable and loved in Julie's cozy cottage.

She was convinced that the house had originally been built for elves. In the first place, it was nestled in the woods. Though not too far back from the road, it seemed more isolated because of the dense growth of trees, mosses, ferns, and other elements of the forest primeval that surrounded it. Then there was the architecture, the sort usually reserved for buildings constructed of gingergread and sugar wafers.

Tonight it provided the perfect setting for warding off the chill December evening. The three women were gathered around the fire burning in the gray stone fireplace, nursing steaming mugs of Julie's special coffee, perked up with just a touch of cinnamon. A large plate offered an assortment of cookies and breads, fresh from Julie's oven.

"And what about you, Laura?" Claire asked suddenly.

Laura glanced at her, surprised. "What do you mean, what about me?"

"When are you going to start dating?"

"Me?" The word came out like a croak.

"Sure," said Julie. "You remember dating, don't you? Flowers, candy, candelit dinners at romantic restaurants —"

"Long, hot nights," Claire interrupted, "entire weekends in bed, whispering sweet nothings, sucking each other's toes —"

"Worrying about sexually transmitted diseases," Laura countered, "waiting for the phone to ring, fighting off macho morons who can't take no for an answer —"

Julie closed her eyes and sighed. "It's such a wonderful experience, meeting someone you're crazy about and falling madly in love. You can't eat, you can't sleep . . . all you want is to be with him."

Claire was wearing a similarly dreamy expression. "The sex at the beginning is always fantastic. Not the first time, of course. That's always awful. But once you start learning the rhythm of someone else's body . . ."

"Frankly, I don't think there's any way I'd ever be willing to go through all that again." The mere thought made Laura shudder. "Putting yourself on the line, taking risks, making sure your hair is clean all the time

. . . It's more than any human being should ever have to endure."

"Now, Laura," Julie scolded, "you have to change your attitude."

"I do? Why?"

"Sex, for one thing," Claire replied. "Don't you miss great sex?"

"I've been missing great sex ever since I got married."

"We have to find you somebody," said Julie. "You know what they say. When you fall off a horse, it's important to get right back into the saddle."

"I'd rather take my car, thanks." Laura sighed. "Look, I know you're both just trying to be helpful. But the way I feel about getting into a relationship is like working in a chemical plant, getting cancer, going through torturous treatments and finally being cured . . . and then saying, 'Gee, think I'll stop over at the nuclear power plant and see if they have any job openings.' "

"Poor Laura," Julie cooed, shaking her head slowly. "Have you really become so disillusioned?"

"Try self-protective."

"You don't want to spend the rest of your life alone, do you?" asked Julie.

Laura was almost embarrassed to admit that that was exactly what she wanted. She had a favorite fantasy she played in her mind several times a day with precisely that theme. Living with Evan in a tiny cottage, not unlike Julie's. There'd be a white picket fence, rose bushes, and a larder full of her favorite cookies. She'd stay up all night watching reruns of classic sitcoms on cable. She'd eat Klondike bars for dinner. She'd luxuriate in a queen-sized bed outfitted with soft flannel sheets . . . blissfully alone.

Such freedom! How glorious it sounded. To be in total control of one's destiny, one's schedule, one's dietary habits . . .

"What's wrong with living alone?" Laura demanded.

"Nothing," said Claire. "Personally, I love living alone."

"You know, Claire," Julie said, her eyes fixed on the edge of her coffee mug, "I've always wondered why you never married again. Or got into another committed relationship."

"Because I'm smart enough to learn from my mistakes."

"Is that really it?" asked Laura. "Or is it that you never found yourself another Mr. Right?"

"Oh, I've come across some contenders. I just . . ." Claire bit her lip. "Never again will I put myself in a position where a man can cause me as much pain as the first 'Mr. Right.' "

There was a long silence before Laura said in a soft voice, "Claire's got a point. Living alone is fine, if that's the choice a woman makes."

"Is that what *you* really want?" Julie asked.

"It certainly sounds safe," Laura said.

"Maybe," mused Julie, "but is 'safe' enough to make you happy?"

"Right now safe sounds more important than happy." Laura sighed. "What about you, Julie? Are you happy, being with George?"

"I love George," Julie said a little too quickly. "Being with him is . . . comfortable."

"Comfortable?" Claire's eyebrows shot up. "That doesn't sound very exciting."

"There's something to be said for comfortable." Julie toyed with the ends of her braid. "We're good for each other. We . . . we fit."

"Sounds like an underwear ad," Claire muttered.

"Oh, it's not perfect," Julie went on. "George and I have our ups and downs. But every couple does. It's part of life."

" 'Every couple has its ups and downs,' " Laura mimicked. "I hate that line. It's right out of the *Ladies' Home Journal.*"

"It happens to be true," Julie insisted.

"Well, the ups are fine. It's the downs I can live without."

"Look," Claire said tiredly, "if you don't want to date, that's fine. Frankly, I couldn't blame you for resisting the advances of the swinging bus driver at the Robin Hood Inn. But at least try meeting some new people. Get out of the house, have a little fun —"

"Join a club!" Julie suggested brightly.

"Sounds like advice from a high school guidance counselor," Laura grumbled.

The wheels in Claire's brain were clearly turning. "Let's see. . . . How about a sailing club?"

Laura shook her head. "I had enough of the open seas with Roger." She held up her left hand, warding off the idea.

"How about golf?"

"I look awful in kelly green."

"You could always go skiing again."

"Going down the mountain was fine. It was standing around the bar, feeling like a seventh grader at her first school dance, I can do without."

Claire sighed. "How about you, Julie? Do you have any suggestions?"

"Hmmm?" She blinked hard, dragging her gaze away from the fire. "Oh, I'm sorry. I guess I wasn't listening. I was thinking about something else."

"Clearly." Claire eyed her carefully, a strange look on her face. "You have that unmistakable glow in your cheeks, that glint in your eyes. . . . Fantasizing about George?"

Instantly Julie turned a deep shade of

crimson. "Uh, no. As a matter of fact, I was thinking about the new patient of mine. You know, Bob."

"Ah, yes," said Claire. "The man with the stiff pectineus. What about him?"

Julie hesitated, casting a furtive look to the right and then to the left as if someone might be eavesdropping. In a hoarse whisper she said, "You're not going to believe this — in fact, I wasn't even going to say anything — but he asked me to have coffee with him."

"Coffee?" Claire repeated, her eyebrows rising. "Is that all?"

"Of course that's all!" Julie's tone was indignant, but the color of her cheeks had deepened into a nice shade of red. "We're just . . . friends, that's all."

"And what did you say?" asked Laura.

"Knowing Julie," Claire said, waving her hand in the air, "she slapped his naughty little face."

"Actually . . ." Julie cleared her throat. "I said yes."

"You said *what?*" Laura cried.

"Way to go, Julie!" Claire sounded impressed. "Good girl. I didn't know you had it in you."

"Well, I didn't *mean* to say yes, it's just that it was so sudden. And I wasn't sure what he meant, and I didn't want to be rude. . . ."

Laura and Claire stared at her expectantly.

"I was working out a knot in his adductor longus —"

"Oh, it's his adductor longus now," Claire interrupted.

Julie didn't even glance in her direction. "I was chattering away about the trip George and I took to Aruba last winter. Bobby had said —"

"Bobby?" Claire interrupted.

Julie bit her lip. "He said that's what all his friends call him."

"Ah," said Laura. "So he's progressed from a client to a friend."

Squirming in her seat, Julie said, "When you're working on somebody day after day, week after week, you develop a kind of . . . intimacy."

"Especially if that somebody has his shirt off," said Claire. "Probably his pants, too, if you've got your fingers wrapped around his longus."

"It's not like that at all," Julie insisted. "Anyway, Bobby had been saying he was thinking about a trip to the Caribbean, and I was telling him how much I'd enjoyed Aruba. He asked me if I remembered the name of the travel agent who'd booked the tour, and I said yes. Then he asked me if I still had the brochure, and I said yes. Then he asked me —"

"I can't wait to hear this one," Claire interjected.

"He asked me if I had any photographs from the vacation, and I said yes." Julie paused to take a deep breath. "And then he asked me if I'd meet him for coffee so I could show him."

"Show him what?" Laura demanded.

"The pictures! And the brochures." With a shrug Julie said, "So of course, I said yes. It all seemed so innocent. Everything flowed so naturally. It wasn't until I got home that I realized how the whole thing sounded."

"You didn't tell George, did you?" Claire was making a statement more than asking a question. "He with whom you 'fit' as well as a pair of Fruit of the Looms?"

"I would have," Julie insisted, her voice strangely high-pitched, "but I didn't want him to get the wrong idea."

Claire leaned forward, folding her arms across her chest. "This is delicious. You *are* going to tell us every single sordid detail, aren't you?"

"You know, Julie," said Laura, "you could cancel. Just call up this Bob —"

"Bobby."

"Call him and tell him you changed your mind. You could even mail him your old travel brochure."

Julie stared at her, wide-eyed. "But I *want* to have coffee with him!"

"What about George?" asked Laura.

Julie hung her head. "I know. I'm a terrible person. I'm bad. I'm a floozy."

"Hell, Julie," Claire said, leaning back in her chair, "the last 'floozy' was Betty Boop. And she was a cartoon."

"I can't help it. I know George and I have a good relationship. It's steady. It's predictable."

"But?" Claire prompted.

"But lately I've been feeling stifled. Hemmed in." She glanced around nervously, then hung her head. "I haven't said this to anyone. I've barely let myself think it, but . . . to be perfectly honest, I'm no longer sure George is the man I want to spend the rest of my life with."

Laura's mouth dropped open. "You never said anything like that before."

"I never felt this way before."

Claire smiled wickedly. "Not until she got her hands on Bobby's longus pectineus."

"It's not like that!" cried Julie. "Well . . . maybe just a little. I couldn't help noticing he has a very nice body. But it's mainly his mind that interests me," she added hastily. "I like the way he makes me feel. We have so much to say to each other. When I'm massaging his rectus femoris and I can feel him relaxing, responding to the motion, it's like . . . like we're doing a wonderful dance together."

"Sounds like a tango," Claire observed. "I say go for it, Julie. Check this Bobby out."

"Poor George," Laura said softly.

While she adored Julie and was willing to support her almost unquestioningly in whatever she did, she couldn't help feeling for George. After all, he was doing his best to make the relationship work, never dreaming for a minute that there were factors at play that could destroy it.

Wednesday night's Divorce and Separation Support Group had become an integral part of Laura's life, giving structure to her week and providing her with a sense of continuity she didn't get anywhere else. She liked having someplace to go.

With the holidays getting closer, she was in need of a support fix. She headed into the meeting room at the Y a week and a half before Christmas, looking forward to being updated on the wild and zany lives of Arnie, Tom, Estelle, and all the others. All in all, she concluded, their adventures were miles ahead of any sitcom characters'.

But the entertainment value was only part of it. Laura found it reassuring that she was not alone in what she was experiencing — or what she was feeling. Often as she lay in bed at night, she pictured Dawn in her bed in Great Neck and Arnie in his in Westbury and Carolyn in Syosset, all of them unwinding after a long day wrestling with the same highs and lows that had sent her diving into the sheets in a state of emotional exhaustion.

Her suspicions that she wasn't the only one who had concerns about how to weather the holidays ahead proved correct. As coffee hour came to a close and the members of Group Two and Three wandered off, she saw that there was a full house tonight. All eleven of the regulars were present, and a few newcomers as well. Merry, in a corduroy jumper and the same thick stockings Laura's grandmother used to wear, took her place at one end of their irregular circle.

"I'd like to start tonight." Dawn had her hand up before Merry had even had a chance to choke out a tearful welcome. Tonight the large woman was decked out in a red sequined sweater and white stretch pants that hid nothing. While the effect was startling, it did scream "festive." "All this holiday business is really giving me the blues. Oh, sure, I'm going through the motions, shopping and baking and going to parties. But I can't get past the fact that I'm going to the parties *alone*. When I bake my famous peanut-butter fudge, there's nobody to eat it but me and the kids. I'm experiencing a kind of loneliness I haven't felt up until this point."

"Yeah, I'm findin' the same thing," seconded Tom. Tonight his work clothes looked spanking clean. "Things at the shop are always kind of quiet this time of year. Nobody wants to have their tires rotated or their oil changed — not that you should ever neglect your auto maintenance, not even during the yuletide season.

"Still, it looks like my customers would rather be at the mall. So I always end up with a lot of extra time on my hands. This year, instead of running around, trying to find the perfect gift for my wife, I'm doing stuff like stackin' up the cans of Valvoline neater."

Merry was nodding sympathetically. "The holidays are an extremely difficult time. Everywhere we go, we're hit with messages that say this is a loving time. A family time. A togetherness time. How do we feel when we see that so many of the people around us are part of a couple?"

Tom shot his hand up into the air. "We feel like crap."

Go, Tom, thought Laura.

As usual, Merry finessed that one. "We experience bad feelings. Negative feelings. We don't always feel very good about ourselves. We may feel alone. We may feel as if we've failed —"

Laura was relieved when Carolyn raised her hand. The tiny redhead was dressed for the holiday season as well. Her green sweater had reindeer on the pockets, and a gold Christmas tree was pinned to the blouse underneath. Even her earrings — a tiny green ornament on one side, a shiny red bell on the other — were seasonal. "This is my first Christmas alone, too. But instead of being miserable about it, I'm trying really hard to look inside myself to find the strength to get through the holidays. I'm reaching out to friends. I'm working at a soup kitchen. I decided I'm going to make this the best darned Christmas my kids ever had. I've been so busy stringing popcorn and going caroling and doing all the things I never managed to find the time for in the past that I haven't had time to feel bad. As a matter of fact, I've been feeling pretty good about myself."

Carolyn's enthusiasm prompted Laura to raise her hand. "I'm feeling pretty good, too," she told the group. "I've barely noticed it's Christmas. I've been too busy discovering that I actually enjoy being single. My husband just moved out of the house a few weeks ago, and since then, I've been exhilarated. I feel so free.

"I can stay up as late as I want and read in bed without anyone complaining about the light being on. I can watch whatever I want on TV . . . and the remote is always in *my* possession." Laura shrugged. "Sometimes I even have ice cream for dinner."

Merry's head was bobbing up and down. She looked as if she were about to burst. "I hope everyone is listening to what Laura is saying. Carolyn, too. We don't *have* to have a mate in order to count. We don't need someone else in our lives to feel whole. We're all capable of enjoying life . . . on our own. Each of us is capable of giving to ourselves."

Arnie looked confused. "Wait a minute. You mean, like, instead of me giving a present to my wife, this year I can use the money to buy something I want?"

"She means we don't need to look to others to make us happy," explained Estelle. As usual, she had kept silent until she was so strongly motivated that nothing could keep her from speaking out. Of course, the members of the group held their breath whenever she took the floor. "We make ourselves happy. We fulfill ourselves. We decide what's important to us, and we fill our lives with it."

"I think I get it," said Tom. "You mean like Carolyn workin' at that soup kitchen."

Merry's eyes were shining. "That's right."

He turned to Carolyn. "You get paid for that?"

"I guess what we need to do," Dawn said thoughtfully, "is think of finding happiness as a challenge. Kind of like a mission. A quest. We have to figure out what matters to *us*, without worrying about anybody else."

"Like hockey," Arnie muttered.

Merry jumped on that one immediately. "Hockey is a good example. When you were married, Arnie, was ice hockey something you and your wife enjoyed together?"

"Hah! You kidding?"

"Well," she went on, growing more excited, "now that you're on your own, you're free to pursue your interest in sports. It's something that matters to you. You don't need another person in order to enjoy it."

"Well, it helps to have somebody else to watch your coat while you're on line for a hot dog. . . . But I understand what you're saying. Really, I do."

Laura did, too. Sitting in the meeting room, for a moment phasing out the voices of the others, she felt a surge of strength rising up inside her. She would get through the holidays. And she would enjoy herself. She'd look to the traditions that had always brought her joy; immerse herself in schmaltzy choral music and fancy cookies and too much tinsel and all the other things that made the holidays wonderful. She'd find the spirit that only came once a year, the real gift of the holiday season.

Besides, she reminded herself, she was

anything but alone. She had Evan. If she couldn't hold on to this feeling of power for her own sake, she'd do it for him.

Chapter Ten

"Okay," Laura said under her breath, rubbing her hands together. "I can do this."

"Are you sure, Mom?" Evan sounded doubtful as he struggled to hold up a seven-foot fir tree. Next to it, he looked as tiny as one of Santa's elves.

"Of course. What's so hard about making a tree stand up in your living room? Mother Nature's been doing it in *her* living room for aeons."

Glancing around the room, Laura had to admit she couldn't help feeling as if she were posing for a Kodak moment. That afternoon, right after she'd picked Evan up from school, the two of them had gone Christmas-tree hunting. Instead of heading for the woods, they opted to trek over to the nearest farm stand, where freshly cut trees were being sold as fast as the men in the red-plaid coats could bind them in twine.

As usual, Evan had set his heart on one so tall owning it would have necessitated cutting a hole in the ceiling. Laura, with her level head and limited budget, patiently led him to the moderately priced trees, the ones that looked as if they needed a little love. Picking out a tree, they'd decided, was like choosing a puppy. You looked and looked . . . and then suddenly you just *knew*.

When Evan insisted on the way home that they set up the tree and start decorating it right away, putting the task even above his favorite six-o'clock rerun, Laura agreed. She was excited, too. As far as she was concerned, it never really felt like Christmastime until the tree was up. And she was definitely in need of a little boost in the spirit department.

She even built a fire in the fireplace for the occasion. She was determined to make her first Christmas on her own as wonderful as possible. The promise she'd made to herself at the support group the night before was still ringing in her ears. She and Evan laughed hysterically as they tried to remember the words of the Christmas carols she insisted upon singing while they carried the cartons of decorations down from the attic. She tried to sing the less familiar ones to keep him entertained.

"Who was Good King Wenceslas, anyway?" Evan demanded, lugging a box down the stairs. Peeking out of the top were tacky gold garlands that Laura loved.

"The man who invented Scotch tape," she replied earnestly. "Think about it, Ev. How could any of us have a real Christmas without Scotch tape?"

With the roaring fire, the fragrance of pine, and the dusty cardboard cartons promising goodies that had been forgotten for the past eleven and a half months, all the elements were in order. Her heart fluttered as she took the brand-new red tree stand, the finest K Mart had to offer, out of its box.

Still, as she contemplated the task ahead, she wished she'd forgone one or two of her college English courses and opted for something more practical — like mechanical engineering. While this was precisely the kind of thing Gertrude Giraffe could carry off without a hitch, Laura was anything but confident about the undertaking. As much as she hated to admit it, she'd always thought of setting up the tree as the husband's job. Taking a deep breath, she pushed the metal tree stand into the corner of the living room. The Christmas tree had always gone next to the fireplace, but this year it would have a new place, she'd decided.

"Bring that baby over here," Laura instructed. "Now, what we need here is a show of upper-body strength. Pretend you're a Ninja Turtle —"

"Come on, Mom. You know nobody likes the Ninja Turtles anymore."

"Okay. Pretend you're He-Man —"

"He-Man's worse. Only babies like him."

"Barbie on steroids?"

"Mo-o-o-m!" Evan chortled. Then, growing sober: "What are steroids?"

"You'll learn all about them when you play high school football. In the meantime let's see if together you and I can lift up that tree and get it right smack in the middle of this — bull's-eye!"

Tightening the screws against the pine tree's trunk, Laura felt a surge of triumph. She really *was* doing it. She'd accomplished this formidable job not only with ease, not only with grace, but without having to argue about which side of the tree had more bare spots.

"Not bad, huh? Not that I can be totally objective, of course, but all things considered, I'd say this is the best tree we've ever had."

"Oh, Mom. You say that every year."

"Sure I do. It's a Christmas tradition, like giving fruitcake to people you secretly don't like." Laura turned to the boxes of decorations lined up along the couch. "Now we can —"

"Mom!" Evan screeched. "Look out!"

Their precious little *Tannenbaum* began leaning to one side, slowly, and then it toppled over, taking the metal stand with it. She could have sworn it was laughing at her. Or at least trying to get back at her for

201

those metal screws she'd slammed into its trunk.

Evan looked at it forlornly. "Dad never had any trouble making the tree stand up."

"Oh, sure he did. Everyone does. We just made a point of protecting you from the more stressful aspects of the holiday." She was on all fours underneath the tree, fumbling with the screws once again, silently cursing the defiant bit of flora, which was rebelling against having been wrested from its natural habitat by sticking its spiky needles into her neck and up her nose.

Yet in the end, the human spirit triumphed over nature. "Voilà! Pretty cool, huh?"

"Do you think we should be careful not to breathe when we're close to it?"

"This tree is as sturdy as . . . as the *Titanic*."

"The *what?*"

"Uh, a famous ship that . . . How about if you try to find the lights? That's the next step. Meanwhile I'll start unpacking the ornaments."

She held her breath as she opened the first box and confronted the ghost of Christmases Past. Taking out the pieces one at a time, holding them in her hand, forced her to reexamine memories that she hadn't had to face since the year before, when she'd packed them away.

Gingerly she pulled out the four ceramic apples she'd bought the first year she and Roger were married. Delving into a clump of tissue paper, she unwrapped a cardboard star, decorated with gold glitter, with Evan's baby picture in the middle. She'd made that one to commemorate his very first Christmas. Underneath was a wooden sailboat with Santa at the helm. She'd bought it for Roger as a stocking stuffer just the year before. She remembered having thought about attaching a tiny wedding ring to the side — as a joke — but in the end had decided against it.

The visions that came to her were not all sugarplums. There was coal in the Christmas stocking as well. Laura reminded herself that even in the best of times, she'd ended up decorating most of the tree with only the help of a toddler who couldn't be trusted to handle anything breakable.

In fact, the norm was for her to spend nearly every Christmas Eve alone. Somehow, Roger had always had more important things to do. For one thing, he left his shopping to the last minute, claiming that the day before Christmas was the ideal time to avoid the crowds. That meant he toiled away late into the night, hiding in the basement, wrapping the presents Laura wasn't allowed to see.

Some years he wasn't in the house at all.

He was out delivering gifts, or helping his mother with the tree, or painting a handmade wooden present out in the cold garage in the hope that it would dry overnight. Laura and Evan were left on their own to admire the sparkling lights on the tree and speculate about whether or not Santa would have managed to get ahold of this toy or that.

That had been the reality. Even so, Laura felt a pang of sadness, becoming suddenly very aware of the fact that she was a single mother. At least this year, doing the tree by herself was her choice. Then she realized something else was missing: the usual knot of anger in her stomach over the fact that once again she wanted something from her husband that she simply wasn't getting. All around the country, happy families were carrying out their traditions . . . together. But no matter how hard she'd tried, her life never quite seemed to work the way she wanted it to.

"Hey, Mom?" Evan's voice brought her out of her reverie. "We got trouble."

"What now?"

He held up the Christmas-tree lights, a tangle of green wires and colored bulbs. "We're never going to straighten these out!"

His voice was quiet, trembling just a little. Laura realized that he was afraid. Afraid that this year the Christmas tree would have no lights or perhaps that there would be no joy, none of that special feeling that made fires in fireplaces glow with holiday magic, and the evergreen come alive, and the simplest Christmas carol resonate like a magnificent cantata.

Maybe he feared that Christmas, like everything else in his life, would never again be as wonderful as it had once been.

"Oh, Evan!" she cried, kneeling down to throw her arms around his bony shoulders. Suddenly he seemed very small and very fragile. "Of course I can fix those lights. And if I can't, we can run out and buy new ones. We're going to have a wonderful Christmas, I promise."

"As good as last year's?"

"As good as last year's. Maybe even better."

Evan pulled away, never one to sustain a hug even a second longer than he had to. "Does that mean you'll get me Sega Genesis?"

"We've been through this a hundred times, Ev." Laura sighed. "You already have Nintendo, and those videogame systems are too expensive to go out and buy —"

She stopped, having recognized the glint in his eye, the hint of a smirk on his lips. "You're kidding, right? You're just trying to give your dear, sweet old mom a hard time, aren't you?"

Grinning, Evan shrugged. "Couldn't resist."

Laura stuck her tongue out at him. When she got the laugh she was looking for, she grabbed the lights and foraged around until she found the plug.

"Here," she instructed, handing it to him. "Hold this, you pip-squeak. I'll bet you a zillion dollars I can have these going within ten minutes."

"Wow! It used to take Dad hours!"

"My fingers are smaller and nimbler. They also happen to be capable of performing magic."

Evan watched with wide eyes as she began straightening out the recalcitrant lights. One by one she liberated the colored bulbs, working until they looked more like the familiar strings and less like a cruel Christmas joke.

"You're good!" Evan said admiringly.

"You're darned right I'm good." Wanting to prove just how good, she undid a knot the size of a popcorn ball. "Hey, Ev?"

"Yeah?"

"We really are going to have a nice Christmas. I'm not going to let you down."

"I know, Mom." He thought for a few seconds, then said matter-of-factly, "I guess you never do."

Laura bit her lip. She pretended she was simply concentrating. It wouldn't do to mix salty tears with electricity.

'Tis the season to be jolly, Laura reminded herself as an enthusiastic shopper jabbed her in the stomach with his elbow. Like her, he was desperately fighting his way through the crowd around a display table in Macy's accessories department. The three simple words printed on the sign rising above it, TWENTY-FIVE PERCENT OFF, evoked in otherwise normal human beings a competitiveness rarely seen off a football field.

She had no choice but to join in the game. Christmas was only three days away, and she had to buy gifts for Claire and Julie. Ordinarily, shopping for her two best friends was one of Laura's favorite holiday tasks. It was almost as much fun as shopping for herself. She loved scouring the bins of leather gloves, the glass cases with rows of silk scarves, and the displays of costume jewelry hanging like baubles and beads at a Middle Eastern bazaar. Her usual strategy was to pick out something she liked, then buy it in the most garish color available for Claire and the most sedate shade for Julie. This year, however, it was turning out to be a chore.

When she finally edged her way to the table, she was disappointed to find only piles of slippers in the shape of barnyard animals.

She turned away, discouraged. The store was too hot and too crowded. Most of the sales help looked as if they were amazed that people had come into the store. She was contemplating giving up, wondering if one of those enterprising mail-order companies could magically whisk some wonderful trinkets to her door overnight, when a display of brightly colored fabrics across the floor caught her eye.

A surge of hope rose up through the despair, and Laura headed toward what looked like silk scarves. It was only after she'd hurled herself through the throngs that she realized the confused masses of color weren't scarves at all. They were neckties.

Laura was in the men's department.

She stood frozen to the spot, blinking, unable to focus on either the decorations or the merchandise. Her surroundings melted into a blur. Instead, what Laura saw were women shopping for presents for the men in their lives.

In an instant her eyes filled with tears. What she had striven so hard to forget had crept up on her here among the piles of silk and cashmere and suede. It hit her on a visceral level, causing her stomach to knot, her shoulders to tense, her temples to throb.

You're alone. It's Christmas, and you're all alone.

Laura found herself recalling the year before. The scene popped out of her memory, playing before her with cruel clarity. She'd been in this same department, in a spot less than fifty feet away, standing in line for what seemed an eternity. Even though the store was as hot as it was today, she'd been wearing her winter coat, preferring that to carrying it. The salespeople, who appeared to have been heavily sedated, moved in slow motion and looked completely baffled every time a customer presented a credit card. The other shoppers were cross, buying gifts for their loved ones with the same spirit and goodwill with which they waited in line at the Motor Vehicle Bureau.

For a fleeting moment it had occurred to Laura that she didn't have to be doing this. But she'd already invested a good twenty minutes picking out the perfect pair of plaid flannel pajamas for Roger. And she had her heart set on buying her husband a three-pack of Calvin Klein briefs — purple, blue, and fire-engine red. Buying Roger racy underwear for Christmas was one of her favorite traditions.

She thought about forgetting the whole thing, dropping her selections on the counter and rushing over to Houlihan's for a margarita and a plate of nachos. But she didn't. She was still throwing herself into all the usual Christmas preparations, last year, going through the motions of creating a holiday in the Briggs-Walsh household that, at least on the outside, *looked* happy. She hadn't yet been able to give up the pretense, or bring herself to admit that she was fighting a battle that couldn't be won.

Now, all of a sudden, Laura could tolerate no more. She turned and fled, desperate to get out of the men's department, longing to leave Macy's . . . yearning to exit her own life. It was not only the haunting memories that sent her racing from the store, but the realization that while she'd rejected her old life, simply picked up and walked away from it, she had yet to come up with any-thing better. She was in a holding pattern. She was waiting . . . but for what?

Ever since she'd been a little girl, organ-ized, conscientious Laura Briggs had made a point of knowing where her life was going, what was coming next. Now, no matter how hard she tried, she couldn't conjure up what her future held. She didn't know where she'd be living. Aside from continu-ing to write, she was unable to imagine how she'd spend her days. And when she tried to envision the faces of the people who would be surrounding her, all she saw were bodies with faceless heads, their features indecipherable.

Would her decision to get divorced really

result in a better life? Or had the choice started her on a road she would one day regret? The roller coaster was fraught with terrifying twists and turns . . . but what was waiting for her at the end?

Rushing through Macy's, Laura was certain she'd never feel settled again. Something had been ripped away from her. A large piece of her life had been declared unviable. She feared that in the process, a wound too large ever to heal had been created. Not only would Christmas never be Christmas again; nothing in her life would ever again be the way she wanted it to be.

As always, Christmas morning was anticlimactic. Still, after the shopping, the wrapping, the decorating, the baking, and the writing of enthusiastic messages on cards, all carried out at the desperate pace of someone told she had only three months to live, Laura welcomed the chance to sit back and reap the rewards.

She sat cross-legged on the floor next to the Christmas tree, a mug of coffee in one hand and a garbage bag in the other, relishing the time spent with Evan. She loved watching as he gleefully tore the wrapping paper off one gift after another. Her anxiety attack at Macy's had already faded to nothing more than an unsettling memory.

"I have a present for you, too, Mom," he

said, pausing to take a break after opening a papermaking kit guaranteed to convert junk mail into greeting cards Rembrandt himself would have been proud to send.

"Evan, that's so thoughtful!" This was the first year he had given her a Christmas present. Still, she braced herself as she undid the small box wrapped in gold paper. For all she knew, it could turn out to be rubber vomit or a whoopee cushion.

So she was as pleased as she was surprised when she discovered Evan had gotten her a necklace with a charm that said #1 MOM.

"Evan, it's gorgeous!" she said sincerely. "I love it. I'll wear it all the time. Here, let me give you a kiss."

He let out a loud groan. "Oh, *no*. I was afraid of that!"

Christmas dinner was a welcome contrast to the quiet morning she and her son had spent at home. Evan went off with his father, excited about spending the rest of the day with his grandparents, Uncle Dirk, and the rest of the Walsh clan. She was free to relax, curl up in front of Julie's fireplace, and enjoy her surroundings.

In a flush of holiday exuberance that would have put Martha Stewart to shame, Julie had decked her halls with a lot more than boughs of holly. In fact, in addition to the perky green sprigs, there were pine garlands, mistletoe, poinsettias, and more Christmas cactus than the Painted Desert. There were also homemade candles and bowls of pinecones and cinnamon-and-clove potpourri. Her collection of hand-crafted Christmas stockings hung from the mantelpiece.

Yet while Julie was playing the role of holiday hostess to the hilt — wearing a red snowflake sweater, serving up a delectable dinner — Laura sensed something was wrong.

George, playing his usual role of pleasant, if somewhat bumbling, host, carved the turkey. An editor at a news magazine for intellectuals based in New York City, he very much looked the part in his wrinkled khaki pants and nubby brown sweater with a tiny moth hole at the elbow. As he sawed away at breasts and thighs, a lock of straight, dark brown hair kept falling over his tortoiseshell glasses.

"If I'd known how demanding this task would prove to be" — he chortled — "I'd have spent last week pumping iron instead of laboring over my scathing review of William F. Buckley's latest treatise."

Laura laughed, but when she glanced at Julie, she saw her lower her eyes. Evidently, creating symmetry in the bowl of string beans amandine was more important to her friend than joining in the appreciation of George's little joke.

Later, when Laura and Claire sat in the living room together, nursing a second glass of eggnog, they overheard Julie and George bickering in the kitchen.

"What are you *doing?*" Julie shrieked. "George, the leftover chestnut stuffing doesn't go in the same container as the sausage stuffing!"

"I'm sorry, Julie," George returned. Peeking through the doorway, Laura saw the bewildered look on his pale, gaunt face.

"Mixing the spices in Tupperware would be a travesty!"

"I said I was sorry." Poor George sounded as if he didn't know what had hit him.

When Julie finally came into the living room, leaving George in the kitchen to abuse spices at will, Laura gently placed her hand on her friend's arm.

"Julie, is everything all right?"

"It would be if George —" Staring into the fire, Julie bit her lip. Laura sneaked a peek at Claire, who looked puzzled.

"Oh, it's not George's fault," Julie suddenly burst out. "It's mine, all mine. I'm just so — so edgy lately." She took a few deep breaths, her thin chest heaving. Then, in a soft voice, she said, "I had dinner with Bobby."

"Dinner?" Claire cried. "What happened to coffee?"

"It started out as coffee. But it went on to dinner."

"Please don't tell me it ended with breakfast," Laura pleaded.

She expected a string of reassurances. Instead, Julie looked at her mournfully. "I can't help it. I'm really attracted to him. It's as if there were something . . . something *magical* between us."

Claire snorted. "Magical? Or chemical?"

Laura cast her an icy look.

"Not that I'm antichemistry," she was quick to add. "I owe some of my most memorable nights to pheromones."

"Julie," said Laura, pointedly ignoring Claire, "do you realize what you're saying?"

"I know what I'm saying," Julie replied in a hoarse whisper. "I just wish I knew what I was doing."

"Cappuccino time!" George chose that moment to burst through the doorway, tray in hand. On it were four white cups arranged around a plate of home-baked cookies shaped like stars, bells, and eight tiny reindeer. "Any takers?"

Laura perked up immediately. "Caffeine, the greatest gift of all!"

"You must have read my mind, you gem." Claire was already reaching for one of the steaming cups.

As for Julie, she simply glanced at him sorrowfully, then pulled her snowflake sweater down over her bent knees. Laura watched her stare into the flames of the fire, left untended for so long they were beginning to die down.

Chapter Eleven

"Don't worry. I'll be fine," Laura assured Julie, cradling the phone receiver between her neck and her shoulder. "New Year's Eve has never been a biggie in my book."

"But you shouldn't be alone, tonight of all nights," Julie insisted. "The whole world is out partying!"

"All the more reason to stay in." Laura nestled against the soft cushions of the couch, tucking the afghan around herself. "Actually, I'm looking forward to a quiet evening all by myself. With Evan at Roger's, I can watch what I want on TV. I can hardly believe I'll actually be able to tune in to something besides *Nick at Night*."

"Won't you be lonely?"

"Not me. I'm armed with a pint of Häagan-Dazs chocolate chocolate chip, the January issue of *Glamour*, and a really juicy novel. I even have the makings for my favorite cocktail for a midnight toast: Southern Comfort and cherry Diet Coke. I call it Janis Joplin Meets Jenny Craig."

"Well, if you're sure . . ."

"I'll be fine. Scout's honor."

Laura really was looking forward to having an entire evening all to herself. When she got off the phone she picked up the spanking-new issue of *Glamour*. Predictably, the cover blurbs promised several articles on how to make oneself over for the new year.

Usually opening the magazine was like taking the cover off a box of chocolates. So she turned the pages, hoping to work up some excitement over the barrage of advice crammed onto them. Moisturizing. Accessorizing. Determining the best haircut, given the shape of one's face. Choosing a jacket that could be coordinated with several different outfits.

Instead of being inspired by the do's, the don'ts, and the don't-even-think-about-its, however, she quickly became discouraged. She tossed the magazine onto the coffee table.

What I need for the new year, Laura told herself, isn't a reminder to put hand lotion on my fingernails. It's not the scoop on the latest trend in belts. No, my resolutions have to go much deeper.

She paused for a moment, thinking back to all the New Year's Eves when she'd dutifully made a list of promises to herself. Why should this year be any different? she wondered. She dragged herself up off the couch to seek out a respectable piece of paper, instead of reaching for the nearest scrap of junk mail. This, after all, was an effort worth legitimizing.

RESOLUTIONS, she printed at the top of the page, underlining the word twice. She was using the first writing implement she'd come across, a neon-green felt-tip pen of Evan's. Directly underneath she wrote, _Be good to yourself._

There, she thought triumphantly. That seems to define a healthy attitude with which to approach the new year. It was certainly better than the old standbys about losing five pounds, getting serious about a savings account, and telephoning her mother more often.

She stared at the words she'd written, thinking hard about their implications. The idea of being good to herself was a novel one. After all, up until quite recently her focus had been on being good to others.

Over the years Laura had found her struggle to prove that she was the grown-up version of the perfect little girl an exhausting, thankless, and ultimately futile endeavor. She resented the fact that while she was married she did so much — pretty darned close to everything, as far as she was concerned. She was the one who made sure there was always milk in the refrigerator and bagels near the toaster. She had dinner ready promptly at six forty-five every night, a three- or four-course meal made entirely with fresh ingredients, since Roger didn't believe in mixes, frozen foods, canned goods, or preservatives. She kept the house clean enough to keep out the board of health. She was the one who made phone calls and wrote letters to the insurance companies, the credit-card companies, the utility companies, and the banks, figuring that all in all she spent more time wheeling and dealing than Donald Trump.

And while Roger was usually good for a few rounds of wrestling with Evan or a long evening of building spindly cities out of Tinkertoys, it was Laura who made sure there was always clean underwear in their son's top drawer. She was the parent capable of reciting in her sleep which days were gym days, which were music days, and which were art days. She coordinated the extensive staff of professionals necessary to keep an eight-year-old in working order: doctors, dentists, haircutters, Cub Scout leaders, baby-sitters, and friends.

In addition, Laura had also been the main wage earner in her household. The success of Gertrude Giraffe and her cohorts not only paid for the basics; it also financed the best nursery school, a ten-day trip for two to Paris, and the countless periods that Roger spent trying to decide what he wanted to be when he grew up.

Just thinking about it all made her tired. But she brushed it aside and jumped into resolution number two.

Get on with your life, she wrote.

Too general, she decided, chewing the end of Evan's pen. *How* can I get on with my life? I already made the most critical move: getting myself out of a marriage that wasn't working.

She closed her eyes and leaned her head back. What *do* I want? Laura wondered. Here I am, back at square one, ready to redesign my life. How do I want it to look?

As always, the first image that came to mind was that of a life of solitude. The one with the cookies in the pantry and the big, empty bed, all to herself. For a few moments she stepped into the cottage she'd created in her mind, thinking about how she'd decorate the walls with sponge-paint borders in the bathroom and a space-age mural in Evan's room. In her dream house, even the little piles of clutter were gone. Not only those made of junk mail and PTA memos, either; more important, her mind would be clear. The emotional turmoil would have been swept away.

Yet there was another image pushing its way through. Laura's attempts at keeping it at bay were in vain. Finally she simply let it come. In this fantasy, she was once again the star . . . but there was a costar, as well. A man. A wonderful man, the 1990s version of Prince Charming. He was smart, of course. Accomplished in his career as well, an important factor not only because he was satisfied with the way his life had turned out, but also because he had no reason to be jealous of the pleasure she found in her work. He also had a great sense of humor, a mellow outlook on life, and, while she was designing her dream man, a great set of buns. . . .

Damn! she thought, angry with herself. Have I learned nothing? Have all those years of mushy movies and breath-mint commercials really had such an impact on me? Could I even entertain the idea of pairing up with a man again?

No, she decided firmly. Not yet. I still want my freedom. I'm not ready to give up this wonderful gift of having no one to think about besides my son and myself.

All of a sudden, having no idea what she wanted out of life didn't feel threatening at all. As a matter of fact, it was actually a relief. The roller coaster was in a state of free fall, heading downward in response to gravity's pull . . . and the sensation was exhilarating. She'd embarked on a real adventure. For a change, Laura realized, instead of gripping the sides so tightly that her knuckles turned white, she willingly threw her arms up into the air, anxious to experience simply letting go and seeing where the ride was going to take her.

Standing beneath a dim porch light that flickered uncertainly, Laura pulled off one of the purple suede gloves that had been her Christmas present from Claire and stuck her hand into her coat pocket. She compared the address handwritten on a crumpled piece of paper with the number displayed on the front door.

This was the place, all right, a row house in Queens. Checking her watch, she saw the time was right as well. In fact, she thought, taking a deep breath and boldly ringing the doorbell, the only thing missing was the conviction that she was really ready for this.

Coming to an orientation meeting for Parents on Their Own had taken every bit of nerve Laura possessed. Following up on the newspaper's suggestion that she *call Dave for information* had been hard enough. She knew perfectly well that, unlike her weekly support group, designed to be therapeutic, Parents on Their Own was a social organization. Still, there'd been no commitment involved in dialing the number listed in the paper. She owed Dave nothing besides listening politely as he rambled on about all the events the group's members were invited to participate in.

She learned that, for single parents and their kids, the organization hosted ski weekends, day trips to amusement parks, and visits to local ice-skating rinks, video arcades, and restaurants. For single parents on their own, footloose and fancy-free while the kids were weekending with the ex, there were dances, rap groups, and Trivial Pursuit nights, which, Dave informed her with pride, had been known to get pretty raunchy on occasion.

It sounded like fun. Good, clean, innocent fun. Of course, with all those singles together under one roof, hordes of people representing gallons of hormones with no outlet, there was a good chance there'd be a lot more going on than pleasant chitchat about which of the new PG-13 videos were worth renting.

Relax, Laura chided herself. You're not here on a manhunt. You're simply following through on a resolution made under the influence of Southern Comfort and cherry Diet Coke.

Her sincere intention in joining this organization was to make new friends — women friends. What she needed was a coterie of divorced and separated women who were up for a Friday-night movie or a raucous Saturday night at Chippendale's, stuffing grocery money into the B.V.D.s of men so young they really should be home in bed, fast asleep. And Parents on Their Own seemed like the ideal place to start.

Laura was tempted to ring the bell again when she felt the vibrations of something large moving on the other side of the front door. Sure enough, when it opened, standing there was a woman who easily hit the two-hundred mark on the scale.

"You must be Laura. Come in, come in! You'll freeze standin' out there!"

Darlene Colletti was either a Brooklyn native or auditioning for the sequel to *My Cousin Vinny*. Her billboard-size frame was draped in a variety of garments, all of them in startlingly bold colors. Her jewelry was also oversized: earrings as big as postcards, an impressive row of bangle bracelets, rings flashier than the pope's.

It's not too late to turn back, Laura told herself. But it was. Her hostess for the evening was ushering her inside, holding out her arms to take Laura's coat.

"You're here for the POTO new members' Greeting Meeting, right?"

Clearly a different language was spoken here. It took her a few seconds to change gears. "Right. Parents on Their Own — uh, POTO. That's me."

Darlene led her into the living room. The way she grabbed her by the wrist made Laura feel she was being dragged off to the principal's office.

She glanced around the room, trying to get a feel for what she'd gotten herself into.

What struck her first was that too much large, dark furniture had been stuffed into too small a place. Huge, overstuffed couches and chairs, covered in brocade fabric with shiny gold threads running through, were pushed into corners and lined up against walls. Wedged between them were ornate tables with marble tops and molded wooden legs, swirled and twisted and ending in shapes that resembled the paws of various animals. Decorating the walls were crucifixes, fifteen or twenty at least, Laura estimated. They covered even the doorframes and major appliances, she noticed as she peeked at the refrigerator magnets in the kitchen.

Well, she'd come to meet and greet, not to redecorate, she reminded herself. Twenty or so people had gathered in the living room. A few of them milled about, but most sat up stiffly, in chairs or on the couch, looking as if they were in the waiting room at a proctologist's office.

They were all wearing name tags with the bright green POTO logo printed across the top. A man with JOE on his sweater sat with his legs spread wide, a big bowl of pretzels balanced in his lap. An older woman sat in one corner, smiling and nodding as she knitted away happily. She was dressed in a hand-knit sweater, a hand-knit scarf, and hand-knit socks. None of the garments hung quite straight. Her name, her tag proclaimed, was Natalie. Another woman, Elsa, wearing a dark, tailored suit, looked very much the banker with her silk scarf fashioned into a natty bow tie and her sensible black pumps. Vince was a male version of Elsa. The two of them sat side by side on the couch like a pair of salt and pepper shakers.

"Come in! Come in! Don't be shy." Darlene gave Laura a push. "This is the first time for everybody. It's as if we were all virgins again. But like anything else, it's only hard the first time."

The man with the Joe name tag snickered. "If you're lucky, it's hard every time."

Suddenly Laura jumped as someone slapped her on the chest.

"There you go." Elsa was grinning at her. "You're Laura, right?"

Peering down, Laura saw that now she, too, wore a name tag.

She was relieved when Darlene glanced at her watch and commanded the last stragglers to take a seat. The setup reminded her of a game of spin the bottle. It took her back, all those nervous males and females sitting in a circle in someone else's living room, waiting for the evening to get started and hoping desperately they wouldn't make complete fools of themselves.

Panic rose inside her. What am I doing here? she thought. I have nothing in common with these people.

But she did. And the name tag that Elsa had so unceremoniously stuck onto her chest was proof.

Laura headed for the last vacant seat, a big upholstered chair that nearly swallowed her up. Its soft bottom placed her about ten inches below the people on either side of her, who were sitting on hard folding chairs.

"Comfy?" the man on her right asked, grinning down at her.

"Uh, I guess so." She studied him more carefully, her interest piqued now that he'd gone out of his way to speak to her. His broad smile was a welcome sight, his friendliness a relief. There was something engaging about him. Open. He wasn't what she'd call handsome, exactly, although his dark, piercing eyes and thick head of dark hair peppered with gray were appealing. It was more that he had a lot of character in his face, she decided.

He stuck out his hand. "I'm Richie. I'm a doto."

"Excuse me?"

"D-O-T-O? Dads on Their Own?"

"Ah." Laura nodded knowingly. "Then I guess that makes me a moto."

Before he had a chance to respond, Darlene plopped down on the piano bench at one end of the room.

"Take a seat, evvybody," she insisted in her loud, gravelly voice. "First of all, welcome." Earnestly she looked around the circle. "And Happy New Yeah. How many of yiz made new yeah's resolutions?"

Amid some tittering, half a dozen hands were raised shyly into the air.

"Now, I'm gonna be nice t'night. I'm not gonna cawl on you and make you tell us what they were. I'm just gonna aks if any of yiz made a resolution to get out and meet some new people. Anybody?"

Four of the raised hands remained in the air. As Darlene's eyes traveled around the room Laura burrowed more deeply into her chair.

"That's a very worthwhile resolution. Much better than losin' ten pounds. But it's not easy, getting back into the social scene after a divorce. In fact, it's very, very hard."

"At least you hope it's hard!" Joe, the man with the lapful of pretzels, guffawed. Laura wondered how many more times he intended to milk that one tonight. She also wondered what he was hiding underneath that bowl.

"But you're all off to a good start. Parents on Their Own is a great place to make new friends. And you're all first-timers here, so there's no reason to feel self-conscious or anything."

"Hey, we don't have to take off our clothes, do we?" Joe called out.

Darlene let out a noise that was more a snort than a laugh, and waved her hands in the air dismissively.

"Then I got nothin' to feel self-conscious about." Joe chortled.

Laura wondered if he'd like to go out for a couple of brewskis with Tom and Arnie from the Wednesday night support group sometime.

"Anyways," Darlene went on, "what we're gonna do, as a way of evvybody getting to know evvybody else, is play a little game."

A groan rose up from the crowd.

"No, no, this is a good game. You're gonna like this one."

"How 'bout strip poker?" suggested Joe.

Richie leaned over so that his face was next to Laura's, no easy feat since he seemed to be well over six feet tall. "I wish somebody'd show that guy the door," he whispered.

"We're gonna play a game I call the secret game," Darlene went on. "The way it works is we go around the circle, one at a time, and evvybody tells a secret about themselves. Something other people wouldn't necessarily find out unless you told 'em."

Whatever happened to name, rank, and

serial number? Laura wondered. Desperately she racked her brain, trying to come up with something revealing enough to be interesting, yet tasteful enough to expose to a roomful of complete strangers.

"Natalie, you wanna start?"

Dutifully Natalie put down her yarn. "My secret is that I love to knit." Conspiratorially she added, "That's something only my closest friends know about me."

Laura nodded politely, feeling like Alice on the other side of the looking glass, when Richie caught her eye and grimaced. She responded with a shy smile.

"Okay, thank you, Natalie." Darlene reached over and patted her hand. "Now we all know you a little better. Who's next? Elsa?"

Elsa tugged at the hem of her skirt, already covering so much of her legs she could have been a member of a religious order. "Well . . . my secret is that even though I'm pretty successful in my job, a loan officer at a bank —"

Laura patted herself on the back for having such an astute eye.

"— what I would really like to be is an exotic dancer."

"I expect some of the men here tonight are gonna want to find out more about that," Darlene said, without a blink. "Vince? Looks like you're next."

Vince looked as if he were about to run from the room. "This isn't really a secret," he said, his face turning red, "but it's something most people don't know about me. I'm an alcoholic. I've been in recovery for two years now, and it's been a real struggle. . . ."

Joe was up next. "Most people think I'm a pretty easygoin' guy," he said. "But they don't realize I got a few — I guess they're what ya'd call compulsions. Like I can't leave the bedroom unless all my underwear is lined up in the drawer exactly straight. I check the front door ten or twelve times every night to make sure I really locked it. And I can't date women with the letter *R* in their names."

I wonder if Phil Donahue's thought about another go-round with Men Who Lead Secret Lives, Laura thought, struggling to maintain a pleasant, nonjudgmental expression.

"I guess I'll take my turn next." Darlene clasped her hands to her abundant chest and raised her eyes upward, as if imploring some higher power to supply her with a secret worth sharing. Finally she looked around the room. "My secret is that I'm very shy."

A reverent silence fell over the room. Or perhaps it was simply incredulity. At any rate, it didn't last very long. It was Richie's turn, and he jumped right in. Laura was so

232

busy trying to slow down her racing heart as she realized she was next, she barely listened to his confession about his passion for skeet shooting.

And then all eyes were upon her. Laura attempted to sit up straighter, struggling unsuccessfully to reach something resembling adult height. "I, uh, guess my secret is that I'm actually enjoying being a single parent. I don't feel lonely on Saturday nights, and I don't feel pressured to find myself a new mate. For years I worried about what it would be like, being on my own again, only this time with a child to take care of. But now that I'm doing it, it's okay."

She was exhausted after her little spurt of honesty. Fortunately, the group had already moved on. Someone named Pete was talking about his passion for buying lottery tickets.

When the group broke up for refreshments, Laura felt someone tap her on the arm.

Once again, Richie was smiling down at her. Only this time they were both standing. She'd been correct in her estimate of his height. He towered above her a good eight or nine inches.

"That was very interesting, what you said before," Richie began, "about enjoying being single again. I've been finding the same thing."

The way he looked at her was disconcerting. He stared with such intensity she felt like a specimen pinned against a tray.

"I'm particularly enjoying getting out and meeting women again, after being married for twenty-two years," he told her, taking a small step forward.

"Really?" Automatically Laura moved back, as if the two of them were doing a dance. As she did she was struck with the alarming realization that this man — nice enough, if a little rough around the edges — was hitting on her.

Oh, my God! she thought. He can't do that! I'm not here for social purposes. I mean, I *am*, but I'm looking for friends, not men. Well, men *friends* would be okay, but I'm not looking for men *that* way. . . .

"Listen, I know this is kind of sudden, but would you like to go out sometime?"

"Excuse me?" Of course, she'd heard him. This man was asking her out on a date.

"Thanks, but I don't think I'm ready to start dating."

"No? How long's it been? Since you got separated, I mean."

"Only a few months."

"Tell you what. I'll give you my number, in case you change your mind." Already he was scribbling across the back of a paper napkin printed with EAT, DRINK, AND BE SORRY.

"I hope I hear from you," he said earnestly.

234

He took hold of her hand and pressed the napkin into her palm, hanging on a little longer then necessary. Laura, trying her hardest to act nonchalant, could feel her cheeks turning as red as if she'd just been asked out on her very first date.

Then again, in a way, she had.

Chapter Twelve

Although Laura tried to suppress her excitement over having had a real live man ask her out for the first time in almost seventeen years, her step was a little more lilting than usual as she sailed past The Limited, past Sbarro, past the Disney Store, toward Macy's. She couldn't help marveling over the fact that even though she'd been around the block enough times to have earned frequent-flyer points, someone actually wanted to take her out on a date. It was precisely what her sagging ego needed.

Valentine's Day was only a few days away, and she'd come to the mall determined to buy something special. After all, this year she was the only one likely to give herself a treat when February fourteenth rolled around.

Predictably, the mall was decked out in hearts: red ones, pink ones, lacy ones, comical ones, none of which resembled the human version that had inspired their creation. She had to admit that the holiday itself was similarly contrived, rooted more in the greeting-card and boxed-candy industries than in the deeply felt emotions of those lucky enough to be in love. Even so, Laura had always found the holiday a welcome break from the doldrums of what was easily the dreariest month of the year.

Tonight, however, instead of being cheered by the plump cardboard cherubs decorating store windows and the bouquets of flowers peddled from pushcarts set up in the center of the mall, she was feeling empty and alone. Even the memory of Richie scrawling his number on a paper napkin didn't help. The world was filled with lovers — or at least the shopping mall was. Laura had never been so aware of all the hand-holding that went on in public. On the bench in front of Woolworth's, a couple in their seventies took turns licking a pistachio ice-cream cone. Two teenagers were draped around each other, their bodies so closely intertwined they appeared to be participants in a three-legged race.

She suspected that even a major purchase, one requiring the use of a credit card, wouldn't banish the dull ache in her heart. Yet she'd come this far. She was determined to go through with her plan to indulge herself.

At the store directory, she fought off a sudden wave of dizziness. So many departments were off-limits. Jewelry, for example. The idea of buying herself a piece of jewelry had a pathetic quality to it. The same went for chocolates and perfume.

Trying to ignore the thought that what she really needed was a new pair of snow boots, she hit upon "Lingerie."

Perfect, she muttered, heading toward the up escalator. Something lacy, silky, or of an otherwise sexy texture, was bound to make her feel desirable. Besides, one day in the future — as difficult as it was to imagine — she might actually have a reason to wear whatever bit of froufrou she bought for herself today.

Visions of low-cut camisoles and high-cut bikini underpants followed Laura up to the second floor. Even if something new couldn't cure her ills, at least it would anesthetize her for a while. A surge of energy catapulted her toward a rack of shimmering pink camisoles trimmed in cream-colored lace.

She checked the tag. The price was within the conceivable range. As she fumbled around for size labels the sound of a familiar voice caught her attention.

"I'm sure she takes a small," a man was telling the salesclerk, a short, round woman who would have done well to shop in her own department with a more discriminating eye.

"She has very narrow hips and an exceptionally tiny waist."

Laura's stomach lurched, and she ducked behind a rack of filmy negligees, pulling back the hangers to peer through.

It was Roger. He was holding up a pair of black bikini panties the size of an elbow patch.

"Those are the silk Countess Ivanna's, right?" the clerk said matter-of-factly. "Forty-nine ninety-nine? Just a minute, sir. I'll see if we have any smalls in back."

Laura stood frozen to the spot, grasping the chiffon nightgowns with hands that were suddenly damp. She was both fascinated and horrified as she watched her husband, standing less than five feet away, run his fingers along the satiny fabric.

In a flash, a picture of Roger with another woman passed through Laura's mind. Naked buttocks, flailing legs and arms, moans and groans and all manner of guttural utterances . . . Jealousy stabbed at her for a moment, but the feeling passed quickly.

Before she had a chance to think about what she was doing, she stepped out from behind the rack. "Roger?"

He glanced in her direction and his expression of surprise quickly gave way to one of guilt. She'd seen that same face on Evan a million times.

"Laura?" He swallowed hard. "What are you doing here?"

"I could easily ask you the same question." She took a step closer, noting how absurd he looked, standing in the middle of the lingerie department, clumsily fondling a pair of coaster-sized underpants. "Actually," she went on in a controlled voice, "I was doing a bit of Valentine's Day shopping. It looks as if you were, too."

"We're in luck!" the saleswoman announced triumphantly, emerging from the back room. With both hands she held up a black silk triangle. "Do these look okay?"

Roger barely glanced at them. "They look, uh, fine."

"Cash or charge?"

"So you've finally found yourself a thin woman." Laura was trying hard to sound haughty, like Bette Davis in one of her finer moments. Instead, bitterness curdled in her tone.

She expected a rush of denials, certain that "It's not what you think" was bound to come pouring from her husband's lips.

Instead, Roger said simply, "I guess we'd better talk."

Laura hovered next to a Formica display of girdles, feigning interest in the instruments of torture. The irony of the moment — that she was waiting patiently for her husband as he bought sexy underwear for another woman — was not wasted on her. Her initial reaction, incredulity and confusion with a chaser of jealousy, had been replaced by simple curiosity. What, when, where . . . and above all, *who?*

Laura followed Roger to a neutral area of the store, the coat department. It took all the self-control she possessed to keep from shrieking, "Who is she?" Instead, standing under a huge FINAL CLEARANCE sign, she remained silent. She'd let him do the talking.

"I've been seeing someone," he said evenly.

A little more than *seeing*, she was tempted to add.

"It started in November. Right around Thanksgiving."

Bingo. Claire had been right. There *was* a woman behind Roger's concession that divorce really was the way to go.

He took a deep breath. "It's Melanie Plympton."

It took Laura a few seconds to process that bit of information. Melanie Plympton was one of the Clover Hollow mothers whom she knew from all the hours she'd logged in at the school yard, waiting for Evan. She was more memorable than most, mainly because she didn't dress in the usual jogging suits, sweats, and oversized tees that looked as if they'd been grabbed off the back of teenage boys. Instead, she tended toward suede jackets with fringe. Floppy felt hats. Clogs. She was also Clover Hollow's resident potter. Melanie taught elementary school children in the PTA's after-school program the ins and outs of throwing clay onto a wheel and forming it into lopsided terra-cotta wonders.

"She's still living with her husband," Roger went on, "but she's wanted to get out for a long time."

"Excuse me?" Laura sincerely believed she had heard him wrong. "Did you say she's *married?*"

Roger looked annoyed. "Gil Plympton is a madman. He rages around the house like a maniac. You may think you and I had it rough, Laura, but it's nothing compared to what's gone on between them."

"She's still married . . . and you're buying her silk underwear?"

"She wants out."

"You're certainly making it easy for her," Laura shot back.

"I don't know why I expected you to understand," Roger said, no longer treating her like a coconspirator. Instead, he was huffing and puffing angrily. "Anyway, now you know."

"Yes," she returned dryly. "Now I know."

Melanie Plympton, a woman she'd barely given a thought to, had stepped out of the mob of Clover Hollow mothers into the limelight.

"A potter?" Claire mouthed the word disdainfully. "Who wears *clogs?*"

"I'm afraid so." Laura clasped Claire's purple throw pillow against her chest.

"I hate to say I told you so —" said Claire.

Laura sighed. "Go ahead. Say it."

"What a way to find out," breathed Julie, curled up on the floor in front of Claire's unlit fireplace, balancing her coffee cup on the Matisse-Goes-Hawaiian ottoman. "Imagine, stumbling upon your husband shopping for sexy underwear for another woman's Valentine's Day present." She hesitated for a moment before asking, "Are you jealous?"

Laura paused for a few seconds, thinking hard before answering. "No, I'm not," she replied sincerely. "I'll admit, my first reaction was to be horrified. But to tell you the truth, part of me actually feels sorry for poor old Melanie. I'm tempted to take her aside and warn her about what she's getting into."

"Sisterhood only goes so far," Claire observed dryly. She paused to take a sip of coffee. "Besides, I doubt she'd believe you."

"Oh, my God; you're right." Melodramatically Laura clutched her hand to her heart. "After all, I'm an *ex-wife!*"

"Technically you're still a wife," Julie pointed out.

"So's Melanie," Claire said with a mischievous glint in her eye. "Goodness gracious, I feel like I'm living in *General Hospital!*"

Laura grimaced. "Pretty sordid, isn't it?"

"Yes, but it could turn out to be exactly what you need," said Claire. "To get you to start giving serious thought to how you're going to get your revenge, I mean."

"Revenge?" Laura repeated. "What good would that do?"

"Make *you* feel better, for one thing. Besides, I have the perfect plan."

"Claire, I really don't see any reason to —"

"Find yourself an absolute hunk. Somebody gorgeous, of course, but also rich. And charming. And funny." Claire frowned. "Where can we find you somebody famous?"

"You know," Julie offered, "Claire does have a point." Ignoring Laura's protests, she went on, "It probably is time for you to start dating again. Not for revenge, necessarily. For your own personal growth."

"Oh, no, you don't." Laura held up both hands, as if fending off an attack. "Don't start on me."

"Roger's ended his period of mourning," Claire pointed out. "And I'm sure the designers of overpriced lingerie couldn't be happier. Now it's your turn to trade in your bedroom slippers for a pair of dancing shoes."

Laura looked at Claire, then at Julie. With a shrug she said, "I — I'm not ready."

"You can't sit home forever," Claire insisted.

"I haven't been staying at home." Laura

stuck out her chin defensively. "In fact, I've even joined a group for single parents."

Julie and Claire exchanged looks of surprise.

"My, my," said Claire. "So our little Laura is spreading her wings."

"What group did you join?"

"POTO. Parents on Their Own."

"I've heard of them!" Julie exclaimed. "They're supposed to be *excellent*. Have you been going to their meetings?"

"One. A welcome party."

"Meet anyone interesting?" asked Claire.

"As a matter of fact," Laura said with a casual toss of her head, "somebody asked me out."

"That's wonderful!" Julie squealed, clapping her hands together with the enthusiasm of a pom-pom girl.

"Who is he?" Claire asked eagerly. "When are you going out with him?"

"Well . . . I'm not. I told him I wasn't really interested in dating yet."

Both Julie and Claire groaned.

"I wish someone would just invent video dating," Laura said.

"There are plenty of video-dating services," said Julie. "But why would you want to go out with a man you've only seen on a television screen?"

"From the waist up, no less," Claire interjected.

Laura waved her hand in the air impatiently. "No, no. I'm talking about an actual *date*. I've got it all planned in my mind. The way it works is that you'd get all dressed up — or not, depending on how much energy you felt like exerting. When you were ready, you'd run the video. It would start with a door opening. On the other side, there'd be a gorgeous guy — one you'd preselected, based on the pictures on the boxes at the video store — holding out a bouquet of flowers."

"Oh, I get it," Julie cried. "The video would show the male half of the date."

"It would be interactive." Claire leaned forward, her eyes bright and her cheeks flushed. "The guy would say, 'Where shall we go for dinner? A fancy restaurant — ' "

"Or a picnic?" Julie supplied. "And you'd push a button to choose. Meanwhile you'd have gotten the food that goes with the type of restaurant you picked."

"Lean Cuisine," Claire suggested. "They have Italian, French, Mexican —"

"The best part," Laura went on, "would be the dinner conversation. The dream date would say things like, 'So tell me about your work' or 'I'd love to hear about your childhood.' Then he'd sit back and give you a chance to talk."

"He'd appear to be genuinely interested," said Julie, nodding. "He'd say, 'Uh-huh' a lot, as if he were really listening."

"He'd look you in the eye," Claire added, "instead of in the chest."

"It sounds perfectly wonderful," Julie breathed. "Romance on tap."

"Better than pornography." Claire snapped her fingers. "Hey, what about that? Sex, I mean?"

"At the end," said Laura, "the dream date could be shown naked, lying in bed, whispering sweet nothings. Things like, 'You were wonderful. What a great body you have!' "

"How about 'I really get turned on by cellulite?' " Julie suggested. "Or 'I admire a woman with stretch marks. They tell me I'm with a woman who's experienced life to its fullest.' "

"Only one problem," said Claire. "You've just left out the best part."

"Remember Estelle, the woman in my support group?" Laura reminded her. "The viewer would simply have to follow her advice."

Claire smirked. "Take matters into her own hands, so to speak."

"Oh, you two!" Julie's cheeks had turned pink.

"Us?" Claire shot back. "You're the wild one, the one who's 'torn between two lovers,' as the old song goes."

"Don't remind me." Julie's expression

clouded. "I feel so bad about what I'm doing to George. Not that George *knows* what I'm doing to him. Not that him not knowing makes it any easier —"

"Julie," Laura interrupted, "what, exactly, is going on between you and Bobby?"

Julie bit her lip nervously. "I've seen him a few more times. We had lunch a few times, and then dinner again —"

"At least he's keeping you well fed," Claire observed. "Soon you'll be able to write a restaurant guide to Long Island."

Hesitating, Julie confessed, "We've been eating at his apartment."

"Don't tell me," said Claire. "You've been treating yourselves to dessert in the bedroom."

"Of course not!"

"You mean 'Not yet.' " Claire smiled wickedly.

Julie sighed, the long, deep sigh of the ambivalent. "I'm developing strong feelings for him. I can't help myself. He's so . . . so alive. His eyes light up when he speaks. He's so animated, so enthusiastic —"

"Sounds like the man's on uppers," Claire muttered.

Julie ignored her. "We have so much to say to each other. And when I talk, he really listens. It's just like Laura's video date. He understands me, too. We're so much in sync it's unbelievable."

Claire was nodding. "*Unbelievable* sounds like the right word."

"What do you mean?"

"I hate to burst your little bubble of denial," Claire explained, "but somebody has to ask the inevitable question. If this Mr. Right of yours is so perfect, why did his ex-wife dump him?"

"He doesn't talk about his first marriage. The few times I brought it up, he simply said that that's the past, and right now he's concentrating on the present . . . and the future."

Laura exchanged a skeptical glance with Claire.

"If there's one thing I've learned," said Laura, "it's that for every eligible divorced man out there, there's a woman who'd be only too happy to give you her side of the story."

"Well, whatever happened, I'm sure it was mostly her fault," Julie insisted. She paused, then added, "You know, it's kind of a funny coincidence, but Bobby's ex-wife's name was Claire, too."

"Oh, no!" Claire groaned. "Another Robert-and-Claire combination. Maybe it's simply inevitable that people with those two names get along together as well as a pack of matches and a stick of dynamite."

"Julie," Laura said gently, "I know you're head over heels in love with this guy, but it might be helpful if you could find out a little more about what went on in his marriage."

Claire nodded. "Have you tried going through Bobby's desk while he's in the bathroom?"

"Claire!" Julie was shocked. "You're joking, aren't you?"

With a shrug Claire said, "You'd be surprised what you can learn about a man by pawing through his paper-clip drawer."

"He was married so long ago, I'm sure he doesn't have anything around from those days. There is one thing, though. . . ."

"Don't tell me. A woman's head in his freezer, sealed up nice and tight in a Ziploc bag."

Julie gave her a dirty look. "There's a little box he keeps on the coffee table. It's hand carved out of a light-colored wood. On the lid there are two birds. Doves, I think. When I asked him about it, he mentioned that his ex-wife had given it to him. It was a birthday present. Or maybe anniversary."

"Sounds to me like there's a sentimental side to this man," Laura observed. "Don't you think so, Claire? *Claire?*"

Claire didn't respond. She was staring at Julie, a look of horror on her face. "Wait a minute. What did you say this guy's name was?"

"His name is Bobby — uh, Robert Weiss."

Claire dropped her coffee cup into its saucer with a loud crash. "This sweetie pie of yours is my ex-husband!"

"But . . . but . . . that's impossible!" Julie sputtered. "Your last name is Nielsen."

"Of course it is! I took my own name back when I left that bastard!"

"Wait a minute," Laura interrupted. "We're still not sure we're talking about the same guy."

"Oh, it's him, all right. And let me tell you something about that darling little keepsake from his marriage that he still displays on his coffee table. That was never his. It was a wedding present from one of *my* friends. I fought him tooth and nail for it. It became the most symbolic issue in our divorce settlement. Finally he stole it. He *stole* it!"

Julie was so flabbergasted she was having trouble forming words. "I can't believe . . . It's just not . . . But he's so . . . ."

"Believe it, Julie. Believe it, and run as fast as your yellow high-tops can carry you."

"Before you do," Laura suggested dryly, "why don't you grab that box off the coffee table?"

"Wait a minute!" Julie protested. "I'm not running anywhere. Bobby Weiss is the best thing that ever happened to me. I'm not going to break up with him because of some silly box."

"In that case," Claire said bitterly, "I can give you an entire encyclopedia filled with despicable things the man did during the eight years we were married."

"Julie," said Laura, "do you really want to date this man now that you know he's Claire's ex-husband?"

"I don't see what that has to do with anything. I was in love with him before, and I knew perfectly well he was somebody's ex-husband. What difference does it make that he's turned out to be Claire's?"

Claire was pacing around the room, her hands clenched into fists. "I don't believe this. Don't you care that when he used to come in late, he'd come into the bedroom and turn on the light, even though I was asleep? Or that he had this annoying habit of walking into the bathroom and trimming his nose hairs while I was in the bathtub? Or that he hung on to the rattiest sport jacket in the entire universe just so he could make me mad by insisting on wearing it every time we went out?"

"I'm a big girl," Julie said crisply, "capable of making my own decisions. I don't need —"

"Julie, listen to me," Claire interrupted. Her gaze was steely, but her voice faltered. "Don't you care that we're talking about a man who was unfaithful to his wife?"

"I don't care," Julie insisted. Her expression was equally hard, her tone much more confident. "With me, he's different."

Chapter Thirteen

"Get on with your life," muttered Laura.

She paused outside the Y's meeting room, where the Wednesday-night Divorce and Separation Support Group's coffee hour had taken on the atmosphere of a happy hour. Despite the fact that January was long gone and even February was beginning to turn into old news, she hadn't forgotten her resolutions.

In the spirit of living up to the promises she'd made to herself on New Year's Eve, she'd decided it was finally time to move out of Group One and into Group Two. While she wasn't quite ready for life in the fast lane, she was at least willing to move off the entrance ramp and onto the highway.

Heading toward the library and a collection of folks noticeably more animated than those left behind in Merry's care, Laura felt a pang of nervousness. A different setting, a roomful of strangers . . . the feeling that too many challenges were being thrown her way, made it a difficult step.

She told herself it was good for her to push herself. That with each new experience, she became a little stronger. A little more independent. A little less the passenger on the roller coaster, holding on for dear life.

She relaxed when she saw how upbeat the mood in the library was. Instead of what she'd grown accustomed to in Group One — dour expressions, heavy movements like a scene filmed in slow motion — here people talked and even laughed as they arranged chairs in a circle. Group Two was much larger as well. Making a quick count, Laura came up with thirty-three.

"Let's get started." A woman's voice, deep and tough with a thick New York accent, broke through the din. The effect was startling, like the *bleep-bleep-bleep* of a truck backing up. "Hello, evvybody. My name is Phyllis, and this is Group Two of the Divorce and Separation Support Group. If you're looking for AA or NA or any other kind of A, you're in the wrong place."

She paused as the group laughed. This woman's working the room like a comedian in Vegas, Laura thought. In fact, she has some of the same glitziness.

Phyllis's makeup was theatrical, her fluffy hair a golden apricot color that picked up the fluorescent light like a reflector. Her fashion choices leaned toward loud colors and stretchy fabrics. Her long fingernails were lacquered bloodred, and her numerous pieces of jewelry seemed big enough to be considered lethal weapons.

"Okay, so who wants to start tonight?" Phyllis looked around the circle, frowning when she got no response. "What, all of a sudden evvybody's shy? Nobody's allowed to be shy in my group. Tell you what: I'll start by telling a joke. What's the difference between a penis that's medium and one that's rare?"

Nervous chuckling followed, along with a few titters, but there was no response.

"This is one that's medium." Phyllis held her hands a few inches apart. Then she moved them much farther apart. "*This* is one that's rare."

Good move, coming here, Laura thought, joining the others in their laughter. Much more therapeutic than Group One's gloom.

"Now that the ice has been broken," Phyllis went on, "who wants to tell us what they've been up to? Anybody here dating? Elaine, how about you?"

She'd zeroed in on a plump woman a few seats away. Glancing up, Elaine grimaced.

"Are you kidding?" she snorted. "All men are pigs. Last week a friend of mine gives my number to some guy she knows from work, right? She tells me he's going through a divorce, he's really hot to meet women. . . . Anyway, he calls me up, what, last Thursday night. We end up talking on the phone for, like, two hours.

256

"So I'm really startin' to think we have somethin' going, you know? And then he says why don't we have dinner Saturday night, and I say fine. . . ."

"So what happened?" Phyllis asked calmly.

"So he asks me where I live and I tell him Deer Park. Well, all of a sudden you'd think I'd told him I had leprosy. I can tell something's wrong, but he won't tell me what. Finally I get it outta him. Turns out he lives in Mineola, like fifteen miles away, and he doesn't wanna drive so far." She shook her head disgustedly. "I'm tellin' ya, they're all slime."

Carolyn, another émigré from Group One, raised her hand. "I had a bad dating experience this week, too." Nervously she smoothed the skirt of her tweed business suit. "Saturday night I went out with a guy I'd met at a singles bar a couple of weeks ago. He seemed okay at first —"

"They always do," Elaine muttered.

"We went out for dinner. That part went pretty smoothly. Then we went back to his apartment. He said he'd gotten one of those new coffeemakers for Christmas, and he wanted to make cappuccino.

"Everything was fine — until I was ready to leave. That was when he asked me to spend the night. I said no. So *he* said, 'Then do you mind if I masturbate in front of you?' "

Laura was considering checking into a convent when Elaine broke in. "Like I said. Men are pigs."

"Maybe we need to hear from some of the men in the group," Phyllis suggested. "Let's get another point of view."

"So both of you happened to meet up with a couple of creeps," volunteered a man who identified himself as Ken, sitting directly across from Laura. He was tall and lanky, with a mustache and a thick head of hair. "But I'll tell ya, there's a lot of crazy women running around out there, too."

"That's for sure," a second man, shorter and considerably less hairy, chimed in. "And if they're not crazy, all they're interested in is the size of a man's wallet. They don't care diddly about what kind of person he really is."

"Sounds like something bad happened to you, Jake," Phyllis prompted.

"You could say that. A couple of weeks ago I went to a party. There were a few women there. But I felt like they were all giving me the third degree. They wanted to know what kind of job I have, what kind of car I drive —"

"Ever get the question about whether or not you own your own home?" Ken was shaking his head. "Half the time, when I take a woman out to dinner, I feel like I'm on a job interview."

"Yeah, right," snorted Jake. "Except no potential employer would dare ask those questions."

"Sounds like there's a lot of mistrust between the sexes," Phyllis observed. "Getting a divorce can do that. It causes people a lot of pain, feelings of betrayal. . . . It makes them reluctant to put themselves on the line again."

My sentiments exactly, Laura was thinking.

"I don't think all men are slime." A lone voice, soft and tentative, broke through the anger in the room. "As a matter of fact, I've started seeing somebody really nice."

A woman who hadn't spoken before had raised her hand.

"I think Dolores has something to share," said Phyllis.

"I met him in the supermarket, of all places. We were both in line at the deli counter. We were waiting for the longest time, and, well, we got to talking. Right from the start he seemed really nice. He was funny, easy to get along with. . . . Anyway, he finally said, 'I don't usually pick up women in the supermarket, but would you like to have coffee?'

"That was about a month ago. Since then, we've been seeing each other every chance we get." Dolores sighed, twirling a strand of long brown hair around one finger. Her eyes were shining. "I feel sixteen again. It's so wonderful, falling in love all over again. I — I never thought it would happen. Not a second time. And it's even better than when I met my husband. I'm older, more sure of myself . . . more certain of what I'm looking for.

"Anyway, it's still a little soon to tell, but . . ." She looked around the circle, her cheeks reddening. "I think I've found myself a good man this time."

Laura's heart fluttered. There it was again, that same haunting image that had forced its way into her brain on New Year's Eve. She saw herself flitting through a field of wildflowers with a tall, dark, handsome stranger. Or maybe he was short and blond. Or medium with brown hair and a distinctive bald spot and a face that wasn't exactly handsome but lit up nicely when he smiled . . .

The details didn't matter. What did matter was that once again, when she'd dared let her guard down, that distinctive longing for some other person with whom to travel through flower-covered fields had crept up on her.

Again Laura attempted to push it out of her mind, calling upon her list of logical reasons why that image was dangerous. And again her attempts failed. Something that defied all reason caused a yearning to well up inside her.

Later that night, as she sat alone in her silent house, Laura found herself staring at the phone. The voices of the other group members echoed through her head like the special effects in a grade-B movie.

Men are slime. . . . It's so wonderful, falling in love all over again. . . . There's a lot of mistrust between the sexes. . . . I feel sixteen. . . . I think I've found myself a good man this time. . . .

Do it, a voice inside her head urged.

What are you, nuts? a second voice countered.

And then she took a deep breath. Rifling through her pocketbook, she found the "Eat, Drink, and Be Sorry" napkin. Her hands trembling, she picked up the phone and punched the numbers Richie had written.

Please don't answer. Please don't answer. . . .

"Hello, Richie? Oh, hi." Nervously she cleared her throat. "This is Laura Briggs. You probably don't remember me, but we met at — oh, you do? I was? You have?"

Oh, boy.

"May I offer you more champagne?" the near-stranger purrs, bending the bottle of Moët & Chandon over Laura's tulip glass, made of the finest crystal.

"Why, yes," she replies. For a moment she gazes at him, overwhelmed by how handsome he is. Even features, a roguish mustache, sparkling dark eyes that fix upon hers with such intensity she feels as if he can see straight into her very heart and soul.

Then she looks past his shoulder — an unusually broad, muscular shoulder, covered in dark blue silky fabric that shimmers with every moment. Not far beyond she can see the sea, a luminescent shade of turquoise. The bright Caribbean sun glints off the gentle waves, rhythmically lapping against the pink beach that lies between the water and the veranda on which they sit, head to head.

"Laura," he murmurs in a thick but exotic European accent, "did you know your eyes are the color of the sea?" He gestures toward the panorama behind him.

"You make me blush," she coos.

He moves closer. She can feel the heat from his body. "Did you know your ears are as lovely as the most delicate seashell?"

"I — I don't know what to say."

Underneath the table, she can feel the hard muscles of his thigh, pushing urgently against hers. He reaches for her hand, gently bringing it to his lips.

"Did you know there's a booger hanging from your nose?"

"Evan!" Laura screeched, turning from the bathroom mirror, mascara wand poised in midair. "How long have you been standing there?"

"Long enough to watch you put that slop all over your face." He was scowling, and slamming his softball into his catcher's mitt over and over.

"Shouldn't you be doing something more worthwhile than playing Peeping Tom? Reading a good book? Memorizing the multiplication tables?" She turned back to the mirror. "Working in a factory?"

"Aw, you don't really have a booger in your nose."

"I know."

Laura had been staring at her reflection for a good fifteen minutes, pawing through the cosmetics piled up in a Rubbermaid storage bin. She only hoped the Clarion computer knew as much as it claimed about matching synthetic makeup shades to nature's own skin tones.

"Where are you going tonight, anyway? Are you giving a speech?"

"No."

"Doing an autographing? Going to a writers' meeting?"

"Not exactly."

Evan was silent, still slamming the ball into his glove. Suddenly he sniffed the air and grimaced. "Hey, what's that smell?"

"Perfume. Beautiful, to be exact. Look, Evan, I'm not going to a writers' meeting or giving a speech or doing anything like that. Tonight I'm going out to dinner with a friend."

"Who, Julie?"

"Not, not Julie."

"Claire?"

"It's somebody new." She could see her son's face reflected in the bathroom mirror. "Somebody you don't know."

"Oh." He looked her up and down. "Gee, you must be going someplace pretty fancy. You're wearing a dress and everything!"

"Actually, I'm not sure where I'm go—"

"Can I go watch *Rugrats?*"

"Sure. Annie's baby-sitting tonight. She should be here any minute."

" 'Kay." He turned away, his interest in Laura's social activities having already waned.

"Hey, Ev?" Laura called after him.

"Yeah, Mom?"

"The person I'm going out with tonight —"

"Yeah?"

"It's a man. He's just a friend," she added quickly. "I met him in a . . . a club I joined."

Evan was silent for a long time. Finally, in an odd voice, he asked, "Is this, like, a date?"

"Not really. Well, maybe in a way . . . He's

just a nice man who I enjoyed talking to, so I thought it might be fun to have dinner with him." She turned around and looked at Evan, hoping to see some understanding there. Instead, his face was expressionless.

"I'm gonna go turn on *Rugrats*." He scampered away.

Just as she had done for her first date back in junior high school, Laura had placed the things she'd need in strategic spots around the room in anticipation of Richie's arrival. She desperately wanted everything to go smoothly. And so she'd slung her jacket across the back of a chair to avoid a wrestling match with a hanger. On a table near the front door she'd placed her purse, her version of a portable disaster kit. In it she'd packed tissues in case the rest room was out of toilet paper. Dental floss, in case spinach was on the menu. A small mirror because of the ever-present possibility of some alien substance coming between her eye and her contact lens. And of course, she'd tucked away enough cash to get herself home in a taxi if her date got drunk, abandoned her, or turned out to be a sex maniac, felon, or insurance salesman.

When she heard the doorbell ring, Laura forced a smile and, trying to ignore the knot in her stomach, flung open the front door. Richie was standing on her doorstep, clutching a bouquet of flowers. It would have been a sweet moment if she hadn't been so nervous.

"Hi," she said.

"Hello, Laura. You look really pretty. Here, I brought you these flowers. Maybe you'd better get them in some water. They're already starting to look a little dry."

Ah. Richie was good at this. He'd done this dating thing before — at least more recently than she had. Laura relaxed.

At least *one* of us knows what he's doing, she thought. Maybe I can get by simply following his lead.

"Thanks, Richie. Here, I'll take these into the kitchen." Leading him into the living room, she nearly tripped over her son, sprawled out on the floor in front of the TV. "Evan, this is Richie. Richie, my son, Evan."

Evan never took his eyes off the screen. "One of his favorite shows," she said apologetically. "I'll, uh, put these in a vase."

In the kitchen, Laura took her time arranging the cheerful bouquet in a crystal vase that had been a wedding present. Meanwhile she kept an ear cocked toward the living room. She was anxious to hear how the two males were getting along. So far, so good. At least no violence had erupted. Instead, the usual banalities were being exchanged, with Richie predictably doing most of the work.

"So, Evan, what are you watching?"

"*Rugrats.*"

"Oh, yeah. I think I heard of that. That's supposed to be a pretty good show."

"Yeah."

Silence; then: "What grade are you in?"

"Third."

"You like school?"

"It's okay."

Another silence. Laura was about to carry the vase into the dining room when she heard Evan say, "My mom's forty, you know."

"Evan!" Laura cried, rushing into the living room.

"I didn't know," said Richie. "Thanks for telling me."

"How old did you think she was?"

"Oh, I don't know. Twenty, twenty-one."

"Evan," Laura protested. "I really don't think —"

"You know my mom's getting a divorce, don't you?"

"I think I'd heard that," Richie said pleasantly.

"Evan, I think it's time for you to go to your room and —"

Pointedly he ignored her. "Did you know she dyes her hair?"

"Evan, *now!*" Catching herself, Laura paused to smile sweetly at Richie. "You'll excuse us a moment, won't you?"

"What do you think you're doing?" she cried once she and her son were behind closed doors. Her tone was somewhere between angry and pleading.

"I was only trying to be friendly." Evan sank down on the bed. Rather than looking her in the eye, he picked up a tiny plastic robot and began rotating its arms. He was staring at it as if he'd never seen anything quite so fascinating. "Do you really like that guy, Mom?"

"Honey, I hardly know him."

"Are you in love with him?"

"Evan, at least let me have dinner with him before you send me off into the sunset."

"Huh?"

"Sweetie," she said, softening her tone as she got down on one knee, "I'm not in love with him. I'm not in love with anybody."

"Not even Dad?"

Laura put her arm around him and pulled him close. He resisted before finally giving in, collapsing against her shoulder.

"Ev, I can't help feeling that, deep down inside, you still wish Daddy and I would get back together."

He nodded.

"Honey, it's not going to happen that way. I'm sorry. In fact," she went on, measuring her words carefully, "Daddy has a new girlfriend."

"Yeah. I know." Evan's words were barely

audible. He kept his eyes on the toy robot, still moving its arms but with much less enthusiasm.

"But you know that no matter what, Daddy and I both still —"

"You both still love me," he finished for her, his tone bitter.

"We really do, you know." Her voice was a hoarse whisper. It was the best she could do, given the sudden thickening in her throat and tears welling up in her eyes. "Maybe you're tired of hearing it, but it happens to be the truth."

He said nothing. Instead, he listlessly twirled the arms of the robot round and round.

Laura's anguish over her son was moved to a back burner as she switched gears from mom to femme fatale. Her first date as a gay divorcée, she soon discovered, wasn't much of an improvement over her first time out as a terrified teen.

As she sat in the front seat of Richie's little red sports car, all the same concerns that had plagued her twenty-five years earlier raised their ugly little heads. She struggled to pull down over her knees the skirt that had looked fine in the mirror but that suddenly reminded her of a go-go dancer's costume. The microscopic tear in her stocking threatened to become a full-fledged stripe. Sneaking a glance in the side mirror, she saw that her hair had suddenly developed a flip. All she needed were a couple of pimples and her look would be complete.

When Richie slid behind the wheel, she recalled one more of the challenges of dating: coming up with a topic of conversation worthy of more than three sentences.

"Where are we going for dinner?" Laura asked. That seemed like a good place to start. She could easily come up with a long list of questions and comments relating to food.

"I know a great Indian restaurant. Not only is the food great. The whole feel of the place is fabulous. It's one of my favorites."

"Do you eat out a lot?"

"Yup. Part of my business is entertaining clients. I've pretty much tried every restaurant on the Island."

"What do you do?"

"I'm in sales."

Keep it moving, thought Laura. "How fascinating."

"I enjoy it. I spend a lot of time on the road, selling supplies to local businesses."

"What kind of supplies?"

"Mortuary."

On the outside, Vishvanath looked like just another overdone, overpriced Indian restaurant. Walking through the parking lot, Laura cringed at the mock Taj Mahal architecture: the exotic raindrop-shaped archways, the columns covered with ornate carvings, the faux marble facade that up close turned out to be brickface. It was precisely the kind of restaurant she detested, her suspicion being that the owners were trying to distract the patrons with a decor so extreme they wouldn't notice the cuisine, which was an Eastern version of TV dinners.

"I love this place," Richie gushed as he rushed to open the door for her. "It's really beautiful. Wait till you see the inside."

Laura stood in the foyer, trying to adjust to the dim light. Sitar music twanged in the background. For just a moment she was back in 1969. She half expected someone to offer her a glass of Boone's Farm Apple Wine.

"Two?" the headwaiter asked. He picked two huge menus off the dais and gestured for them to follow.

"By the way," Laura asked, following him down a short corridor toward the restaurant's main room, "exactly what does the name of the restaurant mean?"

"Ah. Vishvanath is a very famous temple in India. One of many at Khajuraho."

"I see. So it's modeled after a religious building." Strange theme for a restaurant, Laura mused. She noticed that as the headwaiter paused at the entrance to the dining area, he wore an odd smile.

She expected the inside to be more variations on the theme of a Hindu palace gone Las Vegas, but as soon as her eyes adjusted to the dim light, she gasped.

Along the entire back wall of the restaurant, a good ten or twelve feet high and at least thirty feet wide, were bas-relief sculptures, the stylized, somewhat crude forms of men and women. All of them were engaged in different and creative variations on sexual positions.

"Oh, my God."

Richie looked pleased. "I told you this place was somethin' else."

Suddenly it all made sense. Vishvanath, the temples at Khajuraho . . . They were religious buildings, all right. Although what their significance was, other than as a shrine to fertility, no one had ever explained.

She was hardly in the mood to play do-it-yourself archaeologist. When the headwaiter led them to a corner table, Laura darted for the chair that would place her with her back to the wall. Once she was settled in, however, she realized she'd made a mistake. Richie now sat opposite her — with a first-rate view of couples demonstrating the Top Fifty positions of the Kama Sutra. She forced a weak smile as she peeked over her shoulder and caught a glimpse of thighs, shoulders, and taut round breasts. Richie beamed at her. She couldn't tell whether the glint in his eye was because of her or because of the athletic foursome on the wall directly over her head, doing things she'd never dreamed were possible without the assistance of a chiropractor.

"Gee, it didn't even occur to me to ask if you like Indian food," Richie said apologetically.

"Oh, I love it," she assured him. She made a point of keeping her eyes fixed on his. The need to make unwavering eye contact had never been so strong. "In fact, I like all kinds of exotic — uh, food."

She threw open her arms to illustrate just how expansive her taste in international cuisines was. As she did, her left hand hit the wall, coming directly into contact with a bulbous penis, fully erect and pointing upward.

Richie didn't appear to have noticed. "Me, too. I'm one of those people who'll eat anything that's put in front of me. Now, my wife, on the other hand — my *ex*-wife, I mean — she was the pickiest eater you ever saw."

"Really?" Laura folded her hands in her lap.

"Oh, sure. We'd go to a restaurant, even a fancy place, and whatever the waiter brought, you could bet your bottom dollar good old Jeannie'd send it back to the kitchen. Too rare, too well done, too spicy, too bland . . . It was always something."

Laura forced a polite smile. "Perhaps we should order." As she opened her menu, roughly the size of Bangladesh, she was careful not to brush against any body parts.

"The tandoori sounds good," she said pleasantly, scanning the menu. "Of course, Indian curries are always so delicious. . . ."

"Hah! My ex-wife refused to eat curry. She said it was so spicy it made her nose run. I always said, What the hell, let it run. It's like two for the price of one: not only do you get your belly full; you get your sinuses cleared, too.

"Of course, we never agreed on anything. That was the problem. Take where we lived, for example. Me, I love Long Island. As far as I'm concerned, the beaches are the best in the world. You can have your French Riviera, your Waikiki. And on top of all the natural wonders, you're only a short drive from the city.

"But no-o-o, my wife didn't see it that way. She was always nagging me about moving. Her sisters live down in Florida, and she was hot to move down there, too. I used to say to her, 'Look, Jeannie . . .' "

You survived childbirth, Laura reminded

herself. *Without* a spinal. Surely you can make it through one short evening. Just me, Richie, the winners of the Sexual Olympics . . . and, of course, Jeannie.

The next morning, as she sat nursing a second cup of coffee, trying to get rid of her curry-flavored morning-after mouth, Laura vowed never to date again. Nor would she ever again speak to a man who wasn't a blood relative, gaze at someone across a crowded room for longer than a millisecond, or even glance at the personals in a newspaper or magazine.

"Mortuary supplies," she mumbled. "Well, at least it's an honest living. Good steady work. With an emphasis on *steady*."

When the telephone rang, she was tempted to ignore it. It was probably Richie. Perhaps he'd left some important detail out of their conversation — like what color shoes his wife wore on their eighth wedding anniversary.

"Hello?" She was ready to affect an accent and claim she was the housekeeper.

"Is this Laura Briggs?"

A male voice, all right, but one she didn't recognize.

"Yes," she said hesitantly. "Who's this, please?"

"My name is Gil Plympton." The caller paused as if waiting for a reaction. When he was greeted by nothing more than Laura's confused silence, he explained, "I'm Melanie Plympton's husband."

Chapter Fourteen

The Starlight Diner was one of hundreds of such places dotting Long Island, offering in convenience and bizarrely extensive menus what they lacked in charm. Inside, Laura found herself surrounded by the usual glass, chrome, and vinyl. The restaurant had an antiseptic feeling, as if at any moment one of the waiters might suddenly put down his matching pair of coffeepots — brown for regular, orange for decaf — and perform surgery.

Glancing around, she surmised that Gil Plympton hadn't arrived yet, and followed the hostess to a corner booth. She sat patiently while the waiter did his little dance with water glasses, a relish tray, and two red plastic menus.

As she scanned the luncheon selections Laura thought about what a strange encounter this was. How many ex-wives throughout history had shared pickles and coleslaw with the soon-to-be ex-husbands of their soon-to-be ex-husbands' new girlfriends? It boggled the mind. This, she decided, was an occasion that warranted throwing caution to the wind and bypassing the Dieter's Corner.

She was trying to decide between a bacon cheeseburger and a pastrami on rye when the waiter returned. This time he brought with him a man who could only have been Gil Plympton.

"Laura?"

"Gil?"

She was struck by how much the slender, gaunt-faced man sliding into the seat across from her resembled her ex-husband. It wasn't only that his coloring was similar. Nor was it simply that the structure of Gil's face was so much like Roger's. He even dressed the same way. The slightly crumpled khaki pants and the muted green cotton shirt with the threadbare cuffs could have come from Roger's closet.

At least ol' Melanie's consistent, she thought, amused.

What was different was the hangdog expression on Gil's face. Even more than his tense forehead and the lines around his mouth, his eyes betrayed his emotions. The sadness and confusion reflected there were unmistakable.

"Thanks for agreeing to see me." He folded his hands in front of him on the table. Laura noticed that he still wore a wedding band.

"It is a little unusual." Laura closed the menu and put it aside. "I mean, your wife, my husband . . . Hardly the basis for a friendship."

"But we have so much in common!"

Laura blinked.

"I still haven't come to grips with this," he went on. "I don't know how you're handling it, but to me it's like a dream. No, a nightmare. Everything around me has taken on a surreal quality. Even my psychic's commented on it. She says she can see my confusion reflected in my aura."

He shook his head slowly. "I just hope Roger knows what he's got. Although how could he not? In a way, I don't blame him for wanting Melanie." Gil spoke quickly, in a monotone. Laura was finding his stream-of-consciousness discourse disconcerting.

"I mean, what man *wouldn't* do anything to have her? She's got everything. She's beautiful, smart, sophisticated, creative. . . . Let's face it. She's an exciting, desirable woman."

Excuse me? Laura was tempted to say. Are we talking about the same woman here? The one with the pots? The one whose idea of high fashion is kneesocks with clogs?

"Still, even though I can understand why he did it, I can't help being angry. He did break up my marriage, after all."

Laura's eyebrows shot up. "Roger? *My*

Roger? I knew she was still married to you when they met, but do you expect me to believe a man incapable of answering a want ad actually got his act together enough to break up a marriage?"

The waiter chose that moment to return, his pen poised purposefully over his pad. But Laura had lost interest in food. Even the promise of more grams of fat than she usually allowed herself over an entire week paled beside the chance to get the inside scoop on the Roger-and-Melanie scandal. She quickly ordered a salad, then waited impatiently while Gil agonized over the Sandwich Board.

"They met at a PTA meeting, you know," Gil told her when they were alone again.

"I didn't know. In fact, I didn't know Roger even cared about the PTA."

"Melanie's very active in the PTA." Gil spoke with pride. "She runs the arts program, you know."

"Yes, I've heard. Pots for Tots."

"Their most popular program. Anyway, she decided to try expanding the after-school enrichment classes to include sports. Somebody told her Roger was into sailing, so she called him up and invited him to a planning meeting."

"Sailing, huh? Don't tell me. Their eyes met across the crowded school cafeteria and violins played."

"Believe it or not, that's pretty much how it happened. At least, from what I've been able to piece together."

"How did you manage to find all this out?"

"It took me a while," Gil admitted. "Oh, I had my suspicions that something was going on. Melanie was acting distant. Of course, she'd been distant for years, but this was different." He paused. "She started going on these . . . walks."

"Walks?"

"Very long walks. Late at night. She'd leave me home with the kids around seven, then show up at midnight."

"I take it you didn't notice any improvement in muscle tone," Laura commented dryly.

"She didn't give me much of a chance. Whenever she came in that late, she'd sleep on the couch. The next day she'd tell me she hadn't wanted to wake me."

"How considerate."

"Anyway, it wasn't hard to put two and two together, but I still had to find out for sure. So I did what any other self-respecting husband who thinks his wife may be cheating on him does. I went to Radio Shack and bought a bugging device. All it took was listening in on one phone call, and I knew everything I needed to know."

Shades of Irwin Hart, Laura thought in amazement. Maybe the man with the silver balls really did know what he was talking about.

"What exactly did you hear?"

"Not too much, actually. But I could tell by the way they talked to each other that their after-school activities involved a lot more than sports planning."

"I had no idea," Laura confessed. "Of course, by that time, Roger and I were barely speaking to each other. I'd told him I'd wanted a divorce weeks earlier. I wasn't paying much attention to his extracurricular activities."

The waiter returned, plates in hand. Laura had almost forgotten that food was why they'd come here in the first place.

"I can't believe this." She shifted her gaze from Gil to the mound of raw spinach the size of a compost heap that now sat in front of her.

"Believe it," Gil insisted, misinterpreting her comment. "Things between Melanie and me weren't that great; I'm willing to admit that. Still, I had no idea she wanted out. Now she claims that she'd been contemplating divorce for a long time."

"I guess she was just waiting for someone to come along and give her a reason."

"Or make it easy for her," Gil said bitterly. "If only she'd been open with me. If only we'd been able to talk —"

"Gil," Laura pointed out, "the problem

with ninety-nine out of a hundred marriages is that the husband and wife can't talk."

"Well, it's water under the bridge now," Gil said with a sigh. "What I'm left with is dealing with the fact that my twelve-year marriage is over. Melanie's planning to move out — and take the kids with her. By then, our separation agreement should be signed. We've decided that until then, we'll continue living under the same roof, doing our best to keep out of each other's way."

"Who's got the couch?" Laura asked cheerfully.

"Melanie. Laura," Gil continued earnestly, "it's really good to have someone to talk to. Someone who knows the people involved . . . somebody who understands."

Laura nodded. "Maybe it's not a bad idea for us to keep communication open. The more we know, the better off we'll be."

"I think we can do much more for each other than that. I think we can help each other."

"How?"

He cast her an odd look. "By sharing our pain."

Laura was struck by how much further along in the separation process she was than he. Her roller-coaster car was miles ahead of Gil's. She even had her first date behind her.

"We'll definitely have to do this again soon," Gil said earnestly, standing outside the Starlight Diner with his hands stuck deep in his pockets.

"Okay," Laura agreed. "And if you need to talk, feel free to call me anytime. I think you were right, Gil. This is something we're both going through, and I believe we really can help each other —"

She stopped, having realized that Gil wasn't listening. He was looking over her shoulder at something behind her, so fascinating that even gossiping about their spouses couldn't compete.

Automatically Laura turned. "Claire!" she cried. "What are you doing here?"

"Meeting some clients for lunch." Her words were directed at Laura, but her eyes were fixed on Gil. She strode toward them, a startling Day-Glo vision. Against a dreary backdrop of mounds of gray snow, shoved to the side of the parking lot by a snowplow, her choice of blinding colors seemed even more dramatic than usual. With a hot-pink car coat she wore turquoise stretch pants, her long legs sticking out beneath the hem of her jacket like a Barbie doll's. Her white crew cut gleamed in the wintery sunlight.

"Hello," she said, her voice suddenly so deep and throaty she sounded as if she were doing a bad Kathleen Turner imitation.

Gil responded immediately. "Hello. Are you a friend of Laura's?"

"Oh, yes. Laura and I go back to our college days. And you?" As she spoke Claire ran her fingers through her spiky hair.

"We're just starting to become friends," Gil replied.

"Then Laura is a very lucky woman," Claire purred.

Out of the corner of her eye, Laura noticed a pair of men in business suits heading into the diner. The one with more pens in his breast pocket glanced at his watch.

"I hate to break this up," she said, "but I think your lunch dates have arrived, Claire."

Claire just batted her eyelashes at Gil.

"Well, I guess I'd better be going," he said. He took a couple of steps backward, moving with reluctance. "I hope we meet again."

"Claire Nielsen," Laura hissed, grabbing Claire's arm and dragging her toward the diner, "do you have any idea who that man is?"

She watched him walk away across the parking lot. "Superman? Mr. Right? Romeo?"

"*Wrong.* Try Gil Plympton. As in *Melanie* Plympton? The new love of Roger's life?"

"Does he live around here?" Claire asked dreamily.

"You're missing the point." Laura was quickly losing patience. "You're not really interested in him, are you?"

After considering the question carefully, Claire nodded. "I think I could be."

"Oh, no, you don't. This is too incestuous for my blood. Besides, I thought you weren't looking for Mr. Right."

Claire wore a faraway look. "I thought so, too."

"Listen, why don't you just go to a singles bar like everybody else?"

Claire turned, her hands on her hips as she peered down from her four-inch heels at Laura. "Wait a minute. Aren't you the one who encouraged — *encouraged* — your friend and mine, Julie Cavanaugh, to date my ex-husband? Not only to date him, but also to learn to live with his exhibitionistic nose-hair cutting, his Salvation Army jacket, his obnoxious friends, his even more obnoxious relatives —"

"This is different. Believe me, Claire, this man is not for you."

"Why not?"

"For one thing, he's still in love with his ex-wife. He's wearing his wedding ring, for heaven's sake."

"Maybe I could get him to take it off."

"The man is in pain. He's . . . he's vulnerable, he's searching, he's lonely, he's overcome with desperation. . . ."

Claire's eyes followed Gil, who was driving past them, out of the parking lot. He leaned out the window to give them both a big wave. "Great. In that case, he's bound to say yes when I ask him to dinner."

"Television?" squawked Laura, her voice rising a few octaves. She squeezed the telephone receiver more tightly, aware that her palms had instantly become sweaty. *Me?*"

"It's a local station, right on Long Island." Alice was the publicist at Laura's publisher, assigned to promote Gertrude Giraffe and Lenny Leopard and the woman who'd created them. She sounded amazingly matter-of-fact. "Are you available for a taping next Thursday morning?"

Laura paused to catch her breath. *Television.* Instantly she began constructing fantasies of a career in broadcast media. Through her mind raced delicious images of herself as the new Joan Lunden: picked up at dawn by a limo; dropped at the station, where fawning hairdressers, makeup artists, and fashion experts transformed her into a media icon; giggling with Loni Anderson and other celebrities as they shared their innermost secrets, their childhood dreams, their favorite chili recipes. . . .

"It's the Shop-at-Home Network," Alice went on. "Twenty-four hours a day, they hawk polyester pantsuits and exercise machines and fake jewelry."

Laura's vision faded. "How do I fit into this high-tech version of a door-to-door salesman?"

"According to cable-TV regulations, in order to qualify for some financially beneficial status, the station has to offer five minutes of public-service programming for every hour it's on the air."

"How does promoting my books fit in? I suppose I could claim that Johnny Jaguar has polyester fur and that Carol Cobra is covered in faux snakeskin."

"Actually, you're not supposed to promote your books. They just want you to talk about your career as a writer. You know, how you first got into it, how other people can get started . . . Think educational."

Driving to the station later in the week, Laura wasn't quite sure why she was bothering to go through with it. This, her very first television appearance, had already eaten up a good part of her day. She'd spent the entire morning showering and fussing with her hair, makeup, and accessories. What was worse was that short of the night before the SATs, she couldn't remember having ever been as nervous about anything.

She was greatly comforted by the fact that the studio turned out to be in a storefront in a strip mall. She was a long way away from vying for Barbara Walters's job. In fact, she realized, the best part about her television debut might turn out to be the fact that she could combine stardom with the opportunity to stock up on deodorant and dental floss at the CVS drugstore a few doors down.

Pushing through glass doors, Laura found herself in a carpeted anteroom. There were no pictures on the walls, no furniture — only a buzzer. Ringing it, she wondered if an agent of the Great Oz was going to poke his head through the door.

Instead, a man in a well-cut, expensive-looking suit answered. "Laura Briggs? I'm Kirk Brentwood. I'll be interviewing you on the air today."

At least they got my name right this time, thought Laura. She extended her hand and received one of the heartiest, firmest hand-shakes of her life.

An outstanding grip was hardly the only thing noteworthy about Kirk Brentwood, she thought, finding herself in an intense eye-lock that was at least as formidable. Eyes the color of robin's eggs — or perhaps dyed Easter eggs — were fixed upon hers with such an unwavering gaze that she didn't dare look away.

Kirk Brentwood was knock-'em-dead handsome. With his square jaw, perfectly straight nose, and even, white teeth that resembled the keys on a piano, he looked like a comic-book hero come to life. Even his hair fit that image. It was yellow. Not blond; yellow.

Not surprisingly, his voice was as hearty and firm as his handshake.

"I certainly am pleased to meet *you!*" he exclaimed. "Twelve books, huh? Color me impressed!"

He sounded so much like a game-show host that Laura expected lights to flash on, accompanied by a shrill *ding-ding-ding!* Instead, Kirk led her through a maze of corridors, toward a lounge.

"Our green room," he informed her with a Vanna White wave. "Notice anything interesting about it? There's nothing green in it!"

He guffawed loudly. Laura managed a wan smile.

"Goodness," she commented, glancing around, "everything here looks brand-new."

"It is brand-new. The station's only a few months old. I'm new, too. At least, I'm new to the area. I moved out here to Long Island when the station opened. Before that, I was doing a television show in Manhattan —"

"Really?" Color *me* impressed. "What show?"

"It's, uh, one you're probably not familiar with. It was never broadcast out here —"

"What was it called? I have a lot of friends in the city who might have watched it."

"Well, it's not on anymore. I'm sure no one you know —"

"Try me."

Kirk lowered his eyes. "The Pet Channel."

"Excuse me?"

"It was an experimental thing," he explained quickly. "Twenty-four-hour programming on the subject of, uh, pets. I was kind of the anchor for the station."

"The Pet Channel?"

"How to decide what breed of dog's right for you, how to train a new puppy, advice on dealing with the hair-ball problem . . ." He was muttering. Gone was the confident show-biz personality.

"But that was then and this is now," he insisted, sliding right back into his television-celebrity persona. Flashing those two rows of sparkling white teeth that were a toothpaste-commercial director's dream, he added, "I've moved on to bigger and better things."

Right, thought Laura. Like selling faux diamond earrings to Princess Grace wanna-bes.

"Let me ask you something." Kirk leaned forward, his baby blues burning into hers with such intensity that she looked away, afraid of being blinded for life. "I really miss the city. Tell me, how do people stand it out here?"

"Excuse me?"

"I mean, how can anyone with half a brain tolerate living in the suburbs?"

"I *like* living in the suburbs," Laura replied. "Long Island has wonderful beaches, a fascinating history . . . and there's always plenty of free parking."

"Yeah, well, I'm going crazy out here," Kirk insisted. "Frankly, I don't know how you do it. Of course, I'm hoping this stint at Shop-at-Home is only a stepping-stone. I'm not planning to stay out here for the rest of my life, that's for sure."

He was quiet for a moment, clearly brooding over the cards the Great Pinochle Player in the sky had dealt him.

"But the show must go on!" he declared heartily. "Hey, the clock is ticking. I'd better get to the studio and check on things. You wait here, make yourself comfortable, and I'll be back in two shakes of a lamb's tail!"

A very urban expression, Laura thought, picking up a copy of *Fake Fur Times* and thumbing through it.

When Kirk returned, he led her through a control room that looked like something NASA had put together and into a studio. A big room with a lot of lights, it had a video camera with a monitor and a fake-looking living room set, two chairs placed at an unnatural angle on a carpeted platform. Behind her were rows of bookshelves. At least she thought they were bookshelves. When she reached out to grab one of the volumes, she discovered they were really made of papier-mâché.

But there was little time to dwell on the décor. A surly cameraman in a sweatshirt appeared, taking his place behind the lens. Kirk switched on lights so bright and so yellow Laura was certain her carefully chosen lipstick was now the same shade of neon green as Evan's favorite marker. He settled into the seat opposite her and plastered on a smile even wider than those she'd seen before. It was show time.

"Today we're talking with Laura Briggs, author of a dozen books for children."

It was her turn to flash a smile.

"Laura, tell us how you first got interested in writing."

"Well," she began, her voice confident, "when I was a little girl, I thought up a cast of characters, including a giraffe named Gertrude, who solved mysteries, and her sidekick, Carol Cobra. When I was eight or nine, I started writing stories about them. Then, when I grew up, I —"

"Your books are all set in the jungle, aren't they?"

"Yes, they are. Since I write about a giraffe

and a cobra, they really have to —"

"I take it that jungle's in Africa, right?"

"Yes, I —"

"But you live in the suburbs, right? You're a Long Islander?"

"That's right."

"Let me ask you something." Kirk leaned forward. "Isn't it difficult for a creative person like yourself to live in as sterile an environment as the suburbs? I mean, it's so . . . so quiet compared to the city."

Laura cleared her throat. "As a writer, I really enjoy the opportunity to be in a place that's conducive to working —"

"But wouldn't someone like you be better off in an urban environment? There's so much stimulation in the city. Just walking down the street is exciting."

"It's true that every now and then I go into the city to experience some of that street life. But I also enjoy —"

"Even the people out here," Kirk went on. "They're a different breed than the people who live in the city. How do you deal with that?"

"I've managed to find a circle of friends."

"I bet they're all writers."

Five minutes of taping seemed like five years. Laura was in a cold sweat by the time the red light on the camera went off.

"Good interview!" Kirk extended his hand for one more hearty handshake. "Come

294

on, I'll walk you out."

As Kirk babbled on about when the segment she'd just taped was likely to be aired, Laura was lost in thought, mentally reworking her drugstore shopping list.

"You were a great guest," Kirk insisted as she struggled to remember whether or not Evan had used the last of his neon-colored Band-Aids to decorate his nutrition diorama, a 3-D depiction of the food pyramid. "You seem like a very interesting woman."

"Thanks."

"Another problem I've been having out here," Kirk went on, "is meeting women. I got divorced about a year ago. And so far, the women I've met have been —" He chuckled. "Well, I don't have to tell *you*."

"I know how tough it is," Laura told him consolingly. "I've recently gotten separated myself. Frankly, I haven't been trying that hard to meet anyone, but —"

Kirk's expression had changed. "Separated, huh?"

"That's right. Just last fall. Of course, it's been about six months now, but it still seems —"

"How about getting together sometime? Dinner? Lunch? Brunch?"

Laura was speechless. Kirk the Star had evolved into Kirk the Would-Be Dater. In his book, switching roles meant changing postures. Instead of standing up straight and tall in the aggressive stance of someone who'd sell his grandmother to make a quick buck, he was leaning against the doorway, one knee bent, one elbow bent, one eye looking as if it were dangerously close to winking.

It was a surprising transformation. Yet what surprised Laura even more was hearing herself say, "Sure. That sounds nice."

Sure? Where had that come from? She hadn't even liked the guy. Was she so badly in need of a quick shot of Vitamin B_{12} for her ego? Was she more desperate than she'd realized not to spend another Saturday night alone, watching TV and sobbing over *Sisters*? Was she secretly hoping for a free pair of mock-emerald-and-ruby ear cuffs?

No, she realized. The bottom line was that she was on that search for the Other. Like it or not, she was seeking eyes, a nose, and a mouth for that faceless man in her fantasy, the one who would run through a field of wildflowers with her. Her rational side knew chances were slim that Kirk Brentwood was the person to supply the missing features. But another side of her whispered, "You never know. . . ."

"Great." Kirk was beaming. "Then it's a date."

Date. There was that word. A wave of

dizziness came over Laura as she opened her purse to fumble around for pen and paper. Suddenly it occurred to her that *date* was a four-letter word.

This date's got to be better than the last one, Laura thought, studying her reflection in the full-length mirror. It certainly couldn't be worse.

Partly in the name of self-protection, partly because she was having trouble mustering up enthusiasm, she wasn't trying nearly as hard this time around. Memories of her date with Richie had, like an undercooked dinner, left her with a bad case of heartburn. Wanting to make a statement — to herself, if to no one else — she'd chosen an outfit she didn't particularly like. She made a point of wearing the same earrings she'd worn all day. She hadn't even bothered to wash her hair, figuring a recycled do was good enough.

Maybe I'm daring Kirk to like me, she mused. Call me petulant . . . but it could well be the best possible attitude.

Watching Kirk drive up in a sleek black Porsche, the perfect car for an aspiring television personality, Laura was struck by the fact that despite her cynicism, she was still nervous. Some things, she decided, never changed. It was like crying at the end of *Gone With the Wind*: no matter how many times she saw it, she always responded the same way.

Kirk was just as bold and as beautiful as Laura remembered him. He even acted the part of a Ken doll come to life. Standing in the doorway, he flashed his perfect, toothy smile as he handed her a bouquet of flowers.

"I hope you like Japanese food," he greeted her.

What is it with men and ethnic food? Laura wondered, grabbing her jacket from the closet. There must be a rumor circulating that exotic spices are an aphrodisiac.

"Which Japanese restaurant are we going to?" Laura asked once she was in the front seat of Kirk's car. Once again she tugged at the Incredible Shrinking Skirt.

"No," said Kirk.

"Oh. I thought you said we were having Japanese food."

"No."

Laura was silent, wondering how to deal with Kirk's sudden rudeness.

"No," he repeated. "The restaurant is called Noh. Spelled N-O-H. You know, the Japanese theater?"

"Oh-h-h," Laura said, relieved. That's O-H, she thought.

Noh wasn't just any Japanese restaurant, Laura discovered, opening the menu. It was a sushi restaurant. Her policy was never to let any fellow member of the animal king-dom pass through her lips unless it had first been cooked. Desperately she searched the menu for the default section, the en-trées like tempura and teriyaki and cheese-burgers that were geared toward the weak-kneed. Short of rice, there was noth-ing here she could categorize as even close to appetizing.

She was trying to remember the tricks she'd mastered as a child, ways of disposing of food at the dinner table without actually consuming it. Before she was able to dredge up any details, Kirk leaned forward, his intense baby blue eyes glowing like Christ-mas lights.

"So you're a writer," he said. "It sounds absolutely fascinating. I want to hear all about it."

"I must say, it's quite a rewarding career. I —"

"I bet. You know, I'm a bit of a writer myself."

"Are you?"

"I've considered getting serious about my writing."

"Really? Fiction?"

"Fiction based on my life story. A lot of interesting things have happened to me. Zany, too."

"It's an interesting process, the way the author's real-life experiences are incorporated into fiction. I've found that they never come out exactly the same, but —"

"It all began when I was a child." Kirk leaned back in his chair, a faraway look in his eyes. "Sure, I seemed like just another typical American kid. Cuter than most, of course. Blond hair, blue eyes, the whole bit. But inside, I was burning. *Burning.* I knew I was destined for greatness. . . ."

Laura let out a long, deep sigh, not at all surprised that Bachelor Number Two failed to notice. She simply did not have the energy to pretend to be enraptured by a recitation of the Life and Times of Kirk Brentwood. She picked up the menu again, having decided that eating lower life-forms had to be more palatable than conversing with them.

"Dates from hell!" Laura cried, throwing herself on the couch and burying her face in a cushion. The fact that it was spotted with an apple-juice stain dating back to the 1980s didn't even faze her. "They find me. I don't know how they do it, but these guys can pick me out of a crowd —"

"Just because you had a couple of bad experiences doesn't mean you should reject the entire concept of dating," said Julie, sitting cross-legged on the floor, toying with one of Evan's plastic Troll dolls. At the moment she was hopscotching it from square to square of her patchwork skirt.

"Besides, there *are* benefits to dating." Claire, lounging in the chair opposite the couch, ran her fingers through her spiky hair, causing it to clump together. "Even I'm willing to concede that." A dreamy, faraway expression crossed her face.

"Of course," she added pointedly, casting Julie a cold look, "the key is to be dating the right person."

Ever since the true identity of Bobby of the sore rectus femoris had been revealed, a cavernous rift had formed between Claire and Julie. Laura knew they'd been avoiding each other. Yet after her fiasco with Kirk Brentwood, she'd called upon them both, needing a double dose of moral support. Tonight her friends' problems with their social lives had to take second place to hers.

"Never again," Laura insisted, her words muffled by the cushion. "I'm never going on another date."

"What you need," Julie said soothingly, "is a facial."

"What you need," Claire chimed in, "is a shopping spree at Bloomingdale's."

"What I need is to get away from all this." In an abrupt movement Laura pulled herself off the couch and strode across the room. Frantically she rifled through the collection of magazines, catalogs, and assorted pieces of junk mail she'd tossed into a large wicker basket the day before during one of her rare cleaning frenzies.

"Here it is," she finally exclaimed, thrusting a pamphlet at Julie. "*This* is what I need."

Gingerly Julie accepted the pamphlet, an unassuming, handbill-size bit of paper. She studied it for a few seconds, then glanced up at Laura. There was a puzzled expression on her face. "World Watch?"

Laura nodded. "I need to throw myself into something . . . something productive. Something outside myself. Something more important, bigger somehow —"

"Something you need clothes from L. L. Bean for," Claire observed, peering over Julie's shoulder. "Laura, have you completely lost your senses?"

"World Watch?" Julie said again, clearly at least three steps behind. "What kind of organization is this? Laura, you're not going out to sea in a rowboat to terrorize oil tanks the size of Rhode Island?"

"That's somebody else's job," Laura informed her. "World Watch has been sending me unsolicited junk mail for ages. I finally took a break from wrestling with dust bunnies yesterday and read their pamphlet. Apparently this organization was designed for those of us who want to keep our feet dry. It's modeled after the Peace Corps, except it's for people who only have a week or two to donate to a good cause. It's like going on vacation — only instead of touring museums or brushing up on your windsurfing skills, you help out on some worthwhile project designed to help keep the planet going for another decade or two."

Julie blinked. "You mean like scraping high octane off ducks?"

"Now you've got it."

Claire stared at Laura, a look of incredulity on her face. "You're not serious, are you?"

"You know," Julie said thoughtfully, "I think maybe Laura's on to something here." Taking the pamphlet, she skimmed the copy. Then she studied the pictures that Laura had pored over, groups of happy campers dressed in shorts and funny hats holding up fossils or exotic-looking bits of seaweed. "She's right when she says she needs to get involved in something other than her own life. A project like this might help her put things in perspective."

"After all," Laura reminded Claire, "look at the drastic changes you made after you and . . . you decided to get divorced. You cut your hair, dyed it, bought a whole new wardrobe, and began a brand-new career."

"That's not exactly how Bobby tells it," Julie said in a strained voice, "but I suppose such a creative interpretation will do for now."

"Wait a minute," Claire countered. "Robert — *Bobby* — got exactly what he had coming to him. Just because he got hit with a little competition —"

"What about you?" Julie countered. "Laura told me what you've been up to. Throwing yourself at Melanie's ex-husband. The poor man's still wearing his wedding band and you're plotting ways to lure him to your apartment —"

"Hey, guys," Laura broke in, holding up her hands referee style. "This is my midlife crisis we're dealing with here. Let's stick to the subject at hand, shall we?"

Claire and Julie exchanged subzero glares, but lapsed into respectful silence.

"I say go for it, Laura," said Julie. "You've got nothing to lose. And according to the tag line here at the bottom of this pamphlet, 'you've got a whole lot to gain.' "

"That's really their slogan?" Claire asked, incredulous. "Good thing it's not a spa."

She looked at Laura. "Julie's right. You might as well send for more information. Who knows? As crazy as it sounds, something like this could even turn your life around."

Chapter Fifteen

"I hope this wasn't a mistake," Laura said in a thin, high-pitched voice.

She'd paused to study her reflection in the window of one of La Guardia Airport's gift shops. There, superimposed over the "I Love New York" mugs and the Mets T-shirts, was a woman she barely recognized. The blurry, translucent image that hovered behind the display of Big Apple memorabilia like a ghost was dressed in clothing unlike anything she had ever worn. Industrial-strength jeans from L. L. Bean, designed for hauling firewood or clearing the back forty. A red plaid flannel shirt. A navy blue nylon jacket with retractable hood. And the pièce de résistance: stiff, brown suede hiking boots straight out of the box that made her walk with all the grace and dignity of Quasimodo.

Her hair was pulled back into a utilitarian ponytail. Even her face looked different. Her skin had already taken on an unusually healthy glow — and she hadn't even gotten her boarding pass.

"Who is this woman?" she muttered, mesmerized by the image before her, still not quite ready to believe it was really her.

"The new Laura Briggs, that's who." Julie, beaming like a proud parent, had come up behind her. "Off on an adventure. Traveling to an exotic new location, experiencing what few before her have experienced . . . Laura, you look fabulous."

"Very Ralph Lauren," Claire seconded. She, too, had come over to the window. "You're so lucky. Personally, I've never been a plaid person."

"Guys," Laura said in a low, even voice, "I'm starting to feel the way I felt on my first day of Girl Scout camp. The bus was getting ready to leave, and there I was all decked out in my green shorts and crisp white blouse with a string tie, my nose pressed against the window as I watched my parents get back into their car, knowing there was no turning back —"

"You're going to love Alaska," Julie insisted.

Claire nodded. "All that nature!"

"That's right, Laura. You're going to see magnificent lakes and mountains and glaciers and . . . and . . ."

"Grizzlies," Laura mumbled. "And mosquitoes. Don't forget those." She swallowed hard. "It sounded like such a good idea at the time."

Running off to the Last Frontier had, indeed, seemed like the ideal way to break with the past on that Saturday night three months earlier, when the three of them — and a family-size bottle of white zinfandel — had gotten together at Claire's. It had been one of the first spring evenings in March, the kind in which the air positively vibrates with intoxicating sweetness. Soft breezes, wafting through windows opened for the first time since September, carried with them a dangerous impulse to experience life at its fullest.

The three women sat in the living room, poring over the literature World Watch had sent.

"Here's one that sounds good," Julie said thoughtfully after scanning several pages of listings in the World Watch catalog, a book of listings as thick as the telephone book for a medium-sized American city. "It's a research project called 'What Do Iguanas Eat?' The write-up says, 'Spend the month of August studying these fascinating lizards that inhabit the scenic Baja Peninsula, Mexico's playground — '"

"Mexico in August?" Claire shook her head. "Laura will come back looking like a crab-apple doll."

"How about this one? 'The Poisonous Leaves of Papua. Toxic foliage, an important part of every ecosystem — '"

"Have you completely lost your mind?" Claire demanded. "Don't you know that in New Guinea, all the best families serve archaeologists for Sunday brunch?"

" 'Trailing Tarantulas in Death Valley'?" Julie suggested hopefully.

"Ix-nay on the Death Valley bit," said Claire.

" 'Parasites of the Rain Forest'?"

"If the worms don't get her, the guerrillas will." Claire let out a frustrated sigh. "Here. Give me that."

Indignant, Julie handed the catalog to Claire. "I don't know why you think you'd be any better at finding a program for Laura than me."

"At least I'm capable of keeping my hormones from clouding my brain," Claire shot back. She buried herself in the World Watch offerings before Julie had a chance to reply. "Hmmm. No. . . . No. . . . Wait a minute. . . . By Jove, I think I've got it!"

"I'm afraid to ask," muttered Laura. She was huddled in one corner of the couch, hugging the purple throw pillow.

"Alaska!"

"Alaska?" Julie and Laura repeated in unison.

"It's perfect." Claire's eyes were glazed. "This is precisely what we've been looking for, Laura. Think about it. Alaska is part of the United States, so you don't have to worry about the language or the currency or the eating habits of the natives . . . or how loosely the locals interpret the word *bathroom*. But it's still exotic. Wild. Unexplored . . ."

"Exactly what would Laura be doing up there?" Julie asked.

"Working side by side with Dr. Cameron P. Woodward of the biology department of Tyler University."

"Tyler?" Julie repeated. "Right here on Long Island?"

"One and the same. The name of his research project — are you ready? — is 'The Mystery of Motherhood in Sculpin Fish.' Does that sound intriguing or what?"

"Thanks," said Laura, "but I think I'll wait for the movie."

"No, listen. The number of eggs produced by female sculpin, a fascinating freshwater fish that dwells at the bottom of lakes — ' "

Julie rolled her eyes. "I think I'll even skip the movie."

"What's wrong with fish?" Claire protested. "Some of my best meals have been fish."

"But Alaska?" Laura said doubtfully. "Isn't it . . . cold?"

"Not in the summer. At least according to this." Claire paused a moment to check the bible of her newfound field of expertise. "We're talking fifties, sixties, occasional drizzle. . . . Besides, think about how beautiful Alaska must be. You've seen the calendars.

And the back issues of *National Geographic*. And what about *White Fang*? Picture all those magnificent mountains and lakes and fields of wildflowers. . . ."

Sitting in Claire's living room back in March, high on the sweet spring air and the even sweeter cheap wine, Laura had fallen in love with the fantasyland vision of Alaska that Claire had conjured up. She'd also been taken with a brand-new image of herself. This version of Laura Briggs did not spend her days conjuring up the trials and tribulations of fictional others while sitting safely at a computer. Nor was she someone who considered watching two reruns of *Mary Tyler Moore* back-to-back almost more excitement than she could handle.

The Laura Briggs she saw that night grabbed life by the shoulders, looked it straight in the eye, and demanded, "Lead on!" She trekked through the wilderness, a mess kit in her backpack and a hiking song in her heart. She was at one with nature, a daughter of the earth, a friend to the animals, a part of a wonderful ecosystem that even made room for poisonous plants and slithery iguanas. . . .

Now, as she stood in the airport dressed like the centerfold for *Field and Stream*, the song in Laura's heart was more of a dirge. And the idea of being surrounded by any more nature than the plastic ferns decorating the back wall of the airport bar seemed positively ominous.

"I can change my mind, can't I?" she asked meekly.

"Nonsense." Claire grabbed her arm and began dragging her toward the gates. "Everything is set. The check you sent to World Watch has cleared. Evan's tucked away at sleep-away camp, learning vital survival skills like how to make an ice-cream-stick birdhouse. Your flight leaves in less than an hour. The wheels are in motion, Laura. The Earth's future rests in your hands —"

Laura whimpered. "If I hurry, I bet I can still book one of those Alaskan cruises that feature shuffleboard and blocks of ice sculpted into swans. . . ."

Claire gave her a firm push right below her Eddie Bauer tag. "Have a great time, kid."

"Don't forget to take lots of pictures," Julie called after her. "Try to get something besides snow."

"I thought you were my friends!"

Laura's desperate words were lost. A SWAT team of security guards had already surrounded her, urging her through the metal detector as her carry-on bag was X-rayed. There was no going back.

Like it or not, the new Laura Briggs was

about to embark on her great adventure.

Laura had fallen into that lethargic, semi-conscious state that can only be reached at thirty thousand feet aboveground when she suddenly became aware that the floor was falling out from under her. At least that was her initial impression. Snapping back into consciousness, she realized that the plane was simply descending.

Part of her longed to stay right where she was, strapped safely into a comfortable seat on an airplane. How pleasant it was up here, far from anything that even vaguely resembled real life. It was a relief, being tucked in with a pillow, a soft blue blanket, and the current issues of a dozen magazines. Stubbornly she closed her eyes again, not yet ready to face whatever was waiting for her on the other side of her lids.

And then she heard the man behind her gasp. "Look! There it is! I must have seen this a dozen times, yet every time I do, I feel like a little kid on Christmas morning."

With a testimonial like that, Laura couldn't help being curious. She forced her eyes open. Looking out the plane window, she, too, gasped.

Far below, underneath a curtain of clouds parting dramatically, she saw rugged, untamed landscape, unmarked by any signs of humanity. Craggy, forbidding mountains reached upward, their gray stone surfaces pushing out from the snow draped over them. Magnificent glaciers, slicing their way through whatever obstacles dared get in their way, lurked ominously between the sky-scraping peaks that were dwarfed in comparison. Cut into the rocky terrain were spiky inlets, the water murky and dark.

"Snow," Laura breathed. "It's *June*."

As the plane descended farther she was relieved to see green. Large stretches of it, in fact, interspersed with what looked like hundreds of tiny lakes. Lush growths of trees lined the peninsulas that stretched lazily across the sea. The sun glinted off the water in little bursts of light.

"It's breathtaking, isn't it?" the man behind her asked, poking his head between the seats.

"There are no people," Laura mumbled.

"That's the point."

It wasn't until she stood up that she realized how tired she was. The flight from New York had consisted of three separate legs. Stopovers in both Chicago and Seattle, all that deplaning and replaning . . . In total, she'd been in transit close to a full twelve hours. The joints in her legs weren't about to let her forget it. While over the intercom the pilot cheerfully informed them that the time was four hours earlier than on the East Coast, Laura's body insisted it wasn't dinnertime, but bedtime.

Zombielike, she moved through the airport, her tote bag slung over her shoulder as she retrieved her luggage. "There's no place like home," she muttered over and over, not quite able to believe any of this was really happening. It took every ounce of self-control she possessed to keep from clicking her heels together.

She lugged her two heavy suitcases to the exit, speculating that all this could turn out to be nothing more than a cruel joke. Perhaps there would be no one to meet her. Maybe she was destined to spend the rest of her days here at the Anchorage airport, waiting. . . .

And then she caught sight of her contact. He was leaning against a column, holding up a piece of brown cardboard with BRIGGS scrawled across the front in black crayon.

"*Oh,* boy." She swallowed hard.

If she hadn't known he was authentic, she would have concluded he'd been sent over from central casting. Grizzly Adams, right here in Anchorage Airport, waiting to pick up the greenhorn from the lower forty-eight.

It wasn't even the way he was dressed. The plaid flannel shirt, jeans, and hiking boots were pretty much the local uniform, she surmised. What gave him the look of the missing link on the evolutionary scale was the impressive amount of hair above

314

his shoulders. A full dark beard, bushy eyebrows shading intense brown eyes, and a wild growth on his head, as thick and coarse as fur. If this man wasn't Yukon Jack, he was certainly doing a darned good imitation.

Laura experienced a repeat of the dreadful sinking feeling in the pit of her stomach she'd had at the airport in New York. Struggling to keep from panicking, she reminded herself that she was no longer a little girl being forced to fend for herself in a world of plastic lanyards and "Kum-Ba-Ya." She was a full-fledged adult, with traveler's checks, a Visa card . . . and a plane ticket home.

Besides, she told herself, maybe he's just some guy from the local taxi company. There's no reason to assume this man is Dr. Woodward. Surely this . . . this *being* couldn't be my host, my guide, my only link to survival out here in a place so undeveloped they probably don't even have Coke.

"Laura Briggs?" he asked as she approached.

"That's me." She smiled bravely.

Her smile wasn't returned. "I'm Cameron Woodward."

"Hello. I'm pleased to —"

"Is all this luggage yours?"

Laura raised her chin in the air, one of her favorite defensive gestures. "I *am* going to be here a full two weeks."

"What have you got in here?"

"Enough clothes for the entire trip, including an extra pair of hiking shoes," she answered, the impatience in her voice only thinly masked. "Also six paperbacks, a hair dryer, and a jar of peanut butter in case it turns out moose burgers don't agree with me."

Dr. Woodward shrugged. "I carry all my personal gear in this backpack."

Laura couldn't tell if she was only imagining the disapproval she heard in his voice.

She decided to reserve judgment, at least until she reached the parking lot. "I can't tell you what a relief it is to finally be on solid ground. That flight from New York took forever." Laura nearly had to run to keep up with Dr. Woodward as he strode out of the airport. Not even the bulging knapsack on his back and her two heavy suitcases slowed him down.

His response was a noncommittal grunt. Laura, however, struggled to keep up her cheerful chatter.

"I'm exhausted. Oh, sure, I tried to sleep on the plane, but it turned out I was flying with the Vienna Boys Choir. Well, not really; what I mean is, there was a bunch of overly energetic pubescent boys on the flight out of Seattle. They talked nonstop, as if they couldn't quite believe their voices were finally changing. Anyway, I didn't get much of a rest. What I'm really looking forward to is a nice hot shower and a good night's sleep —"

"Sleep? Shower?" Dr. Woodward stopped in his tracks. He turned to face her, his eyes burning into hers so piercingly that for a moment Laura wondered if the devil himself had taken to leading World Watch projects.

"Don't people in Alaska sleep or shower?" Although she was only joking, as she said the words the feeling that she could well be speaking the truth descended over Laura like a chill.

"Not if they were sent here by World Watch. At least, not yet."

"Explain."

"I guess no one told you."

"No one told me *what?*"

"We're driving straight through tonight."

"Wait a minute." To punctuate her words, Laura stopped, put down her tote bag, and folded her arms across her chest. "Who's *we* — and where are *we* driving tonight?"

"*We* is you and me. And we're driving straight to the Kenai Peninsula."

"Which is . . . where?"

"About eight hours away."

"Eight *hours?*"

"It's only seven o'clock," Dr. Woodward informed her with annoying calmness.

"Hold on. It's seven o'clock to people *here*, people who were still wrapped up in caribou fur, dreaming about kayaking, while I was hovering over Chicago with two rubber eggs and a quart of nitric acid disguised as coffee in my stomach. To *me*, it's eleven P.M.!"

"You'll be better off getting used to our time right away. If you have to, you can sleep in the truck."

"Truck," Laura repeated. "You're telling me I'm about to spend eight hours in a truck."

"You probably won't want to, though. Sleep, I mean. Around here, the sun only sets for two hours in June. Between midnight and two, it's dark. Otherwise," he said, gesturing toward the sun, "this is Alaska's version of nighttime.

"Besides," Dr. Woodward went on, "we've got to get down to the Kenai as soon as we can. We've got a long day in the canoes ahead of us tomorrow."

"Canoes?"

"That's right. Wolf Lake is three miles long, and it's going to take the full two weeks to set traps all along the shore. I'm anxious to get a good start, so I figure we'll be out most of the day."

Laura opened her mouth to protest. But before she had a chance, Dr. Woodward flashed her a smile.

"Welcome to World Watch," he said pleasantly. "We hope you enjoy your stay."

"Rise and shine! We're there."

Slowly, reluctantly, Laura dragged herself out of a deep sleep and tried to remember where she was. Even before she opened her eyes, a complicated mixture of emotions — including anxiety, dread, self-doubt, and more than a little fear — descended upon her.

When she did open her eyes, she let out a shriek.

Two large, brown, soulful eyes were staring directly into hers. Between them was a long, furry snout, with a moist nose at the end. At the moment that nose was covering the window that separated *her* from *it* with clouds of moisture. As two rabbit-sized ears flicked at her it let out a bellow.

Before she had a chance to follow up her initial reaction with an appropriate comment like "Get that thing away from me," a hand she recognized as human grabbed the moose gently around the neck.

"Come on now, Mabel. Get away from that car," a female voice scolded softly. "You gave the lady a real start."

I must be dreaming, thought Laura. I'm still asleep. It's the only possible explanation.

But as the panic growing inside catapulted her into full consciousness, she realized she wasn't dreaming at all. She was curled up in the front seat of a Jeep that probably dated back to the Middle Ages, its shredded vinyl covers ineffectually held together by silver bands of duct tape. Her right cheek smarted where it had been dented by the metal pull tab of the zipper on the nylon sleeping bag she'd been clinging to as tenaciously as Christopher Robin hung on to Pooh.

Through the window, she watched Dr. Woodward take fishnets, buckets, and an assortment of metal contraptions that looked like instruments of torture down off the car roof. She blinked, trying to digest the fact that all around her was nature untamed, manifested largely in the form of a veil of mosquitoes that surrounded the Jeep. They'd stopped at the end of a dirt road. Beyond, as far as the half-closed eye could see, was nothing but forest.

And of course, there was the moose standing outside the Jeep, peering at Laura as if she were the oddity.

"Dr. Woodward?" Laura croaked.

"Ummm?"

"Why is there a moose outside the car?"

"Actually, Mabel's just a calf."

"I think we're splitting hairs here." Laura struggled to remain calm. "Why is she — uh, Mabel — standing so close?"

"Relax. We're at Wolf Lake, where I collect

samples. It happens to be in the middle of a moose preserve, about an hour and a half from the nearest town. Chances are you'll be seeing a lot of Mabel and her buddies over the next couple of weeks. Unless," he added with a chuckle, "Elsie here manages to teach them a few commands like *stay* and *lie down*."

Laura sat very, very still as she watched Mabel being led away by a crusty-looking dark-haired woman dressed entirely in denim. Elsie obviously used the same image consultant as Dr. Woodward.

"Why don't you get out and stretch your legs?" Dr. Woodward suggested, poking his head in through the driver's side.

"What time is it?"

"Three."

"Three A.M.? It's still daylight!"

Dr. Woodward chuckled. "I told you the sun only sets a couple of hours a night. Tell you what. Before you grab a few hours of shut-eye, we'll have a little breakfast up at the cabin."

"Cabin? Oh, good." Laura let out a nervous laugh. "Believe it or not, I was actually afraid we'd be staying in tents."

"It's up a ways. Follow me." Dr. Woodward hoisted his knapsack onto his back, picked up his odd collection of fishing paraphernalia and one of her suitcases, and headed toward the woods.

As she trudged after him through the thickly wooded area, dragging her other suitcase along with her tote bag, Laura's spirits were lifted for the first time since she'd landed on Alaskan soil. She was picturing a homey little hideaway: stone fireplace, tasteful knotty-pine paneling, lots of the plaid Claire was so fond of, big beds made of rough-hewn wood and covered with puffy quilts. All that was required to turn her back into a fully functioning human being, she decided, all she needed to banish the cobwebs from her mind and the charley horses from her aching shoulders and back, were a cup of hot coffee, a hearty breakfast, and that steaming shower she'd been craving since somewhere over Idaho.

The building that appeared at the other end of the rocky path put an end to her momentary spurt of optimism. The cabin looked like the one the Billy Goats Gruff had lived in before urban renewal came along. It was small and boxy, made of oversized Lincoln Logs. Hanging over the front door was a pair of antlers. A makeshift porch had been constructed from splintery wood. On it were two different items that told Laura everything she needed to know: a large plastic jug of water and a gas lantern.

"There's no electricity, is there?" she asked dully, even though the answer was clear. "No running water, either."

"We manage quite nicely," Dr. Woodward insisted cheerfully. "Besides, you'll be amazed at how quickly you get used to it."

He was smiling, Laura noted. *Smiling.* As if being stranded a thousand miles from nowhere in the middle of the night were something to be pleased about.

"Of course," he went on, "the outhouse is a little tricky, mainly because it's a good distance away." He chuckled, responding to some inside joke. "Besides, if the smell doesn't get you, the mosquitoes will.

"Come on inside. I'll give you the grand tour. Then I'll see if I can hustle up some breakfast."

Laura lugged her suitcase and tote bag up the stairs, onto the porch. As her right shoulder muscle went into spasm she wondered glumly how much extra weight her hair dryer accounted for.

The inside of the cabin, her brand-new home away from home, was consistent with the outside. The same rough-hewn look — walls capable of scraping off human skin — was repeated there. At least the bare wooden floors had been given the once-over with a sander. There was plaid, all right, in the form of a sagging sofa that looked as if it predated the antique Jeep. As far as amenities were concerned, that was about as far as they went.

"You'll be sleeping up there, with Sandy," Dr. Woodward told her in a near whisper. After dropping his knapsack onto the couch, he gestured toward a ladder that led up to a loft.

"Up there? Sandy?" Laura repeated the words as if she'd never heard them before.

"There's an inflatable mattress up there. A sleeping bag, too, so you'll really be in the lap of luxury. Just be careful you don't hit your head when you sit up. And watch out for the boxes of supplies. The loft's the only place to store them. That is, unless we want the bears to get them."

"Bears? You're kidding, right?"

Dr. Woodward cast her a strange smile. "If I were you, I'd worry more about Sandy's snoring than the bears."

"Wait a second. Sandy *is* female, isn't she?"

"As far as any of us can tell."

At least something's going right, thought Laura.

"Now, about that grub." He opened the cooler that was pushed into the corner, underneath a shelf. On it were half a dozen mismatched mugs, most of them with spidery cracks running up the side. "We're in luck! Sausage!"

"Oh, good." She'd just realized she was famished.

"Great. A little reindeer sausage, a cup of

instant coffee . . ." Dr. Woodward looked over at her and smiled, a gleam in his dark eyes. "If this isn't heaven, I don't know what is."

Laura forced a smile, though she was wondering who she'd be eating for breakfast: Cupid, Donner, or Blitzen.

All her life, Laura had tried to be a good sport. In high school she participated in the school cheer during pep rallies. At beer parties in college, she'd managed to look as if she were having a good time as her date lost his Rolling Rock on the rug beside her. When her wedding ring had become united as one with Lake Ontario, she'd pretended not to care.

Desperately she reminded herself of her masterful past performances as she sat in the middle of a huge lake. There was sunblock on her face and lips, mosquito repellent on every other bit of exposed skin, and hiking boots laced up so tightly over a pair of damp socks that she had no doubt jungle rot was in her future. She'd had so little sleep she was having trouble focusing — both her eyes and her mind. Yet she had no choice but to try her hardest to follow Dr. Woodward's lead in rhythmically paddling a silver canoe, the only thing between the two of them and a lakeful of creatures she was trying hard not to picture.

"Think we'll catch much today?" she called, anxious to hear the sound of a human voice.

"I expect so. We'll set these traps and leave them until tomorrow before checking to see what we've got." He gestured toward the metal contraptions he'd tossed into the rear of the boat.

"Then what?" Perhaps if she had a better understanding of what she was really doing out here, she reasoned, she'd feel better about all this.

"Ship 'em home, back to my lab at the university. They keep fine in gallon jugs, those plastic ones water comes in. I can fit eighteen in a giant cooler.

"If things go smoothly," Dr. Woodward went on, "we should be finished by four this afternoon."

Four o'clock, she thought ruefully. Back in New York, it'll be eight. The time for winding down after a long, leisurely Sunday. Eating bagels and cream cheese left over from brunch. Leafing through those second-string sections of the *Times* . . .

She missed home terribly. Not only home; all the amenities that civilization had to offer. She'd been in Alaska less than fifteen hours, and already she craved so many of the things that up until now she'd taken for granted. Bathtubs. Flush toilets. Dry feet.

Still, she had to admit her surroundings were spectacular. The surface of Wolf Lake was as smooth as a sheet of ice. Long strands of willowy grass stuck out in the shallowest parts, near the shore. There were lily pads as well, with yellow flowers on top that reminded her of icing rosettes on birthday cakes. All around the lake the rich greens and golds of bushes and trees encircled the water like the gilt frame on a Victorian mirror.

The sun felt pleasantly warm on her back. She smiled at the sound of a loon's cry, cutting through the mist rising off the lake. Looking down into the water, Laura could see clumps of underwater plants, undulating gently as the motion of her paddle disturbed what was otherwise complete calm. Down at the bottom she saw something move. Something brown, mottled with tan . . .

"I see one!" Laura cried. "I see a sculpin!"

She never meant to stand up. Yet somehow, in her excitement, she'd forgotten the single most important rule of canoeing. Jumping to her feet, she suddenly felt the earth move. If not the earth, at least the slippery metallic bottom surface of her own personal version of the *Titanic*.

"Aw-ooh-eee!" Laura was vaguely aware that she let out a sound more piercing than a loon ever made as the canoe rolled over.

Out spilled the fish traps, the canteen, the plastic bag containing lunch, the notebook, and Dr. Woodward. The next thing she knew she was sitting in a foot of cold water, her knees sticking out as if she were engaged in some childish game. For a few seconds she remained frozen, aware that water was creeping into every available space between fabric and skin but too stunned to do anything about it.

Then she spotted a little brown fish swimming between her legs, toward her.

"Eeek!" She scrambled to her feet, fighting not only gravity and the awkwardness of a pair of boots as supple as concrete blocks, but also the slippery lake bottom. She knew she sounded like a cartoon character who'd just spotted a mouse. But at the moment her dignity was the last of her concerns.

"Are you all right?" Dr. Woodward asked calmly. He was standing shin-deep in lake water, but otherwise dry as he worked at turning the canoe back over.

"I think so." Unless you count the mildew growing in my armpits, Laura thought miserably.

"Then help me with this. We've got to keep going."

She helped him right the canoe, then eyed it warily. The last place she wanted to be was in that boat. Still, she was about to climb back in when she noticed something black on the back of her hand. At first she thought it was some form of plant life that had mistaken her flesh for a rock.

Then she realized what it was. She let out a scream that cut into the peaceful silence of the lake like an ambulance siren.

"A *leech!*" she shrieked.

Panicked, she flicked at it with her fingers. To her horror, it didn't budge. Again and again she tried to brush it off. But the tenacious little blob refused to move.

"Get this thing off me!"

She held her left hand as far away from herself as she could, unable to look at her own pale flesh blemished by a black smear without her panic escalating.

"It's only a little one," Dr. Woodward said matter-of-factly.

"Get it off! Get it *off!*"

"It can't do any real damage —"

"Get it off me!"

Calmly Dr. Woodward reached over and pulled the leech off her hand. "There. It's gone. There's a little blood, that's all. Your hand might bleed for a while, but you'll be fine. Come on, I'll help you back into the canoe."

As he took hold of her arm she shrugged him off roughly. "I don't want to get back into that stupid canoe!" she cried. "I'd sooner die than get back in!"

"Laura, we're a good half mile from shore, and —"

"I *hate* this! I hate all of it!"

"If you'd like, we can talk about how we can —"

Laura realized that he was speaking, but his words had no meaning. She could neither hear nor see beyond her own desperation. "I haven't slept for two days. I haven't eaten recognizable food since I left New York. I haven't peed in a real toilet since I got off the airplane."

"I don't know what you were expecting, but —"

"I was expecting some basic amenities! Things like normal food, a normal bed, and a normal bathroom. I thought I'd spend a few hours a day looking at fish eggs through a microscope in a lab with piped-in music, then go for a stroll through the woods, stopping for a snack at the vending machines. I thought . . . I thought . . ."

"Perhaps if we could talk calmly about —"

"I don't *want* to talk calmly!" She could feel all her self-control slipping away. "I can't take any more! I hate reindeer sausage! I hate Mabel the moose and her disgusting nose secretions! I hate mosquitoes and leeches and even those sculpin that are so ugly they deserve to live at the bottom of a lake! Most of all, I hate the entire state of Alaska!"

Dr. Woodward nodded. "I see."

"I want to go home. Take me back — *now!*"

He opened his mouth as if he were about to speak. In the end, he clearly thought better of it. Instead, he simply shook his head slowly, drawing his lips into a thin, straight line.

Chapter Sixteen

"Here, Laura."

Out of the corner of her eye, she watched Dr. Woodward set a plate down in front of her. She was sitting at the only table in the cabin, so clumsy and rough it looked as if it had been a Cub Scout project. Pretending to be absorbed in a paperback, she barely glanced up.

Still, she couldn't help noticing that what he'd brought her looked suspiciously like breakfast. "What is it?"

"Bacon and eggs. *Chicken* eggs. There are no surprises this time. I promise."

"I *am* pretty hungry." She hesitated only a moment before picking up a fork and digging in.

The simple meal Dr. Woodward had prepared tasted surprisingly good. She'd also slept well, sinking into a deep, satisfying sleep mere seconds after her bunkmate Sandy began snoring as deeply and loudly as Papa Bear.

"This is wonderful," she commented, already halfway through the eggs.

"I figured you deserved it."

Laura just grunted.

"You'll be pleased to know I finally got

through to the airline," Dr. Woodward went on. "I made you a reservation on the one A.M. flight tomorrow night. You can change your ticket at the airport —"

"Tomorrow night?"

"Tonight's flight was booked. It's probably just as well, since it would've been tough getting you back to Anchorage in time. I'm afraid you'll have to hang around an extra day. We'll leave first thing tomorrow."

"*We?*"

"You and I."

Laura raised her eyebrows. "You're driving me back to Anchorage?"

"I don't know how else you'd get there. There are no taxis on the Kenai Peninsula. Taxidermists, yes . . ."

She didn't laugh. "Why would you go to all that trouble?"

Dr. Woodward shrugged. "As I said, there's no other way to get you to the airport. Besides, as the director of this project, it's my responsibility to get you back."

"I'm sorry you'll have to lose all that time."

His face was expressionless. "Me, too."

"Well, guess I'd better get out there. I promised Elsie we'd all help feed the baby moose this morning before we head out to the lake. Payback for letting us use the cabin." Heading toward the door, he glanced over his shoulder. "Want to come?"

"Thanks. I'll pass."

The solitude of the cabin was oddly disconcerting. Laura reminded herself that she hadn't been alone since Claire had picked her up to take her to the airport, more than forty-eight hours earlier. Sipping her coffee and appreciating the feeling of a stomach full of readily recognizable foods, she leaned back in her chair to listen. What she heard was something remarkable: silence. There were no cars, no lawn mowers, no barking dogs. Complete quiet surrounded her, broken only by the occasional rustling of leaves or the call of a loon. She'd never experienced this kind of peacefulness before.

Coffee cup in hand, she wandered outside. The sun was a pale circle hanging low in the blue-gray summer sky. The dense growth of leaves on the trees that enveloped the cabin, a vibrant shade of green, gave off a rich, fresh smell. She could also smell the dark soil of the forest floor beneath her feet. Laura lowered herself onto the edge of the porch, breathing deeply. Never before had air this clean, this crisp, entered her lungs. She inhaled greedily.

When she heard voices, she was annoyed at the intrusion. Still, she couldn't help being curious. She crossed the rocky path, noticing the scattering of wildflowers on both sides, violet and yellow and tiny clusters of white.

As she came to a clearing she found Dr. Woodward, the caretaker Elsie, Sandy, and the other two World Watch volunteers. They stood beneath a makeshift canopy, sheets of blue plastic propped up with wooden sticks like a tent in an Arabian bazaar. They were bottle-feeding a half dozen baby moose, acting as if they were having the time of their lives. The animals, gangly and wide-eyed, sucked eagerly, stepping all over each other and the feet of their meal tickets in their desperation to eat.

Dr. Woodward glanced up, immediately breaking into a wide grin. "Cute little guys, aren't they?"

Something about him reminded Laura of Evan. His boyish glee, no doubt, the unabashed pleasure he took in this simple yet wonderful task.

"Yes," she admitted, "they are."

"Want to help?"

"No, I don't think —"

"Come on, pick up a bottle. Shakespeare here is almost done with this one. Knowing him, he'll be more than ready for another round."

"Well, I —" Laura hesitated, suddenly self-conscious. Yet she could see that the moose Dr. Woodward was feeding was nearly devouring the bottle itself in an effort to get more food. Awkwardly she reached for one of the bottles standing in a cardboard box on the ground and handed it to Dr. Woodward.

"You do it," he insisted gently.

She didn't have much choice. Shakespeare had already spotted his second helping of Purina Moose Chow or whatever the *soupe du jour* was here at the preserve. He stepped over to Laura and clasped his mouth around the nipple.

"Wow! He's strong!"

Dr. Woodward laughed. "I'd hold on to that bottle, if I were you. Shakespeare isn't the type to take kindly to interruptions."

The baby moose grunted and slurped as he drank. Still shy around the animal, Laura reached over and cautiously stroked his head. "He's so bony. I expected him to be soft." Moving her fingers over his long ears, comically jutting out at two different angles, she found that parts of Shakespeare were reminiscent of a big stuffed animal, after all. "How old is he?"

"Four weeks."

"Was he born here?"

"Up on the Yukon. A team from the preserve went out in planes and picked up one moose in each set of twins it spotted. They were brought here so the people at the preserve could try out an experimental diet."

"Shakespeare seems to like their cooking." Feeling braver, she ran her hand along the soft fur of his neck. "Isn't it mean to separate a baby moose from its mother?"

Dr. Woodward shook his head. "When a mother moose gives birth to twins, one of her babies will die. She can only feed one. All the moose you see here have a twin somewhere. That short airplane ride, terrifying as it was, was their only chance for survival."

"They seem to be doing more than surviving. They look like they're thriving."

"Yup, they're a pretty hardy lot," Dr. Woodward agreed. "I guess this secret formula's doing the trick."

"It must be really fascinating to be involved in something like —" Laura stopped herself. She could feel her cheeks reddening.

"Looks like Shakespeare's all done," Dr. Woodward said, ignoring her comment. "Sure, he'd be willing to go for three, but that's not what's on the menu today. Here, I'll take that empty bottle."

"So we're finished?" Laura was surprised by the disappointment in her own voice.

"That's it. Too bad you won't be here tomorrow. Shakespeare's taken a real shine to you."

Dr. Woodward had already moved away, joining the rest of the party gathering up the empty baby bottles and tossing them back into the cardboard cartons. Laura paused, watching from the sidelines for another minute or two before she finally stepped away and retreated to the cabin, alone.

Night fell gently, lazily creeping across the sky, gradually dimming the indefatigable daylight. Lying in her loft bed that night, gazing out the window as sleep eluded her, Laura watched the darkness come. It was after midnight, she knew; it had to be for the sun to take a break. That meant she'd been lying there for more than two hours.

At first, she'd been hiding, avoiding the others. They came in from a long day's work on the lake, setting traps and hauling in fish, then bottling up the day's catch to be shipped back to Dr. Woodward's lab.

Grueling, thankless work, Laura thought. She could hear them chatting in stage whispers as they passed below her, getting ready for bed. I'm glad I opted out.

Even so, once the cabin was quiet, with all the World Watchers snuggled up in their beds — or at least their sleeping bags — she still couldn't fall asleep. She'd thought she was exhausted, tuckered out from a long day trying to keep herself occupied. But something was nagging at her. It was the feeling she'd had earlier that day when a moose named Shakespeare had sucked greedily at the bottle she held in her hand. For the first time in her life she saw herself as simply one more element of the natural world. As corny as she felt for even thinking it, she was related to that silly moose with the crooked ears and the knobby knees.

Suddenly her own problems seemed very far away — and very trivial. For the first time in nine months the fact that she was in the middle of a divorce wasn't what mattered most. There really was life beyond, she realized. Not everything revolved around the fact that her situation in life was shifting — or, more accurately, undergoing an earthquake. The turmoil *would* die down. A new equilibrium would be reached. Sooner or later the roller-coaster ride really would come to an end. And as difficult as it was for her to admit it, she had Alaska to thank for this newfound ability to put things into a more reasonable perspective.

Climbing down the ladder, out of the loft, Laura was careful not to wake the others. Solitude had already become comfortable. Having acknowledged her restlessness, accepting the fact that sleep wasn't going to come, she was anxious to head outdoors. Here in Alaska, she had yet to experience the night.

She started when she opened the cabin door and saw the shadowy outline of a large form. Bear, was her first thought. But bears didn't perch on the edge of a porch, staring out at the night.

"Dr. Woodward?" she called softly.

"Hello, Laura." He didn't sound at all surprised.

"I didn't know anyone else was awake."

"Can't sleep?"

Laura shook her head.

"You sure it's not Sandy's snoring that's keeping you awake?"

"I don't know what it is. I thought I was exhausted."

"The beauty of this place is starting to get to you." Dr. Woodward lapsed into silence. His eyes were raised toward the horizon. Laura sat down a few feet away from him, gazing in the same direction. She was already growing accustomed to the darkness. Off in the distance, she could see jagged mountain peaks topped with snow, cutting across a dark sky that seemed to go on forever.

Her companion glanced over in her direction. "It's magical, isn't it?"

"Yes, I guess it is," Laura agreed. "You know, Dr. Woodward —"

"Cam. I think it's about time, don't you?"

"Okay, then. Cam." Her sudden wave of self-consciousness passed quickly. "I was going to say that it's funny how being in a place like this, where everything exists on such a grand scale, is helping me put things in perspective." Shaking her head slowly, she added, "It's all happening exactly the way my friends said it would."

"Your friends?"

Laura nodded. "They were hoping that coming up here for a couple of weeks would help me put some of the emotional chaos of my divorce behind me."

"You're getting divorced?"

"Smack in the middle of one."

"I wish you the best. I went through all that myself recently."

"You?"

He cast her an odd look. "World Watch leaders do have a personal life, you know."

"Oh, I didn't . . . I wasn't . . . It's just that you seem so *solid*."

"What does that have to do with getting a divorce?"

"Nothing, I suppose. But up until now, I've been imagining you as someone who had his life entirely under control. I mean, you are a scientist, after all. Someone who deals in facts, not emotions. Your life should be orderly."

"It is. At least, as much as is possible with three kids."

"Three?"

"Last time I counted. How about you?"

"One. A boy, eight."

"How's he handling it?"

341

"Okay, I think. Most of the time, anyway."

"Guess you'll be glad to get back to him."

"He's at sleep-away camp for another few weeks."

"Well, then, I guess you'll be glad to get back to whatever's waiting for you. Which reminds me. We'll be leaving in just a few hours. Probably be a good idea to get a few hours sleep."

A long silence followed. Laura's heart was pounding as inside her there raged a debate as heated as any she'd ever had with herself. "Cam?" she finally said.

"Ummm?"

"I think I want to stay."

"If you're sure."

"I'm sure. And I think I owe you an apology. We got off to a bad start. It's important to me that you know I'm not usually like that."

She held her breath, expecting a barrage of recriminations. Instead, Cam Woodward nodded. "Divorce can do funny things to people."

"Yes," she agreed, raising her eyes to the lake once again, its smooth surface reflecting the moon as clearly as a mirror. "But I'm hoping some of it's finally behind me."

Over the next few days Alaska underwent a dramatic transformation in Laura's eyes. Slowly, cautiously, she allowed herself to look at her surroundings differently. Before, it had been a forbidding place where danger and discomfort lurked behind every tree, bush, and outhouse. But once she let down her guard, she began to see it was a glorious wonderland.

Trees were no longer simply trees, but proof that the world had been around for a very long time — while she was merely a short-term visitor here, one who'd do best to take advantage of a limited-time-only stay. The wildflowers vainly sunning themselves, standing tall and proud as if saying, "Look at me!" reminded her that good things could be found anywhere, if only she was willing to look. And the sheer size of everything that surrounded her, mountains and glaciers and valleys bigger than anything she'd ever imagined, assured her that in the grand scheme of things, her own problems, her ruminations about lost wedding rings and fine china and even moving on from one chapter of her life to the next, loomed large only in her own mind. She never left the cabin without her camera, determined to capture on film whatever small piece of the place's power she could.

In this environment she discovered a brand-new skill: the ability to let go. Laura found herself able to enjoy even the simplest things in a way she never had before. Bacon-and-egg breakfasts were just the beginning. The sensual side of her had been awakened. She luxuriated in the feeling of a cool breeze on her skin as she labored in the sun, freeing fish from their traps and packing them up to be shipped home. She took the time to sniff the air, never ceasing to appreciate the fragrance of the forest. She paused to pay attention to the subtlest sounds: the call of a bird, the chirping of an insect, the lapping of the lake against the shore.

She'd also come to value the people around her. The other members of World Watch, she discovered, were actually quite fascinating. Marion Slesinger, a retired librarian from Tacoma, could do things with Spam that would have impressed the Cordon Bleu. She'd traveled all over the world, doing offbeat things like climbing the Himalayas and boating up the Amazon. Hal Bottoms, an accountant, was so good at organizing information that Cam bestowed upon him the honor of keeping the daily log. Sandy North, the woman with the overly enthusiastic nasal passages, had yet to decide what she wanted to be when she grew up, even though she was pushing fifty. But her tales of the variety of jobs she'd held, related with the finesse of a stand-up comic, kept everyone in stitches. For the first time in her life Laura was a member of a cohesive group of energetic souls, committed to doing something that mattered.

Sitting behind Cam in the canoe, expertly paddling across Wolf Lake, she took a mental inventory of all the changes she'd gone through as a result of being in a world so different from her own. By this point, the sight of the back of his head, the thick, dark, wavy mane that peeked out from under the wide-brimmed green felt hat he wore on the water, was a familiar one. She watched his broad shoulders tilt one way, then the other, as he effortlessly paddled through the water.

"You know, Cam," Laura confessed, "whenever I think back to that first day, I feel really foolish. I acted like such a baby. I guess it was culture shock."

"Can't blame you. Alaska's not like any place else. It's hardly surprising that someone like you would react strongly."

" 'Someone like me'?" Laura repeated teasingly. "You mean someone whose idea of roughing it used to be drinking out of a coffee cup that didn't match its saucer?"

"I mean someone who's in the middle of a divorce. I've already told you I went through it myself. It was without a doubt the most difficult thing I've ever done." He glanced at her over his shoulder. "Just keep in mind that sooner or later this period of your life will end. You'll come through it. And you'll establish a brand-new life for yourself, one that's a lot better than the one you had before."

Laura shook her head. "I can't envision that yet. The part about the new and improved life, I mean." She squinted her eyes to close out the glaring morning light as she gazed across the lake. "It's scary, not knowing what's going to come next. For the first time in my life I have absolutely no idea where I'll be a year from now. Not even in six months."

"Actually, that could be liberating."

"Sometimes it feels that way. But there's still this uncertainty that gnaws away at me all the time. Am I going to end up living all alone in a room with cracked linoleum and peeling wallpaper, eating off a hot plate for the rest of my life? Or am I going to establish a comfortable life alone, with a double bed all to myself and kitchen cabinets full of every type of junk food I've ever craved?"

Cam laughed. "Probably neither. Who knows? Maybe you'll even get married again."

"No, thanks," she shot back.

He laughed again. "Give yourself time, Laura."

"I know that's what I need. In fact, that's partly how I ended up here. I desperately wanted some time to myself, in a situation unlike anything else I've ever been in. I wanted to take myself out of my normal routine and force myself to sit back and take stock of my life. Of myself, too."

She shook her head slowly. "You know, I've spent most of my life running around like the proverbial chicken with her head cut off. I've constantly been in a hurry — and always looking over my shoulder to see if what I was doing was okay with everybody else. First it was my parents. Then my teachers and my college professors. Finally, it was Roger.

"Now, for the first time in my life, when I look over my shoulder, there's nobody standing there. Nobody's watching me. It's an amazing feeling. The problem is, I've spent so much of my life trying to second-guess what other people wanted out of me that somewhere along the way I lost the ability to figure out what *I* want out of me."

She let out a deep sigh. "And so I developed this idea that what I needed was a block of time to ruminate. To stop thinking about the deadline for my next book and whether or not there were enough dirty clothes to do a load of laundry and what time I was supposed to pick my son up from Cub Scouts. If I could only concentrate long and hard enough, I decided, I'd have this . . . this vision. All of a sudden, through some mysterious process, I'd know exactly who Laura Briggs is. Not only know her, but also have the courage to *be* her."

Cam stopped paddling long enough to turn around and give her a long, hard look.

"You're certainly full of surprises," he said gently.

She could feel her face turning red. She hadn't meant to go on like that, pouring her heart out to someone she barely knew. But perhaps that was why it had felt so safe. She was out in the middle of nowhere with no one to hear except a few fish, a lot of mosquitoes, and more leeches than she cared to think about.

Yes, Laura insisted to herself, earnestly studying the ripples the paddle made as she plunged it into the water, that was probably all it was.

"It's hard to believe I'll be going home in just three more days. This past week and a half went by so quickly." The deep sigh Laura let out had nothing to do with the fact that she was trudging along the edge of the lake, struggling with her half of the heavy fishnet that was Cam's latest toy. "It's funny; looking back, I see that every day was pretty much the same. But each one felt so different. All the new things I did, the new things I saw . . ."

"I knew we'd turn you into a nature lover." Cam flashed her a smile. He had a particularly warm smile, Laura noted, not for the first time. It lit up his whole face, its sincerity clearly reflected in his brown eyes.

"Well, I can't deny that I still have dreams about the feather pillow I left behind," she admitted. "And as much as I hate to admit it, I miss my microwave almost as much as my friends."

"No doubt they're all waiting for you."

"Yes, I suppose they are." She paused, experiencing a wave of sadness.

It wasn't as much that she didn't want to return to her real life as that she was reluctant to abandon the new equilibrium she'd established. She loved the daily routine. The whole crew was up early for coffee and a lumberjack-sized breakfast, followed by a full day on the lake collecting fish. The evenings were just as busy: packing and labeling the day's samples, making dinner in the makeshift kitchen, eating together, then cleaning up. Afterward it was time to sit back and appreciate the feeling of being physically exhausted, inventorying the aches and pains of overworked muscles and then finally giving in to the intense craving for sleep, knowing it was all the result of having put in a good day's work. Laura had never been more relaxed . . . or invigorated.

She even looked different. She gasped when by chance she caught a rare glimpse of herself in a mirror. She hadn't even noticed it, propped up on a shelf in the small cabin that housed supplies, machinery, and a rusty metal shower stall that was something out of a grade-B women's prison movie. Instead of looking uncomfortable and out of place, the way she'd looked when she'd peered at her reflection in the window at La Guardia, she looked as if she belonged here.

Her skin was glowing, its healthy color heightened even further by the pink tinge of her cheeks and the smattering of freckles strewn across her nose. She'd taken to wearing her hair in a ponytail all the time now, which gave her the look of a spirited cheerleader. Her clothes, a mix of plaid flannel, cotton knit, and denim, had lost their stiff fresh-out-of-the-box appearance. After a week and a half her shirts were pleasantly rumpled and her jeans had conformed to the shape of her body. Somehow, the old Laura Briggs had evolved into the new Laura Briggs.

She tried to concentrate on the good points about going home. Her passion for her microwave aside, she couldn't wait to tell Claire and Julie every single detail of her trip — with a good deal of embellishment, of course. And in two more weeks, when Evan got back, it would be great fun to show him the pictures she'd taken and tell him that his mother, a woman who'd nearly had heart failure the time a frog got into their basement, had actually had a leech stuck to her hand.

But it wasn't only playing Daniel Boone that she was going to miss. It was Cam, too. Swallowing hard, she realized that whenever she felt a pang of regret over how quickly the time was going, it was partly because of him.

You've been out in the wilds too long, she scolded herself. Before she could add on half a dozen more arguments, a fat, cold drop of water snaked down the back of her shirt.

"Oh, no!" she gasped. "It's starting to rain!"

"It's just a drizzle. No big deal." Cam was already folding up the net. "Besides, I seem to remember Elsie mentioning something about an outbuilding around here. A storage shed. I'm pretty sure she said it was up this way. Here, let me help you."

He took her by the hand, helping her across the rocky terrain densely overgrown with a variety of plants. There were no paths on this part of the shore surrounding Wolf Lake. Twice she stumbled, grabbing on to his sleeve, grateful for his surefootedness.

"It's raining harder," she commented, ducking her head.

"The shed's right up here." He pulled her up a slope, then led her to the door of a small log cabin that looked as if it had been created by the same person who'd conceived the shoebox design of the main building.

Once inside, out of the rain, Laura breathed a sigh of relief. Distractedly she pushed her damp front locks off her forehead. "Safe," she announced, leaning against the wall.

There was little in the place besides some old tools, most of them rusty or broken. Still, she was glad to be out of the rain. Big drops pounded noisily against the roof. Outside, they made a soft rustling sound as they hit the broad leaves of the trees.

Cam stayed in the doorway, looking out. "It's beautiful in the rain, isn't it? A whole different world, compared to the way it feels the rest of the time."

"You certainly seem at home here." There was an undertone of admiration in her voice.

"I love it. I feel more alive when I'm up here in Alaska than anywhere else."

"You're lucky to have a place like this, one that means so much to you."

"Now you do, too."

Laura was silent for a long time. When she finally spoke, her voice was thick and odd sounding. "Cam?"

"Ummm?"

"I feel as if I really owe you a lot. I — I

want to thank you for being so patient. And, well, thanks for giving me all this. Alaska, I mean. You're right; it is a place that'll always be special to me."

"The pleasure was all mine." He turned away from the doorway and came over to her. The shed was so small that he had no place to stand except right across from her. Laura felt her heart shift into overdrive. Looking into his eyes, she had the sensation she was floating.

"I bet you say that to all your World Watch volunteers," she quipped, anxious to mask her sudden self-consciousness.

"No, Laura, I don't. I really mean it. I enjoyed sharing it all with you. This is a special place, but not everybody's capable of enjoying it. I've come up here five or six times, but having you up here this summer made this visit really special."

Suddenly the fact that she was leaving soon, that this magnificent respite from her real life was about to end, infused Laura with a burst of courage. She lifted her face to his, standing on her toes as she placed a gentle kiss on his lips.

When she drew back, she didn't know who was more surprised. But Cam hesitated only a moment before encircling her with his arms and drawing her close. This time their kiss was nothing like the shy, tentative one she'd offered. She got lost in the sensation of his mouth against hers. For a few moments everything else disappeared, everything else ceased to matter. The rain, the shed, even the fact that she was in Alaska, all faded into the background.

"That was so nice," she said, leaning her head against his shoulder.

"I've wanted to do that for a long time," he returned.

"Why didn't you?"

"I wasn't sure if you wanted me to."

She chuckled softly. "Then I'm glad I finally threw myself at you." Laura ran her fingers along his face, curious about how his beard would feel. "I like the way your face feels. I've never kissed anyone with a beard before."

"You'd better get used to it. If things go the way I hope, it'll become commonplace. That is," he added solicitously, "if that's what you want."

Laura shut her eyes, wanting to concentrate on how it felt being so close to a man — a man who made her feel good about him, a man who made her feel good about herself.

"It's what I want."

Chapter Seventeen

"Ee-e-ek! Ee-e-ek!"

With all the squealing and hugging and jumping up and down going on at the edge of La Guardia Airport's baggage claim, Laura was sure onlookers would assume she'd just been released from a Turkish prison. Two weeks wasn't very long at all, yet now that she was back on New York soil, the time she'd been apart from Julie and Claire suddenly seemed like aeons.

"You look fabulous," Claire exclaimed, giving her the once-over. "You're actually tan! And are those *freckles?*"

"You look really healthy, Laura." Julie was beaming. "Happy, too."

Claire leaned forward to peer at her more carefully. "It's just jet lag."

Laughing, Laura slung one arm around Julie, the other around Claire. "It's so good to see you guys."

"Tell us about your trip!" Julie cried. "I can't wait to hear every single detail."

Claire was nodding. "Don't leave out a thing."

"Did you see any bears?"

"How about moose? Did you see Bullwinkle?"

"As a matter of fact," said Laura, "I stayed on a moose preserve and —"

"You know, you're not the only one who had an exciting couple of weeks," Claire interrupted. "Gil and I saw each other every chance we got. We went to the beach and strolled through the surf at sunset. We had a picnic in the woods. We went roller-skating. We danced under the moonlight —"

"We can talk about that later," Julie insisted. "Right now I want to hear about Laura's trip. Did you see any dogsleds?"

"Did you see Mount McKinley?"

"Was it like *Northern Exposure*?"

"It's funny," Laura began. "It was surprisingly like —"

"Actually, this has been an important time for me, too," Julie said. "I made a major decision three days ago. To be exact, three days, four hours, and —" She glanced at her watch. "Well, I'm not exactly sure how many minutes. And I suppose it doesn't matter, except that I like to keep track of things like that. It helps me feel centered. Anyway, I . . . I decided to break up with George."

Laura gaped. "Are you serious?"

Julie nodded. "It's not that George isn't sweet and dependable and a whole list of other admirable qualities. It's just that Bobby is . . ." She was glowing like a chunk of plutonium. "Bobby is *special*. He makes me feel alive. He fills me with joy."

"You broke up with George?" Laura was still having trouble digesting that fact. She'd expected to experience culture shock upon her return, but this was ridiculous. All of a sudden the entire cast of characters was changing. In a quiet voice she added, "I always liked George."

"You'll like Bobby, too," Julie insisted.

"*I* don't," muttered Claire. "Besides, I'm not interested in the sordid details of your personal life. I want to hear about Laura's trip. Did you sleep outdoors?"

"Did you walk in the snow?"

"Did you see any Eskimos?"

"Actually," Laura said casually, "I met someone."

Time stopped. She'd muttered the magic words. Through her lips had passed the four simple syllables that were guaranteed to turn any woman at an all-female gathering into the center of attention. Claire and Julie suddenly focused on her with new intensity, forgetting about their own love lives.

"You're kidding!" Claire squealed. "Who is he?"

"Tell us everything!" Julie chimed in. "What's he like?"

"Where should I begin?" Laura was aware that a broad smile was creeping across her face. "He's smart and funny and easy to be with —"

"Does he live in Alaska?" Claire sounded alarmed.

"As a matter of fact, he lives right here on Long Island."

Julie blinked. "You had to travel five thousand miles to meet someone from Long Island?"

"Who is he? What's his name?"

"His name," said Laura, "is Cameron P. Woodward."

Julie gasped. "Dr. Woodward?"

"The *fish* guy?"

"None other."

"You had an affair with your World Watch leader?" Claire said breathlessly. "Wow!"

Julie looked doubtful. "Isn't that against the rules?"

"We're all mature, consenting adults. Well, maybe Sandy wasn't quite what you'd call mature. . . . Anyway, I didn't exactly have an affair with him."

"No sex, huh?" Claire was clearly disappointed.

"Not yet, anyway."

Julie nudged Claire with her elbow. " 'Not yet,' she says. That means she's planning to see him again."

"Go back to the beginning, Laura," Claire insisted. "Tell us everything."

"Where should I start? Do you want to

358

hear about how the sun never set before midnight? Or how I bottle-fed a four-week-old moose? Or about the time I fell into the lake and ended up with a leech stuck to my hand?"

"We want to hear the *good* parts," Claire said impatiently.

"You can tell us about that other stuff later," Julie agreed. "We want to hear about Dr. Woodward."

"Cam," Laura corrected her.

Julie and Claire looked at each other and giggled.

"Is it serious?" asked Julie.

Claire nodded knowingly. "It must be, if she's getting together with him here in the civilized world. So when are you seeing him again?"

"When can we meet him?"

"He'll be in Alaska until the end of the summer. We're planning to see each other as soon as he gets back."

"How romantic!" Julie breathed. "A reunion of two lovers, kept thousands of miles apart for weeks on end, all because of the cruel hand fate dealt them, the dedication he has to his work, the . . . the . . ."

"The return date on her airline ticket," Claire finished. "I just hope this love affair doesn't turn out to be nothing more than a summer fling."

Laura remained silent, not daring to admit that ever since she'd boarded the plane in Anchorage, her heart turning a few somersaults as she watched Cam wave good-bye, she'd been worried about the very same thing.

Laura sat at the dining-room table with the page proofs for her latest book, *Riddle-Dee-Dee,* spread out before her. Her eyes remained fixed on the typeset pages, but she was incapable of focusing enough to give her bouncy prose one final proofreading before handing it over to the printer. How could she, when every two minutes she had to look at the clock?

Tonight she was seeing Cam again. He was due in just fifteen minutes. All the details were worked out. They had an eight-o'clock dinner reservation at the Sassafras Café. Evan was spending the night at Roger's. She'd showered and shampooed and put on makeup and wielded her hair dryer — with stellar results, if she did say so herself.

She seemed to remember that a single young woman about to embark on a night on the town with a special beau was supposed to be bubbling over with gleeful anticipation. Why, then, was she so filled with anxiety? She pushed away the page proofs, finally admitting they were a lost cause.

She knew the answer. She'd been wrestling with this one for weeks now, and her ruminations had escalated over the past twenty-four hours — ever since Cam had stepped off an airplane, onto Long Island.

This was much more than a date. Seeing Cam again was a far cry from choking down five-alarm chicken with Richie and a roomful of oversexed statues. It had little in common with picking at food that looked as if it were still breathing with Kirk Brentwood, the man whose three favorite words in the English language were *me, myself,* and *I.*

On those occasions Laura had little emotional investment in how the evening proceeded. Tonight, what happened with Cam really mattered.

What was really going on between them? Was it love . . . or just a distraction? Had she merely picked out the first available man who'd come along and latched on to him, being careful to gloss over faults that would one day come back to haunt her?

During those last days in Alaska, she'd felt as if she were living in an MTV video. She and Cam did all the things lovers were supposed to do — with an Alaskan twist. Instead of a candlelight dinner, they split a fistful of beef jerky and a can of diet 7-Up out in the woods. There were no sunsets to gaze at, since the sun didn't set until way after they'd reached the point of exhaustion, so they settled for watching hordes of blackflies hovering in the sky. Instead of walking hand in hand through grassy fields, they'd slogged through layers of peat, ankle-deep in muck that sucked at them hungrily.

It had all been so unreal. What was the vague threat of bears compared with the unavoidable presence of lawyers and ex-spouses? With no telephones, no fax machines, no mail service, she and Cam had been free to concentrate on each other. In a world like that, how could she possibly be expected to separate out feelings she really had from feelings she *wished* she had?

Stay tuned, she thought ruefully. All this will be resolved soon enough. She only hoped her heart, barely patched together, could stand another pummeling.

And that wasn't all. The issue of whether or not what had started five thousand miles away would continue here on the home front was only part of what had kept her preoccupied over the summer. She'd also struggled endlessly with the question of whether or not she even wanted it to.

It was so easy being alone, and a comfortable rhythm had developed between Evan and her. At camp he'd acquired much more than seventy-nine mosquito bites and an impressive repertoire of disgusting songs. He'd also gained self-assurance. He seemed happier than she'd ever seen him. With minor exceptions, conflict and compromise were no longer a part of Laura's life.

But whenever Cam called, the part of her that thrived on being alone was silenced. Their last long-distance conversation, two nights earlier, had been no exception.

"I can't wait to see you," he told her. "It's hard to believe that in forty-eight hours, I'll be back home. The first thing I want to do is take you out on a real date."

"A date?" It was midnight in Laura's neck of the woods. A call so late, from such a faraway place, cloaked the two of them in intimacy. She sat in bed, wearing her sexiest nightgown, wishing desperately she were curled up with more than the telephone.

"That's right. I'm talking about a good old-fashioned traditional date. You know, flowers, a candlelight dinner, a movie . . . and a good-night kiss."

"It sounds wonderful."

"I want to court you," Cam insisted. "I want to win your heart. I want to hold your hand and whisper sweet nothings and cover the back of your neck with wet kisses."

Maybe it was his words, maybe it was the deep, sexy voice in which they were delivered, but goose bumps sprang up all over Laura's body.

Yet now that the time for their reunion had arrived, Laura could scarcely remember the yearning she'd felt lying in bed with a phone at her ear and lust in her heart. She was too busy trying to calm herself down.

When the telephone rang at twelve minutes to seven, her stomach lurched.

"He's not coming," she muttered, racing to the phone. "He changed his mind. He decided he prefers redheads. He joined a cult."

She was wondering whether to feel dismayed or relieved when she discovered it wasn't Cam on the other end of the line, but Roger.

"What is it?" she demanded, hardly in the mood for sparring with her ex.

"Evan needs his Roller Blades. We're coming over to get them."

"*Now?*"

"We'll be there in five minutes."

Laura hesitated. "I'm expecting someone."

"We'll be out in two minutes. I promise."

Laura tried to suppress her annoyance. Roger had managed to put her in a no-win situation — again. If she said no, her poor son would be deprived of the use of his skates. If she said yes, she risked breaking rule number one on the list of dating do's and don'ts: Never introduce your ex-husband and your boyfriend on the first date.

Please be late, she silently begged Cam. Standing at the window, staring out into the street, she hoped he'd get lost on his way over — not enough to put a damper on the evening, but enough to keep an unsavory encounter from ruining an event she'd been agonizing over for six weeks.

When she heard the sound of tires crunching in the driveway, Laura moaned.

Seconds later Evan came bounding joyfully into the house, exuding energy and enthusiasm. Her husband's entrance was a sharp contrast. Roger was so good at playing the role of wet blanket she was surprised he didn't leave a trail of water on the floor.

She struggled to remain calm. "This really isn't a very good time."

"We'll be fast. Get your skates, Ev."

Roger glanced at Laura, an odd look on his face as he gave her the once-over. She could feel her cheeks reddening. Makeup, freshly washed hair, the silver earrings he'd given her for their fifth anniversary . . . Was it obvious that it was all for another man? She chafed under his steady gaze, feeling as if, in addition to her favorite string of beads, a scarlet *A* decorated her chest.

"Did you get your hair cut?" he finally asked.

"Da-a-ad, my Roller Blades aren't in the closet."

Reminding herself that at one time she'd been considered someone who worked well under pressure, Laura willed herself to remember where she'd last seen Ev's Roller Blades. The clock was ticking, the danger was mounting, her panic was escalating. . . .

"Under the bed!" she cried, having just had something as close to a vision as possible without having been nominated for sainthood. She took the stairs two at a time, nearly decking her son as she zoomed into his room. Falling to her knees, she stuck her arm under the bed. Socks, an empty Cheerios box, comic books . . . Eureka! Never in her life had she been so happy to make contact with round pieces of molded plastic.

"Voilà!" she announced, dragging the Roller Blades out from under the bed. She brushed off the colony of dust bunnies. "Now off with you, pumpkin. Have fun skating."

"Oh, Dad's not taking me skating until tomorrow," Evan said offhandedly. "Right now we're going to Friendly's for dinner."

Seconds after Roger's car had disappeared down the street, a second set of tires crunched in the driveway. Standing by the window, Laura watched Cam get out of his car and stroll toward the front door, the requisite bouquet of flowers in hand. An alarming thought entered her mind.

I want this man.

Quickly she banished it from her consciousness. That was no way to embark on a first official date. Instead, she tried looking at him objectively.

Here in the civilized world, she observed, Cameron Woodward looked considerably more conventional. Thanks to a haircut and a beard trimming, he'd lost the look of someone who'd been raised by wolves. Instead, he looked like a college professor. Of course, he was also dressed differently, having traded jeans for khakis, a plaid flannel shirt for striped cotton with a button-down collar, and hiking boots for loafers.

Yet there was something that hadn't changed. And that was the way Laura felt all fluttery inside when she looked at him.

Flinging open the front door, she was overcome with shyness.

"Hi." She could feel her cheeks turn what was no doubt a garish shade of pink.

"Hi." Cam hesitated before leaning forward and planting a chaste kiss on her cheek. "Brought you these."

"Thank you." As she reached over to take the flowers her hand brushed against his. He stepped toward her, putting his arms around her and pulling her close.

"I missed you, Laura."

"I missed you, too."

Once she was in his arms, she realized just how much. The sensations of being with him were still new, yet already they were threatening to become addictive. The way his broad shoulders felt beneath her fingertips, firm and curved a certain way. The softness of his beard against her cheek. The barely perceptible scent of his skin.

"I've been a nervous wreck over the prospect of seeing you again," she confessed.

"Why?"

"I was afraid it would be different."

"Is it?"

"No," she said softly, raising her face to his. "It's exactly the same."

Late that evening, as the rest of the world either slept or stubbornly prolonged the day with the help of the late-night talk-show hosts, Laura and Cam sat curled up together on the couch. She longed to lose herself in the complete bliss of being in his arms, her head tucked between his shoulder and his soft beard. But an ambivalence nagged at her.

While she yearned to take their growing level of intimacy one step further, she was terrified. For one thing, the possibility of rejection was overwhelming. Rationally she knew it was unlikely Cam would burst out laughing upon being confronted with a naked Laura Briggs. Even so, she was hardly immune to the inferiority complexes inflicted on the female half of the population by the Claudia Schiffers and Kate Mosses of the world.

Then there was the issue of performance — a word that invariably made Laura cringe. It conjured up images of an act that required bangles, a tambourine, and a backup band. Yet looking back at her own experience, she realized the label wasn't entirely inappropriate. During her fifteen years of marriage, she'd routinely been scrutinized by a critic who sat in the front row taking notes, handing down reviews so negative the whole production was nearly shut down.

Almost as if he'd been listening in on her ruminations, Cam suddenly said, "I've thought a lot about what it would be like to make love to you."

"I've thought about it, too," said Laura. "But I have a confession to make. I'm as jittery as if I were the lead in the school play on opening night."

"You're already my favorite star," he assured her, stroking her cheek lightly with one finger. "You can do no wrong."

"Oh, Cam," she breathed, "I lo—"

She stopped herself, nervously searching his face.

"Do you mean it?" asked Cam, his voice gentle.

"Yes," she said without hesitation.

"Then say it."

"I love you."

"I love you, Laura."

Going into the bedroom a few minutes later with what was left of the Chianti from dinner, she found Cam lying in bed waiting for her, his clothes off, his head propped up by his bent arm. In the flickering light of the candles burning on the night table, his eyes looked more intense than ever, their dark brown color contrasting dramatically with the light reflected in them. The expression on his face was earnest. Deep shadows played over his face, emphasizing the strength of his features.

"I brought the rest of the wine," she told him, suddenly shy. Turning away, she pulled off her clothes with abrupt, jerky movements, not wanting to give him the opportunity to see her faults. She crossed the room quickly, sliding into bed. Without looking at him, she pulled the sheets up over her. The sensation of his thigh brushing against hers made her jump.

"What's the matter?" he asked in a gentle voice.

"Nothing," she replied too quickly. "I'm just cold."

"Cold . . . or unsure?"

370

"Well, I . . ." She couldn't lie to him, she realized. Feeling her cheeks redden, she told him, "It's been a while."

"I want to look at you."

Laura swallowed hard. "Okay."

Slowly Cam pulled back the sheets. Laura held her breath — partly in an attempt at flattening her stomach, but even more as a means of bracing herself against whatever criticisms might be about to fly her way.

"You're beautiful," he breathed. Already he was running his hand lightly across her nipple, down her stomach, inside her thigh.

She realized at that moment that she truly trusted him. *Trust:* a word she'd thought would never be part of her vocabulary again, at least with respect to a man. Yet her gut reaction was that she was safe with him. She'd felt it in Alaska, where she'd not only entrusted him with her very survival, but poured out her heart to him as well. She'd felt it that evening over dinner, as she told him about all the fears that had plagued her since she'd left behind the romance of Alaska and come back to real life.

Lying there beside him, gazing into his eyes, she felt all her nervousness slip away. She could feel herself letting go, allowing that feeling of complete trust to be her guide. For the first time she could remember, Laura was able to concentrate on the man beside her instead of watching herself, monitoring every move she made . . . trying to view herself through someone else's eyes.

She closed her eyes as he kissed her cheek, her forehead, her neck, her ear. His kisses, first light, became more ardent. Eagerly she reached for him, suddenly craving the sensation of his skin. So warm, so smooth, so surprisingly soft . . . Marveling over every sensation, she traced the line of his shoulder, his neck, his jawline. Boldly she ran her fingers down his back and across his buttocks. Through it all, she was struck by the fact that this all felt so new, as if she were with a man for the first time.

Had it ever been this good with Roger? Laura wondered. Had she ever been so aware of the smallest sensation: the softness of the hair at the back of his neck, the tenderness of the skin near his throat? How wonderful it was simply to enjoy the sweetness of each moment . . . and to make pleasing herself as much a priority as pleasing her partner. She reveled in the feeling of her breasts pushing against the hardness of his chest, the delight of running her tongue along the delicate ridge of his ear.

Had she ever before felt this close to someone? So much at ease, so much at peace . . . so happy?

She could feel her entire body opening up

to him. She pulled him close, no longer able to be apart from him. Clasping his body tightly against hers, she could hear her own breaths, quick and sharp, and throaty sounds that reminded her of a cat's purr. All the clichés she'd ever come across in a romance novel came back to her. Surrender. Release. Ecstasy. She was experiencing them all.

He slid inside her, his eyes locked in hers. As she and Cam moved together, their bodies so completely and so magnificently in sync, Laura was struck by the fact that what they were doing truly deserved to be called "making love."

Chapter Eighteen

"Today we're taking a departure from our usual format," says Robin Leach, clasping a microphone in his hand as he stares directly into the camera. "Instead of visiting with the Rich and Famous, we're here with lovely Laura Briggs at her lovely home in scenic Clover Hollow, located on the lovely north shore of Long Island."

He takes a few steps toward the back door, his eyes never wavering from the camera. "Laura is a bright star in the great publishing sky, the author of more than a dozen successful books for children. Yet it's not her career that's responsible for her being our guest today. It's the unnaturally high level of satisfaction and contentment she's achieved. Laura's got it all — at least she thinks she does. And so we're retitling our show. Welcome to Lifestyles of the Deliriously Happy . . . !"

The shrill ring of the telephone catapulted Laura out of her reverie. Her fantasy wasn't the only thing she was reluctant to abandon. The idea of climbing out of the warm bathtub in which she lay, surrounded by more bubbles than she'd ever seen outside a Doris Day movie, was even worse than giving up her starring role in a delicious daydream.

But figuring it was probably Cam calling, Laura leaped out of her sudsy sanctuary. Quickly she wrapped herself in a towel, then dove for the phone. Standing in the middle of her bedroom, watching drops of water slide off her skin and onto the carpet, she felt like the heroine in a movie, risking cold and flu and permanent rug stains in the name of love.

"Hello, Laura. It's Roger."

Suddenly she felt like a cold, wet puppy cowering between two trash cans.

"We need to talk. I'll be right over."

Her heart sank. Even her half hour of self-administered hydrotherapy was of no use in warding off the instant tensing of her muscles.

It couldn't possibly be good news, she thought, giving herself a cursory drying off, then pulling on jeans and a T-shirt.

Sitting at the kitchen table with Roger, her stomach in knots as she waited for a bomb to drop, was painfully familiar. Yet even in the midst of the familiar tableau, Laura recognized that something was different.

He no longer belonged here. He was out of place among the coffeepot, the canisters, Evan's paintings stuck on the refrigerator with magnets shaped like Hershey's Miniatures. He was no longer a part of her life. The time for her to be sitting opposite him, waiting for the answer to the question *What now?* had passed.

Slowly her ties to him were unraveling. With each week that went by, with each day, she grew more and more distant from him. She became less the wife. She even became less the ex-wife. Instead, she got that much closer to being simply Laura Briggs.

With that realization, Laura felt the roller-coaster car soar upward. And the sensation of the wind in her face was exhilarating.

Still, something was up. Roger sat a few feet away, his expression earnest. The bomb he was carrying, she suspected, was of nuclear proportions.

Like any good general, he wasted no time.

"I want to buy out your share of the house."

Laura blinked, taking a few seconds to absorb what he'd just said.

In a calm voice she asked, "Can you afford it?"

He shifted his eyes downward, away from her gaze. Suddenly he'd developed a new fascination with the pepper shaker.

"I'm not buying it alone."

Laura swallowed hard . . . and waited.

"Melanie and I are moving in together."

She stared at him, a thousand different thoughts flitting through her head. I can't let this happen! screamed a voice only she could hear. It's *my* house! Why should he live in it? Why should that woman live in it?

She also heard the voices of her friends. "I told you so," Claire told her in the fantasy that played through her head, her voice hard with disdain. "That's so typical. Men can't bear to be on their own, so they grab the first welcoming pair of arms that comes along."

She could imagine Julie's sympathetic clucking as well. "Oh, Laura. You must be terribly hurt. But keep in mind it's only because he's so needy. The man's still in shock."

Yet through her initial jolt pushed another thought, one that was much more rational. Shedding the house would be almost as liberating as shedding Roger.

It was true that part of her longed for the familiarity of the place she'd lived in for close to a decade. It was also the only home Evan had ever known. The idea of staying put, madonna and child in their natural domain, seemed like the path of least resistance.

Yet staying here would tie her to the past. This, after all, had been *their* house. First

Roger and Laura, then baby made three. The further she got away from playing the role of the heavy in a rather lopsided triangle, the more enticing the idea of shedding all the trappings of her past became. If she really was going to close the book on this chapter of her life, it made sense for the next chapter to have a completely different setting.

The daydream she'd played over and over in her head, of packing up her things and walking out, was about to become real. She imagined herself outside in the yard, peeking into the window. From there she watched Melanie Plympton, living in this house. She saw her sleeping in her bedroom, showering in her bathroom, making coffee in this very kitchen. Laura expected to be jealous. Instead, the feeling that rushed over her was more along the lines of glee.

It's as if she's stepping into my old life, she thought. Melanie's moving into *my* house with *my* husband . . . and, at least part of the time, *my* kid. She probably thinks she's getting a great deal. But along with the Italian bathroom tile that's perfectly aligned only because I nearly got into a fistfight with the contractor, and the miniblinds that got sent back to the store three times before they were finally right, she's inheriting all the dissatisfactions and disappointments that I put up with all those years.

Melanie, Laura thought, trying not to look smug, you want my old life? You've got it. Let's just see if it makes you any less miserable than it made me.

After Roger left, one more ramification of his sudden and completely unexpected announcement hit Laura. If he was moving in, *she* was moving *out*.

Sitting at the kitchen table, looking around at what up until this moment she'd thought of as "her kitchen," an old fantasy of where her life would end up as a result of having made the decision to leave Roger came back to haunt her. She saw herself in a tiny apartment — a walk-up above a deli, or worse yet, in someone's basement. Her new kitchen would have cracked, yellowed linoleum, faded wallpaper featuring dancing fruits and vegetables, an eternally dripping faucet, and a refrigerator that dated from the Great Depression, its freezer possessing a special snow-making feature.

The longer she sat at the kitchen table, the more colorful — and disastrous — the image of her nightmare apartment became. The shower would produce hot water only on alternate Tuesdays. Cockroaches would regularly hold conventions in her pantry. A motorcycle gang would move into the apartment next door. . . .

When the phone rang, she raced to answer it. She hoped it was Cam, calling to scare away the demons. Instead it was Gil Plympton, suggesting they get together for lunch again — same time, same greasy spoon. She was glad for the chance to have someone to commiserate with — especially someone who was a party to all that was going on. A sympathetic ear was precisely what she needed to counteract the terrifying sensation that the rug was being pulled out from under her — not only the rug, but also the floor, the basement, and the foundation.

Driving to the Starlight Diner, she glowered at each house she passed. Why were *those* people able to live in nice, comfortable homes — homes with linen closets and crawl spaces and water heaters — while she was about to find herself without an address?

It wasn't fair. All her life she'd been a respectable citizen who toed the line, filed her taxes on time, paid her parking tickets the very same day she found them tucked into her windshield wipers, and even used tongs to pick out her bagels and rolls at the supermarket. Yet it was she, not they, who was being forced to move in with the cockroach motorcycle gang and the antique kitchen appliances.

Hurrying inside, Laura spotted Gil sitting at the same table as last time. He looked considerably more cheerful as he nursed a cup of coffee and perused the encyclopedia of selections that constituted the Starlight's menu.

"Hey!" he greeted her, standing and kissing her on the cheek. "Thanks for coming."

"It's good to see you, Gil." Sliding into the booth, she studied him carefully. There was a light in his eyes she knew hadn't been there the last time she'd seen him. "You look great."

"I feel great. In fact, I've never been better." He was so animated that Laura suspected the cup of coffee in front of him wasn't his first.

"No one has a right to feel this good on a Tuesday," she countered, pulling off her jacket.

"These days I find myself feeling good on Tuesdays, Thursdays, Sunday nights, Monday mornings. . . ." Wearing a lopsided grin that gave him a charming Mr. Potato Head look, he shrugged. "Laura, I've got to thank you for introducing me to Claire."

Ah. So it wasn't the caffeine. "You're welcome, but it's not as if I invited you both over for the home version of *Love Connection*."

"I'm convinced it was some kind of cosmic thing," Gil said, his eyes rising up toward that great dating service in the sky. Suddenly he leaned forward. "Has she said anything to you about me?"

"Oh, you've come up in the conversation once or twice." Laura didn't dare let on that she already knew his favorite color, his favorite song, his favorite TV show, and what kind of underwear he wore. "It sounds like you two are really hitting it off."

"Why not? I'd be a fool not to fall for a woman like Claire." A wide smile crept slowly across his face. "She's amazing. She's soft, she's sensitive, she's loving —"

"Claire?" Laura blinked. "*My* Claire?"

"— so giving, so caring —"

"Wait. We're talking about Claire Nielsen, right? A woman who was no doubt a Roller Derby queen in a previous life?"

Gil had a faraway look, as if he were barely listening. Then his smile changed. "Did I mention that she's also a very . . . *passionate* woman?"

"Ah-h-h," Laura said knowingly. "Now I'm beginning to understand."

"Don't get me wrong," Gil protested. "The fact that she's able to express herself so openly during our most intimate moments is only a small part of our relationship. She and I click on a much grander scale. My psychic says our auras are so perfectly matched that they mesh like the pieces of a jigsaw puzzle."

"Gil, the last thing I want to do is rain on your parade." Laura spoke slowly, choosing her words with care. "But let me play devil's advocate for a moment. Isn't it possible — just *possible*, mind you — that your interest in Claire is at least partially rooted in the fact that you're feeling kind of . . . hurt right now? You're still in shock, recovering from what happened with Melanie, and —"

"Don't mention that woman's name to me." The expression on Gil's face suddenly matched that of the most despicable character in Evan's most violent video game.

"See that? The fact that you're so angry makes me think you haven't yet gotten over her."

She was expecting a string of protests. Instead, Gil lowered his eyes. "You're right. Sometimes I manage to forget her — when I'm with Claire, mostly. But other times . . ."

When he looked at Laura, there was fire in his eyes. "But I've figured out what I need to do."

Laura shrugged to show she didn't understand.

"I have to get revenge."

"Revenge?" Just hearing the word made her think of Claire. "What does revenge have to do with anything?"

"In the cosmic scheme of things, a lot."

She was tempted to make a joke about Gil having spent too much time with his astrologist. But his steely look told her this was no laughing matter.

"There's got to be some way of getting back at Melanie," Gil insisted.

"You mean like trampling her flower beds?"

"Nothing that tame."

"How about . . . I don't know, running a bulldozer through her pots?"

"Not even close."

Laura was growing uneasy. "Surely you're not thinking of turning her in to the IRS."

"Now you're thinking along the right lines.

"I've thought of turning the kids against her," he said, staring off into the distance. "But that would hurt them. She *is* their mother, after all. No, they've already been victimized enough."

"Tell me about it," Laura interjected.

"I've thought about trying to break up her relationship with Roger."

"Hah! Believe me, being with him is punishment enough."

"They're all good ideas, but not great ideas. Still, there's got to be a way —"

"But what's the point?" asked Laura. "Why is revenge so important?"

Gil blinked. "For closure, of course."

"Closure," she repeated, not understanding.

"I need a way to get past my divorce, Laura. I have to let go. That chapter of my life is over. It's time to move on. The question is, how?

"And then I figured it out. I need a way of evening up the score. Of doing to Melanie what she did to me. If only I could make her suffer a fraction of the pain I've suffered, if somehow she, too, could be forced to deal with the same feelings of loss . . ."

"Do you really think that would make you feel better?" Laura asked earnestly.

"The idea is not necessarily to feel better. It's to feel you've come full circle. That there's finally an ending to what's been going on for so long."

"You're not getting that from your relationship with Claire?"

"Claire is wonderful. She's easily the best thing to come out of my divorce. But this has nothing to do with her. This is between Melanie and me."

Laura took a deep breath. "I'm sitting here wondering if I dare fill you in on the latest gossip about the Clog Lady."

"What now?"

"This morning Roger came over to announce that he wants to buy me out of our house."

"And?"

Laura took a deep breath. "He wants to move back in . . . with Melanie."

"They're moving in together?"

The vehemence with which he summarized the recitation she'd just given made her recoil, hoping he'd remember not to shoot the messenger.

"That's what Roger told me."

He was staring straight ahead, his eyes glazed, his hands clenched into fists — even the one still clutching his coffee cup. "I'll kill him."

"Be my guest," said Laura. "But please wait until he's taken out the life-insurance policy my lawyer's insisting on."

He didn't laugh.

"Look, Gil," she said, her voice much softer. She sympathized with the turmoil — and the pain — he was so clearly experiencing. "I know this is hard to take. It's as obvious to me as it is to you that Roger and Melanie are acting in a way that's thoughtless, impulsive . . . and just plain stupid. They hardly know each other. They're gambling not only with their own lives, but with the lives of our kids.

"But the bottom line is that whatever cockamamie schemes Roger and Melanie come up with from here on in are not our problem. The kids are our concern, of course, but it's inevitable that all of us divorced folks end up dealing with the fall-out from our ex-spouses' follies. You said yourself that you've got to let go of the past, to accept the fact that your life with Melanie is over. And that you really are better off without her."

Gil's eyes were clouded. "My head hears what you're saying. But my heart wants to crawl into bed and pull the covers all the way up."

"Trust me, Gil. You'll get through this."

"She ripped my family apart! Oh, sure, I get to see my kids every second weekend. And on Wednesday nights I'm allowed to take them out to McDonald's. But I miss seeing them in the morning before school and watching TV with them in the evening and . . . and just doing normal, everyday stuff. . . ." His voice got thicker and thicker until it trailed off.

"Look on the bright side," said Laura, doing her best to sound encouraging. "You're building a new life. You've already found someone new. You've got" — she paused, still incredulous — "Claire."

"I know." He swallowed hard. "She told me you've met somebody, too."

Laura nodded. "I'm crazy about him. I feel as if I'm finally figuring out what love is supposed to feel like, twenty-five years after everybody else."

"Better late than never, I suppose." Gil stared thoughtfully into space. "I wonder if I ever really loved Melanie."

"Of course you wonder. Everybody does. When your marriage falls apart, you can't help thinking it must not have been built on a very strong foundation. You especially have to be suspicious if you want to believe you'll ever get a second chance to fall in love again and start a new relationship — this time one that lasts."

"I guess you're right. Besides, my astrologer's been telling me all along to stay clear of Pisces." Gil laughed, a little embarrassed chuckle. "How'd you get so smart, anyway?"

"Easy," Laura replied, waving her hand in the air. "I write fiction. I just make up this stuff as I go along."

"Somehow I don't think it's that simple. Hey, this new guy of yours . . . ?"

"Cam?"

"Cam. Would you give him a message for me?"

"Sure."

"Tell him he's very lucky."

"Do me a favor, Gil," she returned, smiling. "Pass that same message on to Claire."

Laura wasn't surprised to see new faces at the support group the following Wednesday night, nor that some of the familiar ones were absent. Sitting in the circle, making small talk with Carolyn as she waited for the evening to get under way, she wondered what it was about the group that kept her coming.

It wasn't that she needed a diversion. Since Cam had come into her life, she'd spent nearly every spare moment she could with him. Nor was it merely that the weekly update of other people's ups and downs was much more engrossing than the Wednesday-night lineup of sitcoms. She couldn't attribute her loyalty simply to habit, either.

What kept her hooked in was the feeling that she was still on that roller coaster. True, the ride was easing up. The highs weren't quite as exhilarating, the lows not as devastating. As for the parts in between, they continued to set her heart pounding . . . but at least these days she was able to catch her breath. Even so, her car was still very much in motion — and she was still struggling to hold on.

Glancing around the circle as she tuned out Carolyn's discourse on creative ways to doctor up Campbell's Soup for One, Laura found comfort in both the familiar faces and the new ones. One of the new faces was particularly intriguing. Bright green eyes shone out from an abundance of wrinkles as the woman who was easily the oldest in the room joked with Ken. Laura could have sworn she was flirting.

"I see we got some new members tonight," Phyllis began in her gravelly voice. "Why don't you introduce yourselves? We'll start with this lady over here."

The silver-haired woman glanced up. Her chair was pushed up so closely against

Ken's that they sat thigh to thigh. "My name's Daisy."

"Hello, Daisy. Welcome. Before we get started, I gotta tell you rule number one."

"What's that?"

"We don't touch. Is there anything you'd like to say to help us all get to know you?"

"Let's see. How about I just left my husband after fifty-two years of marriage?"

"Why?"

"He was getting old. Acting old, I mean. He didn't want to go out anymore. He wouldn't do any of the things we used to enjoy together. Bowling, golf, skydiving . . ." Daisy waved her hand in the air. "He kept giving me these cock-and-bull stories, claiming he was developing a whole list of aches and pains." She rolled her eyes. "First this hurt him, then that hurt him."

The look on Phyllis's face was one of incredulity. "Isn't it possible he was telling the truth?"

"Naw. He was just making excuses. His doctor told me he was fit as a fiddle. I figure you're only as old as you feel. And Clyde started acting *old*."

"I'm sure you'll find plenty of support, Daisy. There are so many seniors groups doing interesting things. Weekend trips, volunteer work —"

"Hah! I got no time for that stuff. I'm too busy taking tango lessons with my new boyfriend. He's a younger man, only sixty-three." There was a devilish twinkle in Daisy's eyes. "You should see him dip."

After a few more members introduced themselves, Phyllis looked around the circle. "So what's new? Who's got something interesting happening in their life? If it's of a sexual nature, so much the better."

Laura raised her hand. "Something's come up in my life. A few days ago my ex-husband told me he wants to buy me out of our house." She glanced around the circle, hoping that making eye contact with a sympathetic audience would boost her flagging confidence. "He's moving in with his new girlfriend."

"Men," Elaine muttered. "They're despicable."

"Hey, there's nothing despicable about that," Ken countered. "The guy's just getting on with his life."

"I think the issue here isn't what Laura's ex is doing," Carolyn interjected. "It's how Laura feels about it."

"How *do* you feel about it?" asked Phyllis.

"I feel . . . I feel . . ." Through Laura's mind raced all the emotions that Roger's announcement had elicited. "Mostly I feel afraid."

"I hear ya," commented Jake, Ken's sidekick. "The day I moved out of my house was one of the worst days of my life. And the

391

whole time I was packing up my stuff, my wife was standing there, watching. *Gloating.*"

"Hmph," said Elaine. "You're lucky she gave you a chance to pack. I took all my ex's junk, threw it into the car, and hauled it off to the Salvation Army." With a gleam in her eye, she added, "If you guys hurry, you can pick up Giorgio Armani suits for ten bucks."

"Things between my husband and me are a little more civilized," Laura said. "Don't get me wrong; there's still plenty of anger. But I keep telling myself that this move is probably for the best."

"Any kids?" asked Carolyn.

Laura nodded. "A boy, eight."

"So how come you're not staying in the house with the kid?" Elaine demanded. "Isn't that the way it's usually done?"

"That's what happened in my divorce," said Jake. "My wife got the house, the kids, and the Volvo station wagon. I got the beat-up Honda and the child-support payments." He shook his head. "And she's the one who had the affair."

"My husband and I are pretty good about each spending time with our son," said Laura. "I'm glad Evan'll still be able to spend part of the time in what's always been his house."

"Let me get this straight," Elaine interjected. "Some new woman is moving into *your* house, with *your* husband and *your* kid. . . . How about you and me get together for pistol practice sometime?"

"She probably feels this new woman is welcome to her old life," Daisy interjected.

"That's exactly how I feel," Laura agreed. "You know, it's amazing how many times I've imagined this exact scenario. When I was married, packing up and moving out was one of my favorite fantasies. And now it's really happening."

"You know the old saying," Carolyn observed. " 'Be careful what you wish for because you just might get it.' "

"But I want it!" Laura insisted. "I really do. I'm anxious to get on with my life. I feel as if the rest of it is a wonderful adventure, lying ahead of me. It's as if I'm sitting in front of a blank page, with a pen in my hand, and I'm free to write anything I want on it."

"That's a positive way to approach all this," said Phyllis, nodding approvingly. "Divorce is a time of endings. Painful endings. Sometimes endings that are abrupt or unexpected . . . or unwanted. But it's important to keep in mind that it's also a time of beginnings."

"Maybe you'll meet somebody nice," said Daisy. "Make a new life for yourself and your son. Create a new family."

"I have met someone," Laura admitted, suddenly shy. "To tell you the truth, I can't quite believe I'm letting down my guard. Trusting him, wanting to be with him more than anything else in the world . . . I'm doing all the things that, six months ago, I swore I'd never even consider. I was so determined to protect myself. Committed to never being vulnerable again. Yet here I am, jumping in headfirst. . . ." She laughed self-consciously. "I keep wondering if I'm crazy."

"Not crazy," Daisy said softly. "Just human."

"Besides," said Ken, "hopefully you learned something the first time around."

"Yeah," Jake agreed. "If you keep your eyes open, you won't make the same mistakes."

Laura just nodded, not wanting to admit that while she'd had the exact same thought, deep down she didn't quite believe, given her track record, that she was someone who could be trusted with the responsibility of masterminding her own life.

Chapter Nineteen

"Think Mary Poppins," Laura muttered to herself, lifting a shopping bag of homemade goodies out of the trunk of her car. "Better yet: Mrs. Doubtfire."

It wasn't that she didn't have experience with children. Eight years with Evan, after all, had provided her with an impressive array of skills, everything from wiping noses and making the perfect peanut-butter-and-jelly sandwich to intelligently discussing the *Wayne's World* films and holding her own in video games.

But meeting Cam's kids was different. She wasn't trying to be their mother. Or their friend. Not even their au pair. As a matter of fact, her relationship with them wasn't one that she'd read, heard, or even thought much about. She was their father's girlfriend, a role that in the movies was invariably played by a gum-chewing actress with a Marilyn Monroe body and a bubble of bleached-blond hair.

At least she didn't fit that image. Dressed in jeans and her funkiest T-shirt, she looked more like a camp counselor. Even so, the fact that no amount of shopping at The Gap could override was that she was an outsider. And what she was attempting to do was impose herself on a close-knit group united by blood, common history, and its own glossary of terms for bathroom functions.

She wanted them to like her. She was *desperate* to have them like her. And that, she knew, put her in a difficult position. The danger of trying too hard — with disastrous results — loomed forbiddingly.

Warily Laura eyed the bag of treats she'd brought. She'd spent the entire day before in the kitchen. For weeks now she'd listened carefully as Cam talked lovingly about his kids, recording their likes and dislikes in the recipe-card file in her brain. For their initial meeting, she'd baked gingerbread for Cam's oldest boy, fifteen-year-old Simon. She'd even packed a carton of heavy cream, hoping to impress the Woodward clan by inviting them to jump head-first into decadence. For the others she made Toll House cookies — half with nuts, for twelve-year-old Zach; half without, for seven-year-old Emily. As an afterthought she stuck half a dozen copies of her books into the bag. If she couldn't win them over, maybe Gertrude and Lenny could.

You can't buy their love, an internal voice had warned.

No, came the response, but you can fill them so full of sugar and dairy fat that the idea of tolerating you seems palatable.

Laura was both dreading this first meeting and looking forward to it. She and Cam had decided that their relationship felt firm enough to assume it was going to continue for some time. So that meant including the junior members of each of their families.

"I'll go first," Laura had offered, wishing she were as brave as she sounded.

In a way, bringing Evan along would have made it easier. He was certainly good at providing distraction. Still, in their lengthy discussion, she and Cam had agreed that it made sense to let his kids get used to her before she brought in her sidekick. As for Evan, she decided, it couldn't hurt to give him more time before forcing him to grapple with the fact that his mom had a new man in her life. His turn would come soon enough.

Laura lugged her hostess gift toward the front door, sneaking a peek through the living room window. There was one more aspect of this visit that made her apprehensive. She'd never seen Cam's house before. Being with him in Alaska had been one thing. And that same sense of unreality — the feeling that this man, this magnificent man, had dropped from the sky, into her life — lingered as she saw him at her house, at restaurants in her area, at the movie theaters near her.

Now she was about to take her first peek into the real life of Dr. Cameron P. Woodward. His house, after all, was his nest. His kingdom. A reflection of his true self, the one reserved for the hours behind closed doors. What if she hated what she saw? What if his home revealed a side of him she found repugnant? Maybe the decorating theme was Early Pretentious or he left plastic slipcovers on the couch, cellophane on the lampshades, those annoying warning tags still attached to the throw pillows. Or maybe he'd surrounded himself with tackiness that would set her teeth on edge. Paintings of Elvis on velvet. Wooden magazine racks with appliqués of the Confederate flag. Shag carpeting.

And what if he *acted* different? So far, Laura had seen Cam in the roles of scientist and lover. Both were important, but they were only part of the whole man. What about Cam Woodward, father? What if he turned out to be too strict or too indulgent or guilty of a host of other parental offenses?

What if, upon seeing this contender for Mr. Right in his natural habitat, she wanted nothing more than to flee?

That might happen, she told herself, ringing the doorbell. But sooner or later you've got to find out.

The front door was opened not by Cam,

but by a little girl with big brown eyes and long, dark brown hair. She was dressed in jeans, cowboy boots, and a ruffled pink blouse.

"Hello," Laura said gently. "You must be Emily. I'm Laura."

"I'm not supposed to talk to strangers."

"That's a very good rule. But I'm not a stranger. I'm a friend of your dad's —"

"Daddy told me not to let people I don't know into the house." Emily studied Laura solemnly.

"Didn't your daddy tell you I was coming over today?" Laura's cholesterol-laden shopping bag was getting heavy.

"Are you the giraffe lady?"

Giraffe lady, giraffe lady . . . Suddenly Laura understood. "Gertrude Giraffe? Yes, that's me. I write books for children about Ger—"

"How do I *know* it's you?"

"Emily, who's at the door?" Cam appeared behind the little girl. His expression softened the moment he spotted Laura. "Hi. I thought I heard your voice."

"She *says* she's the giraffe lady," Emily explained, eyeing Laura warily. "But she couldn't prove it."

"This is Laura, Emily. She's my new friend, the one I told you about." Cam opened the door, giving her an apologetic look. "Come on in, giraffe lady."

Walking inside, Laura smiled at Emily. "I brought chocolate-chip cookies. They're made the way you like them, without nuts."

Emily glanced up at her, suddenly shy. "Is that how Gertrude Giraffe likes them, too?"

Cam's house, Laura was relieved to see, was as comfortable and easy as he was. There was an abundance of natural wood, showing up in the highly polished floors, the window frames, the simple furniture. Splashes of color dotted each room, mostly in the form of Mexican folk art. The various pieces had been picked up on field trips when he was a graduate student, long before his Alaska days, he explained as he gave her a quick tour. Colorful yarn paintings and *molas* hung on the walls, and pillows covered in bright Guatemalan fabrics were nestled into the corner of the couch. Scattered throughout were bits and pieces from his work: fossils framed and hung on the walls, photographs of past field crews, the occasional animal skull.

"This is the boys' room," Cam announced after leading her upstairs. "Simon and Zach are up here, watching the game."

"Hello," she said stiffly, sticking her head in the doorway. She smiled again, feeling like a contestant in the Miss America Pageant. "Nice to meet you."

The two boys, one sprawled on the floor,

the other draped across one of the two single beds, grunted without glancing up. Like their sister, they had Cam's dark eyes and hair.

"Want to see my room?" Emily asked.

Laura hadn't even been aware she was behind her.

"Sure, Emily. I'd love to."

Emily slipped her hand into Laura's. "I'll introduce you to my dolls. But you have to be very, very quiet. They're sleeping."

That's one for female solidarity, thought Laura, heading toward the pink-and-lavender wonderland that was Emily's room. If only I'd once been with the Miami Dolphins, maybe I'd be able to win over the whole lot.

"It's good to have you here," Cam told her once they were alone in the kitchen.

When he wrapped his arms around her, she clung to him tightly. "This is hard. How am I doing?"

"You're doing great. Besides, you don't have to knock yourself out trying to impress my kids."

"I want them to like me."

"They'll like you. Once they get to know you, how could they not?"

Laura sighed. "I'm not sure it's that simple. But I came prepared. Just give me a few minutes with my electric beater."

"What have you got in there?" Cam peered into her shopping bag.

"Enough sweets for an all-you-can-eat dessert bar. You don't mind if I make myself at home, do you?"

"Be my guest. In the meantime I'll just run out for a minute. We're out of milk. Besides," Cam said, giving her a peck on the cheek, "having me out of the way will give you a chance to get to know the kids."

Emily walked into the kitchen just as Laura had finished whipping the cream. The little girl stopped in her tracks, watching with wide eyes as she ran her finger through it, then took a lick.

"You can't use that bowl," Emily announced firmly.

"I'm sure your dad wouldn't mind."

"But it's not yours! You can't use it!"

"Emily," Laura said patiently, "I'm just mixing some whipped cream in it. I promise that as soon as I'm done —"

"It's Nathan's bowl."

"You can assure Nathan I'm always very careful with other people's things."

"But Nathan's not a people," Emily protested. "He's a snake."

Laura looked down into the clear glass bowl, filled with whipped cream that only seconds before had been so appetizing. Given the way Emily was staring at her, she suspected that her face had turned green.

"It doesn't have his germs on it or anything," Emily reassured her. "He doesn't eat out of it."

Laura swallowed hard. "Uh, exactly what does Nathan use the bowl for?"

"To take baths. Before it was Nathan's bathtub, Daddy used it in his lab at school. Do you want to know what he kept in it then?"

Laura stared at her finger, still partially covered with whipped cream. "Maybe you'd better not tell me."

"Oooh, look! Here's Nathan now! Oscar, too."

"Oscar?" Laura repeated weakly.

"They're named after hot dogs," Simon explained. He walked into the kitchen with a snake coiled around his neck. Its narrow head was next to his cheek, its tongue darting out every few seconds. His brother, Zach, wore a matching reptile.

"Aren't they cute?" Emily reached for Simon's snake. "I want to hold Nathan."

"It's my turn," Simon insisted.

"Can I hold yours, then?" Emily had turned to Zach. *"Please?"*

"Let's let Laura hold him," said Zach.

Suddenly three pairs of eyes were on Laura. Five, if she counted Nathan and Oscar's beady black ones.

"Gee, I really don't think —"

"Please!" Emily pleaded, clapping her hands and jumping up and down.

"They can't hurt you," said Simon. "They're only babies."

"Exactly what kind of, uh, snakes are Nathan and Oscar?" Laura was stalling, anxiously hoping Cam would appear.

"They're boas."

"Boas? As in boa constrictors?"

"Yes," said Emily. "Please hold one!"

Laura swallowed hard. "I've never held a snake before. I wouldn't want to hurt them."

"You won't," Emily assured her. "Just sit down and I'll put Nathan on you. He really likes crawling around on people. Just hold out your hands like this. . . . There!"

Laura sat very still, her mouth stretched into a stiff smile as she watched the baby boa slither around her wrist, through her fingers, onto her lap.

"See? He likes you!" Emily announced triumphantly.

Looking up and finding all three of Cam's children watching her with approval, Laura felt it was almost — *almost* — worth it.

At least one thing's becoming increasingly clear, she thought, bracing herself as Nathan began crawling up her forearm. This must be love.

"Hello, Appleton Realty? I'm calling about your ad in today's paper for the two-bedroom in Clover Hollow. . . ."

Laura doodled nervously on the classified

ads page of the Sunday paper as she listened to the nameless, faceless real estate agent at the other end of the line describe an apartment that sounded ideal. Brand-new kitchen, washer and dryer, gas and electric included . . .

"By the way, how many people is this for?" the agent asked, cutting into her own spiel.

"Two."

"A husband and wife?"

"No, my son and me."

"Son?" Her tone suddenly had an icy edge. "How old?"

"Almost nine."

"Sorry. The landlord specified no children."

Before Laura had a chance to protest, the line went dead. Laura's doodles went from decorative curlicues to angry slashes that spiked out from the classified ad that began *Too Good to Be True!*

Laura rubbed her eyes. Her fifth phone call . . . her fifth rejection. She was learning quickly that when it came to renting an apartment, having a child was even worse than having a bad credit rating.

It's not enough that I'm moving out of the only home I've known for ten years, she mused, letting out a long, frustrated sigh. Now I'm finding that even the wretched apartment I've been imagining in my worst nightmares is beyond my reach.

Disgusted, Laura threw down her pen. She stood up, intending to fill her cup from the coffeepot. But she walked past it, and instead wandered through the house.

She was seeing it the way it had looked the first time she'd seen it. She and Roger had been living in Manhattan then. One balmy Sunday afternoon in early May, on a whim she'd opened the *Times* to the real estate section, running down the Long Island column. She wasn't a serious shopper. In fact, she practically dared one of the ads to catch her eye.

YOUNG COUPLE'S DREAM. The catchy headline made her heart flip-flop. She held her breath as she read on. Two-bedroom starter house, one and a half baths, charming garden . . . Even the price sounded just right.

Her thoughts were racing as she glanced over at Roger, stretched out on the couch in the living room of their one-bedroom apartment. When she'd lived there alone, she'd luxuriated in all that space. But ever since he'd moved in, a curse had befallen it: every day, those three and a half rooms grew smaller and smaller.

Perhaps her new interest in real estate was a result of the *Twilight Zone*-esque manner in which the walls of the apartment were closing in on her. Or maybe it was just that she'd recently turned thirty. At any rate, the nesting urge had hit her hard. All of a sudden she caught herself fantasizing about vegetable gardens, kitchens with breakfast nooks, and big bay windows just the right size for spray-painting snowflakes.

The biological urge to choose wallpaper had apparently bypassed her husband.

"A house?" Roger had said the first time she'd brought it up, his face twisting into a scowl. "You have no idea what being a homeowner entails. Overflowing cesspools. Freezing pipes. Leaks. Termites. Real estate taxes." Shuddering, he added, "People like us are much better off renting."

And so she'd thought long and hard before finally daring to say, "Roger, listen to this." Immediately she launched into an animated reading of the four-line ad.

Much to her amazement, he responded with, "Sounds interesting. Want to check it out?"

Perhaps it was because it was a warm spring day, with crocuses just beginning to peek their purple and yellow heads out of the ground. Maybe it was the way the sunlight streamed in through the kitchen window, like a scene out of a Windex commercial. Or maybe once Roger realized that owning his own home was a real possibility, even he was unable to resist.

The house itself was charming. From the start it seemed to invite them in, throwing its arms around them and snuggling up close. Now, walking slowly through the dining room, Laura remembered the flowered wallpaper that had covered the walls, big yellow cabbage roses splashed across a pale blue background.

The print made her cringe. Her mind had clicked away, trying to decide which neutral shade of paint would work best in that room. Even so, looking at that wallpaper that day, she'd appreciated the fact that this house had been some other couple's refuge, a place that long before had been decorated to fit their taste. Now it was her turn. The maze of rooms waited for her and Roger to put their imprint on it, to make it into *their* home.

There was another reason for wanting to buy a house. She'd imagined that changing their status from apartment-renting city slickers to a suburban couple who owned a snow shovel would bring Roger and her closer. Perhaps if they had something to build on, a dream to work on together . . . That same image of all those families, snug and happy in their warm houses as Laura the little girl peeked through their windows, gave her hope. Maybe all they needed to be a real family was a real home.

Yet thinking back over the years as she wandered into the living room, running her fingers along the nubby fabric of the drapes, she understood that even though she'd worked long and hard to make this place feel like home, it never had. There was too much unrest here, too much unhappiness. The feeling that things weren't quite right couldn't be covered up with paint or carpeting or a brand-new layer of wallpaper.

No, Laura realized, sinking onto the couch, taking a good hard look around, this wasn't her home. And just as she'd told Gil, it was time to let go.

She sat still a few minutes longer, trying to conjure up some feelings of regret, to dredge up something positive from her past, some sweet memory to cling to. When she realized her efforts were futile, she pulled herself up and headed back to the kitchen.

"Hello, North Shore Realty? I'm calling about your ad. . . ."

"Just wait till you see this place, Ev. You're going to love it."

Laura threw open the door of the apartment on which she'd just signed a one-year lease. Finding it had been a tremendous relief, after the others she'd seen on her quest for a new residence. Her worst nightmare about where she and her son might end up turned out to be quite plausible, she discovered once she began making the rounds.

The first apartment she'd looked at wasn't technically a basement; it only acted like one. It was on the first floor of a small apartment building — one that happened to be way below street level. Looking out the living-room window, she couldn't see the cars she heard whooshing by; she saw only piles of dirt.

The second one was considered a three-bedroom. What that meant, in real estate–ese, was a maze of tiny rooms, each of which was just big enough to squeeze in a single bed. Aside from the fact that it presented a true decorating challenge — especially for someone who owned dressers — she couldn't help noticing that three or four mousetraps had been discreetly pushed under kitchen cabinets. She decided to keep looking.

Numbers three and four weren't much better. By the time the real estate agent begrudgingly brought her to the last address on her list, Laura was close to tears. And so she was relieved when she found herself on the second floor of a private house, a perfectly symmetrical arrangement of four square rooms. Not only were there two bathrooms, wall-to-wall carpeting, and a kitchen that looked as if it was actually meant to be used, there were no signs of any furry roommates. After what she'd been through, this one seemed nothing short of Barbie's Dream House.

Walking around the empty rooms, she'd instantly begun imagining her own things filling the bare space. The couch would fit right in there, the Matisse poster would be perfect on that wall. . . . If she squinted just so, Laura could actually picture herself living there.

When she saw the room that would be Evan's, she was sold. It was big and bright, with two good-sized windows. There were also built-in bookshelves, enough to store a good portion of his toys, books, and space-age video equipment.

Now, looking at the apartment through her son's eyes, she wasn't so certain. On her first trip, she hadn't noticed that the bathroom door didn't quite close. Or that the window in her bedroom had a tiny crack in the glass. Here a scratch, there a dent . . . Still, she glossed over it all as she went from room to room — manically chattering away. She drew Evan's attention to all the good points, giving him more of a hard sell than any self-respecting real estate agent would have dared.

"So," she finally asked, ready to burst, "how do you like it?"

Evan shrugged. "It's okay, I guess."

"Okay? Is that all?" Laura's spirits

drooped. "But your room is so big. And there's all that sunlight, and all those shelves. . . ."

"I like our house better."

"Oh, Ev, you'll still live in the house part of the time. But when you're with me, we'll be here. We'll make this our home."

Please like it! she was tempted to exclaim, throwing herself at his size-four feet. Say it's all right. Tell me I did the right thing.

But she remained silent as she watched him shuffle from room to room, cloaked in gloom. She swallowed her misery, wondering if she could get out of the lease. After all, they hadn't moved in yet. Maybe if she pleaded or argued or threatened to hire a lawyer . . .

"Hey, Mom! Check this out!"

Laura was snapped out of her anxious reverie by Evan's cry. He actually sounded excited — in a *positive* way.

"Look over there! Out that window!"

"What? Where?" Craning her neck to see over the kitchen sink, all Laura saw was her car, parked in the driveway. That, and the man who lived downstairs, ambling down the front walk, toward the street.

"You didn't tell me this place had a dog!"

"I had no idea —"

But Evan had already taken off, bounding down the stairs, out of the house.

"Hey, mister! 'S that your dog? Can I play with him? Can I walk him? What's his name?"

Laura watched as a black-and-white spotted mongrel came loping toward Evan, a tennis ball in his mouth. Their friendship was instantaneous. Walt Disney himself couldn't have done a better job of creating the scene: a boy and a dog, two pals who acted as if they'd spent their entire lives searching for each other.

She'd locked up the apartment and was heading toward the car when Evan came running over.

"Are we leaving?"

"For now."

"But we'll be back, right?" Evan asked anxiously.

"As soon as we can pack up our stuff."

"Mr. Ross said I can walk Spooner anytime I want," Evan told her, scrambling into the backseat. "He's a really smart dog. He can sit and beg and roll over . . . and boy, can he play ball!"

"He sounds like quite a pup."

Evan turned around as she drove away, looking back at the house longingly. "That place is pretty neat."

"I'm glad you like it."

"I think my room at your house is bigger than my room at Dad's."

"I think you're right."

He was silent for a while before saying, "Hey, Mom?"

Laura peeked at him through the rearview mirror. "Hmm?"

"I think it's gonna be okay, you and me living here."

"You know, Evan," she said sincerely, catching his eye in the mirror, "I think so, too."

Chapter Twenty

"Have you got it? I got it. Higher, now more to the right . . . watch that corner. . . ."

With a loud bang, the edge of the love seat crashed against the corner of the house. Laura cringed, wondering which was worse: smashing the arm of the couch or taking a few shingles off what was about to become her new home.

"How bad is it?"

"Not bad at all," Cam assured her. He was at the rear, bearing most of the weight as the two of them struggled to lug up to the second floor a piece of furniture clearly never intended to ascend a flight of stairs. "Just a little tear. You can hardly see it."

"I'd been thinking about slipcovers, anyway."

"Hey, if this is the worst casualty of the move, you'll be lucky."

"Lucky," Laura muttered, hoisting the love seat with every last bit of energy she had. All her muscles ached, some she'd never dreamed she possessed. She was covered in sweat, though the temperature on this November afternoon was just hovering above thirty-two degrees. Still, it was warm enough to keep the persistent drizzle from freezing. The only thing worse than moving all her worldly possessions in the rain, she told herself, would have been moving them in the snow.

At least the truck's almost empty, she thought, trudging across the lawn one more time. A few more trips and we'll be done.

"I'll get those lamps." Cam hopped into the Ryder truck.

"Great. I'll finish off these toys."

Laura lifted a pile of games out of the back of the truck. Firmly she clutched Monopoly, the foundation of a leaning tower of kiddie entertainment. Balanced on top were Candyland, Life, and half a dozen others. At the pinnacle were a pair of five-hundred-piece jigsaw puzzles, one a picture of Snoopy having a meaningful dialogue with Woodstock, the other the four Teenage Mutant Ninja Turtles doing serious damage to their arteries by devouring a pepperoni-and-sausage pizza. She shuffled toward the house, marveling over how heavy all those cardboard boxes filled with nothing more than plastic pieces and bits of paper were.

Cam reached the door before she did. Juggling two living room lamps, he propped it open for her. "Are you sure you can manage?"

"Yup. I've got it." Moving in slow motion, she began her ascent.

"Here, let me help you —"

"No, really," she insisted, feeling her way with her toe. "I'm fine."

She'd just reached the second-floor landing and was about to bend over to deposit her load on the floor when she felt it shifting. Still clutching Monopoly, she watched in horror as the entire stack of cardboard boxes tumbled down the stairs, their contents flying. A thousand cardboard puzzle pieces mixed with pink and blue plastic cars, Candyland cards, Chinese checkers marbles, and dice.

"Oh, no!" Laura moaned.

Dropping Monopoly on the floor, she sank to her knees. A jolt of pain shot through her. One of the Monopoly pieces, a tiny silver top hat, was embedded in her knee. She covered her face with her hands, succumbing to a crying jag she realized had been floating close to the surface all day. Then she felt Cam's arms encircling her, the softness of his beard against her cheek, and she opened her eyes.

Chaos surrounded her. Boxes were piled up everywhere. They covered the kitchen counters. They lined the walls of every room — even the bathroom. She'd packed in a hurry, tossing things into whatever box they fit into. Towels were stashed with mixing bowls, bottles of shampoo with Play-Doh, cookbooks with pillowcases. At the time her method had seemed to make sense. But here at the other end of the one-mile trek to her new home, she realized the contents of each box would need to be sorted out before being tucked away.

As if that task weren't daunting enough, the apartment itself had a long way to go before it would be livable. The bathroom and the kitchen needed a scrubbing. No curtains were hung, no pictures, not even a calendar. Her furniture looked much too big, and much too plentiful, for the compact rooms. Besides, none of the pieces were in quite the right place. Lamps had been set down unceremoniously on the floor of the hallway, end tables were clustered in Evan's room. Somehow the kitchen table had ended up in the living room.

Yet the turmoil of the apartment, Laura knew, was only partly responsible for reducing her to tears. Nor could she blame the stress of leaving the familiarity of her house and moving into a place where she couldn't even find the electric sockets. Three days earlier, the paperwork on her divorce had been finalized.

She'd expected to be matter-of-fact about it. Instead, she was overcome with a dozen different emotions, ranging from relief to sadness to fear. She tried to push them inside, to busy herself by throwing out a decade's worth of telephone bills and finishing off an entire freezer full of food.

Now, suddenly, all the emotions she'd tried to ignore were rising to the surface, jumbled together. She realized that while she'd tried to believe that the pieces of the puzzle that constituted her life were starting to fit together, in reality they were no more organized than the Snoopy-and-Woodstock puzzle at the bottom of the stairs.

"I can't do this," she gasped, her voice muffled by Cam's shoulder.

"Can't do what?"

"I can't live here. This doesn't feel like home. No place feels like home. I don't live anywhere. I don't have a life. Everything that was familiar is gone."

Cam kissed her gently on top of her head. "You must be exhausted. We've been lugging stuff all day. Tell you what. You go lie down, and I'll do something about dinner."

"I can't lie down," she protested. "There's too much to do."

"Just twenty minutes," said Cam. Glancing around, he added, "Now all we have to do is find the bed."

Laura hadn't realized just how tired she was until she lay down and closed her eyes. Almost immediately her aching muscles melted into the mattress. Succumbing to the thick sleep that wrapped her in its insistent arms was a relief.

When she opened her eyes, afternoon had

been replaced by night. Unfamiliar shadows painted the walls. She lay still for a long time, listening to the strange sounds that invaded the room: the clicking of the radiators, the dog downstairs barking, a train whistle in the distance. Peering at her watch, she saw she'd been asleep for almost two hours.

"Cam?" she said sleepily, shuffling out of the bedroom. "Are you still here?"

She heard him bustling around in the kitchen. She wandered in, bracing herself for the disconcerting dishevelment she expected to find. She stood in the doorway, amazed.

Instead of looking like a warehouse, the kitchen was a kitchen. The cardboard cartons were gone. In their place stood the kitchen table, with all four chairs pushed underneath. The small appliances had been unpacked and lined up on the counters. One of the cabinet doors was open, and she could see dishes and cups stacked neatly inside. Even the refrigerator magnets were in place.

The table was covered with a tablecloth, set for dinner. In addition to two place settings there was a pair of candles, their tiny flames oddly cheerful. There was even a bunch of flowers, stuck into an NFL glass that had been a freebie from a local gas station.

Cam stood at the counter, wrestling with cartons of Chinese take-out food. Glancing over his shoulder, he smiled at her warmly.

"If it isn't Sleeping Beauty. I was just about to wake you with a kiss. Did you have a good rest?"

"Mm-hmm. Goodness, the elves have been busy. Or should I say Prince Charming?"

"You might want to hold off on characterizing me as charming until you've sampled my taste in Chinese takeout. I order from the hot-and-spicy column."

Laura crossed the room. Going up behind him, she put her arms around his waist and leaned her cheek against his back. "You've thought of everything. You're even going to feed me."

He turned around and hugged her hard.

"I'm sorry about before," she said. "I guess I kind of lost it."

"Who could blame you? I know how hard this was."

"You made it a lot easier."

"I'm glad. Now, enough mushy stuff," Cam insisted. "I don't know about you, but I'm starved. Carting around furniture is hard work." He ushered her toward the table. "Chopsticks or fork?"

"The world looks considerably brighter now that I've got some prawns in me," Laura observed a few minutes later. She

421

glanced around the room. "Wow. You really whipped this place into shape."

Cam shrugged. "I did my best. You'll probably want to redo some of it. But at least the shampoo's in the bathroom and the silverware's in the kitchen."

"It's starting to look like a place where human beings reside. I don't know how you found the energy to do all this."

"This move didn't wear me out as much as it did you. I didn't have your emotional investment in it."

She reached across the table and took his hand. "Thanks, Cam. This really means a lot to me."

"All I did was unpack a few boxes."

"No, you did a lot more. You saw that I was having a hard time and you bailed me out. I'm not used to having anyone do that for me."

"Hey, I'm trying to be one of the good guys. You've spent enough of your life having showdowns with the bad guys."

Looking around, he added, "But you're right about this apartment starting to shape up. You found a good place for yourself and your son, Laura."

"I wonder how long it's going to take me to get used to it," she mused.

"I predict a week, tops."

"You know," Laura mused, glancing around, "I remember reading this story when I was a kid. It was kind of corny, but for some reason it stuck with me all these years. It was about a pioneer family that traveled across the country in a covered wagon, a mother and a father and a couple of kids. They suffered terrible hardships, but managed to build a sod house in the middle of the prairie. Even though they were barely getting by, the mother of the family insisted on making a real Christmas. She said, 'A house isn't a home until you've spent your first Christmas in it.' "

Cam looked confused. "Are you saying this apartment won't feel like home until Christmas?"

"Sort of. Actually, I have my own theory." Still clasping his hand, she led him toward the bedroom. "Come on. I'll show you my idea of how to break in a new place."

Laura stood at the kitchen window, washing breakfast dishes and gazing out at a view that was still foreign to her. Through the black, leafless branches, stark as a skeleton, she watched a pale sun struggling to brighten up a gray November sky.

The dreariness of the day was a dramatic contrast to her lighthearted mood. Happily she puttered around the kitchen. Having just dropped Evan at school, she was now free to luxuriate in the still-new feeling of having the apartment all to herself. When a favorite oldie from the seventies came on the radio, she couldn't resist singing along.

Slowly she was coming to grips with the idea that *this* was home. She was full of plans and ideas of how to turn these four rooms into a real home. Her mental shopping list kept growing: shelf paper for the kitchen cabinets, a new rug for the bathroom, new sheets for her bed so she could finally throw away the ones that had been hers and Roger's. Even more, she dreamed up extra touches she wanted to add to her life, little niceties she'd never bothered with before, like indulging in a mud pack once a week and keeping a bottle of champagne in her refrigerator.

Suddenly Laura chuckled. She'd just realized, as she rinsed out her coffee mug, that she was smiling. Cam had crept into her thoughts. He'd been so helpful, getting her settled in. Considerate as well. He truly understood how hard this move had been. She reached over and with a sudsy hand touched the bouquet of flowers he'd picked up for her on moving day.

My goodness, she thought, incredulous. I'm happy. I'm really happy. I've made the move. I've left my house behind . . . along with that part of my life. It's over. I actually managed to get through it.

Her son had also survived. Evan was excited about living in a new place, and full

424

of plans of his own. He'd taken great pains to tape his collection of posters up on the walls of his room, becoming so absorbed in getting them just right that he actually chose wrestling with a roll of masking tape over watching television. He'd also gone through the list of his school friends to decide who should sleep over which weekend and help break in his new home.

Laura sensed that Evan's enthusiasm went beyond the novelty of having a brandnew space to nest in. He, too, had experienced a sense of closure. The period of transition was over. He had to have been dreading this move — if not actually fearing it. It had finally come to pass. He now had two separate homes: Mom's house, Dad's house. This was what divorce looked like. Not only was it probably less painful than he'd imagined, it may have actually been a relief.

When the telephone rang, Laura dashed into the living room. She was anxious to feel that even though she was living in a new place, the rest of the world hadn't forgotten her.

"Hi, Laura. I hope I'm not calling at a bad time —"

"Julie!" Laura cried. "It's so good to hear your voice."

"I figured it was about time I gave you a call at your new home. I can't wait to see it. How's it shaping up?"

"Well . . ." Laura looked around at the pile of boxes that was still pushed against the living-room wall. The couch was covered with sheets, washcloths, and enough towels for her to open her own Turkish bath. Every single item needed to be refolded and stacked up in the linen closet. Jammed between the chairs and the end table were framed posters and photographs, a hammer and a box of nails. Several piles of toys, most of which Evan had outgrown long ago but nevertheless refused to part with, decorated the corner.

With a deep sigh Laura admitted, "Right now this apartment looks like it's been done in Early Warehouse. But I'm full of plans."

"How exciting! Your very own place. Are you ready for visitors yet?"

Laura's eyes rested on her unhung art collection. "How well can you handle yourself on a stepladder?"

Julie brought along a tin of Scottish shortbread cookies and a brand-new teakettle. She also personally brightened up the apartment with the day's fashion statement, a garden medley that included a full skirt of flowered fabric, a T-shirt with daisies all over it, and a silk rose worn behind her ear.

Laura bustled around the kitchen, chattering away as she filled the kettle and arranged the cookies on a serving tray. For a moment she felt as if she were seven years old again, having her teddy bear and her Betsy Wetsy doll over for tea. Reaching up into the cabinet above the stove for the Earl Grey tea bags, she was again struck by the realization that living on her own was going to be just fine.

"This place is *you*, Laura," Julie insisted, sitting down at the kitchen table. "Or at least it will be by the time you get done with it." Giving her the once-over, she added, "And you look radiant."

"You look good, too, Julie." Laura paused for a moment, trying to remember where she'd put her fine china. When she realized she had yet to unpack that box, she settled for coffee mugs. "I take it things are going well in the romance department?"

"Oh, Laura," Julie said with a sigh, "Bobby is so wonderful. Things with him are great. Perfect, in fact, if I dare use that word."

Peering over at her, Laura saw that her words didn't quite match up with the earnest expression on her face. "I keep waiting for the *but*."

Laughing self-consciously, Julie admitted, "There is one thing."

"What's that?" Laura asked, expecting some deep, dark revelation.

So she was disappointed when Julie replied, "Claire."

"Is that all? Giving you a hard time again, is she?" Laura waved her hand in the air dismissively. "Whatever it was she said, Julie, don't listen to her. She's just . . . well, she's just being Claire."

"It's not anything in particular she's said," Julie hastened to explain. "It's not even that she's constantly on my case. You know that 'don't say I didn't warn you' attitude of hers."

"Only too well."

"It's that . . ." Julie's voice trailed off as she carefully arranged her flowered skirt over her knees. "It's that I can't help wondering if I'm making a terrible mistake. Or to be more accurate, if I'm repeating Claire's mistake."

She looked at Laura with large, soulful eyes. "Claire's my friend, for heaven's sake. She's not some . . . some psychopath, or some princess, or some unreasonable person. If she couldn't manage to make a go of it with Bobby, what on earth makes me believe I could do any better?"

Laura was taken aback by Julie's words. They sounded all too familiar. Nodding understandingly, she said, "That's the problem with getting involved with someone else's ex. You can't help wondering if there's something you're missing — something his ex-wife found out once good old Mr. Right let down his guard."

"That's part of it. There's also the question of whether *I'm* capable of doing it right." Julie shook her head. "I'm beginning to think the world would be a better place if we left matchmaking up to computers. We humans certainly haven't had a very impressive track record."

Laura stopped fussing with tea bags and dessert plates and sat down opposite Julie. "Has something happened to precipitate all this rumination? Or is this just an ongoing existential crisis?"

Julie cast her eyes downward. "Last night Bobby asked me to move in with him."

"That's wonderful!" Laura exclaimed. When she saw that Julie's face was still tense, she asked, "Isn't it?"

"I don't know if it's wonderful or not. My heart says, 'Go for it.' But my head says, 'Whoa.' Frankly, I'm not sure which organ to listen to."

Julie's words hit Laura close to home. She'd mulled over those same thoughts, wrestled with the same doubts. Perhaps it really was impossible. Maybe men and women weren't meant to pair off, two by two. Those animals on the ark didn't do much together besides produce a few baby animals. No one expected them to spend the rest of their lives together, refinancing mortgages and agreeing on where to go for vacation. Why should human animals be any different?

Yet the urge to find a mate, a better half, was as strong in people as it was in every other species. Even though she'd sworn off men forever, determined not to bring on any more heartaches, headaches, or dents in her savings account, only minutes before she'd been thinking of Cam, feeling all warm and tingly inside.

"You're not the only one," she finally said.

"You, too?" Julie perked up.

"You'd think it would be easier, now that we've got all these years under our belts," said Laura. "You'd think experience would count for something."

"It seemed so simple when I was young," Julie said thoughtfully. "I slipped in and out of relationships as easily as I slipped in and out of different pairs of shoes." With a shrug she added, "Now that I fully under-stand the cost of making a mistake, I'm gun-shy."

"Still, we should be better at making choices now," Laura mused. "If nothing else, we've got more information."

Julie frowned. "I don't follow."

"Look at it this way. When two people are young and getting married for the first time, they're both chock-full of potential. That's exhilarating . . . but dangerous. Neither of them is fully formed yet, so neither of them really knows what they're getting. That was certainly the case with Roger and me. I married what I thought he was going to become.

"But the second time around, after a couple more decades have gone by, it's pretty safe to assume that what you see is what you get. There shouldn't be that many surprises down the road."

"I think Bobby's a different person now compared to who he was when he was with Claire. They were both so young. Not even out of school yet." Julie thought for a few moments. "Still, I keep wondering if I'm a fool for thinking things could go better for us."

"But people pair off in different combinations all the time," Laura interjected.

"Right . . . and how many of those couplings actually work out?" Julie shook her head. "Sometimes I think I'm guilty of incredible arrogance. I mean, who do I think I am? What makes me think I could possibly succeed where so many before me have failed?"

"Maybe it's just the chemistry of different pairings," Laura suggested. "Look at Roger. He and I couldn't make a go of it. But maybe he and Melanie will do better."

Julie blinked. "Do you really believe that?"

"Not for a minute. But he's hardly the best

example," Laura was quick to add. "For one thing, I'm biased. For another thing, I don't think Roger learned anything from the failure of our own marriage."

"Does anyone?"

"I like to think so." She thought hard for a few seconds. "I believe I did."

"Do you think you made a good choice with Cam? Are things still good?"

There was that smile again, creeping slowly across Laura's face. She could feel it. "Things are great. But that doesn't mean I don't have my doubts. About myself, about buying in to the bit about 'boy meets girl and finds happy ending' . . . certainly about the wisdom of ever again believing that business about 'forever.' "

"That's a dangerous word," Julie observed. "It should be banished from the English language."

"Well, diamonds are forever, or so they say. Tattoos, too. Maybe the notion of permanence should simply be banished from marriage ceremonies. I always thought that part about 'till death do us part' was a little macabre, anyway."

"How about 'For better or for worse, in sickness and in health, for as long as we can both sit together in the front seat of the car for more than fifteen minutes without arguing'?"

Laura laughed, then quickly grew serious

432

again. "So what are you going to do? Are you going to move in with Bobby?"

Julie gave her a rueful look. "Give me two minutes with a crystal ball. Then I'll give you my answer."

Chapter Twenty-one

"I'm amazed at how quickly I'm getting used to this apartment," Laura mused, tucking her toes underneath Cam's legs and snuggling a little closer.

The two of them were lingering under the covers late on a Sunday morning in December. A tumultuous rainstorm raged outside, providing the perfect excuse. She peeked out from under the down comforter she'd splurged on, her idea of the ideal housewarming present to herself, to survey the room.

Having all her furniture in place helped, as did the sampling of artifacts from her forty-odd years, trinkets picked up along the way since childhood. Evidence of the important people in her life stood on top of her dresser; half a dozen photographs in colorful frames of Evan, her parents, Julie and Claire, and other friends. Her computer was set up in one corner, with a copy of each book she'd written displayed on a shelf next to it. Her signature was even on the walls: she'd finally gotten the pictures hung.

"This place definitely has your stamp on it," Cam commented, his fingers twisting a lock of her hair as he surveyed the room.

"Remember a couple of weekends ago, when Evan was at Roger's and I spent the whole weekend at your house? When I came back here that Sunday night, I felt as if I'd come home."

She expected Cam to burst forth with an exclamation of joy over the fact that after so many months of uncertainty, she'd at last found a comfortable place. But he said nothing. Instead, he simply continued with the rhythmic stroking of her hair.

Trying to keep her tone light, Laura said, "I figured you'd be happy for me."

During the long silence that followed, she could practically hear the wheels turning in his brain.

"Of course I'm glad you found an apartment you're pleased with." He ran his fingertips along her shoulder and down her arm. "But at the risk of sounding selfish, I have to admit I'm kind of hoping you don't get *too* settled into this new life of yours."

"You mean the swinging life of Bachelorette Number One?"

He didn't laugh. "Look, I know it's important for you to find a new equilibrium, Laura. You need a breathing period, a chance to be by yourself. It's just that I've been thinking that one of these days you might want to — you know."

"Might want to what?" Cam had never

been so evasive before.

"Move in with me."

It took her a few seconds to digest what he'd said. "Are you looking for a way of lowering your monthly mortgage payments?" she finally asked. "Or are you looking for somebody to mate with for life?"

"B."

"If that's your idea of a proposal, Dr. Woodward," said Laura, her voice strangely high-pitched, "I suggest that you hurry over to the romance section of your local bookstore."

"I'm not proposing." He hesitated before adding, "Not yet."

"Gulp," Laura joked. She was barely able to get the single syllable out.

"Surely you must have thought about the possibility of us living together at some point. And, well, getting married."

"Sure I've thought about it." Laura didn't bother to mention that every time she did, she had to administer chocolate immediately.

"I'm forty-seven years old, Laura. And my differences with my ex-wife aside, I basically *liked* being married. I need someone I can count on. What I want is a commitment. I'm not interested in dating forever. I want to settle down."

He paused before asking, "What about you? Is that what you want?"

"To tell you the truth, Cam, I'm not sure what I want. Whenever I try looking into the future, all I see is a big blank."

"What about having a man in your life?" Cam's voice was strained. "What about *us?*"

"What *about* us?"

"Exactly what do you want our relationship to be?"

Laura thought for a moment. "Most of all, I want something comfortable. Romance is lovely. But the flowers and the candlelight dinners are only temporary.

"It's also the easy part. Even first dates, no matter how horrible, are nothing compared to that first fight. Or realizing for the first time the person you thought was perfect has a big fat glaring flaw right smack in the middle of his personality. The way I see it, any two people in the world can have fun together — provided they agree not to discuss politics or religion and to steer clear of ethnic food. It's the hard times that determine whether or not they're going to make it."

Laura shook her head slowly, and continued. "Even Roger and I managed during those rare times there were no problems, no pressures. It was trying to get through the rough spots that was our downfall."

"You won't get any argument from me," said Cam. "The question is how to accomplish that."

"I believe what's most important is for two people in a relationship to want the same things. To share a vision of what life should be like. It may sound terribly unromantic, but I believe that when you get right down to it, if a couple agrees on the really important things, it doesn't matter if he remembers to buy her flowers on her birthday or if she can keep track of whether it's the big football game or the big basketball game that's on TV that night."

"You do sound just a touch unromantic," Cam teased.

"Don't get me wrong. I recognize that there's got to be something magical between two people. That chemistry that's so easy to recognize — but so difficult to define."

"Do we dare label that 'something magical' *love?*"

"Love's great," Laura replied. "But there's got to be something more. Look at all those couples who started out so crazy about each other that they were willing to declare their love in front of a roomful of people sitting there with tears in their eyes and gift-wrapped blenders in their laps. Yet a few years later those same two people end up at some lawyer's office, screaming at each other from opposite ends of a conference table."

"Not that you're cynical," Cam observed wryly.

"I'm not cynical," Laura insisted. "I'm afraid. And that fear is making me tread very carefully. For fifteen years I tried to find answers. I thought about what makes a marriage work — or not work — every single day. I knew what I had was making me miserable. But that didn't mean coming up with a definition of what I did want was easy."

Cam kissed the top of her head. "I don't want you to be afraid. Not with me."

"It's not you, Cam. I'd be afraid with anybody."

"Okay, so maybe it's too soon to talk about sharing a mailbox. Believe me, the last thing I'd want to do is pressure you. But would you do me a favor?"

"Hmmm?"

"Think about it. When you're lying in bed late at night with nobody but David Letterman to keep you company, try to picture a life with you and me together. One in which I have the privilege of keeping your feet warm every night, not just on weekends."

His tone growing more serious, he added, "And one in which I can be more than just a guy you have fun with. I'd like to take a stab at working out some of those rough spots with you."

Puzzled, Laura glanced at him. "Why?"

"Because I believe that you and I could actually do it."

Legions of window decorators, interior designers, and city employees had made a full-scale effort at converting the island of Manhattan into a living, breathing Christmas card. Laura stood at the edge of Rockefeller Center, her eyes greedily taking in the festive accoutrements of the holiday season.

Every window and doorway in sight was strung with lights. At Saks Fifth Avenue, right across the street, the windows were filled with robotic elves assembling quaint wooden rocking horses and dollhouses. A special vibrancy filled the air — maybe because the sidewalks were jammed with desperate shoppers, maybe because the thick clouds in the eerily white sky promised snow.

Viewing New York City in one of its finest hours had been Laura's idea. It wasn't just the chance to mainline a little Christmas spirit that had prompted this adventure, however. She'd decided it was time for the two most important men in her life to meet.

She'd already established a comfortable relationship with Cam's children. On occasion she had even carried on a conversation with the boas, Nathan and Oscar, although only when the glass wall of their tank was between them. Even so, when it came to thrusting her own son into a new situation, presenting him with Cam and his brood and asking him to accept them, perhaps even to go so far as to like them, she was filled with apprehension.

She'd been nervous that morning when Cam swung by in his station wagon. It was packed, not only with his three children but also with Zach's Game Gear video system, a substantial portion of Simon's comic-book collection, a stuffed bear almost as big as Emily, and two large thermoses, one filled with coffee, the other with hot chocolate.

"I can't help treating every outing like a field trip," Cam apologized as she climbed into the car. "Force of habit."

Once she was settled in the front seat, Laura glanced back at Evan, anxious to see how he was reacting to being thrust into a car filled with activity. His eyes had lit up as if this year Christmas had come a week early.

"Evan," she said casually, "this is Simon, Zach, and Emily. And this is Cam —"

He didn't seem to have heard her. "Oh, boy, Sonic Chaos! Can I play?" he asked Zach eagerly. "I can get up to the leader of the game, on level six!"

Laura breathed a little easier. This was a nine-year-old boy's version of heaven: a carful of kids *and* video games on tap. She realized she'd been foolish to worry so much.

Tripping up Fifth Avenue, all six of them more or less together, she observed that the mood was comfortably upbeat. Having this first meeting in New York on the flashiest holiday of the year had been pure inspiration. So far, the only tense moment had arisen over the issue of whether or not the children should each get their own three-dollar pretzel — or whether the ho-ho-ho prices called for some holiday sharing.

"Look!" Emily suddenly cried, skipping ahead of the others. She headed toward one of the eight-foot candy canes growing out of the sidewalk that led into Rockefeller Center. "Is it real?"

"Why don't you bite it and find out?" Simon suggested.

"Yeah, right," said Zach. "Try that and you'll end up getting arrested."

"It's not a real candy cane," Evan explained with uncharacteristic patience. "It's made out of plastic or something. And don't worry; nobody's gonna arrest you. You're just a little kid."

He was fitting into the role of big brother nicely, Laura observed. She and Cam exchanged knowing glances. Or perhaps they were looks of relief.

"There it is," Laura finally announced, gathering the others around her. "The famous Rockefeller Center Christmas tree. When I was a little girl growing up in the suburbs, my parents brought me into the city to see it every year. It was always the second most exciting part of the holiday, after opening presents on Christmas morning."

As she stood in front of the tree Laura was surprised to find that her heart fluttered in the same way it had when she'd stood in this same spot decades earlier, wearing a spiffy pair of patent-leather Mary Janes and white tights that kept creeping downward. It was funny how Christmases were strung together, like the bulbs on those strings of lights. Each one was connected to the last, providing a sense of continuity to years that often fit together as haphazardly as patches in a crazy quilt.

What a difference there was between this year and the last. She remembered how braving the holiday season alone had made her feel like the gutsy heroine in a TV movie of the week. When she took on that string of recalcitrant Christmas lights and emerged the victor, she'd felt like Spartacus. She'd been so proud of herself. Not only had she made it through the month of December with no more holiday headaches than in any other year, she'd actually managed to put together a warm and memorable Christmas for herself and her son.

This year, orchestrating a merry Christmas was a piece of mince pie. Evan had settled comfortably into their new life, and she had Cam. Reaching for his hand now, she gave it a squeeze.

"This was a great idea," he commented, leaning over and sneaking a quick kiss. "I hardly ever get into the city."

"You're such a country boy," she teased. "But you're doing fine. I must confess, I never thought a plaid-flannel guy like you could look so much at home on Fifth Avenue."

"See that? I'm pretty versatile."

"Hey, you don't have to convince me."

"Don't leer. There are children present."

"Fortunately, they've got so many stars in their eyes they'll never notice."

"Can we get our pretzels now?" Emily suddenly piped up. "I'm hungry."

Laura looked at Cam and laughed. "So much for the wonder of Christmas."

As they stood at the pretzel vendor's cart the man in the apron hummed a carol.

"Merry Christmas," he said, counting out their change. "You and your family have a nice holiday, now."

An hour later, as Cam zigzagged through the heavy holiday traffic, those words continued to echo through Laura's head. Glancing over her shoulder, she saw Simon staring out the window, half-hypnotized by the steady stream of cars. Emily was asleep, her head leaning against his shoulder. Behind them, Zach and Evan were engaged in a video game, the long, tiring day having taken some of the competitiveness out of them both. And she and Cam, cast in the roles of Mom and Dad, sat at the helm.

"Did you hear what the pretzel guy called us?" Cam suddenly said, his eyes fixed straight ahead. "He thought we were a family."

"Yes, I heard that."

He reached over and put his large hand over hers. "Think he knows something we don't know?"

Laura rested her head back against the seat, closed her eyes, and smiled mysteriously. She hoped that in the dim light of dusk, Cam would mistake her uncertainty for Mona Lisa serenity.

Laura sat at her word processor, transfixed by a blinking cursor. Unwilling to allow herself to be dragged down by January doldrums, she'd coped with the inevitable postholiday letdown by throwing herself into a new writing project. Yet when it came to cooking up a new scheme for a giraffe who'd seen too many *Hart to Hart* reruns, she was stumped.

The ringing telephone was a welcome interruption. It was Claire, wanting to lure her away for another ladies' lunch at the Sassafras Café.

"Claire says she's got good news," Julie announced the moment Laura sat down. "But she hasn't breathed a word. She insisted on waiting until you got here."

Glancing over at Claire, Laura saw she looked like the proverbial cat after he'd polished off a canary sandwich. "Is this news I should be sitting down for?" she asked.

Her heart was pounding. Please, *please*, don't let it be what I think it is. . . .

Claire was beaming. "Here's the clue. Something old, something new —"

"Oh, dear," Laura muttered. "I hope you're planning a garage sale."

"Gil and I are getting married!"

"Oh, Claire!" Julie stood up and rushed over to throw her arms around her. "I'm so happy for you! How incredibly romantic!"

"How incredibly *rash*." Laura remained firmly glued to her seat.

"When's the big day?" Julie demanded.

"As soon as I can throw together the most magnificent wedding since Lady Di's."

"And we all know how well *her* marriage turned out," Laura mumbled.

Claire hadn't heard her. She was too busy pulling a stack of glossy magazines out of her tote bag. All of them featured cover girls wearing bits of white fluff on their heads.

"These magazines are an absolute life-saver." Claire's tone was edged with giddiness. "They tell you everything you need to know. I've got them all: *Bride, Today's Bride, Bridal Monthly, Bridal News.* . . ."

"My goodness," Laura commented. "How many articles on 'Honeymoon Do's and Don'ts for the Recycled Bride' can these editors come up with?"

Despite her cynicism about the precipitousness of Claire's decision to become Gil Plympton's better half — or to accept him as hers — Laura had to admit that she'd never seen Claire so happy. She couldn't help wondering, though, was it real happiness . . . or merely some weird hypnotic state, induced by the promise of a cake with more tiers than a Hyatt Hotel and a complete collection of pasta-making machines, fondue pots, and coffee grinders.

"What kind of wedding are you planning?" Julie asked. Her cheeks were glowing with the same vibrancy as Claire's. Grabbing one of the magazines, she fixated on a four-color spread of garters.

"Don't tell me," said Laura. "Ultramodern. I can see it all now. A rap ceremony, synthesizer music, a wedding party clothed entirely in baggy shirts and jeans that are falling off . . ."

"Oh, no!" Claire looked horrified. "I'm planning to have the wedding every little girl dreams of! The first time around, I eloped. This time I intend to do it right."

A faraway look had come into her eyes. "I'm going to wear a long white dress with a train and a veil that trails behind me. There'll be flowers everywhere. And music. I want a live orchestra. I'll march down the aisle to 'Here Comes the Bride,' of course."

"It sounds absolutely lovely," Julie breathed.

"And so original!" Laura couldn't resist adding.

"But the *best* part," Claire continued, "is that I want you both to be part of it!"

"Bridesmaids?" The word caught in Laura's throat.

"Long dresses, coordinating bouquets . . . the whole kit and kaboodle!"

"Oh, wow!" Julie replied.

"Oh, no!" Laura moaned.

"I haven't decided what kind of dresses you'll wear yet," Claire went on, "but I promise they'll be something out of a story-book."

"What about shoes?" Julie asked excitedly. "I've never worn dyed-to-match."

"I hate to be a wet blanket," Laura drawled, "but may I ask a question?"

Julie and Claire looked at her expectantly.

"If we can forget about playing Martha Stewart for a moment, can I ask how carefully you've thought all this through?"

Claire fingered her copy of *Bridal Monthly* defensively. "I've been faithfully following the step-by-step 'Guide to Planning Your Wedding' —"

"I'm not talking about the decision to go with the chicken cordon bleu or the roast beef au jus," Laura replied. "I'm talking about the decision to get married again."

"I think it's wonderful," Julie insisted.

"But look at the evidence!" Laura cried. "Claire, your first marriage failed. *My* marriage failed. Julie and George were together for years . . . then broke up." She shook her head. "How can you take a risk like this? How can you be sure?"

"I feel it in my heart," Claire replied.

"Since when are hearts capable of making critical decisions?" Laura countered. "All they do is go thump-thump, thump-thump."

"Oh, Laura," said Julie, "at some point you've got to let go of all the debating, the weighing of the pros and cons, the endless obsessing. You've simply got to have faith."

"Wait a minute. Aren't you the one who not long ago told me you were concerned about Bobby being someone else's ex-husband? It just so happens that Gil is somebody else's ex, too."

"What about Cam?" Claire demanded. "He's somebody else's ex."

"As a matter of fact, he is," Laura said. "And you don't see me rushing around.

hiring a five-piece combo and renting a wedding dress —"

"I don't rent," Claire said indignantly. "I buy."

"You're right, Laura," Julie said softly. "Gil and Bobby and Cam are all someone else's exes . . . but so are we. Just because our last relationship didn't make it doesn't mean we don't deserve a second chance."

"What about all the doubts you've been having about moving in with Bobby?" Laura demanded.

"I'm simply taking my time about making my decision," Julie declared loftily.

Laura just stared at Julie. I thought you agreed with me. I thought I wasn't the only one who was afraid to take another gamble . . . one in which the odds were anything but favorable.

Laura could see she was putting a damper on everyone else's fun. So she sat quietly as Claire and Julie continued with their gleeful plans, marveling over what she was witnessing.

Julie, Claire . . . even Cam. They're all falling into the same trap, Laura thought morosely. There seems to be something in human nature that makes us willing, even eager, to take the risk, to go for the long shot. Some stubbornness that believes sooner or later, if we try hard enough, we'll finally get it right.

Chapter Twenty-two

Laura pulled up in front of the curb, killed the engine, and jerked up the parking brake. But instead of hurrying out to retrieve her son, she sat at the wheel, staring out the window. Through the relentless drizzle that cast the evening in gloom, she studied the house that used to be her home.

It was Roger's house now. Roger's . . . and Melanie's. She studied the changes they'd made in the past four months. The front door used to be painted white; now it was bright yellow. The front steps had two potted plants on them. Running along the front windowsill were ten or twelve pieces of handmade pottery, their glazes the subtle tones of the earth, their silhouettes sleek and perfect.

Staring out through the mist, Laura was amazed at the fact she felt nothing. Not anger, not envy, not even resentment. Instead, she observed the changes with a cold objectivity.

It's only a house, thought Laura, surprised by her detachment.

The true meaning of that phrase, one she'd repeated to herself over and over, was suddenly glaringly clear. The wood and bricks and shingles and glass were no more than building materials, brought together to create a collection of rooms. Once, those rooms had been the setting for her life.

Now, she reflected, that had come to an end.

As she climbed out of the car an icy wind stabbed at her, a reminder that February held the world firmly in its merciless grip. Laura barely acknowledged it. She was pre-occupied with more pressing concerns.

Walking up to the front door, she wondered again what the proper etiquette was for picking up one's son after his weekend stint with Dad. Staying in the car and honking was the coward's way out. While that wasn't entirely without appeal, she had too much pride to be so overt about avoiding Roger. It was even worse to imagine herself face-to-face with the brand-new lady of the house.

And so Laura was relieved that Roger, not Melanie, answered the door. Her good feelings, however minimal, were short-lived. The tension in his face instantly put her on edge.

"What's wrong?" she demanded.

"It's nothing, really. Only that —"

"I'm never coming back here again!" Evan shrieked. He came hurtling toward her, his jacket unzipped, his backpack falling off his shoulder. Behind him he dragged his canvas overnight bag, stuffed with balled-up clothes that threatened to tumble out of the gaping opening. "Let's get out of here, Mom. I wanna go home!"

He was already halfway to the car. Laura stared at Roger, searching his face for an explanation. Instead, he simply looked irritated.

"I don't understand what his problem is," he grumbled. "He just can't seem to adjust."

In the car, the rhythmic whooshing of the windshield wipers punctuated Evan's silence. Sneaking a peek in the rearview mirror, Laura saw he was staring out the window, brooding.

"Want to talk about it?" she finally asked.

"I hate it there. I'm never going back."

"Honey," she said gently, "he's your dad. You have to go back. We've told you all along that just because we're divorced doesn't mean —"

"Yeah, I know. It doesn't mean you stopped loving me." He spat out his words. "Well, Dad has."

"Stopped loving you?" Laura turned to look at him. "Why would you ever think that?"

"For one thing, he gave my room to Lindsay."

Laura stepped on the brake. "Dad gave your bedroom to Melanie's daughter?"

"When I showed up on Friday, Melanie

had already painted it."

"He gave your room away?"

"They told me they'd decided it was best for everybody." Evan's voice wavered. "It's *pink*."

"Oh, Evan, I'm so sorry. You must feel terrible!"

"Dad's always saying that. 'It's best for everybody,' " Evan mimicked, his voice mocking. "It's like there are two sets of rules in that house, one set for me and one for Greg and Lindsay. Dad's always siding with them!"

"Honey, I'm sure it's difficult, trying to merge two families under one roof —"

"Yeah, right. Like it's gonna help that I'm not allowed to play with Greg or Lindsay's toys, even though they're allowed to play with mine. I'm not allowed to play with their cat, either."

"You're not? Why?"

"Because Melanie wants it that way," Evan reported in that same bitter voice. "I don't count in that house! And it's my house. At least, it used to be."

"Oh, Evan. How awful!"

"Like this weekend? Greg played with my Sega the whole time. He wouldn't give me a single turn. He was being really mean."

Laura was trying her best to remain calm. "What did Dad say?"

"He said I have to learn to share. So I got

454

really mad and said I didn't think it was fair. And he said . . . he said . . ."

"Yes, honey?"

"Dad said I'm the reason the five of us can't be a real family!"

Instant rage nearly choked Laura.

"I don't have to go back there, do I?" Evan pleaded. "Please, Mom. Don't make me!"

"I'll talk to your father."

"I don't understand why you and Dad had to get divorced in the first place. Why can't you two get back together again? Why did this ever have to happen?" Evan choked out a loud sob. "Why can't everything just go back to the way it was before?"

Evan's words were still playing in Laura's head half an hour later when she picked up the phone to call Roger. Her son's fury gnawed away at her, as raw as if it were her own. As she dialed, her hands were shaking.

"Roger," she began, struggling to stay calm, "exactly what is going on over there?"

At the other end of the line, Roger sighed tiredly. "Nothing, really. We're simply trying to come up with a way for all five of us to live together."

"Then why is Evan so angry?"

"He's just having a hard time adjusting."

"And Melanie's kids? How are they adjusting?"

Snorting, he replied, "A lot better than our son."

"I wonder how much Lindsay's new bedroom helped," Laura shot back.

Roger paused. "I guess Evan told you about that."

"You could say that. It's more like he shrieked it."

"It's a decision Melanie and I came to together," Roger said matter-of-factly. "We concluded it was the arrangement that made the most sense."

"Not to Evan."

"Look, I don't want him to think he's getting special treatment. We're trying to create a new family here. I'm making a point of treating all three kids exactly the same."

"And you're doing an excellent job of it," Laura replied tartly. "I particularly like the part about how Evan's not allowed to play with Greg and Lindsay's toys, but they're allowed to play with his."

"He has an important lesson to learn."

"What's that?"

"Evan needs to start respecting other people's property. He broke one of Greg's toys. That's why he's not allowed to touch their things."

"And the cat? Since when is he off-limits?"

"A few weeks ago I caught Evan trying to stick a Cheerio in Bozo's ear. For heaven's sake, these new rules really are for the best. I don't see what the big deal is."

Laura knew that tone of voice well. Roger's defenses were so firmly in place that not even the Pentagon's most powerful missiles would have been capable of penetrating them.

"So this is all supposed to be for Evan's good."

"That's right. And the good of the entire family."

"If you ask me, it sounds like they're a teensy bit imbalanced."

"That's your opinion," Roger shot back. "I have good reasons for every one of the new rules we've made."

"I'll bet." Laura's tone was bitter. "Why do I have the sneaking suspicion good old Melanie's behind all this?"

"I'm not going to pretend that Melanie and I don't agree."

"Don't you see what's going on here?" Laura demanded, all her frustration suddenly pouring out. "Have you no concept of the fact that you and the Wicked Stepmother are turning our son into Cinderella?"

"There's no reason why I should have to listen —"

"Roger," Laura interrupted sharply, "is it true that you told Evan he's the reason the five of you can't be a real family?"

"You don't know what's been going on here," Roger barked. "Evan's been belligerent, uncooperative, unwilling to share his toys —"

"He's a child!" Laura cried. "Besides, he's smart enough to see that you and Melanie have two separate sets of rules in that house."

"That's *his* perception."

"His perception matters, Roger! If those are his feelings about what's going on over there, his reaction is perfectly valid. He thinks you're pushing him away, and that feeling didn't just fall from the sky. You're treating him like an outsider. Naturally he's afraid he's losing you to Melanie and her kids. You've got to acknowledge that, Roger. You have to listen to him. Most of all, you've got to start treating him like a member of your family."

"I don't have to put up with your laundry list of all the things I've 'got to' do, Laura. It's too late for that."

"That may be true," Laura replied. "But let me give you a piece of advice. Keep on like this and it won't be long before it's 'too late' for you to have any kind of relationship at all with your son."

I can't protect him from this, Laura told herself, lying in bed that night, unable to sleep. Sooner or later Evan was bound to find out who his father really is. That would have been true even if Roger and I had stayed married.

Her arguments were perfectly logical. Yet even as she repeated them to herself, clinging to them as if they were a life raft in a tumultuous sea, Laura knew her mind didn't have the power to banish the angry feeling rooted in the pit of her stomach.

This was what the divorce was doing to her son. Her actions had brought this about. If she hadn't chosen to leave her marriage, if she'd somehow found a way of hanging on, Evan would never have had to deal with the miserable situation that Roger and his new ladylove were inflicting on him.

But of course, that would have been impossible. Even lying wide-awake, struggling to keep her mind from racing, she knew she'd done the only thing she could do. She had to get out of a situation that was smothering her. For her, it had turned out to be the best thing. Even Roger had survived. He'd probably even managed to convince himself he'd moved on to something better.

It was Evan who was paying. Her son — who'd never asked for his mother and father to get divorced, who'd never even asked them to get married in the first place — was bearing the brunt of his parents' mistakes.

Why did doing what was best for her have

to cost Evan so dearly?

When the telephone rang, Laura was almost pleased to have a distraction. Still, she was instantly on guard. It was two o'clock in the morning, an hour when people rarely called to report good news.

"Hello, Laura? I'm sorry to be calling so late." In the darkness, Julie's voice sounded faint and faraway.

"Believe it or not, I was still awake." Laura sat up in bed, pulling the covers around her. "What's going on? Are you all right?"

"I'm fine. But —"

"What's wrong?"

From the other end of the line came a loud sniffle. "Oh, Laura. Claire was right."

A dozen different possibilities played through Laura's mind. What was Claire right about? That chicken was a better choice than roast beef? That a parade of rainbow-garbed bridesmaids really was the way to go?

And then, in one terrible flash, Laura understood.

"Oh, no." The words came out like a groan. "Bobby?"

"I'm in a phone booth downstairs," Julie said in a thin, little-girl voice. "Can I come up?"

Laura had thrown on a bathrobe and put a kettle of water on the stove by the time Julie appeared on her doorstep. Clearly,

Julie had been crying; while tears no longer lined her face, the trails of mascara they'd left behind gave her a ghoulish appearance. Her distraught look made an odd contrast to her party clothes. She wore a slinky black dress that wasn't at all her usual style, along with heels so high they could have been borrowed from Claire's closet. And the makeup. Laura couldn't remember having ever seen Julie in makeup before, aside from the time she'd filled in at Evan's birthday party after the hired clown came down with chicken pox.

Laura sat down opposite Julie at the kitchen table. "What happened?" she asked gently.

"It was that stupid box, of all things." Julie shook her head slowly. As she spoke she kept her eyes fixed on the mug Laura had put in front of her. An herbal tea bag was already balanced against the side. "Remember? The one Claire told us about?"

Laura nodded. "Two doves carved into wood, right? A wedding gift from one of Claire's friends?"

"That's the one." Julie took a deep breath. "Bobby and I had just come home from a party. He'd dragged me off to meet a bunch of his clients. I tried so hard to fit in!"

That explained the makeup and heels.

"The evening went really well. Bobby and I were all snuggly in the car ride home.

Then the subject of me moving in with him came up again. You know I've been going back and forth with it for a long time. But by the time we got back to his apartment, I was ready to say yes.

"He went into the kitchen to pour us both a glass of wine. I was on the verge of giving him my decision. Then, while I was sitting on the couch, waiting for him, I happened to pick up that box of Claire's."

She hesitated, her eyes welling up with tears. "That was when I saw the hair."

"The hair? What hair?"

"A very long, very blond hair. Definitely not one of mine."

"Julie, I understand that you're upset, but there could be a hundred different explanations."

"There's only one." Julie drew in her breath sharply, her eyes still fixed on the mug. "And Bobby had no qualms about giving it to me. He said it was all my fault, that I was responsible for driving him into the arms of another woman.

"He blamed his infidelity on the fact that I was taking so long to decide whether or not I was ready to move in with him. He told me he was hurt. That he felt rejected — so much so that when this woman came on to him, his bruised ego couldn't possibly turn her away."

Julie glanced at Laura for the first time

since she'd begun her discourse. Her pain was clearly reflected on her face.

"He'd been sleeping with one of his clients." Her hoarse voice was nearly a whisper. "It happened exactly the way Claire said it would. The same way it happened to her."

She shook her head. "She was right all along, Laura. He hasn't changed. He is still the same person he was when he was married to Claire. And I fell for it."

"Oh, Julie." Laura went over and threw her arms around her. "You had no way of knowing. You wanted to believe it could work. You were crazy about the guy. All you did was follow your heart."

"It was worse than that, Laura. I was dumb enough to believe it could be different. That I could *make* it different by being better than Claire. I thought if I were nicer, sweeter, prettier, less demanding, more interested in sex, more attuned to what he wanted . . ."

Julie buried her face in her hands. "I was such a fool!" she sobbed. "How could I ever have been naive enough to believe that fairy tale endings really exist?"

"Maybe it's because you wanted one so badly." Stroking Julie's back soothingly, Laura added, "No one could blame you. It's a mistake we all make."

Chapter Twenty-three

Laura leaned her head back and closed her eyes, telling herself that the setting was perfect. She lay naked in Cam's arms, the two of them on a rug in front of the fireplace, their skin glowing in the flames' flickering light. The house was silent except for the crackling of the fire, the ticking of the clock on the mantel, and next to her ear, the beating of Cam's heart.

Before making love, they'd made a substantial dent in a bottle of champagne — their way of celebrating having an entire weekend to themselves, with no children, deadlines, work obligations, luncheon dates, doctors' appointments, or phone messages to return. In fact, in the past twenty-four hours, the most demanding thing they'd done was decide between pizza and Chinese takeout.

It was a scene out of a fantasy. Yet Laura's attempts at losing herself in the moment were futile. The events of the weeks before — Evan's anger at his father, Julie's crushing discovery about Bobby — had left her reeling. Everything suddenly seemed much too complicated: her relationship with her son, her romance with Cam, her inability to put her divorce behind her once and for all. She was juggling too many balls, each one getting in the way of the others, the whole thing threatening to come tumbling down.

She was wondering whether the unrest rumbling inside her showed when Cam leaned over and planted a kiss on the back of her neck.

"Happy?" he asked.

"I can't imagine a more idyllic moment," she replied diplomatically.

"Good. You look happy." He snuggled up even closer. "You know, I could get used to this."

"Lying on the floor stark naked?"

He laughed gently. "That, too. But what I meant was, I could get used to having you around."

Laura's muscles tensed.

"I want you to move in with me, Laura, for you and Evan to be part of my life. Emily's and Zach's and Simon's, too. I want to know that no matter how bad a day I have, I can always look forward to curling up with you in bed at night. I want to wake up in the morning and see you with your hair all messed up and your eyes half-closed. I even want to argue with you over whose turn it is to empty the dishwasher and who's stealing the covers."

"Cam, I —"

"Look, I know you were terribly hurt by your marriage. I know what it did to you. But that's all in the past. It's time for you to get on with your life, Laura. And I want you to do it with me."

"You know I —"

"No, Laura. I don't want an answer right now. I know you've been grappling with this. That you've given us — and our future — a lot of thought. But so have I. And I want you. I want Evan, too." He took a deep breath. "I want us to be a family."

She was silent for a long time. She couldn't imagine a man more perfect than Cam. Nor could she envision a relationship more joyful, more rewarding . . . more comfortable. It was the romance she'd day-dreamed about — maybe not Julie's storybook version but one about which she had no uncertainty, even in her most private moments.

It was making the commitment to trying again with another man that gave her pause. Not only taking a risk for herself, but for her son as well. The stakes were so high. One marriage had already failed. Recovering had been an excruciating process. The emotional cost was higher than she'd ever anticipated.

"I need more time, Cam," she said.

He said nothing. Instead, he simply

wrapped his arms around her more tightly.

*She tries to run, but her feet are leaden.
It — the terrible nameless faceless it —
is getting closer and closer. She knows
she has to get away, that her very survival depends upon being able to escape
. . . but her feet are so heavy, so very,
very heavy. . . .*

Laura's eyes opened to a room so dark
she was unable to make out anything familiar. Her heart pounded. Rushes of adrenaline shot through her. The fear
engulfing her was so strong she could
hardly breathe.

A dream, she told herself. It was only a
dream.

She knew she was awake. The demons of
the night had vanished. Yet while she
struggled to orient herself, too much champagne and not enough sleep clouded her
brain. Blinking hard, she made out the
outline of a window. The light of the moon
was too dim for her to recognize any of the
silhouettes around.

And then she realized she wasn't alone.
She could feel the heat from someone else's
body, hear the rhythmic breathing of someone who slept. Abruptly she turned her
head.

A man was lying with his back to her. His

broad shoulders, covered in a thick blanket, jutted upward.

Roger, she thought.

The panic of the dream followed her into consciousness.

I have to get away. I don't belong here.

The terrible feeling of being trapped washed over her. Suddenly all that mattered was escaping. Her panic rising, Laura threw back the covers and leaped out of bed. She had to get away. . . .

"Laura?"

The sound of Cam's voice, so thick with sleep it was barely discernible, pulled her into the present. She was with Cam, not Roger. She was at his house, in his bed. She was safe.

Yet instead of feeling comforted by the reality of the situation, the panic deepened.

"Are you all right?" he asked, concerned. He leaned over and snapped on the light. Squinting, he reached for her. "Do you need anything?"

"No. Yes, I —" Laura took a few deep breaths, waiting for the panic to subside.

It's Cam, not Roger, she kept telling herself. It's all right.

But it wasn't.

"Come back to bed," he said, turning off the light.

"I can't sleep. I'm going downstairs."

Lying on the living room couch, curled up

under two coats she'd pulled out of the front closet, Laura waited for the panic to subside. She was calmer now. The acuteness of the moment had passed. But fear still gnawed at her.

What am I doing? she thought. I've barely gotten out of a marriage. Why am I rushing into another relationship? Why am I daring to trust?

How could I possibly believe it could work out better this time? The hurt look on Julie's face as she'd told Laura the tragic ending of her love story still haunted her. With years of anger and sorrow and disappointment to look back on, the idea of ever taking a risk like that again was terrifying.

Hours earlier Cam had invited her to live with him. He'd asked her to share his life. It was what he wanted . . . what he deserved. Yet the fear that gnawed away inside her kept her from being able to give it to him.

We're at different points in our lives, Laura thought miserably. He's prepared to dive back in again, while I'm still trembling at the edge of the pool.

She was still awake when the room began to lighten, the early morning sun gradually revealing that the ominous shapes surrounding her were a chair, a plant, a wooden trunk. The fear had stayed with her. But instead of inhibiting her, it enabled her to think clearly — more clearly, she decided, than she had in a very long time.

When she heard Cam coming down the stairs, the fear gave way to dread. She sat up in time to see him come into the room. The expression on his face was grave.

He sat down on the edge of the couch, far enough away so they weren't touching. He looked at her expectantly, his eyes clouded, his expression troubled.

He knows.

"I was up most of the night, thinking," she said in a quiet voice.

"You must have been wrestling with something very difficult."

Laura nodded. She couldn't bring herself to look him in the eye. "I was thinking about . . . us. About me, really," she added quickly. "Cam, I can't do this. I'm not ready. I thought I was, but it's just too complicated."

"It doesn't have to be complicated," he insisted.

"I don't mean logistically. I mean emotionally. I don't know what I want. I'm still too confused, sorting through too many feelings. . . ." She took a deep breath. "I guess the bottom line is that I'm simply too afraid."

"I'm sorry if I've been moving too fast. I'm not looking for a commitment — at least, not yet. But I'm also not looking for something casual. I need to feel you and I are moving toward something."

"I know. And you deserve that." Laura lowered her eyes. "But I can't give it to you."

She expected him to protest. She braced herself against a barrage of recriminations. Instead, he nodded sadly.

"I understand."

It was only then she was able to look at him.

"I'm sorry," she said, her voice breaking.

It was Cam's turn to look away. "I am, too."

Laura sat in front of the computer, pretending to be working. She was too numb, however, to concentrate on anything that required more brainpower than choosing what color socks to wear.

Ever since the weekend before, she'd been acting like a zombie in a bad voodoo movie. That wasn't entirely coincidental, since she felt like the walking dead. Her emotions were turned off like a light switch.

Still, she welcomed her inability to feel. Not far below the surface, she knew, was a terrible pain. Once it got her in its grip, it could very well strangle her.

It's for the best, she told herself for what had to be the millionth time. It's simply the way it's got to be.

With a deep sigh, Laura forced herself to

concentrate. The words *Gertrude said* stared back at her from her screen. Her hands were poised above the keyboard. The problem was that she had no idea what Gertrude said. Nor did she care. The world of imaginary jungle animals, meeting with ups and downs but invariably heading toward a happy ending, was suddenly alien.

When the telephone rang, she barely glanced at it, and let the answering machine pick up. Lately, lifting the receiver had required too much exertion. Still, she couldn't help hearing Gil's voice, chirpier than she'd ever heard him.

". . . And I was wondering if you were free for lunch today — oh, hi, Laura. You're there."

"Hello, Gil. Yes, I'm here. I've been screening my calls."

"Up for lunch?"

Her first impulse was to say no. But there was something appealing about the idea of a shoulder to cry on. "Lunch sounds like precisely what I need."

She felt considerably more energetic an hour later as she pulled into the parking lot of the Starlight Diner, "their" restaurant. Getting out was probably a good idea. She especially appreciated the predictability of the situation: meeting Gil at the same time, at the same place . . . probably sitting at the same booth, ordering the same lunch.

He was waiting for her, menu in hand, cup of coffee at his side. As she slid into the booth and exchanged the usual pleasantries, Laura felt grateful he'd called. Wading around in the details of someone else's doings had to be better than sitting around her apartment, drowning in ruminations about her own. She was already feeling better.

"I guess I should congratulate you," she told Gil after flagging down a coffeepot-bearing waiter and requesting her own jolt of caffeine.

Gil was beaming. "Claire told you, huh?"

Laura chuckled. "I'm surprised she hasn't taken out a full-page ad in *The New York Times*. Seriously, I haven't seen her this happy in years. She's really crazy about you, Gil."

"I'm crazy about her. You're coming to the wedding, aren't you?"

"Are you kidding? I'm in the wedding party!" Laura wondered if Gil had some pull as far as that business was concerned. Ever since Claire had broken the news to her that her duties as best friend included dressing up in an obscene amount of ribbons, lace, and ruffles, in some impossible-to-wear color like salmon pink or burgundy, she'd been desperate to find a way out.

Then she remembered it was Claire she was dealing with. And this wasn't even the strong, levelheaded version. This was Claire under a powerful spell, one that had her obsessing over things like the latest innovations in veils and the number of second cousins one was obliged to invite.

"I know Claire's really into planning this wedding." Gil actually sounded proud. "And if I know her, it's really going to be something. Hey, will I finally get to meet this Prince Charming of yours?"

Laura looked down, suddenly feigning great interest in the ring of coffee that had spilled onto her saucer. "I'm afraid not."

"Too bad. He can't make it?"

She shook her head. "I sent the prince back to the castle."

"Gee, Laura, I'm sorry to hear that. For a while it sounded as if you two were really hitting it off."

"We were."

"I guess that's just how it goes sometimes." Gil shook his head sympathetically. "You think things are great, you think you really know the other person . . . and then something happens, totally out of the blue. He reveals something about himself or does something that exposes a different side —"

"It wasn't like that at all." Laura hesitated. "It was me."

Glancing up she saw Gil was looking at her expectantly. "I just wasn't ready to be in a relationship."

"That's too bad. From what you said, he sounded like a great guy." Laura could tell he was choosing his words carefully. "But hey, if the timing's not right, what can you do? When you're ready, you'll find somebody."

She swallowed hard and nodded. She wasn't about to admit that she doubted she'd ever feel ready.

"Well, you're a good example," she said. "Finding Claire, deciding you were ready to jump in, feet first . . . Although I must admit, I was a little surprised when she told me the two of you were getting married."

"Really? Why?"

Laura hesitated. "Because you had such a hard time getting over Melanie."

"Ah," said Gil, shaking his finger at her, "but I finally did. And it's all because I finally got my revenge."

Laura's eyebrows shot up. "What did you do?" Images of pizzas being delivered to the house every hour on the hour were already running through her brain.

"Simple. You've heard that expression 'Living well is the best revenge'? Well, falling in love with Claire has turned out to be the best possible way of getting back at my ex-wife. That combined with the fact that from what I can tell, Melanie's absolutely miserable with Roger."

"It does seem as if my old residence has

become the Clover Hollow Horror." Remembering Evan's angry tirade, Laura shivered. "I suppose you're right about Melanie not being any happier living with Roger than I was."

"Are you kidding? She's taken to calling me on the phone, complaining about him. If I know my ex-wife, her new hobby is banging her head against the wall, moaning, 'What have I done?' " The look on Gil's face was one of absolute triumph. "There really is such a thing as justice."

After lunch, Laura sat in the car for a long time, thinking. For Gil, feeling that the score had finally been evened up had enabled him to let go of the past. "Living well" — especially when Melanie's experience was turning out to be exactly the opposite — turned out to be just what the therapist ordered.

Then why isn't it enough for me? Laura wondered, frustrated.

Chapter Twenty-four

Laura lay across a wrought-iron chaise lounge, sipping her breakfast coffee. She delighted in the fact that it was once again possible to be outdoors for more than five minutes without developing cold symptoms.

Only weeks earlier the ornate lawn furniture, tucked into one corner of her landlady's backyard, had been heavily shrouded in snow, looking like props in *Dr. Zhivago*. But spring, that insistent little devil, was once again fighting off Old Man Winter and pushing its way in. All but a few clumps of soot-dusted snow had melted. Even the monumental deposits left behind by the snowplows, white fortresses that had lingered like insensitive guests, were now little more than molehills.

Relief sweetened the air. The feeling reminded Laura of dozing off with a terrible headache, then waking up to discover that, miraculously, the throbbing pain was gone. There was also a bittersweet element to the balminess. A year earlier, when the world had felt this fresh and new, she and Julie had descended upon Claire's apartment to pore over the World Watch literature and design the next chapter of Laura's life.

Suddenly her eyes filled with tears. It had been a month since she'd broken up with Cam. Twenty-six days, to be precise. She'd counted them carefully, like a prisoner making chalk marks on the wall. In an effort to lessen the pain, she'd packed away most of the things that reminded her of him. The photograph of the two of them standing at the edge of Wolf Lake, taken by Sandy the day before Laura left Alaska. His Christmas present to her, a gold charm shaped like a tree to commemorate their day at Rockefeller Center. The T-shirt printed with BOAS ARE BEAUTIFUL.

Even so, the sadness lingered. It's for the best, she told herself a hundred times a day.

Besides, she couldn't complain. She and her son had settled into an easy routine. On mornings like this, when Evan was at school, she was nearly overwhelmed by the exhilaration of total freedom. She was still close enough to her marriage to appreciate having escaped. By comparison, her present life was as fresh and new as the spring air.

Taking another sip of coffee, Laura thought about Gil and his obsession with getting revenge. She'd been skeptical at first, but lately she'd turned his idea into a sort of game. Lying in bed at night, she let her imagination run wild, concocting various schemes designed to even the score with Roger. Usually they came out like something Johnny Jaguar would've dreamed up. After indulging in a good chuckle, she'd finally drift off to sleep. By morning, her schemes were forgotten.

Still, indulging in vengeful fantasies didn't hurt anyone. Perhaps, she reasoned, they would even prove helpful in putting the past behind.

Laura was about to go back into the house when Roger's car turned up the driveway. "Speak of the devil," she muttered.

Through the windshield, she could see how earnest the expression on his face was. She automatically tensed.

"Hi," he called, climbing out of the car.

As he walked toward her Laura was struck by how haggard he looked. His shoulders were slumped, his gait tired. His face, which she'd found handsome even during their worst arguments, looked drawn.

In a flash of understanding, Laura knew what Daisy, the seniormost member of the Wednesday-night support group, had meant when she'd complained that her husband was getting old. Roger, too, had gotten old. He looked defeated, as if something inside him had simply given up.

"Top o' the morning," she quipped. "I'd offer you some coffee, but this is the last of it."

"That's okay. I just had some."

He stood in front of her, shifting his weight from one foot to the other. An awkward silence hung over them.

"Is this purely a social call?" she finally asked, her tone pleasant.

He cast her a wary glance.

"Maybe you'd better have a seat," Laura suggested.

Roger lowered himself into the wrought-iron chair next to her. She was struck by the contrast between the tension in the air and the picniclike setting of their tête-à-tête.

"There's something I've been wanting to say to you for some time, Laura."

Instantly the level of tension jumped from medium to high. She braced herself for the worst.

Roger took a deep breath, keeping his eyes on the dry clump of grass beneath his feet. "Laura, letting you go was the biggest mistake of my life."

She simply stared.

"It's only now, when I'm trying to start all over again, that I'm starting to appreciate you. I've been having a really tough time. And taking on a whole new family, shouldering the responsibility of owning a house all by myself, is only part of it. I'm also wrestling with all kinds of internal demons." He paused. "I'm beginning to face the fact that maybe you were right about some of the things you complained about when we were married.

"Melanie's saying the same things you used to say." Roger shook his head slowly. "We had a big fight last night. It was about me working. At first I was so angry I couldn't see straight. But slowly, through the barriers I'd put up, I heard her saying the exact words I'd heard you saying for years."

Taking a deep breath, he added, "I can't simply blame it all on you anymore."

Roger's voice had gotten lower and more controlled. "You know, Laura, when you told me you wanted out a year and a half ago, I should've insisted we give it more time. I was wrong not to try to get my act together. I should've worked on our relationship instead of simply letting it die.

"I know it's too late now — for you and me, I mean. But I realize I have to step back and take a good, hard look at myself and the part I played in the failure of our marriage. Melanie and I are determined to stick together, to try to work it out. As painful as it is, I'm going to have to start making some changes."

He stood up, his head bowed. "That's all I wanted to say. This wasn't easy for me, but I felt you deserved that much."

Laura simply nodded. Her throat was so constricted she couldn't speak. It hardly mattered, since she wouldn't have known how to respond.

She sat very still as he walked back to his car. Watching him leave, she suddenly had a sense of ties breaking, of being released . . . of letting go. He'd opened the car door and was about to climb in when she stood up.

"Roger?" she called after him.

He stopped and turned. "Yes?"

"Thank you."

After he'd left, she sat down in one of the wrought-iron chairs. For a long time she stayed very still, her hands folded on the table in front of her. It wasn't Roger she was thinking about; it was Gil. Gil — and his longing to get revenge, hoping it would bring about the closure he so badly needed.

She realized that she'd exacted her revenge. And it hadn't come from smashing pottery or calling in the IRS or playing manipulative games. Instead, it came from having finally been acknowledged.

"So who's having good sex?" Phyllis had an innocent look on her face as she glanced around the circle at the Wednesday-night support group. "Decent sex? Half-decent sex? Any sex at all?"

Her opener for the evening elicited the usual round of laughter — some of it embarrassed, some relieved. Laura, wedged between Ken and Elaine, settled back in her chair. All day she'd been looking forward to coming to the support group. Tonight she had something to share — something important.

Over and over in her mind she'd replayed the scene with Roger. She'd gotten her revenge — and her sense of closure. What surprised her most was that she wasn't gloating. Instead, she felt cloaked in serenity.

Beside her, Elaine waved her hand in the air.

"Elaine," demanded Phyllis, "are you one of the lucky ones or are you drying your nails?"

"I have something I want to tell the group."

"It doesn't look as if any of us could stop you."

Elaine's round face was flushed. "I met a man."

Everyone in the room gasped. The reaction couldn't have been more dramatic if she'd announced she was placing them all under arrest.

Even Phyllis, whose job was to act unimpressed, was unable to contain herself. "No!" she cried, clutching her hands to her heart.

"Who's the sucker?" demanded Jake.

"Give us his phone number," Ken joked. "We want to warn him."

"Come on, now," Phyllis insisted. "Let's give Elaine a chance. Besides," she added, leaning forward, "I'm sure we're all anxious to hear the details."

"Well," Elaine began, her eyes glowing, "I met him at the auto-parts store where I work. He's a salesman who comes in every few weeks. He's been around for months now, but it was only last week that he finally got up the nerve to ask me out. At least that's what he admitted Saturday night." She sighed. "His name's Hal."

"Poor Hal," breathed Ken.

"Anyway," Elaine went on, pointedly ignoring him, "we went out to dinner Saturday night. It was fantastic. Hal and I clicked like you wouldn't believe. We like the same movies, the same kind of food . . . we've even gone on vacation to the same places." With a little shrug she added, "We're seeing each other again next weekend."

"Going out to dinner again?" asked Phyllis.

"No. Cancún."

"Excuse me?"

"We're going to Cancún for five days. We decided it's a good way to get to know each other. Besides, I figure there's nothing wrong with getting a head start on my tan."

"I think there's a lesson for us all to learn here," said Phyllis. "Even Elaine has found someone new."

" '*Even*'?" Elaine repeated, indignant.

"Well, you gotta admit you been kind of angry since your divorce," said Jake.

"Well, maybe a little." Elaine was pensive for a moment. Then her face lit up. "But just because I'm dating doesn't mean I don't still hate my ex-husband."

As the group went on to give Elaine advice on how to conduct her newfound social life, Laura let her mind wander. So Elaine — angry, disillusioned, man-hating Elaine — had met someone new. It was almost inevitable, she mused, that no matter how bad the first marriage, no matter how deep the wounds, eventually the heart healed. In the end, it almost always went back for more.

And where does that leave me? Laura wondered.

Ever since the day before, when Roger had talked to her, *really* talked to her, for what was perhaps the very first time, she'd basked in the sense of release. Her situation was suddenly different. *She* was different. She'd been freed from her past. What she had to decide now was how to proceed with her future.

Tuning back in to the group, she was surprised to hear Ken agonizing over some event that had occurred between him and his wife years before. Somehow they had moved back into the past again. For them, she realized, the disillusionment of their marriages was still very much alive. For the first time since she'd started coming to the group, hearing about the others' past disappointments made Laura impatient.

At that moment she understood she wouldn't be back. Her roller-coaster ride wasn't quite over, but the end was finally in sight. From where she sat she could see that the bends and twists that remained were much less frightening than those she'd endured.

Something had become clear to her suddenly. And that was that she wanted a man in her life. She missed Cam desperately. Her fears were no longer forbidding enough to keep her from jumping back in feet first, knowing she'd initially be shocked by the coldness of the water but still confident about her ability to stay afloat.

Her only worry now was whether it was too late.

Laura was nervous as she climbed out of her car late Saturday morning. Driving to Cam's house, she'd battled a host of butterflies fluttering around in her stomach. She felt the same way she'd felt the first time she'd made this trip, when she'd been worried about how his children would respond to her. This time her concern was how Cam would react.

The air was still bursting with that dangerous spring freshness that made people do impetuous things. Still, her actions were anything but rash. Ever since Wednesday night she'd been ruminating about making a commitment to another man, to another relationship . . . to Cam. She knew that this time she had to be sure. It wouldn't be fair to call him back, only to get cold feet once things started heating up again.

She'd decided she was sure.

As she was crossing the lawn, heading toward the front door, she heard voices coming from behind the house. In the backyard, Cam was celebrating the arrival of spring with his children.

She hadn't intended to sneak up on him, but standing outside the fence, she realized he hadn't noticed her. So she hung back, watching.

He stood at the barbecue, a striped dish towel tucked into the waistband of his jeans to create a makeshift apron. A pair of orange-and-white gingham oven mitts on his hands, he tended the row of skewers laid out on the metal grating.

Behind him, a redwood picnic table was set for lunch. Next to each of four mismatched plates were plastic cups: one from Pizza Hut, one from Six Flags, one printed with the NFL logo, one picturing the Little Mermaid. Silverware was lined up at each place setting, the forks, knives, and spoons clumped together in creative combinations. The mismatched dinnerware, as well as the bouquet of weeds stuck in a Smucker's peanut butter jar, made Laura smile. Emily's handiwork, she guessed.

Zach and Simon were tossing around a football, whooping and hollering as if they'd both been gripped by spring fever. Emily was on the swing set, performing a gymnastics routine that involved more twirling round and round a horizontal bar than any Olympic committee was ever likely to sanction.

"Watch me, Daddy!" she cried, going for rotation number six. "Watch me!"

Cam glanced over his shoulder. "Way to go, Em. You're doing great!"

"Hey, Dad! Play catch with us!" called Simon.

"You got it. Just give me a few minutes. It's almost time to turn these. . . ." Cam bent over the barbecue, carefully realigning his shish kebobs.

It was a touching domestic scene: the loving father relaxing with his three children, all of them sincerely enjoying each other's company. They seemed so comfortable with each other, so comfortable in their lives.

Laura was struck by how badly she wanted to be part of it. She wanted it for Evan as well. Her son deserved more than just a mother who thought the world of him. He deserved a family.

And then she realized exactly why this scene felt so familiar. Cam horsing around with his children, their easiness with each other . . . For a moment she was ten years old again, walking home through the dusk, longingly looking through the windows of other people's houses.

What was missing from this particular scene was the woman of the family. Laura ached to play that role — in this setting with these people.

Her heart pounding, she stepped forward.

"Cam?" she called softly.

He glanced up, shock registering on his face for just a moment. "Hello, Laura."

She laughed, suddenly self-conscious. "I guess you're surprised to see me."

"Surprised . . . and pleased." He gestured toward the barbecue. "Staying for lunch? I'm told I make a pretty mean shish kebob —"

"Look!" cried Emily, ceasing her whipping around the metal bars of the swing set. "Laura's here! Watch me, Laura!"

"Where's Evan?" Zach asked, the football poised over his shoulder.

"He's with his dad this weekend."

"Too bad." He looked sincerely disappointed. "Hey, want to play catch?"

"No way. First she's got to see what I can do," Emily insisted. "Laura, watch how fast I can flip over!"

"Give Laura and me a few minutes to talk," Cam told them. Turning back to her, he said, "I presume you came here to talk."

Laura nodded.

"Let me take these off." He pulled off the oven mitts. "I don't know about you, but I don't think I could ever have a serious conversation dressed like Betty Crocker."

"I don't remember Betty having such a full beard," Laura countered.

Cam laughed. "There. I guess we've successfully managed to break the ice." He'd led her over to the side of the house, out of earshot of the children. "Should I be happy to see you, or would I just be setting myself up?"

"It depends on how you're feeling about me these days." Laura kicked at a small clump of dry brown grass, keeping her eyes fixed on the new spurt of green pushing its way up beside it.

"I don't know how I dare feel. If I admit to myself that I still care, I could end up getting my heart broken again." He stared off into the distance. "And it's not even close to being mended from the last time around."

490

"I'm sorry about that, Cam. I —"

"What happened before doesn't matter, Laura." He placed his hands on her shoulders, turning her gently so that she faced him. "It's what's going to happen from here on in that counts."

"What do you want to happen?"

"I want you back," he said simply. "That hasn't changed."

"I want to come back."

"You're sure this time?"

"I'm sure."

"No more running away?"

She shook her head. "I'm yours. That is, if you want me."

"I want you," said Cam, taking her in his arms.

Laura leaned forward, resting her head against his chest. I'm home, she thought. I've finally come home.

Chapter Twenty-five

"I can already see the write-up in tomorrow's paper," Laura told Julie, her voice low. " 'The bride wore white, the same shade as her hair — and the effect was nothing short of blinding. Several guests complaining of severe eye pain were rushed to North Shore Hospital —' "

"Oh, Laura," Julie said breathlessly, "Claire looks lovely. Every bride is beautiful."

Laura was about to mutter some comment along the lines of *bah, humbug* when she noticed that her friend's eyes were shiny with tears. Instead, she fussed with the folds of her lavender satin skirt. The dress, cinched at the waist with a tight cummerbund, had a row of froufrou along the hem. Her dust ruffle, she'd nicknamed it. Fortunately, it covered the pair of black patent-leather Little Bo-Peep shoes that laced up her ankles.

The dress, the shoes, the lavender wide-brimmed hat, the parasol . . . every element had been carefully chosen for the June extravaganza. Even the location fit right in with Claire's image of a dream wedding. The Crystal Inn catered to sweet sixteens, fiftieth anniversaries — and the weddings of grown women anxious to combine Mardi Gras, Halloween, and the dress-up corner of the kindergarten classroom. Frowning, Laura glanced at her reflection in the line of floor-to-ceiling mirrors in a dressing room that seriously rivaled the palace of Versailles.

"I feel like Scarlett O'Hara's body double," she muttered. She tugged at the low-cut neckline that revealed considerably more than she felt comfortable showing to anyone who hadn't at least bought her dinner.

"I think Claire's choice of bridesmaids' dresses is lovely," Julie insisted, twirling before the mirror.

Laura had to admit that Julie actually looked good in her mint green version of the outfit. She resembled the tiny doll on an old-fashioned music box, come to life. Her long red hair was twisted into dramatic frankfurter curls, tied to one side with a perky green ribbon. The other bridesmaids also looked the part: Claire's seventeen-year-old cousin in tangerine, her nineteen-year-old cousin in lemon yellow, even her plump sister-in-law-to-be in baby pink.

Laura was wondering if she was being a trifle unfair to Claire, the institution of marriage, and parasol manufacturers when the bride clapped her hands for attention.

"Okay, everybody," she announced crisply,

hiking up her long skirt so she could pace around the room in her white satin four-inch heels. Her dress was the most elaborate of them all, lest anyone be unclear about whose day this was. Made entirely of lace, dotted with roses and ribbons and seed pearls, it swished and swirled with every movement Claire made. "We've got a job to do here. I want everyone to stand tall. Look alert. Chin up, shoulders back . . . and walk, don't shuffle."

" 'The bride wore combat boots,' " Laura mumbled.

She was prepared to remain encased in her armor of cynicism during the ceremony, the reception, and even the rehashing of highlights on the telephone with Julie. So she was surprised to find that as the opening bars of Wagner's classic wedding march filtered into the dressing room, her heart launched into a gymnastics routine. As for the tears welling up in her eyes . . .

All right, so I'm not immune, she admitted, taking her place in the parade that began with a flower girl scattering rose petals and ended with the baby pink sister-in-law. There's something about a wedding — any wedding — that brings out everybody's romantic side.

The ceremony contained every cliché in the book. But the look on Claire's face, and Gil's as well, elicited a brand-new wave of mistiness in Laura.

"You look beautiful," Cam told her later, at the reception. Coming up behind her with two glasses of champagne in hand, he leaned forward to plant a kiss on her cheek.

"What I look is *lavender*," she insisted, accepting the glass. "Very, very lavender."

"You could have done worse," Cam insisted. "Have you seen Claire's new sister-in-law?"

"All that pink should only be worn by someone who still travels in a stroller."

He chuckled. "I don't suppose there's any other color you'd prefer to be wearing today."

"Just about any color in the rainbow."

"I was thinking about white."

"A great color for picket fences."

"You know what I mean. And I bet you'd look great in white." When Laura remained silent, Cam said, "Well, Laura, I know you won't give me a yes. How about a maybe?"

She glanced toward the doorway of the reception hall. Gil and Claire had just come in. They stood together for a moment, shoulder to shoulder, thigh to thigh, their hands clasped together so tightly they looked as if they had no intention of ever letting go.

The look on their faces was the same Laura had seen during the ceremony. There were stars in their eyes. Maybe, just maybe, those stars weren't blinding them, but were actually helping them see even better.

Laura reached over and took hold of Cam's hand.

"Cam?" she said softly.

"Hmmm?"

"Maybe."